like me

like me

a novel

Hayley Phelan

Published by Lake Union Publishing, Seattle

www.apub.com

Amazon, the Amazon logo, and Lake Union Publishing are trademarks of Amazon.com, Inc., or its affiliates.

ISBN-13: 9781542037785
ISBN-10: 1542037786

Cover design by Faceout Studio, Spencer Fuller

Printed in the United States of America

For Amit and Ajooni

Content warning: The following story contains scenes of violence and abuse and depicts issues that may be sensitive for some readers.

PART ONE

From the bathroom, where I was perched in front of the toilet, I could hear Gemma Anton laughing. Gemma was on her way to a party. Not now. Last night. I'd left her on my bed, imprisoned in the two-by-six-inch screen of my phone, as she was goofing around and singing to Bob Marley in the back of a taxi. Her giggle reverberated through my shitty studio's thin walls in a tinny, mechanical loop.

I was kneeling in a pose of abject submission, my forehead pressed against the cool plastic seat of the toilet, hands clammy against its sculpted porcelain. This was how I spent most of my mornings that summer—the summer that concerns us, the summer that Gemma disappeared—hunched in my bathroom, waiting for the bile to climb. I had convinced myself that I'd developed insomnia and needed to drink at least two bottles of wine, or the equivalent, to fall asleep. Although what I called "falling asleep" was what medical professionals would probably term an alcoholic blackout. I often woke fully clothed, reeking of cigarette smoke, the chemical aftertaste of cocaine in the back of my throat, with only the dimmest idea of how I'd gotten there. Of course, I slept worse and worse, and drank more and more, and somehow failed to see the connection between the two.

At nineteen, I was already well trained in the school of hangovers. They were worth it, too, I thought, for those few blissful hours asleep, swimming in the inky black void, falling through nothing. So, on this particular morning, I did not hesitate to act: I bravely lifted my head and, bracing myself with one hand, delicately probed the velvety flesh at the back of my throat. It was like fitting a key into a lock with the lights out. I closed my eyes, feeling for the give, and then—click—it came in a gush: relief awash in soured vodka soda.

Satisfied with the purge, I leaned back and surveyed my reflection in the shallow oval of milky pale water below me. I tore off two squares of toilet paper and cleaned my fingers, tossed the refuse into the bowl, and flushed.

Standing up, I stretched my arms toward the ceiling. Beautiful little fireflies, the kind that signal intense dehydration and hunger, danced in front of my eyes. Reaching past the shower curtain—depressingly mass-market white, mildewed on the bottom—I turned on the shower, pushing it as hot as it would go. The rushing sound drowned out Gemma's laugh and calmed me, making my scalp tingle. I stripped naked, leaving my clothes in a puddle on the floor, and examined my body in the full-length mirror, waiting for the steam to fill the room. I ran my hands along the length of my sides, pinched the skin on my stomach, tapped my hip bones, running my inventory. All the products were in place: flat stomach, skinny arms, ribs that protruded ever so slightly, white skin. I thought of my body as a tool, something I owned. I could rent it out if I wanted to—which is more or less what I did. For all that talk about selling one's soul, no one seems to be in the market. It's the body that everybody wants. The body is a currency everyone can understand.

The steam clouded over the mirror and swallowed me. I stepped into the shower, closed my eyes, and finally lost sight of myself. I felt empty and pure.

I still remember the very first image I saw of Gemma, staring out at me from the kaleidoscopic Grid of my Popular page on Instagram. I had moved to New York City six months before, and it was only just beginning to become obvious that the lucrative modeling career I'd been promised would never materialize.

The image was a close-up of her face against a black backdrop. The first thing I thought was *This girl looks a lot like me.* I, too, was blond and thin, with overlarge pale-blue eyes and a wide, round forehead. It was unnerving, as if I were looking into the face of an intimate or family member whose name I couldn't place, and who had shown up somewhere they weren't meant to be. But once that brief instant had passed, her face seemed to bloom and I saw that though our features were similar, the effect they gave in Gemma was somehow far more captivating. In the image, she was wearing gold, sculptural earrings, and her white-blond ringlets had been pulled into a bun, laying bare her impeccable bone structure. Her head was tilted to one side, and one hand rested lazily on top of her head, two fingers pulling gently at the tender skin of her left eye, which peered out at me frankly. They were intelligent eyes and there was a naked quality to them, framed as they were by pale, white-blond eyebrows. That was one of the differences between us. The eyebrows made her look Nordic, pure, childlike. Her pose was almost surreal, a cubist flourish to the kind of portrait we've seen ten hundred times before. Her skin was perfect. Freckles dotted her nose and cheeks. Between her slightly parted lips, you could see her strong white teeth, which had a small gap between them. There was a nobility about her bearing. I can't quite explain it, but there is something about Gemma. She just looks like a *someone.*

I once overheard a client explain to the casting director that had brought me in for a go-see: "She's too bland. Too safe, not enough personality." What he meant, of course, was that my *look* had no personality. And the thing was, I agreed with him. I knew I was attractive. I wasn't dumb. But for a long time, I'd felt there was an indefinite quality to my face, like it was a blurred outline that some other girl could fill just as well. Perhaps it's a function of the job: my face is a blank canvas on which any fantasy may be projected. Then again, it probably goes back further, to growing up the only child of P. T. Heffernan, erstwhile king of the North Shore, the Bernie Madoff of Illinois, as the local press dubbed him. For the record, we were never as rich as the Madoffs, not even close. But we were certainly wealthy—and my father was certainly a crook. It's possible that being raised by a fraud imparted a certain veiled quality to my expressions. In any case, the fact remains: people see many things in my face, but what they never seem to see is me.

Gemma, on the other hand, is different. Once I'd seen her, right away I started Following her on Instagram. Soon, she was everywhere. On billboards. Magazine covers. All over Instagram. I watched her Follower count rise to 20K, then 50K, then push past 100K. I was completely riveted. I probably clocked an hour or two every day on her feed, poring over her photos. It was intoxicating watching her perfect life unfold, this stranger who looked so much like me; I suppose it made me feel as if my dreams were within reach, like I, too, could be famous, rich again, and loved. Instead, things continued to look grim for me. I knew if they didn't change, if I continued to get passed over for those big-name jobs, if I couldn't scrape together more than a few thousand Instagram Followers, Jason, my agent, would eventually— with sugar-sweet apologies—drop me. And then politely but firmly inform me that I owed thousands of dollars to the agency, interest in loans that I'd unwittingly accepted. Part of me resented Gemma, of course. I was jealous. But I didn't hate her—it might be difficult for you to believe that now, but it's true. I didn't hate her. I was fascinated by her; I thought if I studied her closely enough, something would be revealed to me, a way forward, a way to not be who I was. By that summer, when this story begins, I'd been in New York two years. I didn't have a high school diploma. And if I had to move back in with my mother, I thought I would probably die.

Any sensible person would have gotten a day job; I could have become a barista, or waited tables part time. Then maybe none of this would have happened. But I wasn't a very sensible person back then. I had been bred for the easy life. And because I was pretty and white and had once known what it was like to be rich, I felt entitled to it, as if I were recapturing what was once mine, rather than taking what I didn't deserve. Besides, I had met Julia and Blake—my best friends at the time—shortly after I moved to New York City, and they had shown me how to get on in the city with very little money. It involved rich men and copious amounts of alcohol. We thought it was a bargain.

After I felt I had sufficiently sweated out most of the alcohol from the night before, I gave myself one final blast of cold water—I'd read somewhere it decreased the chances of developing cellulite—and stepped out of the shower. I wrapped a towel around my hair and again positioned myself in the mirror. I cleared a space in the fog, just where my head was: my reflection showed a ghostly face floating in midair. One of my great hobbies at the time was picking my skin. I was prolific. But I had a casting that morning and couldn't afford to go in with a splotchy face—I desperately needed the job—so I resisted, fleeing the bathroom and heading for the kitchen, which was also the living room and the bedroom. Everything in my life fit into a cramped 350-square-foot space. It was pretty bleak in there: blank walls, dust in the corners, a mattress on a box spring, an IKEA dresser. The one thing I liked about my apartment was that its only two windows faced a brick wall. No one could see in.

I filled a glass with water from the tap and guzzled it. I looked at the clock on my microwave: thirty minutes before I had to leave for the casting. As if drawn like a magnet, I went back to bed, back to Gemma, where I'd left her, imprisoned in her little rectangular box, maniacally reenacting the night before. I picked up my phone and watched the rest of it unfold.

Yes, Gemma had gone out last night. I didn't know where. She'd worn a silky camisole, silver, that dipped and pooled beneath her impressive clavicle; if you looked closely (and I always did) when she lifted her glass up, as if to cheers the thousands of strangers that watched her Stories, you could see the faint outline of her ribs on the front of her chest. As her gesture became grander—the arm sweeping around in an exaggerated, grandiose arc—it seemed that it was the bones themselves that moved, furtively, under the skin. Automatically, my hand lifted to my own chest, feeling for the same bones. I pressed my thumb against her body, pinning it against my screen so it went motionless, and raked my eyes over it, looking for more information. She had not tagged the brand of the blouse or anything else she was wearing, which frustrated me.

I'd gone out last night, too, as I did every night, with Julia and Blake. I can't now recall how the three of us met, nor what initially drew me to them; I suppose, like most things in my life then, the friendships evolved largely out of a sense of convenience. We liked each other enough, each of us could take down a bottle of wine without beginning to slur, and we enjoyed doing the same sorts of things, had the same sorts of priorities. Julia was what I came to call rich-adjacent: she'd no real money of her own, but because her father was a well-liked studio musician who occasionally played with famous people, she'd grown up around enough wealth that she felt accustomed to it, entitled to it. Yet she was also enormously resourceful; out of all of us, she was the scrappiest, the most shameless, a fantastic liar, always finding ways to make money. She had three thousand Followers, and even though I knew she had bought a few hundred of them in the early days, most of them were legit, and either way it was still three times the amount of clout I had online.

Blake, on the other hand, poor dear Blake, who went to great pains to disguise her freckles and orange-red hair with self-tanner and $300 highlights, was one of the most insecure, aimless people I'd ever known.

Not that you'd be able to tell upon meeting her: much like her natural physical appearance, she hid her rampant insecurity under layers of self-invention, adorned herself with all manner of baubles and decoration. She was brash, she was loud, she was often irritating, particularly when she was drunk or coked up, which was often. She only had two hundred Followers, though you'd think by the way she posted—*Here's a pro health tip I swear by: try adding coconut oil to your coffee!* Or *I absolutely love rainy days! What's your favorite kind of weather?*—she had closer to two million. It was an embarrassment I found hard to stand sometimes.

The three of us had gone to Parlor, as we always did on Tuesdays, and, as always, we sat at Joe's booth and pretended to listen to what the men were saying in order to fuck us while we steadfastly consumed all their booze until the only mixer left was cranberry juice, which we would not drink, and then we'd turn down, ever so slightly, the wattage on our pliant smiles, and look bored, and then they'd order another bottle of vodka, and we'd ask for more soda, please, and do it all over again. We weren't prostitutes or escorts or anything as tawdry as that, but the fact of the matter was that Joe—one of the biggest club promoters in the city, a squat, bald-headed guy from Long Island with a goofy sense of humor—relied on us to join him and whatever group of rich men he was entertaining at whatever club. We didn't have to *do* anything with these men, per se. We were simply decoration. But sleeping with one or two could be useful. Money would always find its way to us.

I peered more closely at Gemma's Instagram—it was difficult to tell in the photos, but it seemed she might have been at Parlor last night, too. I turned onto my side and tucked my knees to my chin. I had never seen Gemma in person, even though I often saw later on social media that we had been in the same place at the same time. She had ended her night with pizza at Artichoke; there she was, under the vaguely sinister yellow light particular to one-dollar-slice places at three in the morning. She held the pizza aloft and let its floppy tip dangle tantalizingly close to her bottom lip. Her mouth was open. I could see the wetness of her pink tongue. Normally, she said something funny or witty or self-deprecating, but this time she'd only put up an emoji of a crystal ball, a hieroglyph whose meaning I could only begin to parse. Was it an in-joke? A pop culture reference I didn't get?

I thought about what I had eaten during the day yesterday: two boiled eggs and a cup of tomato soup. I often didn't eat a proper meal until nine or ten p.m., when Joe and his benefactors would take a group of us to dinner before the club. Last night, it was Mr. Chow—one of my favorites. After I polished off my plate of noodles, and devoured a good portion of the crispy duck, one of the men had looked at me appreciatively and said: "Man, it's so sexy to see a girl that can eat!" These kinds of idiots, who I privately despised, and openly derided the next day with Julia and Blake, were my main source of nutrients at the time. They probably kept me alive.

Gemma didn't need to bother with such buffoons. She had been with Hans Benoit, the famous photographer, for almost two years. Benoit had taken last night's pizza photo, too. I knew just by looking at it. Whenever he shot nightlife or candids like this, he always used a high-watt flash that blew everyone out, making the girls look like the girls you see on missing persons posters and the men look wild-eyed and like they were on more drugs than they probably were.

I lay back in bed and took a few photos of myself naked, half-wishing there were someone to take them for me. Benoit took photos of Gemma constantly. Gemma in the shower, tufted in soapsuds. Gemma asleep in the late afternoon sun. Gemma eating cereal on the couch. Even Gemma pissing, her cute white panties making a garland around her ankles, a sheepish grin on her face. That's what I thought love was: someone who constantly wanted to take your picture. My mom had been like that with me when I was little. She had about a dozen photo albums, completely filled with snapshots of me. Now, though, I get so annoyed with her asking me to pose, she hardly takes any photos of me at all. She still tells me I'm pretty all the time, though. *I'm so jealous,* she'll whisper, stroking my hair or eyeing my body, which is the highest compliment coming from her.

I studied the nudes I'd taken of myself. I didn't look bad. I selected them all and clicked Hide so no one could see them in my photo roll but I could still visit them privately, peer at my body—you never know when you'll want to evaluate it again, so it's good to have photo evidence on hand. Then I began scrolling through the last few photos in my camera roll. There was one of Blake and me before the night really got started, walking arm in arm on the sidewalk on our way to Parlor. I was wearing Levi's Premium Wedgie Fit jeans in Charleston Moves in Medium Wash, a Stelen Open-Back Spaghetti Strap Camisole in Ivory, Topshop Oversize Gold Hoop Earrings, and Steve Madden Kandi Black Slip-On Loafers, which, if you squinted, looked like Gucci. Blake wore the Reformation Christine Dress in Lemonade, and Converse Low-Top Sneakers in Canvas. We'd found an empty champagne glass tucked neatly beside the staircase of a brownstone, and, tipsy and giggly, I had scooped it up and toasted it toward the camera. After we'd taken the picture, I'd tossed it on the street and watched it shatter.

I put on a few filters and cropped the picture so you couldn't see my thighs. I typed out a caption: *3 a.m. pizza never a bad idea, especially when you bring your own champagne.* Jason had said I needed to think harder about what I was putting out there on social media. *Who are you?* he had asked. *What's your personality? Are you funny? Serious? Interested in social justice?*

Gemma's lucky. She grew up between France and California alongside four boisterous brothers, one of whom is now paraplegic and gives talks to high schoolers about the dangers of drunk driving. Her father's a professor of French literature, and her mother is a potter and florist who recently launched a modestly successful small-batch organic wine label. Gemma grew up playing piano and doing ballet.

I'm an only child, and my father is a crook. I deleted the caption and typed: *Grateful for this human champagne bubble, my wife, @ BlakeyBlake.* I bit my lip, thinking.

Gemma almost made it to the American Ballet Theater, but decided to go to college instead: NYU, as a poli-sci major. "I always felt very deeply the injustices of the world, and knew from a young age I wanted to make a difference," she'd once said in an interview with Net-a-Porter, alongside images of her stretched out on the Italian Riviera somewhere, modeling the new Saint Laurent collection. She got discovered freshman year. Gemma never dreamt of modeling, but it helped pay off her student loans. Gemma says her whole life she's been plagued by anxiety. It runs in her family. Her brother, after he became paralyzed, attempted suicide, and that was a real wake-up call for Gemma. Now, she posts all the time about mental health, and occasionally details her own struggle with depression. She wants to raise awareness, to show that depression can affect anyone, even her. Except it only winds up making me feel worse about myself because if Gemma is depressed, then I might as well just go and jump off a bridge. Still, I wished I had something to care about like Gemma had. Jason was always telling me that I needed to be realer. That's what everyone loves so much about Gemma. She's authentic. She's just being herself. You can tell.

I deleted the caption again and typed: *When the whole country's going up in flames, sometimes you just have to take the champagne to the pizza, y'know?* I added an emoji of a crystal ball, and tagged all the brands we were wearing.

Gemma's body is perfectly arranged under the gentle slopes of her recently purchased Parachute duvet. She sleeps on her back, her face exposed and open to the world, like a child. One of her arms is flung lazily up behind her head, and a fan of wavy blond hair spills over it, creating a halo around her face. She begins to stir, a beam of golden sunlight slicing through her blinds at the appointed hour, the end of what she likes to call her "disco nap." She stretches both arms overhead and shakes away one of her signature white-blond curls. Propping herself up on an elbow, she rubs one eye sleepily.

"Mmm," she says, clearly savoring the moment. Her eyes are open now, and light refracts off the pale-blue irises, giving the impression of unbounded depth, like the inside of a glass marble. She laughs sheepishly. "Naps, man," she says, though it is unclear to whom she is speaking. "Still the best."

Possibly, she is speaking to no one.

Later, on the roof of her West Village apartment building, Gemma fills a mason jar with rosé. It is her favorite time of day. The windows of the office building across the street reflect the sun, little squares of burning gold and ombré pink framed in steel. Snake Oil, an under-the-radar band that I have not heard of but that sounds a little like The Smiths, plays in the background.

Gemma rests her head on Benoit's shoulder. So it was to him that she had been speaking, back in the bedroom. That should have been obvious. Both of their faces are bathed in soft pink. They look happy in the calm way that I have always longed for. Gemma is wearing a worn-in men's button-down shirt and layers of fine gold necklaces, one of which is a locket that Benoit gave her four months ago. Their anniversary. It cost $1,200 and was hand-crafted by a husband-and-wife design team in Istanbul. Benoit is wearing a denim jacket and dark sunglasses. He takes a swig of his beer, and looks out into the distance.

But Gemma, Gemma looks right at me.

I was late to the casting that day. Not that it mattered. They always made you wait at least an hour before they called your name, and I wasn't too excited about the gig anyway—it was for a no-name lookbook shoot, and would probably pay pennies. But Jason had urged me to go in for it because he said the designer, Julio Ronaldo, was about to be the next big thing, and because it was being shot by Billy Pierce, who was still a big deal even if he really did rape all those girls. "Well, it wasn't real rape," Jason had chided me. "Just statutory. And anyway, all the charges were dropped."

After following the direction of the meekly extended finger of the front desk receptionist, I found myself in a long, mirrored corridor where the other girls were waiting, legs limply crossed or stuck out in front of them, on stackable plastic chairs. Their reflections—attenuated frames and dazed expressions—repeated ad infinitum on either side. I hung back, leaning against an empty sliver of wall, away from the mirrors and the other girls. I didn't recognize any of them, though they were instantly familiar to me—the same horde I saw at all of the castings: tall, perilously thin, and white, white, white, just like me. Some of the higher-end labels had started casting models of color in campaigns (usually surrounded by a halo of white girls), but the mall brands and beginning designers that I went up for apparently lacked the imagination, or the courage, though it shouldn't have required either.

I was wearing BDG High-Waisted Contrast Stitch Skate Jeans in Black, the Urban Outfitters Novah Ribbed Tank Top, also in Black, and Converse Chuck Taylor All Star Sneakers in Black.

I had picked up a copy of the latest *New York* on my way over. Gemma had posted about it, and one of my resolutions that summer was to read more. Feeling smug, I unfurled it, and started with the table of contents. Then my phone dinged. Blake and Julia were discussing what Blake should eat that morning, whether she should go out for breakfast alone (Julia was still in bed with one of her suitors) or just order in, and if she ordered in, what she should order. After typing out my vote (order in), my fingers magically carried me to the web browser on my phone. I checked the *New York Times* home page. I read the news, switching to Instagram as the pages loaded. The photo I had posted had gotten 112 Likes so far. There was a bombing in Ukraine that killed nine people, including a child. Kendall Jenner had dyed her hair blond. Donald Trump had mocked a female TV presenter. One of the Likers was Sam, a boy I had once kinda liked. I clicked on his profile. Brazil was struggling to identify a new disease, characterized by mild flu-like symptoms and an asymmetrical rash, that could be accompanied by seizures and temporary dissociation or amnesia and had so far sickened seventy-three people in São Paulo. My best middle school friend went to an amusement park with her boyfriend and he won her a bear (lame). A Brooklyn teen had fled the States to join ISIS. There was a meme circulating, a baby wearing Nikes and nothing else dancing to "Old Town Road." Gemma had taken her little black poodle, Pancakes, for a walk along the West Side Highway. She was wearing denim shorts and a vintage T-shirt, neither of them tagged. I studied her legs—long, pale, and thin, slightly bowed, her thighs like elegant brackets—and the space between them: that yawning distance that seemed to represent the chasm between the two of us. She had the best thigh gap. Conclusion: I needed a pair of denim shorts. Blake had decided to go out after all, to Mogador, the Moroccan joint on St. Marks. Urban Outfitters was selling a pair of shredded Levi's for $49.99. I couldn't decide between white and the light blue. Blake had ordered the Mediterranean breakfast. My horoscope said that today's new moon signaled a journey inward. A new beginning. Julia said I should get the light-blue wash.

I don't know how long I waited, but when they called my name, it was like I heard it from some great distance, even though it was just coming from the end of the hallway, where a soft, stout woman stood, dressed in Eileen Fisher billowy sails and holding a clipboard. Legally, my name's still Michaela Heffernan, but I started going by Mickey Jones—my mother's maiden name—shortly after my dad got arrested, and it still rang a little unfamiliar in my ear. Reluctantly, I rolled my *New York* back up and stuck it in my purse. I hadn't gotten any further than the table of contents. I walked quickly through the corridor, past the girls repeating infinitely on both sides, and had the disconcerting impression that I was passing through a thicket of my own body.

The woman was smiling a chipped-tooth smile, which deepened the crow's-feet around her eyes. She told me her name was Joni and, with a moist palm against my shoulder, ferried me into the next room.

Sunlight poured sideways through the large warehouse windows, creating a golden quadrangle on one side of the wall in which I saw a galaxy of dust swimming. No one else introduced themselves, but I could tell who Julio was right away: a small man with smooth brown skin, a black mop of curly hair, and a startlingly handsome face made all the more compelling by the two large moles that punctuated his right cheek. He had that air of ownership and frenetic energy I'd come to recognize in designers. He paced the room, while the others—a trim man with rangy tattooed arms and chunky black glasses, and a minis-cule woman with a mullet and an aura of keen efficiency—sat at a large conference table. Joni took her seat beside the woman.

Everyone looked at me. When I'm at a casting, I try to go com-pletely empty. I am just a body, and what they say isn't personal. It's business. I can still feel my feet on the ground, and hear the words coming out of my mouth, but other than that I've gone; everything is happening on the outside, and I'm just watching, empty as a shell. (I've since come to understand, from the court-appointed therapist, that this is called dissociation.)

Inevitably, though, snippets of conversation slip through. There was some discussion over whether my thighs were too fat. One of them was concerned I didn't look upmarket enough. *Generic, mall-brand catalog . . .* these are the words they used. *Not at all,* said another. *In the clothes, that sort of blank Americanness will be exactly right. Perverse, almost . . .* Then Julio was standing very close to me, his breath on my neck. Gently he turned my cheek, examining my face in the light.

"Y'know, there's something almost Gemma about her," he said.

The one who had called me generic scoffed. "Really? I'm . . . not sure I'm seeing that."

Julio continued looking at me thoughtfully. "With a few changes . . ." He tucked my hair behind my shoulders and smoothed it down on either side of my head. It was nice being looked at like that.

"She only has eleven hundred Followers," said one of the others. That was something they'd started doing, giving your social media stats alongside your height, weight, and shoe size.

Julio sighed. "You're probably right. But let's at least see how she looks on film. Even just for my own personal amusement." He winked at me and laughed, his fingertips still lingering on my throat and collarbone. He gave me one final examination. Then, with a perfunctory, quick gesture, he clasped my nipples between his thumb and forefinger and pinched—a trick, I knew, for making them hard in the photos. "There," he said, finally stepping away, satisfied. I was careful not to wince.

Soon, I was dazzled by the flash.

When I was dismissed a few minutes later, Joni caressed my cheek gently, called me darling as if she were my own mother, and called the next name.

She'd told me they'd be in touch. But I knew they wouldn't be.

There had been a time when I actually went to castings with some hope. I was seventeen and thought I'd be a star, even though I was then living in a one-bedroom model apartment with six other girls who all thought the same thing and were arguably more talented than me, whatever "talent" means in this industry. I had some luck early on; I was cast alongside five or six other models (guys and girls) in an Urban Outfitters campaign. We pretended to skateboard in an empty swimming pool and sat in plastic folding chairs, drinking from cans that looked like beer without the label (they were actually empty, so when we pressed them to our lips, we only took in air). I guess that gave me confidence. It was enough that Jason took me on as a client, promised me opportunities, consistency. I used to prep for the castings he sent me to, made an effort to be on time, well rested, with absolutely nothing in my stomach, and for a while, it worked; I booked a few more mid-level gigs, and some catalog work that paid well. I thought I had a chance at finally recapturing what had been stripped away from me at my father's trial. Wealth. Ease. The delusion I was somehow special. But soon even those mid-level jobs grew few and far between. I wish I could point to something dramatic that happened, like that I told a photographer to go fuck himself, or showed up to work wasted, but it wasn't anything like that; it was more of a slow fade into nothingness, invisibility. The last casting I'd gone to with a shred of hope, I'd waited seven hours in a cramped hallway, and they didn't even call my name; they packed up and left without even seeing me, and I didn't realize it until a security guard who was closing up for the night had to tell me to leave.

There is a large box, tied with a pale-green silk ribbon, waiting on a sunflooded windowsill. Outside the window: quaint West Village brownstones. Gemma pulls at the ribbon, at first teasingly, and then with abandon.

Inside the box: filmy white tissue paper, which she impatiently tosses aside, revealing a fluffy white robe from Parachute, a thank-you note from the company for posting about it.

Gemma slips on the robe. It looks big on her, but this only accentuates her charm, like she is a little girl playing dress-up in her mother's robe. Underneath she is naked. Surely, she is naked. She wraps her arms around herself, hugging the robe in tight and squealing with delight. Pancakes wags his tail excitedly. He trots over and licks her feet.

Hands clasped together, on a leather car seat. Benoit's tattoo is visible, just above his wrist. Her fingers, delicate and white, are cradled in his. Such a lazy handhold, as if holding each other's hand were the most basic thing in the world.

They are on their way to a lunchtime benefit, in honor of a black woman who died while in police custody. This is a cause dear to my heart. The words are written in a white font, positioned diagonally in the top right corner so that they do not obscure the primary object of the image: the hands holding each other, their love for one another, a delicate gold bracelet from the brand Lorelai.

On the step and repeat, Gemma's body is riddled with flashes. Her hair is wild. A curl, loosening itself from the white-blond mass, blows in the breeze across her face, and she tucks it behind an ear. She is wearing wide-legged, cream-colored trousers, and a matching silk blouse. Thank you Ganni for letting me steal this v v comfy v v cool fit from the shoot! *reads the text, stationary and white over a black scribble in the corner. Hovering near her hip is another string of words: the names of brands, including Ganni, attached to @ signs, each one clickable. As the flashes crescendo her expression says:* Who, me? Well isn't this ridiculous.

That night I dined on squash blossoms, burrata, and stewed plums, and split the branzino with Blake, with a side of green beans. I was wearing a Topshop Ruched Mini Dress in Lime Green that I'd shoplifted earlier that week, the Brandy Melville Gold Double Chain Crescent Charm Necklace, Converse Chuck Taylor All Star Sneakers in Black, and Forever 21 Oversize Hoops. There were eight of us there—Julia, Blake, and me, of course; three men, including Joe; and two other models, neither of whom spoke very much English. I remember being jealous of that; they chewed their food slowly, and smiled, and did not have to say anything much. I, on the other hand, ate and drank voraciously and kept up a steady patter. I told no one about the casting. If I had, Julia might have suggested that I try doing something else, like she'd done last time, and I'd have to pretend I didn't hear her and go to the bathroom, my cheeks burning with shame, because how could I explain to her that I needed this job, that I didn't have anything else—no education, no talent—when I myself had gone to great pains to mislead her about that? She and Blake assumed I had a regular father and a high school diploma just like everyone else.

Though I did not think it at that very moment, I was angry. It was an anger that was loose and unspecific, a faint tint that had spread like dye in water. It encompassed all men.

There was only one way I knew how to seek revenge. Make the men want me. I scanned the room, looking for prey. The man seated across from me was in the midst of a monologue, something about his home in Montauk. He was neither ugly nor handsome, probably in his midforties, balding a little bit on the top of his head, short, narrow-shouldered, but muscular and compact. Yes, he might do. A long aquiline nose, tanned olive skin that looked soft, shirtsleeves rolled up to reveal dark, hairy arms. He was wearing an awful gold watch, terribly gaudy. A turnoff. Good. It's better if you're not attracted to them.

I leaned forward and gently squeezed his wrist.

"Sorry, what's your name again?"

He faltered momentarily, then looked flattered. "Andrew," he said.

"Andrew." I smiled sweetly at him. "Hi."

After dinner, the night proceeded in the usual fashion. Joe ordered an UberXL and we all piled in, tacitly arranging ourselves so that those who had the likeliest chance of fucking later that night were closest to one another. When we arrived at La Boîte, Andrew grasped my hand as I stepped out of the car, an unnecessary act of chivalry that both stirred me and made me think less of him. It was already past midnight and there was a long line outside. Dozens ballooned out near the door, ignoring the line: men in fedoras insisting they were on the list; drunk girls whining into their cell phones, *Can you come out and get me, pleaaase?*; others just looking shamefacedly at their shoes. Ignoring them all was Michael, the tall, elegant black man who managed the door at La Boîte. He was happily chatting away with one of the stout bouncers who acted as his muscle, but, true to his preternatural talents, he glanced up just as we were approaching the melee and, with one fluid motion of his hand, parted the crowd. Walking through those sweaty hopefuls to casually kiss Michael on the cheek and disappear beyond the graffitied metal door, I felt my sense of worth skyrocket.

I can't recall exactly what happened next, but as I said, it was a regular night: we can assume that within minutes of walking through the door, the eight of us were comfortably ensconced in one of La Boîte's semicircular booths, which were tastefully upholstered in pale-gold velvet, and within another minute, one of us, probably Joe, cracked open the bottle of vodka waiting in its ice bucket and began pouring. I wouldn't remember this if it weren't for the photographs posted on Instagram the next day, but apparently we developed an ongoing joke that we were all, in equal turns, in love with our waitress, making embarrassing overtures to her with little regard for how she might have felt about our intrusive attentions. There are several photos of us mooning over her, including one where Joe is on bended knee, as if proposing, and one where Julia is wrapping her arms around the server's waist. In the back of one of them, I'm nuzzling Andrew's neck. I don't remember that either.

Soon, we would have gotten up to dance. Or, in any case, at some point we found ourselves on the dance floor, perhaps better characterized as the tiled space between the booths and the main bar, a massive marble job with the bottles all lit, pink and gold, behind it. This, at least, I remember: Blake, Julia, and me dancing, bodies loose with booze, the lights sliding over our faces, reminding me of the bottom of the ocean the time I went scuba diving in Anguilla, the way the light refracted through the water to create a subtle strobe effect along the ocean floor. I felt I was swaying in the current. Julia's hands were above her head, her wrists swiveling as she made slow semicircular turns with her ass; Blake, who had been raised on jazz and tap-dancing classes, punched and kicked the air aggressively to the beat. We were dancing with each other, yes, but we were also putting on a show; I closed my eyes and imagined us as glimpsed from afar, through the crowd. With each languorous turn of my hips, I felt I was drawing eyes toward us, irresistibly, as if on an invisible string. There was a rushing sensation inside of me. I opened my eyes slightly and looked at the crowd through a sultry, half-lidded gaze. People *were* looking. I wondered if Andrew was. I scanned the crowd, looking for him. My eye caught instead on a particular shoulder, smooth and white in the strange light, like a river rock, just brushed with a tousle of blond curls. I craned my head to get a better look, and at that moment she turned her head, quickly and nervously, as if to find someone in the crowd. Somewhere inside of me a bell rang. Gemma. It was Gemma! My whole body seemed to swim in the proximity of her image, and I had to blink—hard and fast—to maintain my equilibrium. I had often fantasized about seeing her in person, had in fact viewed it as an eventuality, yet now, in the presence of her corporeal reality, the sensation was uncanny, the way it is when you finally visit a famous monument or painting after having seen thousands of images of it, an unnerving blend of familiarity and novelty that made everything feel unreal, as if the presence of the thing flattened everything into the two-dimensional realm in which you'd so often engaged with it. Gemma waved to someone on the other side of the dance floor, and her face broke into a smile. I was relieved to notice she was not more beautiful in person. But she did have a haunted, hunted quality to her expression, and a way of carrying herself that reminded me of other famous people I'd seen, a way of holding her head up high, looking only at what was directly in front of her—nothing in her peripheral vision—which simultaneously acknowledged and ignored the fact that everyone in the room was looking at her.

"What's the matter?" Julia asked.

I realized I'd been standing stock-still, staring off into the distance. I shrugged my shoulders, trying to appear casual. "I just saw Gemma Anton."

Blake was too involved in her performance to take note, but Julia looked around curiously.

"Over there." I pointed, but Gemma had been swallowed up by the crowd. "Oh, you can't see her anymore, but she's there."

Blake, noticing the two of us talking, forever paranoid that she should miss something between us, however minute, stopped her show. "What is it?" she asked.

"Mickey thinks she saw her girl crush."

"She's not my girl crush," I snapped.

Julia smiled and tilted her head like, sure, sure, whatever you say, and Blake asked if I was talking about Gia Ronaldo, an actress I used to like but now hardly even remembered and certainly wouldn't care about seeing, which just goes to show you how much Blake knows about anything.

Julia rolled her eyes. "She's talking about Gemma, *duh*."

Blake scanned the crowd. "I don't see her."

"I didn't either," said Julia. "It was prob just some other blond chick. God knows they're a dime a dozen." She said it sarcastically, while bugging her eyes out at me, trying to be funny.

"It was definitely her." Frustrated, I pulled up Instagram and went to her profile. She'd posted only thirty minutes ago: she was lying in bed, wearing a thin cotton T-shirt through which you could see her erect nipples; Charles Bukowski's *Hot Water Music* covered half her face. The one eye that did show looked out mischievously. The caption read: *Raging night in.*

"See?" said Julia.

"It wasn't her," said Blake.

But I knew it was.

The thing most people don't understand about going out and getting wasted every night is that it's not easy. It's not always fun. It can be hard work. It takes discipline. It takes substances. Of course, we'd been doing bumps all night, turning to one another and ducking our heads to inhale off keys at the booth, in the back of the Uber. But I'd reached a point where I knew I needed more than that: a big fat line to myself. Remember, I was not sleeping well in those days, and so I was often tired by two in the morning, just when the night's unhinged sense of possibility was reaching its peak. Without saying so, I'd looked for Gemma. I'd walked the perimeter of the dance floor, peered into all the banquettes. I supposed she had left. Still, I wanted to stay, because seeing her felt like an omen. It meant I was somewhere where things could happen. But now I was sequestered in a booth with Andrew, leaning in close, my eyelids beginning to droop. He was off, again, on some soliloquy about Montauk, how he liked to surf, his childhood in New England, a difficult father, yada yada. I listened only enough to give vague responses. *Yes, totally, you're so right.* Finally, when it seemed he was letting up, I excused myself for the bathroom, feeling I was close to passing out. He tugged on my hand.

"Don't be long," he said.

There was a large bathroom with six stalls on the other side of the dance floor, but if you were a regular—and no doubt I was—you knew there was also a smaller, two-stall bathroom down a short set of stairs near the coat check. It was often empty and therefore cleaner, quieter. There'd been nights when Julia, Blake, and I had all but commandeered it, pouring out lines right there on the sink countertop—marble, like the bar—not even bothering to go into the stalls. We loved that bathroom. As I snaked my way through the dance floor and the inevitable crowd huddled near the bar, then past the coat check girl, framed in her little window like a painting, just as stuck and stationary, I hoped that the bathroom was empty. It was. I wasted no time: I slipped into the first stall and, with a practiced economy of movement, poured out a sprinkle of coke on my faux-gold cosmetic case and snorted. It hit my brain like soda water bubbling up to the top, making those little snaps and pops.

On my phone, I stared at the image of Gemma in bed. It was the same image. But I kept staring at it as if my intense scrutiny might have the power to make it morph and reveal something new. I spread my fingers over the cool, glassy surface, zooming in until the edges of Gemma's face grew blurry and I could make out the freckles and uneven skin along her cheeks.

She was lying. I knew she was here.

I felt a tingling of anger. Maybe that's what made me do it. A feeling not so much of betrayal, but of moral outrage. Gemma was not allowed to be a liar. I wanted to show her that.

Or maybe it was the coke and the seven vodka sodas that did it. In any case, I can't now claim I was thinking straight. I clicked Message on her profile, and my screen opened up onto a blank vista: uncharted territory. The white space encouraged me. It was impersonal, and at the same time intimate: it was the same white space in which Blake and Jules and I exchanged stupid memes, or my mother sometimes sent me little inspirational quotes. I wasn't really expecting a response. She didn't even follow me; it would go right to her slush pile of DMs. Still, my heart hammered in my chest knowing that the message would be waiting for her, should she happen upon it. It would be waiting there forever in her inbox, a place I knew very well did not exist physically but which nonetheless seemed in closer proximity to her. And perhaps she would see it. Anything was possible with this device in my hand, everything reachable and identifiable, all of us equalized by the algorithm. Gemma was savvy; maybe she made a point to respond to messages in order to keep engagement up. Regardless, I knew I was going to do it, and I knew what I was going to say, too. An older guy I had hooked up with in high school had given me a copy of *Hot Water Music*, believing, I think, that I would be impressed with his taste in literature. He told me his favorite quote from the whole book was Bukowski's advice to young writers: "Drink, fuck, and smoke plenty of cigarettes." He wrote this on the title page in pen. It was the only part of the book I read. The guy stopped texting.

I wrote to Gemma: *I read that book in high school.* And to prove to her I had, I quoted my ex-boyfriend's favorite line. Then I wrote: *Wish I was at home reading it, instead of at La Boite. Funny, actually, because I thought I saw you here tonight . . .*

My thumb hovered over the Send button. Jason's words kept running through my head: *Who are you? Are you sweet? Are you earnest? Sarcastic? Ballsy?*

Someone came into the bathroom, startling me and making me feel claustrophobic. I deleted the ellipses and added an exclamation mark. My heart was beating faster. *Am I funny?* I added *lol* to the beginning of the message. I could see the girl's feet in the stall next to mine, pale in Chanel ballet flats, watching me. I deleted all the punctuation, removed all capital letters, and, before I could change my mind, hit Send, hoping that the lack of grammar would make me seem insouciant and cool.

I took a long time washing my hands. The girl came out of the stall and stopped short. I met her eyes in the mirror. We both started, our mouths forming little *o*'s, and then the girl's face darkened and she rushed out.

It took me only a moment to realize. My hands were still wet, the tap still running. I had been in the same room as Gemma and I had let her go, had only stared at her in the mirror like an imbecile. I went out to see if I could catch her before she disappeared into the crowd, not even bothering to dry my hands, just wiping them against my dress. I made my way through the tumult, straining my eyes to pick out any of her distinguishing features through the crush of bodies.

"There you are!" Andrew cupped my shoulder and smiled like he wanted to eat me.

"Here I am," I said distractedly.

"I was looking for you!" He handed me a vodka soda.

I mashed the straw until it was a narrow slit, then sucked hard at it while continuing to scan the crowd. Andrew gently led us away from the crush that had gathered around the bar, toward an open nook between the booths and a potted plant.

"I just wanted to say—thanks for listening earlier."

"Of course." I kept replaying the moment in my head. Looking for clues in her face.

"How old are you again?"

"What?"

"How old are you again?"

"Eighty-two."

He laughed. "No, seriously."

"Nineteen."

He whistled. "Man, nineteen. *Nineteen.* Fuck."

My vodka soda was almost finished and I shook it gently like a little bell, the ice cubes rattling. I was thinking of Gemma looking at me. I was thinking of her reading the message I had sent. When she made the connection, *if* she made the connection, I would look like a stalker. I would look malicious. I didn't know which was worse: Gemma thinking ill of me, or Gemma not noticing me at all.

"You're an old soul," Andrew said, interrupting my thoughts. He wagged his finger at me as if to say *I got your number.* "The way you process pain . . . it's beyond your years. I just feel like you really *got me*, you know."

I wanted to slap the poor man in the face. Instead, when he leaned in a second later, I let myself be kissed. I let his mouth expand over mine until our teeth were mashing, and I bit his lip and pressed my body against his, as one flings oneself off a cliff.

The next thing I remember, I was in Andrew's bed and we were having sex. I felt badly for dozing off. It wasn't his fault. I was so drunk, everything felt dull and numb. The only thing I could feel was the sharp metal of my bra strap digging into my back. So I started moaning. Soft at first. Just so he wasn't offended. But after some amount of time—it might have been one minute, it might have been fifteen—I had somehow fallen asleep again.

I forced myself awake with a jolt and screamed: "I'm cumming!"

That put an end to it.

Afterward, he crawled up to me on his elbows and kissed me on the cheek, obviously pleased with himself. I knew I had to leave soon. I have a rule about sleepovers: I don't do them. But I was already under the spell of sleep. My body felt weighed down, and the idea of flinging it up and out of doors felt impossible, brutal. *Let me doze just for a little,* I thought. *Twenty minutes. Then: Uber.*

"Hey." Andrew nudged me.

I mumbled something, half-asleep.

"Don't fall asleep on me now!" he said playfully, nuzzling my neck. I groaned. "Tell me something about you. I want to know everything there is to know about Nicky."

I laughed.

"What! I'm curious. I feel like I just talked your ear off all night."

Oh, the poor idiot. I started the clock in my head. "What do you want to know?"

"Where'd you grow up?"

"All over."

"Like where?"

I sighed. "Virginia, Texas, California. One year in Mexico. Most of high school was in Santa Fe."

"Army brat?"

"Just poor. My dad died when we were little."

He made a regretful clucking sound with his tongue and stroked the top of my head. Men are so gullible; they believe whatever phantoms they project onto your face. I ask: How can I respect a species so easily deceived? "I'm sorry," he whispered.

"My mom raised the five of us, which is crazy for me to think about now. I don't know how she did it."

"She must be one strong lady."

"She is."

"And your siblings?"

"Four brothers." I yawned and turned on my side, and Andrew wrapped his arm around me and I thought about my fictitious brothers and felt safe. "I'm the baby. So you can imagine how protective they are. They'd probably kill you if they knew about this."

"I better be careful then." He nudged my earlobe with his nose. Sixteen minutes.

"Oh, I wouldn't bother. You're as good as dead already."

He turned me over, and ran his palm against my face. "I'll take my chances." He kissed me and I tasted salt. "Nicky James. What a woman you are."

I left shortly afterward. Outside, it was gray and bleary: the sun was just starting to rise. I heard birds chirping and pretended not to notice. My Uber driver's name was Jesus, a handsome thirtysomething with dark, tired eyes. I wondered what he'd think if he knew where I'd just come from, what I'd been doing: Would he be appalled or turned on?

You're in a take-charge cycle for career and responsibilities, dear Aquarius, but today's energies may pull you back a little. Kylie Jackson, a former Disney star, did a pole-dancing routine in a music video for Jay Real, a white pop star, and the Internet couldn't decide if it was co-opting black culture or promoting pedophilia (Jackson was fifteen) or if it was actually totally okay, avant-garde even, but I was jealous of the way she looked in the screenshot, her breasts straining against the teal Lurex of the self-consciously trashy bikini top. I wondered if she had implants; if she did, they were good. Julia had posted an image to her Stories of Blake and me on the dance floor. In a series of quick taps, I dispatched one of the Quick Reactions that had popped up on my screen as suggestions, not even really paying attention to which one I selected, because it didn't matter, they'd all been equally vetted by the algorithm.

SÃO PAULO

To Fernanda Silva, headmistress of Santa Maria College, an international all-girls boarding school located in the upscale neighborhood of Alto da Boa Vista, it looked as though the flu season, which typically gets underway in June, had begun early this year. Then, an alarmed classmate reported that her friend, who had been one of the dozen students taken ill following the school's May 1 Labor Day celebrations, was acting strangely. When Ms. Silva and the school's nurse visited the young woman, fifteen, she did not appear to recognize them. Confused and disoriented, the student asked where she was. When told, she said she had never heard of the school. Ms. Silva's student is one of eighty-five known cases of a bizarre new disease the Brazilian government is racing to identify. The sickness, which—

MILEY CYRUS'S HOT GIRL SUMMER HEATS UP.

It's Miley's party and she can do what she wants. The pop songstress continued her so-called "hot girl summer"

campaign on Instagram, showing off her toned physique in
a racy two-piece—

MILEY CYRUS'S DIET & EXERCISE ROUTINE
REVEALED.

Miley Cyrus has been in the headlines recently for her
romantic shenanigans following the sudden split from her
ex-husband. But, here at *Star Daily*, it's her bod that's really
caught our attention. Below, how she got her "hot girl summer" physique. Miley is an avid yoga fan—

SIXTEEN SCARY SKINNY PICTURES OF
CELEBRITIES.

Our weight-loss expert EXCLUSIVELY reveals which stars
have lost weight the unhealthy way, and which are—

Outside my door, I fiddled with my keys, dropping them in front
of a homeless man who was sitting on two pieces of cardboard, passed
out. His palms were open, facing up on his thighs, his legs splayed out
in front of him. I thought he looked dead.

When I got into bed, I opened up Instagram again. It was then
I noticed the familiar sight blaring in the upper right-hand corner of
my screen: a smooth red bubble signifying a new message. I clicked on
it with no particular urgency, not expecting anything. The night had
been so overshadowed by my encounter with Gemma in the bathroom,
and I was so tired and drunk, that I had momentarily forgotten that I'd
DMed her. After all, I'd figured the chances of her replying were slim.
So when the screen slid by and I saw her name at the top of my DMs,
bolded, *1 new message*, my heart stopped. She had actually written back!
Gemma Anton wrote: *Funny, must have been a mirage ;)*

The words on their own could have meant anything. But the winky face suggested mischief, complicity. An admission. Gemma knew that I knew she had lied. It was no big deal. Just a bit of fun. Still, it was something. A connection.

I thought for a moment, then typed out a response: *musta been*. I added a winky face, the mirror image of Gemma's.

It was past five in the morning. I knew Gemma wouldn't reply until later, if at all. In gray script, my screen informed me she had been *active 1h ago*. But I was unsatisfied and wanted more. I visited her profile. She had no new posts, so I placated myself by poring over her tagged images. There she was, sitting cross-legged on a dock somewhere, smile-squinting into the sun, freckled nose under one of those cool-again bucket hats, a child who would twist her body away from her parents as they apply sunscreen, a loved child, a spoiled child, long, glorious limbs glistening in the sun, compact waist, and those incongruous breasts, soft fruits blossomed from that ascetic tree branch. A whiff of fresh grass mingled with a milky, sweet smell, a cooking smell—she used extra-virgin coconut oil in place of lotion, I knew. Ralph Lauren campaign. Paid nearly a million, I'm told.

Gemma was eating a plum somewhere outside, it seemed, though it could have been in a studio, properly lit; her face, that newborn face, took up nearly the whole frame. Her lips pressed against the pulpy flesh of the plum; I could feel the slight resistance as her teeth pierced its skin and her tongue pressed against its insides. Juice dripped down her fingers. Her eyes were mischievous, guileless, as if she were unaware of her beauty.

Gemma was walking down the street in New York City; faded Levi's, a men's button-down, long, bushy blond hair, air-dried, obviously. This was her, the real her, as captured by paparazzi a few months ago. Her arm was wrapped loosely, carelessly, around the neck of Benoit, who was scruffy-faced, tired-looking. They looked serious, cool, like they didn't care about being famous at all, like they stayed up late reading to each other—she had a book in one hand, I couldn't see which one—and shared their dreams in the morning.

Gemma was sitting in a café, wearing wire-rimmed glasses, reading Joan Didion, absorbed and studious; croissant (one bite out of it), café au lait. Gemma was on the beach, a surfboard balanced on her head, her body bathed in the clear, golden light favored by certain photographers. Gemma was at a dinner table covered in white cloth and littered with fine wineglasses. She was laughing with another young woman, a model with dark-brown hair, full lips; her elbows were on the table, her hands clasped as if in prayer. Gemma was wading into the ocean. Gemma was in church, dressed as a nun. Gemma was walking out into the sky, clouds so puffy they could hold you up.

Gemma was

Gemma was

Gemma was

I'd fallen asleep.

The next day, I put up an Instagram of me wearing a Forever 21 Tie-Dye Cross-Strap Bra Top and Zara Tie-Dye Leggings, both knockoffs of Outdoor Voices' Tie One On tie-dye collaboration with graffiti artist Ha-Ha. Caption: *Repent for the sins of your forefathers, Grey Goose and Patron.*

In the picture, I'm standing in my bathroom, looking bored and casual and good-looking. It was the fifteenth one I took, and I chose it because I'm arching my back just enough that you can't actually tell I'm arching my back, but my ribs still protrude slightly and my thigh gap looks bigger.

With today's energies, dear Aquarius, it may be a better time to decompress and regroup. Fourteen Likes. Netflix announced it would allow users to stream videos at 1.5 times the regular speed, a more efficient way to binge-watch as long as you considered efficiency to mean the attenuation of the time and effort required to complete a task, and as long as you considered finishing a series a task that needed to be ticked off, rather than something to be milked and enjoyed. *Kylie Jackson Defends Pole-Dancing Video: "It's Art."* Seven Likes. Comment, from @ LaurenKombi: *hi, can I have your body, pls & thnk u.* Gas prices jumped thirty cents. A decision had been reached in the Eric Garner case: no charges were to be filed against the police officer who choked Garner to death. Sixteen Likes. A comment from my mother, who once came close to winning Miss New Jersey and who always takes great pride in my appearance: *Gorgeous!* Next to the word she put a smiley face with hearts for eyes. *See you in a few! Love, Mom.*

As per our arrangement, my mother came into town every other Thursday from Newark, where she'd taken over her older sister's empty apartment, since Auntie Joey and her husband had recently moved to Florida. The apartment in Newark was a considerable downgrade for her—the spare bedroom was nearly as big as her former dressing room. But I knew she was happy to get out of Illinois. In Newark, no one's heard of the Heffernans. But in the country clubs and department stores and fancy grocers up and down the North Shore, the name still slithers on people's tongues. My father had "misappropriated" the $30 million his real estate development company had raised to build condos in the area, defrauding his investors, many of whom were our neighbors—his drinking buddies, the parents of my school friends. Of course, I'd hated him long before this awful disclosure. He was a drunk, and while he had his magic—drunks often do—and could be impossibly charming, by the age of ten, I'd decided I could no longer ignore or forgive his rages, his philandering (I occasionally came across a Polaroid of a seminude woman, tucked into the papers in his briefcase), the bruises that every so often appeared on my mother's body. When they fought, I would hide out in the apartment above the garage, which belonged to Inna, our "live-in," as they were called, and collapse into a fit of such grandiose, self-righteous pity as only a spoiled teenager could summon. If Inna was there, she'd give me a glass of tap water from the sink, stroke my back, and let me watch whatever I wanted on a small TV that looked like it was from the 1980s. I didn't know it then, but I loved Inna. She had three grown sons back in the Philippines that she hadn't seen in nearly fifteen years. She probably thought I was crazy. Of course, we had to let her go when my father got arrested. I haven't spoken to her since.

My mother and I had agreed to meet at The Coffee Shop in Union Square; she'd already seen my apartment, and I knew she was not eager to return to it. It was a reminder of how much we'd lost, the physical manifestation of how small we'd become. The day I'd moved in, when we'd finished unpacking, I remember her saying, in a strenuously cheerful voice, that minimalism was coming back in, that it had better feng shui, as if the space's depressing barrenness were an aesthetic choice instead of one of necessity. We'd christened the apartment by cracking open a bottle of gin (her drink of choice) and, a little tipsy, she'd looked around the apartment and said, "It reminds me of the little place I used to live in in Jersey City." She never spoke of her youth in New Jersey. "I was probably about your age." She sighed. "Well, it's only temporary."

"What?"

"This apartment." Then she had glared at me. "Your age." When she left there were tears in her eyes.

There was still no response from Gemma. I kicked myself for not writing something wittier or more interesting. She might have read my message and thought I didn't even care to keep the conversation going. It was so *blah*. I should have asked a question, made a joke, *something*. I took a deep breath and began typing. *Woof, so hungover. How are you feeling this morning?* I bit my nail, deleted what I wrote. I went to her profile, looking for clues. She had 1,324 posts. 468K Followers. 881 Following. Beneath her name was a series of symbols and phrases; they were obscure in meaning on their own but, taken together, created a certain effect. Two miniature flags hung just below her name, announcing her national identity: French and American. The text beneath read

Esprit Universel, which I knew from Google Translate was the French word for jack-of-all-trades. Then there was a procession of shooting stars, nine in total, followed on the next line by the words *love, love, love, always love*. Next to Gemma's handle at the top was a small circular mark, simple in design—a white check mark on a blue background— yet deeply significant: this was Instagram's hallowed verification badge, signifier of the Followed vs. the Follower. It meant the social platform recognized a need to authenticate the account, separate it from the fakes and the copies. It anointed only the truly influential and famous, and seeing it again on Gemma's page reinforced the gravity of my missed opportunity last night. Fleetingly, I imagined a white check next to my name, and felt myself swell with the importance and authority it conferred. I went back to our DM thread. Everyone knows that white checks beget white checks. I thought for a long time and then typed out what I thought was a perfectly charming message. *Question: Do mirages get hangovers? Cuz I am definitely *feeling* it this morning.* I threw my phone onto my bed and tried not to think about it again.

I had a few hours to kill before I had to meet my mother, so I took off the yoga gear and put on Brandy Melville Molly Denim Shorts in Faded Blue, a vintage T-shirt I'd stolen from Julia that said *The Specials* on it, Topshop Porto Buckle Sandals in Tan, and Thomas James LA Tiny Hexagonal Furious Sunglasses in Gold. The man was still there on the broken-up cardboard, his hands resting on his thighs, palms up. I got a coffee, black, at Think Coffee, even though Dunkin' Donuts was closer and cheaper. I couldn't be seen walking around with a Dunkin' Donuts cup. Then I went to the Duane Reade on the corner, my favorite place to float.

When I was growing up, my mom and I always went shopping together. It was "our thing." My mom said it was like sports, but for women. We'd drive back from the city at dusk, the back seat heavy with shopping bags and a sense of accomplishment. My mother really blossomed when she shopped. Around the house, she was like a nervous ghost, constantly walking up and down the halls but never really doing or saying anything. She had few friends in Barrington but all of the salesgirls at Neiman's knew her and *loved* her. Walking in with her was like walking in with a celebrity. Now she avoids the place like the plague. Even though she can still afford to buy some of the cheaper brands in there, she can't show her face. It's not like she'd be recognized by other shoppers or something, but the salesladies—they *know*. We tried window-shopping in New York a few times after I moved, but I could tell it depressed her. So now we just do lunch.

Walking through the automatic doors of Duane Reade immediately calmed me: the bright lights, the antiseptic white floors, the shelves and shelves of colorfully packaged products, the frisson of possibility. It's the only place I can really afford to shop, so I go every so often just to relax. I wandered through the hair aisle. Gemma washed her hair every other day. She used an all-natural brand, and a shampoo for dandruff. I ran my fingers over the bottles, smooth as pearls. Inside, the goo would be pearly, too, white and uniform. Gemma doesn't really wear makeup, but once, when she put up a picture of herself from the bathroom, I zoomed in and looked at all the labels on the bottles. I couldn't afford any of them, but after some research, I found out that L'Oréal makes a pretty good dupe of the Clé de Peau she uses. Almost everything has a dupe nowadays, thank god: if a product is popular enough, it's bound to get knocked off. The developers at other beauty brands can just buy it right in the store, distill it down to its most essential components, then repackage and sell it. Two bottles of foundation, under two different labels and with a fifty-dollar price differential, can look nothing alike from the outside, but inside they're exactly the same. There was something about this that I found poignant and beautiful. When I found the foundation I was looking for in the makeup aisle, I squatted down, furtively unscrewed the cap, and squirted some of it into my hand. It smelled like baby powder. I closed my eyes and spread it over my skin. Still squatting, I looked all around. Then I slipped it into my purse.

On my way out, a pimply girl standing in the acne aisle, wearing a Brandy Melville dress I had tried on and rejected, looked at me forlornly. I knew she envied me, as I envied Gemma. Life is sometimes too funny and too cruel.

When I got to The Coffee Shop, my mom was already waiting for me, as I knew she would be, sitting in a tucked-away booth at the back, examining her nail beds. She was wearing a lightweight camel coat, even though it was eighty degrees out, and her hair was blonder, almost platinum, and frizzy in the heat, puffing out around her shoulders like cauliflower florets. Her face lit up when she saw me. I leaned in to kiss her on the cheek, and she put her hand around my neck and clutched me there. I had to wrench myself away before sliding in.

"Oh, honey, you look beautiful."

"Thanks."

"Is that a new shirt?" It was the threadbare vintage band T-shirt I'd stolen from Julia. Neither of us knew who the band was.

"It's Julia's."

Her brows furrowed. "Who?"

"Friend." She should have known who Julia was. She should have remembered that.

"I went blonder," she said, as if it were a major disclosure.

"I see."

She waited.

"It looks really good," I said.

"You think?" She touched the ends self-consciously. "It's not too blond?"

"No. I like it."

"Single process. Upkeep is easier."

"How's Alison doing?" Alison was my mother's longtime hair colorist and stylist. My father, who was nominally an Irish Catholic and liked to remind us of it every once in a while, as if to claim some moral high ground, called Alison my mother's priest and confessor. Mom countered that she had nothing to confess, and the sad thing was, I didn't think she did. What she and Ali mostly talked about, I suspected, was other people. Other people were my mother's favorite topic. When I got old enough I started seeing Alison too ($250 for a teenager's highlights, thank you very much), though we never became close, and I sensed that secretly pleased my mother. She had so few true friends, I think she wanted Alison all to herself. All throughout my father's never-ending court proceedings, my mom never once missed her monthly appointment.

"Actually, I didn't go to Alison."

I pulled a face. "Why?"

"I thought it was time for a change," she said breezily, suddenly becoming fascinated by the menu. "Oh! The omelet looks good!"

"Who'd you go to then?"

"Actually, I did it myself," she said nonchalantly. "It was easy! There's this new company that makes salon-quality dye—you order it online. It's better for the environment, too. And it only took fifteen minutes! Which is crazy when you think of how many hours I'd spent in that chair, not that I regret it—" My mother prattled on, but I was so depressed by the image of her bending over the sink in her pink bathrobe and those awful plastic gloves, biting her lip while the peroxide stung her scalp, that I could hardly follow her. I know it's difficult to pity her. Hadn't she gotten what she deserved? When people began showing up outside our house—it was a mansion, really—in the North Shore, carrying signs like *PONZI SCHEME FRAUD!* and *The 99% Say: Guilty*, they sometimes yelled things at my mother. Once, when we were inching out of our driveway, reporters and photographers crowding around our car—my mother refused to honk; she thought it was undignified—a man with mad-scientist hair and a rumpled business suit yelled at her to "Get a job." But what could she do? She wasn't qualified for any kind of job, and who would hire her—wife of the famous P. T. Heffernan—anyhow? Even if she somehow managed to get one, the truth is my mother *couldn't* work a job. She wouldn't know how. It'd be like asking a monkey to drive a car.

I realized my mother was looking at me pointedly.

"Huh?" I asked.

"What are you going to get?"

"Oh, um—" I looked at the menu and said the first thing my eyes set on. "The fruit salad, I think."

"That's it?"

"I'm not that hungry."

"I think you should get the omelet. I don't want you to get too thin."

"I'm not too thin."

"It doesn't look good, you know, to be that thin. I know. I was really thin when I was younger—everyone was always telling me how thin I was and yet I was always trying to lose weight. You're the perfect weight right now. What are you, one-twenty? That's what I used to weigh."

"Somewhere around there." I was 117.

"Don't try to lose any more."

"I'm *not*, Mom."

"I just want you to be healthy."

When the waiter finally arrived, I ordered the omelet with home fries just to get her to shut up. My mother got the fruit salad. "*I* need to watch my weight," she said, though she spent most of the meal spearing various bits on my plate and ferrying them to her mouth quickly as if I wouldn't notice. Eventually, talk turned to my father, as I knew it would.

"You should call him," my mother said. I was busy mashing the remaining potatoes with my fork and didn't answer. She went on: "We've filed another appeal. Saul has a good feeling about this one."

I put my fork down. "Why keep trying? Everyone knows he did it."

"Don't say that!" she shout-whispered, looking over her shoulder.

I rolled my eyes. "No one's listening."

"You don't know that." She clasped her collar together against her throat. In a whisper she continued: "People are looking for any excuse . . . You saw what happened. Making a big deal out of everything."

"A big deal? He defrauded people of hundreds of thousands of dollars! Families lost their homes! Kids can't go to college!"

She waved that away—the fact of his conviction, his crimes—as if it were all a misunderstanding. "It was an accounting strategy," she said. "He was always going to pay it back, he just needed to move the money around first. It would have been in everybody's best interest if they'd just let him continue—"

"Mom! Let him continue? He was stealing."

She sighed. "It's not so cut-and-dry, Mick. These things are complicated."

"Jesus, Mom, when will you stop believing his lies?"

"He's your father, Michaela."

"I know. I have no choice in the matter. You do."

"What do you mean?"

"You should divorce him!" I hadn't meant to yell it.

She looked stricken.

"I'm sorry," I said.

"Oh, honey." She covered my hand with hers. She still wore her wedding ring: an obese diamond, haloed by chubby children and set on a thick platinum band. If I looked closely, I could see the outline of tender pale-white skin underneath the band. Otherwise her hands looked like those of someone much older: blue veins crisscrossed them like highways, and age spots had appeared as constellations sometime over the past few years. Her knuckles, too, had swollen. It occurred to me that perhaps she wasn't able to slide the ring off anymore. She said: "I couldn't do that to him."

I stared at her. I still remembered the time he gave her a black eye so big she had to get new sunglasses the size of flying saucers (Chanel). I still remembered when, shortly after his mother died of a sudden stroke, he'd absconded for a week away in the Caribbean for "some alone time to recover." Only we found out later he'd gone to Atlantic City instead, returning bleary-eyed, ten grand poorer, and with a case of crabs. I knew all these things and more. I was like a spy in my own house. My favorite place to sit when I was little had been a window seat tucked into the corner of our living room. And though it was comfortable and had a view of the garden, what I really liked was that when I sat in it, I felt like I disappeared into the walls of the room. It wasn't just my imagination. Because of the large drapes on either side, it was easy to miss the small person with her knees tucked up to her chin, sucking on a piece of her hair, staring dreamily out the window. My parents often did.

I don't remember the first fight I saw—the violence and anger between them was always there, *had* always been there to my knowledge, so that it took on the constant hum of white noise—but I am pretty sure it happened in that room. Anyway, many more were to come. At first, I sat motionless out of shame; I didn't want them to see me because for some reason I felt embarrassed, as if what they were doing wasn't wrong until I witnessed it. But then I stayed because I wanted to know; I wanted to know what the fights were about, what made my father spit things from his mouth I had thought unimaginable, what made his hand shoot out like a whip and slap my mother across the face, what made my mother collapse into herself, lips trembling. I don't know why they thought it okay to fight in front of me like that—for surely, they saw me eventually. I guess they thought I wouldn't understand. But I did. I made a point to. I saw the violence that roiled my father and mistook it for power. "He's who you inherited your rage from, isn't he?" the court-appointed therapist asks me now. Yes, it's true, I learned the language of violence from him. But back then, I never had an outlet for it. Learning, knowing, that was the only power I had.

Still, I somehow managed to miss the nature of my father's dealings, a crucial element of our lives, the genesis of our wealth. Friends used to ask, *But didn't you* know? *Didn't you guess?* I honestly didn't. That's the thing about money. It insulates you from certain truths. If ignorance is bliss, then it's also the greatest luxury money can buy.

The week after my father got arrested, I went back to that window seat. Our house was surrounded by a thick stone wall, and behind it was a semicircular lawn my mother had just that summer planted with roses: showy pink, white, and red blooms. There had been a big oak tree in the corner of the lawn that I'd played on as a child, but it'd died the year before—we never figured out why—and my mother had used its removal as an excuse to get the whole lawn redone. Hence the roses. If you looked closely, you could see a large circle of grass just a shade brighter and more uneven where the oak had been ripped out. It reminded me of a poorly concealed zit. Beyond the wall, and through the gate, I could see the crowds of photographers, reporters, protestors with their signs. Watching from my half-concealed perch at the window, I was transfixed. It all seemed to have nothing to do with me. I had to remind myself: this house, that oak tree, those roses, the very hair on my mother's highlighted head, all of it had been bought and paid for with those people's money, and now that money was gone. *Poof.* I may not have personally done anything wrong, but my entire life, my very existence, had been built on the back of others' sufferings. And that made me complicit. It is immoral to be rich; if being rich means having more money than you need, more money than you know what to do with, who do you think is paying that price? The epiphany hung around until I was broke. Yes, it's immoral to be rich, but it's worse being poor.

I put my hand on top of my mother's and we held each other there for a few moments, each lost in our own galaxy of thought, until she, looking down, said, "I like that nail polish. Is it Essie?"

"OPI." It was pale gray, and called Take No Prisoners.

On the way to the PATH station, we stopped to buy magazines. My mother must have been boiling in that silly coat, though she showed no signs of it.

"Oh look, they have all the foreign ones!" she said, beelining for a wall on which dozens of frozen smiles gleamed from brightly lit covers. I picked up one of the fat avant-garde titles and leafed through it, settling on a long profile of a famous female artist, in which she herself was not pictured but a teenage model posed, as if in mid-brushstroke, in front of her abstract canvases. My mother peeked over my shoulder. She had a stack of magazines cradled in her arm and wordlessly fanned them out so I could see her selection.

"These get me so excited!" she said giddily. Her eyes fell on a magazine with Gemma on the cover, staring icily at the camera. Then she looked at me adoringly: "You know, you're so beautiful. I knew you were going to be a model, even when you were little. Everyone was always telling me how beautiful you were."

"We should go." I made a show of checking the time. "You'll miss the 2:16."

Outside, my mother tucked her arm into mine. I could hear the rhythmic *thwap* as the plastic bag full of magazines hit her calf. The streets were crowded and the air was thick with the caramelized-sugar smell of roasted nuts, and strangers' sweat. I thought everyone looked particularly gross and ugly. A homeless woman sat cross-legged on a blanket, next to a flea-bitten dog, and looked at us plaintively. My mother fished through her wallet and gave her a carefully folded one-dollar bill.

"Can't you just see yourself on the cover of one of those someday?" my mother asked me suddenly, continuing a conversation she must have been having in her head.

"Maybe."

"Well, *I* totally can. You should send your picture to *Vogue*."

"That's not how it works, Mom."

"The important thing is to just be seen."

"There are castings you go to. My agent sets them up."

"People like eagerness. That you take the initiative."

"Mom. Stop."

"I just want you to have a career. I gave up mine when I married your father, which of course I don't regret at all, because I had you." She cupped my cheek briefly in her palm. "But, still."

"I know."

"Any exciting gigs coming up?"

"It's pretty slow in the summer."

We came to a stop outside the PATH station. My mother squeezed my hand. "Well," she said. "There's a second bedroom at Joey's—we just have to move the exercise bike and clean out the closet. It's mostly dog toys in there anyway."

I looked up at her sharply but she wouldn't meet my eye. "I thought the deal was, you guys could keep helping me out for the next six months, possibly a year." I measured the words carefully.

"I know, sweetheart, but that was when we were winning the last appeal."

"And now?"

She sighed. "Saul is the very best, the very best, everyone says—"

I cut her off. "So?"

"Well, he's not cheap." She touched the ends of her hair again with her fingertips and added, almost to herself, "You get what you pay for."

"Mom, this appeal bullshit has to stop."

"I can't," she said. Her cheeks were red, and her eyes watery. "It's the only way we can ever . . ." She faltered.

"Ever what?"

She rifled through her purse and took out a tube of ChapStick, running it over her lips in a manner so familiar to me that it instantly took me back to childhood: one rough glide, sealed with two silent smacks. "Things will go back to normal," she said finally, "after this appeal. In the meantime, don't worry about it, lovey. Joey's isn't so bad, and Newark is just a train ride away. We'll figure something out."

I watched her descend the stairs into the PATH; with each step, a feeling of dread tightened further around my neck like a noose. Since my father had gone to jail, I'd only visited him twice, and both times were awful. I knew my mother saw him every weekend and that it was only a matter of time until she made me go, too. If I lived with her, there would be no escape. I couldn't breathe. A woman sighed loudly and made a show of stepping around me. *Fuck her*, I thought, and stamped my foot as I turned to start the walk home along Fourteenth Street. A couple of tween girls gave me an odd look, and giggled conspiratorially. *Fuck them, too.* My stomach seemed to have expanded with the weight of breakfast, what my mother made me eat, and that fullness began to feel like the dread itself: heavy and nauseating and inevitable. For a moment, I was terrified I would throw up—and that was like the dread, too, because, as much as you feared it, you knew what was going to happen, and a part of you wanted it to happen, just so you could get it over with. Instead, I stopped at a halal truck to buy a bottle of water. I chugged it while speed-walking until it was gone, then chucked it without breaking stride onto a convenient mountain of trash. I could tell I was shaking, and that my eyes were not focusing properly—they kept darting around unbidden—but I pretended not to notice. I imagined, for the benefit of those passersby who occasionally glanced my way, that I was in a rush to meet my boyfriend, and that he was very worried about me, because I'd recently been hospitalized with a mysterious illness that kept me bedridden and emaciated. My phone had died, and now he was sick with worry because he had not heard from me. He was worried the illness had taken me again. I had to get to him. A bike messenger whizzed by me just as I was stepping off the curb, lifting my hair briefly from my shoulders. I didn't even pause; I angled my body so I could glide among the sweaty throng, but I had lost hold of the boyfriend fantasy and the dread returned, swiftly cycling through to anger, fear, despair, and back again.

$13,827. The number flashed in my head like a neon sign. It was how much I owed my agency. They'd loaned me money to live off while I "found my feet" in the city, and I had been too stupid and naive to ask if there'd be interest. Jason had been texting me these past few weeks, too, asking me to find a time so that we could *have a coffee and chat.* I had been putting it off, knowing what he was going to say, the way he would squeeze my thigh in that overly familiar way of his and say, *Sugarplum, you know I love you, but . . .* My vision blurred, and I was struck with sudden vertigo. When I steadied myself, there was an intense aura of familiarity. I had returned to the spot where the woman was sitting, cross-legged, with her dog on a dirtied fleece blanket. She was exactly as she had been before—except now there was a lanky blond woman crouching before her. My ears buzzed as a profound feeling of confusion rankled me and then quickly diffused like a puff of black smoke.

It was Gemma. She was wearing the Outdoor Voices Classic Two-Tone Leggings in Black/Blue, an Entireworld Organic Cotton Tank in Navy, and—I squinted—Gucci Birkenstocks, and her hair bounced as she stood, then formed a curtain in front of her face as she dipped it toward the woman. The woman beamed up at her, thanking her. Gemma laughed lightly as they said goodbye—and then she was off down Fourteenth Street, a Whole Foods tote bag swinging at her shoulder. The woman began to pick at the plastic wrap of a premade sandwich. I watched, frozen, as Gemma rounded the corner, turning down Broadway and out of view.

I took off at a run.

I hadn't intended, at first, to actually talk to her. Truly. I only wanted to see her. To observe her at close range. But by the time I'd followed her a few blocks down Broadway and into the Strand bookstore, a plan had taken shape in my mind. I would bump into her casually and, naturally enough, squint my eyes in recognition. *Were you at La Boîte last night . . . ?* Or, *Ah, what's this, another mirage?* Then we could get to talking. I watched her as she browsed the books on display at the New & Noteworthy Fiction table, hefting them in her long, thin hands as if weighing them and then putting them softly back down again, her sensitive eyes processing each of the brightly designed covers. She seemed in a pensive, almost sad mood, and for a moment, I faltered. Perhaps she didn't want to be bothered. Then again, I was allowed to be there just as much as she was, and if we happened to run into each other, well, it was nobody's fault. Besides, I reminded myself, she *had* messaged me. While I was thinking this, though, she looked up and, catching on something just behind me, abruptly put down the book she was holding and walked off, disappearing between the bookshelves.

It took me a moment to find her in the labyrinthine grid of stacks. When I did, she was tucked up at the end of an aisle, an open book cradled in her hand. Her back was to me, her head dipped forward studiously. She'd tied her hair back into a messy bun, something I did when I wanted to concentrate. Seeing her there, with her hair up, back and neck exposed, daubs of light dancing off the knobs of her spine, I felt nauseated again. My palms were wet, and I realized I'd forgotten to put on deodorant that morning. My own rank animal smell prickled the insides of my nostrils. But I had come too far. I was almost beside her . . . I pretended to study the names along the shelf she was facing . . . I would crouch slightly, as if trying to get a better angle at the titles she was blocking, mutter *excuse me*, our eyes would meet, and then—

"Babe?"

Both of us turned and I, already unsteady on my feet, wobbled and almost fell into our interloper.

"Whoa." Benoit steadied my shoulders, then looked from me to Gemma. He was dressed in all black and wearing tinted aviator frames and a baseball cap. I muttered an apology, blushing, and though it would have been natural for me to turn away, go about my business, I didn't move.

Gemma laughed but she looked annoyed. "I was looking for you."

"And now I'm here."

"Yeah . . ."

"Baby, you know I don't control time." He leaned in and kissed her gently on the cheek and she visibly softened. "Are you . . . ?" He drew an invisible line between Gemma and me with his finger. Gemma turned to look at me, seemingly for the first time.

"Oh, we—" I stammered.

"We don't know each other," Gemma finished, a little too firmly for my liking, though I was too concentrated on the way Benoit seemed to be looking at us through his aviator frames to really care.

Benoit took a step back, and I tried, through sheer will, to force his eyes to stay on me. "But my god!" he said. He had a faint Germanic accent I couldn't quite place. "The resemblance. Like sisters or—"

"Oh no." I laughed self-deprecatingly, so that Gemma wouldn't be insulted. "No, please, I don't."

Gemma fixed me with a thoughtful gaze. "Well," she said carefully, "I guess I could see it." My heart skipped a beat.

"Of course, are you kidding?" Benoit exclaimed. "You could be twins."

"The hair's different," Gemma said. "And the eyebrows."

"Here—" He took out his phone. "I must capture this."

"Babe, I'm sure this girl"—she looked at me pityingly, beseechingly—"doesn't want to have some stranger take her picture." Her eyes flashed back at him with barely concealed annoyance. *Ah*, I thought wisely, *trouble in paradise.*

He turned to me and stuck out his hand. "Hans Benoit. And you?"

"Mickey, Mickey Jones," I said, shaking his hand.

"Nice to meet you, Mickey," Benoit said. Then he turned to Gemma, and I felt the absence of his eyes on me like a sudden drop in pressure. He said to her: "Strangers no more."

She sighed loudly. Benoit had already taken a few steps back and was looking through the camera on his phone. Gemma said to me: "You don't have to, if you don't want to."

"Of course she wants to," said Benoit. "Look at her."

"Whatever," I said, shrugging. "I don't mind."

Benoit motioned with his hands for us to get closer. "Smile," he said, and we did. "Actually, don't," he said, and then we didn't. "Now just look over there, yes, exactly, my god, it's uncanny."

He showed us the results on his phone. I cringed. I thought we looked nothing alike; it must have been some joke, Gemma had been trying to protect me, I was nothing next to her.

"You model?" he asked.

I nodded, feeling chastised.

"Never seen your book around. What agency you with?"

"Would you *stop* harassing the poor girl?" Gemma said.

Trying to regain my composure, I forced myself to smile and said, "Jason at Elite."

Benoit shook his head. "All agents are the devil."

He peered back at his phone. Gemma hooked her arm in his.

"I'll AirDrop it to you," he said. "Mickey's Cell Phone, right?"

Before I could even respond, my phone dinged, and I accepted the photos with a light tap of my thumb. Gemma started to pull him away.

"Nice to meet you," she said to me, and added, rolling her eyes, "*twin*." She could be funny like that. A real dry wit.

Benoit laughed and said over his shoulder, "The question is, which one of you is evil?"

Gemma hit him on the arm. "Stop!" She laughed, then looked back at me warmly, and I thought maybe, actually, we could be friends, I'd misread the interaction. She'd never been more beautiful than in that moment. "Anyway, *I'm* obviously the evil one."

I winked at her and said something, hoping to be funny, about how only time would tell. They walked away and I stood there for a long time, my heart beating as fast as a criminal's.

It wasn't until later, when I was safe at home under the covers, that I dared to look at the photos again. Though I looked pale and waxen next to her, there was indeed, upon closer inspection, a kind of familial resemblance.

Eagerly, I opened up Instagram, and went to Benoit's profile. He had posted the series of photos on his Stories, sandwiched between a photo of smoke billowing from those orange funnels that sprout up around New York City in the summer, and a close-up of Gemma's face backlit by the late afternoon sun. He hadn't tagged Gemma or me, but he had written *SISTERS* on the last photo, the one of us looking off into the distance. I felt lightheaded. I remember thinking the really weird thing was that we looked so comfortable with each other, like we'd known each other for years. My therapist now flags this as an "interesting observation," but all I thought at the time was that Jason would be thrilled.

I responded to Benoit's story: *Ha! So nice meeting you two!*

Then, perhaps against my better judgment, I decided to post the picture he'd sent of the two of us smiling. It took me a long time to think of a caption. But when I did I laughed out loud. I wrote: *Which one of us is evil, though?*

Gemma leans in close. Her mouth is slightly parted, her lids low; beneath them her eyes are unfocused, staring off into the distance. With a graceful flick of the wrist, she applies mascara from a pink tube to her eyelashes as a warm, artificial light suffuses her face. The motion is repeated again and again, with such precision it becomes clear it is the work of a machine, a Boomerang.

Never leave home without a flick of @Glossier mascara. *A link is provided to purchase. Just swipe up.*

Gemma is standing at an angle, one foot thrust forward, an arm at her hip. She is wearing the Paco Rabanne Embellished Chainmail Dress and Totême Flip-Flop Heels in Black. A phone obscures her face. The photo is dim-lit, and there is a diagonal line running through it, the edge of a mirror. All of it is a reflection.

She is on her way to the opening of a new club, The Rising. Everyone is going to be there.

A storefront emerges out of the blackness of a New York City street, teetering back and forth before growing stationary. A neon sign announces Bethune Street Body Work. *In the window is a diagram of a human body, the major organs and veins shown in vibrant colors.* One Hour Massage = $45, *another sign reads.*

"Brb, getting a late-night massage," Gemma's voice trills, though she is still nowhere to be seen.

As the door grows closer, a sign comes into focus. CLOSED, *it reads, in all caps.*

"Psych!" Gemma says, and a hand, glowing ghostly white in the evening light, appears at the bottom of the screen, reaching for the door. It swings open before she can reach it, and a stocky man in a suit greets her.

"Welcome to The Rising," he says.

The room is spinning. Light filters in from the street, and the neon sign in the window casts a pink glow on several potted plants, a golden Buddha, and a reception desk with a little bell on it.

"How cool is the supersecret entrance to The Rising?" Gemma asks.

She walks toward an elevator at the end of a hallway. A hand depresses the arrow denoting up.

Gemma's face appears in the near-dark, her eyes large and shining.

"Okay, my sweets, that's it for now—no phones allowed in the club!"

The doors slide open, and she walks in.

Two days later, I watched as Julia glided a butter knife into the soft white flesh of her poached egg, splitting it so that the tangerine-yellow yolk spilled forth, dressing her avocado toast. Blake climbed onto her chair and took pictures, balancing on her knees.

I was thinking about what had come out of my body that morning: a white pearl of sebum, hard and perfectly round, from a tender pink bump between my groin and navel that I'd been worrying for days. I had rolled it between my fingers appreciatively, thinking how mysterious the body could be, how many secrets it hid from us. Then I tossed it. It almost seemed a heartless thing to do now.

Once Blake was satisfied, she climbed back down and sat in her chair, studying the photos. "Mmm, it looks so good," she said, meaning the food in the photos, not the food on our table, which we all knew she wouldn't eat.

Julia forked a gooey piece of avocado toast into her mouth.

Blake looked up. "Want me to send you one?"

"Nah," said Julia, through a mouthful. "Brunch isn't my *brand*."

"Ha! And what is your brand, pray tell?" I asked archly.

"Drinking, fucking, and smoking."

We laughed. I sliced off a piece of one of Blake's gluten-free waffles and slid it into my mouth.

"So good, right?" Blake asked, even though she hadn't tasted them yet herself. I'd lied and said I'd already eaten, knowing that I could eat whatever was on Blake's plate for free. This secretly pleased her, as if I were not just consuming her food but eating up her fat right off the bone, and she pushed her plate toward me. "Have more," she said. "I'm not that hungry."

She toyed with the photos on her phone. "Which one's better?" she asked us, toggling between two identical and uninteresting photos of our brunch table. Blake had no eye. It was quite sad. Arbitrarily I picked the first photo, then I made her take a picture of me with my fork hanging out of my mouth and my eyes giving a look like *fuck my life*, or whatever, and I looked depressed and skinny and cool. I was going to caption it *waffle monster*, but before I could even post it, I noticed I had a new direct message.

It was from Benoit: *hey m we met in the bookstore . . . would love to shoot u . . . u in?*

My heart leapt into my throat, and I looked up as if I'd seen a ghost. Julia and Blake both gawked at me.

"What is it?" Julia asked.

Silently, I showed them my screen. They both let out surprised puffs of laughter. Julia leaned back in her chair. Blake leaned forward. I hunched over my phone protectively and began typing. I don't even remember what I said. But the answer, of course, was: Yes. Yes. Yes. Yes.

Gemma is staring directly into the camera, the beginning of a smile, or what I think is a smile, playing on her face. She is on a pier somewhere, high above the sea. Behind her, the ocean glitters like a thousand diamonds before cresting softly onto the golden shores.

"I think true beauty is about being real," she says. "Authenticity. That's the most beautiful thing in the world to me."

She is wearing a ribbed white T-shirt, jeans, the gold locket that Benoit gave her. Her lips are painted red, and her blond curls bounce gently in the breeze.

The camera blinks.

She is standing in almost the same spot—only slightly different. She's leaning farther against the railing behind her, looking just to the left. "The advice I would give my younger self is . . . it doesn't matter what anyone thinks. It only matters what you think." *She is speaking strangely. It becomes clear she is being prompted, asked to repeat the question within the answer.* "Oh," *she says, her face lighting up.* "And don't get the gap in your teeth fixed." *She makes air quotes around the word* fixed. *This is a part of her story I know very well: Early on in her career, it was suggested she get the gap in her two front teeth closed. But Gemma refused. Gemma persisted. Gemma won.*

The camera blinks.

"Am I living my truth?" *Gemma laughs. She gestures at the surroundings behind her.* "I'm definitely living my dream. Hopefully that's the same thing."

The camera blinks.

"My big break came when I was working in a cheese shop." *She giggles.* "That was my part-time job in college. It was a very Gouda job." *She pumps her pale-blond eyebrows at the camera ironically.* "That's a cheese industry joke for you. We used to make up puns all day to amuse ourselves. Anyway, one day Hans Benoit came in, the photographer? And that was kind of it."

The camera blinks.

"My secret talent is ballet. And that I can touch my tongue to my nose." *She demonstrates the latter, tilting her head back and making herself go cross-eyed. Gemma describes herself as a nerd. Though it's obvious to anyone with eyes she isn't.*

The camera blinks.

Her hands are on her hips. Her face mimes someone deep in thought. "My motto is . . . beauty is in the eye of the beholder. I guess that goes for everything, not just beauty. Like, different strokes for different folks."

The camera blinks.

"The one beauty product I definitely can't live without is Kleenex Pure Beauty Wipes. I'm legit obsessed with them."

The camera blinks.

Now Gemma is holding a colorful plastic package in the palm of one hand. She peels back the top of it and extracts a Kleenex, which billows in the wind. The Kleenex is Millennial Pink.

"I'm really obsessed with being clean. If I have stuff on my skin for too long, it drives me nuts. Obviously, in my line of work it happens, so I always keep a pack of these in my purse to use on the go." She flourishes the Kleenex in front of the camera and it flutters dramatically. A thought seems to occur to her. She smiles slyly. "In fact . . ."

Gemma begins polishing her red mouth, following the contours of her lips carefully. When she is finished, she waves the Kleenex in front of the camera, showing what she has done: a bloody gash where her lips have pressed into the delicate tissue. She smiles triumphantly, her lips naked and pale.

The camera blinks.

Gemma leans far over the railing, looking out at the horizon. The Kleenex is gone. Her lips aren't quite as pale. They've been touched up with something pink and natural-looking. "My biggest dream," she says. "Hm . . ." She looks genuinely perplexed. "I just want to be happy, you know? Happy in myself. Sometimes that's the hardest thing to do."

The screen dissolves to black, and the credits roll. Gemma is gone. The interview is over. If you'd like to know more about Kleenex Pure Beauty Wipes, click here.

My shoot with Benoit was four days away.

I promised myself I would tell no one. *No one.* And then, after a few drinks, I told a lot of people. *Benoit is going to shoot me.* All of the struggle I'd faced—the dead-end casting calls and god-awful penny-pinching shoots, the fear that I'd never be anything, would be broke for the rest of my life, a failure like my father—was validated in those six words. It had all been worth it. Even the people who didn't really know who he was knew enough to pretend to be impressed. *Benoit is going to shoot me in four days. I have a shoot at Benoit's studio.*

That was all I knew. Benoit communicated in short Instagram DMs, laced with charming grammatical errors common among ESLers. It would be "intimate and low-key," a "super chill vibe." I figured that meant it'd pay pennies and I might have to take my top off. That was fine. I was no prude. I thought about messaging Gemma. I spent a lot of time staring at the white space under my last message to her, trying to penetrate its emptiness, bore past its glassy surface and directly into Gemma's brain. What was she thinking? Had she said something to Benoit about me—endorsed me somehow—that made him want to work with me? Did she even know about the shoot? I wanted to reach out to her but could think of nothing to say, no way to bring it up.

So I watched the Kleenex video on repeat. It had come out just a few days before. I had, of course, already read and reread the little Q&As and profiles of her that I could find online. But this was one of her first video interviews, and it was interesting to watch those words coming out of a moving mouth instead of marching across a screen in tiny black-and-white lettering. It felt almost unnatural. There seemed to me a great significance buried deep within the video's pixels, a meaning behind her dreamy expression, the ocean behind her, the fact that the beach she was on, as I learned later, when I googled it, was called Paradise Cove. I wondered what she was thinking about when they asked her if she was living her truth. I wondered if the sun was in her eyes. I wondered if she really *was* living her truth and, if she was, what the fuck that even meant.

The Kleenex wipes smelled like strawberries. Good at first, and then nauseating. I wrapped my fingers in them and ran them across my brow, along my jawline, between my breasts. I put on red lipstick and watched myself take it off in the mirror.

The day before the shoot, Benoit's production assistant, Kiki (@ KissKiss), emailed me. I'd already tried to elicit what details I could from Benoit without seeming overeager, but he was incapable of giving a straightforward answer. Finally, now, I had some concrete information: Call time was nine a.m., and hair and makeup was to begin promptly. The shoot was expected to last until sunset. Lunch would be catered. A car was coming to pick me up at 8:15 in the morning. Any hair around my bikini line, arms, and underarms should be removed. *Also,* she wrote, *Benoit is very sensitive to scent.* She warned me against wearing any perfume or scented lotion or eating onion or garlic within twenty-four hours of the shoot. Even deodorant was discouraged. *Benoit recommends using lavender oil,* she wrote. *Anything too artificial kills the vibe. Vibe,* I was already learning, was a key word in Kiki's and Benoit's vocabulary.

She didn't tell me what the shoot was for, and I didn't ask.

While early today there can be a tendency to worry or stew if you're in limbo on a matter, dear Aquarius, the day shapes up to help open communications. Benoit was a Leo. I knew his birthday because last summer, when they were very much on, Gemma put up a photo of him blowing out the candles on a Momofuku sprinkles cake. He's wearing a wifebeater and the aviators and there's a sheen of sweat over his tattoos. *43 years young! Happy birthday, my love.* Gemma's birthday was November 7, a Scorpio. They had an 83-percent compatibility rating, whereas I had a 76-percent compatibility rating with Benoit, and an 85-percent with Gemma.

How to Attract a Leo Man:

1. *Stand out from the crowd but only have eyes for him.*
2. *Tease him but remain direct.*
3. *Be natural and a little sensible when in private.*
4. *Get rid of your complexes and be ready for games.*
5. *Be there when he opens up about his emotions.*

I imagined celebrating Benoit's birthday, him, Gemma, and me, the three of us all together. Maybe we'd even go away somewhere for the weekend, or I could help host a party, maybe even at The Rising, which we still hadn't been able to go to; Joe said the manager was being lame about it and we weren't about to try if we didn't already know we were on the list. But it was frustrating. Gemma had been going every Thursday and I hadn't even been inside. I went to the club's Instagram page. The bio read *Local watering hole. Dance floor. Rec center. All about community.* The last post featured an artful black-and-white photo of a black person and white person hugging, naked, their bodies pressed together. *Love is love is love. Together we stand.* #solidarity #speakup #justiceforEricGarner, the caption read, though it was unclear what it was actually saying or how it related to the image. It was the kind of thing brands had started posting recently, as if they were moral entities instead of capitalist enterprises, as if they had values beyond customer retention and profit margin. We'd come to expect this from them— they were now our legislators, our educators, and, most importantly, our friends. As people began to think of themselves more and more as brands, brands started to feel more and more like people. The next image in the Grid showed Gigi and Bella Hadid at the *JOY Magazine* party hosted a few days before. I swiped through the carousel clocking the celebrities: Christina Aguilera, Mark Ronson, Sasha Velour, Kylie Jackson (who was suddenly everywhere, even though she was still only fifteen), Pharrell Williams, DJ Khaled. Blake began an Instagram Live video, as part of her Thirty Days of Abundance meditation practice. I tuned in briefly, to show support, and sent her a hands-clapping emoji. She was wearing the same Forever 21 Tie-Dye Crop Top—the knockoff of Outdoor Voices—that I had. São Paulo had issued a shelter-in-place order for residents, trying to quell the spread of the disease, which the press had dubbed the Brazilian flu even though it wasn't technically a flu. A model I'd worked with two years ago, once, had made spaghetti for her boyfriend. She was now a licensed nutritionist and, from what I could tell from her photos, still anorexic. Two of Jeffrey Epstein's abuse victims had asked the judge to deny the billionaire bail. Protests had erupted outside the court, railing against the ruling in the Eric Garner case. Madewell wanted me to buy something from their new summer collection. Julia texted me: *Sup slut?*

She came over later that night. I checked, for the ten thousandth time, to see if Gemma had started Following me yet. She hadn't. I wondered if she knew that Benoit was shooting me, and if she didn't, whether I should tell her about it or not.

"Meh," said Julia, after we'd had a few shots of vodka and I'd felt it increasingly difficult not to say anything about it. "Who cares?" She was hunched over my puny kitchen island, hands clasped together, her cleavage like an axe cut, sucking on an edamame pod.

She pushed the tinfoil container in my direction but I waved it away, terrified of accidentally ingesting trace amounts of garlic or onion.

"It just seems weird because I met them together, you know?" I had told Julia and Blake about the bookstore encounter, omitting the part about how I'd followed her in there and making it sound completely coincidental. "And when I DMed them, it was to both of them," I added defensively. "But then when Benoit messaged me, it was just to me."

"He probably wants to fuck you."

"No way. They're *insanely* in love."

"Insanely codependent, more like it."

"They do things apart. I think she's on vacation right now without him." In fact, I *knew* Gemma was on vacation. She'd put up a photo of herself in a terry-cloth robe, sipping tea, her feet in those plastic sandals that spas give you. *Our society programs us to just go-go-go, nonstop,* she wrote in the caption. *But we aren't robots. It's important to take time to really just BREATHE and BE. Have the courage to just STOP. This is NOT a luxury. It is a vital part of maintaining a healthy mind and a healthy heart.*

"Interesting she's on vacation," said Julia, tossing the eviscerated edamame onto a pile of its fallen brothers.

"Whatever. I just don't want her to think that *I* approached *him*."

"I wouldn't worry too much about it."

"So you don't think I should, like, message her or something?" If Julia had seen my face, she would have seen that my eyes had grown wide and shiny, like a puppy begging for food. But she was looking at her phone, sliding her finger rhythmically up and down its glassy surface.

"Nah, I wouldn't," she said, her eyes still fixed on the screen. "Anyway, it's better if she doesn't know. She might be jealous."

I shut her down, loudly and emphatically. Completely ridiculous, I said. Gemma could not possibly see me as a threat.

Secretly, though, the idea thrilled me. And after Julia left, my heart was still thudding so loudly in my throat that, even though I'd sworn I would not drink too much the night before the shoot, I poured myself another few shots of vodka, mixing them with lukewarm tap water. An agent, the one I'd had before Jason, had told me once that vodka soda was the only thing I should ever drink. I was seventeen at the time. She said, "It's like drinking skinny. I never touch anything else." I thought it tasted like nail polish remover. But soon, inevitably, I was guzzling it down just like the rest of the girls, while the men drank beers or whiskey sours, things that actually tasted like something, filled the glass with color, weight. Vodka soda no longer tasted like nail polish remover to me—it tasted like nothing, looked like nothing, and smelled like the void. Drinking it was like drinking emptiness. How many did I inhale over the years? Millions, it felt like. Gallons of emptiness.

I drank down the last shot in one gulp, then turned off the lights.

Benoit's studio was housed on the third and top floors of a small converted warehouse in Bushwick. Even now, I can still picture it exactly. Cement floors. Big windows. Fifteen-foot ceilings. It had been divided up by a series of temporary walls that stopped a foot from the exposed ceiling, so that you entered into a long, blank hallway with identical, flimsy-looking doors and cheap gold doorknobs. *The moon spends the day in your spirit sector, dear Aquarius, encouraging you to seek new ideas or approaches.* I was wearing Reformation Cynthia High Relaxed Jeans, an Urban Outfitters Mesh Ruched Cami in Snakeskin, Converse Chuck Taylor All Star Sneakers in Black, Farrow Sandra Semi-Hoop Earrings in Brown Tortoise, and *New York* Magazine Tote Bag in Natural Canvas. Three protestors had been arrested at the Eric Garner demonstrations. *Brazilian President Makes Statement on New "Flu": "It's Not Serious."* Miley Cyrus kissed another girl.

Kiki met me at the door. She was petite and skinny, with ropy arms covered in black-and-white tattoos. Her features were small and ferrety, and her sharp eyes scanned my body and face with the practiced precision of a high-powered machine.

"This way," she said, pressing her lips into a thin line that I realized, a little too late, was a smile. I knew from her Instagram that she didn't shave her armpits, and as I followed her down the narrow hallway, I noticed the dark, fecund patch of hair hidden like a shadow in the crevice of her white skin.

The room she ushered me into was small but well lit, with large, warehouse-style windows that were flooded with light. Jack, the hair guy, and Sylvie, the makeup girl, introduced themselves to me. The stylist, Andy, stopped furiously unzipping a limp garment bag to look over his shoulder and nod. It was hot and smelled like hairspray. A steamer hissed in the corner, billowing mist. House music bounced softly over the speakers. Really, it was nothing special. But I recognized it anyway, from her pictures. I recognized the radiators, which were covered in dust, and the metal grid of the windows. I recognized the skyline: a patchwork of industrial-looking buildings and gray water towers. *So this is where it happens,* I thought. Surreptitiously, I ran my hand along the white wall, the white wall that Gemma and all the other models had posed in front of. Benoit lived in the apartment directly below. I had figured that out from Instagram, too, but even if I hadn't, the buzzers were labeled.

One of the doors opened and Benoit strode in. "See?" he said. "We're very informal here."

Despite the heat, he was wearing a navy sweatshirt and matching navy sweatpants cuffed at the ankle, revealing a braided anklet above his Gucci loafers. Astonishingly, he also wore a light cotton utility jacket, navy too, with large pockets. I hadn't seen him without his aviators before—he was never photographed without them. And now I knew why. His eyes had a hard and dull look about them, making him appear almost stupid. I smiled, and he kissed me on the cheek, and I thought he smelled me, too, sniffed near my mouth and neck, but I couldn't be sure.

"Welcome, darling," he said warmly. "Don't you look peachy." Benoit liked to use anachronistic expressions like this. I never figured out if it was an affected quirk, or because he'd grown up in Soviet-era Bulgaria, where Western culture was stuck in a time warp. "Are you wearing any makeup?" he asked, holding me by the shoulders.

I shook my head no. For someone as vain as I was, I wore surprisingly little.

"Swell," he said. "I hate makeup." He leaned away from me and whispered something quickly into Jack's ear. To me, he said: "If I had my way, I'd shoot you just as you are, like this. But, the camera, she loves makeup. You see? So we do just very minimal. Just a little here, here." He touched me gingerly on the lips, by my temples. "We fluff the hair a little. But it's still you. Okay!" He clapped his hands suddenly, signaling he was done with me. "See you soon."

Jack led me gently by the arm and put me in front of a mirror and a long countertop. His tools were laid out on a white towel. I liked the way Jack looked at me. Like he couldn't wait to touch me, rake his fingers through my hair. Though it wasn't in a creepy, sexual way. You could tell at a glance that Jack was gay.

"Hi, beautiful," he said, not smiling and not taking his eyes off me in the mirror. He kept up a steady chatter while he operated on my head, brushing my hair and slicing it into sections with a skinny comb that looked more like a knife. He had tiny hands, smooth and brown, a compact frame, something altogether childish about him: an innocent eagerness to his face, like if you slapped him, he'd just blink really hard, surprised but not broken, still willing to trust. I thought you'd either have to be very green or very good to keep that face in this business, and for a second I worried that Jack was going to do something really bad, like scorch my hair and completely fuck me for the shoot. But I learned, as Jack's life story unspooled while he clipped and coiled my hair, that he was actually thirty-seven and had been doing hair for nearly two decades.

"It's those gaysian genes. I still look like I'm twenty, right?" he asked.

"Lucky you," I said, meaning it.

I leaned back in my chair and relaxed. It had been a long time since I'd worked with someone who was proud of what they did. I felt a rushing sensation inside of me. Something kicking to life in the pit of my stomach. Nervousness, but without the sharp metallic sting that usually accompanied it. What was this? Happiness? I watched as the girl in the mirror smiled. Jack installed curls with a gleaming rod that radiated heat against my skin. Occasionally he would stop, make a low, guttural noise, almost carnal, and sigh, "Such *gorgeous* hair." I smiled, looked down modestly. It felt good to be admired in parts like that.

"So where you from, hon?" he asked.

"California."

"I used to live in LA!" he said, as if this were the world's greatest coincidence. "Man, I miss that place. I mean, the weather, right?"

"Yeah."

"You miss it?"

I nodded.

"Your family still there?"

"Uh-huh."

"There many of 'em?"

"Three sisters, but one of them is my twin."

"Oh my god, you're a twin!"

I laughed. "Yeah, we're not identical or anything."

"I always wanted a twin."

"It was nice, growing up. Like a built-in best friend, you know, someone who is always just *there*."

"You must miss her."

"I do," I said. "Very much."

When Jack finished with me, my head was exploded in tightly coiled curls.

"Don't worry, it'll go down," he said. "We set it now, and comb it out after the face. Then it'll be perfect, I promise."

I closed my eyes and let Jack douse me in hairspray.

"Don't breathe for a sec," he said, unleashing a fresh torrent across my face. But it was too late and I'd already inhaled a mouthful of the tacky, powdery stuff, making everything taste slightly tainted for the rest of the day.

Sylvie scraped a stool over. She took my face in her tender, capable hands, exuding the kind of professional warmth characteristic of nurses. She sprinkled pale-blue water onto a puffy white cotton ball, caressed my face with it. Purifying me like the holy water at my father's church the few times he dragged me along, probably (it occurs to me now) following some particularly slimy episode in his life. I was never christened. My parents had planned to do it, but they'd just never gotten around to it. That happened a lot with them. They meant well and then they got distracted.

I stared at Sylvie's peaceful, nun-like face, inches from my own. Her long black hair was pushed back with a thick black band that resembled a habit, and even though she was large, she still had incredible bone structure and perfect cheekbones. She sort of looked like a chubbier Naomi Campbell. Her fingers were long and delicate, the nails unpolished. She poured out a quarter-sized amount of foundation on the back of her hand, a circle of pearlized skin, and began spreading it over my face with a soft triangle sponge. Unlike Jack, she worked in almost total silence, a beatific look on her face, completely absorbed in her work, opening her mouth only to whisper directives in hushed, maternal tones: *Close your eyes, dear. Smile, dear.* Other than that, it was like I wasn't even there. Just my skin was.

"Wooow," said Jack, when Sylvie had finished with me. "Look at Ms. Pretty."

"Beautiful," said Sylvie, earnestly.

Jack combed out my hair roughly with his fingers. "See? Didn't I promise?"

They spun me around so I could see myself in the mirror, and the fireflies swarmed around the edges of my eyes and I thought I might faint and the first thing I thought when I saw my reflection was: *Gemma.* I tried to hide my excitement, but I laughed, lightly, in spite of myself. When I saw my teeth, gray and even and utterly pedestrian, I closed my mouth quickly, not wanting to ruin the effect. *Gemma,* my heartbeat seemed to thud, *Gemma.*

"Do you like it?" asked Jack.

I nodded vigorously, smiling a closed-lip smile. "Very much so."

I had to resist the urge to run to the bathroom and study my face in private, as if I couldn't fully possess it until I was alone. My skin was luminous, my mouth looked just kissed. Jack had been right: the waves had mellowed into a soft, golden cascade as natural-looking as

Gemma's signature curls. My eyebrows had been lightened like hers, too, using skin-colored pressed powder, so that they nearly vanished into my forehead. Without them, my eyes had that childish, naked look that made Gemma so penetrative in photos. Sylvie had lined my eyes in soft brown, not black, and painted a hint of blush on my cheeks. It all looked so natural, and yet so utterly unlike me. I found that when I moved my head quickly, the effect was even stronger, like it really was Gemma in the mirror. That made me feel powerful and unstable at the same time, like I was up somewhere really high and looking down.

"Gemma," I whispered, though it seemed to come out louder than I'd intended.

Jack, still beaming at me in the mirror, called over his shoulder: "Andy, she's ready!"

I thought Sylvie looked uncomfortable then, and I couldn't understand why.

"You did such a good job," I said, trying to put her at ease.

She thanked me but she looked embarrassed. Then she said she had to go outside to call her daughter.

Andy undressed me quickly and efficiently. When I was naked he slid a bag over my head. He began dressing me again. The bag was there to protect the clothes from the makeup painted on my face. It was loose and easy to breathe under, but still I sucked in air greedily, feeling giddy. *It's really happening,* I thought. *Benoit is really going to shoot me.* I tried to picture what it would be like, what I might be like on set, but I could only see a blond woman with an indistinct face, and arms and legs that looked a little like mine.

At some point, without me realizing, Andy had floated away.

"Can I take this off now?" I asked, to no one in particular, touching the top of my bag. There was no answer so I just stood there, swaying, listening to my heart beat. I was smiling under that bag, like an idiot. Just so happy to be there.

Eventually I felt Andy come back to me. He laughed.

"Oh, sweetie, you can take that off now."

He lifted the bag slowly and carefully from my head so it didn't mess up my hair. I was wearing full-bottom silk panties in pale lavender (ERES), and a thin white wifebeater that scooped low toward my breasts (James Perse). Andy had me brace myself against his back while he helped me into a pair of white socks, which he folded down around my ankles. I'd forgotten about this: how people stopped expecting you to complete basic tasks like putting socks on by yourself once you entered set as a model. I pretended I was a queen, being dressed by her servants.

Andy stepped back and looked at my body. He wet his ring finger with the tip of his tongue and dabbed at something on my collarbone. He yanked at an errant thread frayed at the bottom of the tank top, his breath hot in my face. He squatted on his knees and ran his hands gently and efficiently along my crotch, smoothing the silk. Still on his haunches, he turned me around and slid two fingers under the waistband of my underwear, straightening it. He moved one side of the underwear up, so that it was slightly higher on my butt cheek.

"There," he said finally, and stepped away.

I felt the equilibrium in the room shift, and looked toward the door. Benoit emerged, looking calm and self-possessed. I held my breath, waiting for the moment when his eyes would fall upon me, and when they did, a jolt of electricity ran through my body.

"Wow," he breathed. "Fantastic."

I got that up-high feeling again, like I might fall over. I realized I was grinning and, remembering about the teeth, forced myself back into a tight, close-lipped smile.

Kiki walked over and looked at me with her hands on her hips. "It looks good."

Benoit touched me delicately on the cheeks and shook his head, grinning. "I love it!" Gently he turned me so that we were facing the mirror and he was standing behind me with his hands on my shoulders.

"Doesn't she look just like a child?" he gushed. "This innocence! Barely sweet sixteen."

I didn't feel like a child, and I knew I wasn't innocent, but I liked that Benoit was excited about how I looked. My desire to please him was so persuasive that I felt myself ease, almost seamlessly, into someone who was younger and more innocent than I really was.

"Dear, do you not love it?" he asked.

I nodded yes, slightly embarrassed by how stupidly happy I looked in the mirror.

"That makes me happy. That makes me happy, because when you're happy the camera is happy."

"We want you to be comfortable," added Kiki, in a maternal voice.

"Comfort is the *most* important thing. If you aren't comfortable, you can't be vulnerable for the camera."

Kiki asked if I'd ever seen *Lolita*.

"That's a key inspiration for us," explained Benoit.

"A modern-day Lolita, a teen girl in her bedroom," elucidated Kiki.

"Virginal and pure and sensual. A child-woman, the object of obsession—but totally unawares, totally innocent."

I smiled. Benoit kept talking: "So you're lounging around in your bedroom, totally unawares. Natural. We want very natural. None of this posturing that we have today. None of this Kardashian bullshit." Though he himself had said it, he was viscerally upset by the suggestion. "What kills me is that *that* is what passes for sexy today, that kind of plastic blow-up doll. Who wants to go to bed with a blow-up doll? How fucked up is that?"

I wasn't sure it was any less fucked up to want to go to bed with a sixteen-year-old, but I remained silent. He went on: "You know what the plastic surgeons are saying? They're saying that people are coming in and asking for fake tits that actually look fake. They're saying, 'Doctor, I paid good money for these, I don't want people thinking I just got them for free!'"

Benoit, I was beginning to learn, didn't necessarily require a response in order to have a conversation with someone. Before I could open my mouth, he had begun again: "It's ironic, no? Women are paying hundreds of thousands of dollars to look like sex dolls, but if you so much as hug them without written consent, it's a criminal offense. The most basic, most pure form of affection is demonized, criminalized, and yet—"

"Hans." Kiki interrupted, shooting him a warning look.

"I am merely pointing the irony," he said. When she continued to glare at him, he laughed helplessly. He looked me in the eyes in the mirror and said, in a conspiratorial voice: "Kiki's afraid I'll get myself in trouble. But she doesn't have to worry, does she? You and I understand each other."

"Perfectly," I said.

"Ah, beautiful!" He clapped me lightly on the shoulder. "Beautiful. Beautiful. Beautiful. I thought so."

Kiki eyed us both, and I knew she was sizing me up, though I wasn't sure if it was a disapproving look or if she only pitied me. Either way, I didn't like it. "We should get started," she said finally. "We're behind."

Benoit nodded. He placed both hands on my shoulders and fixed me with a caring, paternal look. "You're going to do wonderfully, my dear. Just relax, and be natural. Be yourself."

And because I knew I looked like Gemma, I thought I actually could.

The set had been styled to look like a quaint New York City apartment, some cool girl's bedroom. I actually thought it looked familiar. Or maybe it was just that everything had started to look the same, an algorithmically optimized aesthetic that lacked any border or definition so you could move through spaces as frictionlessly as you could scroll through Instagram, and you could never really tell whether you were in a certain place, or in a place that looked like a certain place, or in a place that looked like a picture of that certain place. Like how it was getting difficult to remember someone's face without accidentally starting to picture a photo of them.

The bed was unmade, with a fluffy white duvet and white linen sheets piled up in an inviting dollop. It was pushed up against the windows, which were hung with light, filmy curtains and crisscrossed with unlit multicolored Christmas lights. A stack of books served as a bedside table, on which rested a coffee mug, a vintage lamp, a tattered journal, and more books. On one of the windowsills was a mason jar filled with dried wildflowers. Kiki bent over the duvet and fussed with it. She fluffed the pillows. Benoit was fiddling with his iPhone. I understood, now, why he was dressed so unseasonably. The air conditioning was blasting and the room was like a refrigerator. I shivered, resisting the urge to cover my bare arms.

"What do you like to listen to?" he asked, causing the name of every song or band I'd ever heard to flee my brain. I made an indeterminate noise with my mouth.

"C'mon, what're you listening to right now? What's your go-to?"

"Snake Oil," I said, even though I didn't really like them and had only listened to them on Gemma's Instagram.

Benoit smiled at me a little weirdly, and I was worried that maybe he knew why I'd said it, but all he said was "Excellent choice." Then he clapped his hands together and began looking through the lens on his camera, setting the flash off while Kiki held a light tester. Even though I'd done dozens of shoots before, I'd never done one that was supposed to look natural, and I realized I didn't know how to act that way. I looked at the bed stupidly, like it might give me some sort of direction.

"Go on," said Benoit. "Get on."

I clambered on awkwardly, aware of every inch of my exposed skin, the pebbled texture of my upper thighs, the crease formed at my waist when I twisted my legs around. Even though I hadn't eaten all day, I wished I'd somehow eaten less. I leaned back on my hands to try to elongate my body, like I'd seen Gemma do in some of her shoots.

"Yes, that's it, relax, get comfortable."

"Holler if you need anything," Kiki said to Benoit, closing the door behind her. I knew from the interviews I'd read with him online that Benoit almost always required a closed set. *I can have more intimacy that way. The camera does not like crowds.*

I surveyed the room. I noticed that one of the books at the bedside was Bukowski's *Hot Water Music*. The coffee mug was made by a Brooklyn ceramicist that Gemma was friends with. She owned a full set of them.

Now I knew why the apartment looked so familiar.

"So just pretend you're at home, hanging out. Zoning out. Unhunch your shoulders, please. This is your bedroom. Stretch the leg a little. You strung up those Christmas lights last year with your best friend, Chloe. That's your diary, over there. You hide it under your mattress when you go out so your mom won't read it."

After a few minutes of that, Benoit paused and called for Kiki. She came in immediately—she must have been waiting by the door—and after one quick gesture from Benoit, she came over and placed the covers haphazardly across my body. Gently but firmly she pushed me back so that I was lying, half-upright, against the pillows. She peeled back the top of the covers to display my torso, and disappeared out the door again.

"That's it, yes. You're just waking up, you came home past curfew last night and your stepdad is pissed." I tried to look like a girl worthy of being kidnapped. I looked at the ceiling and imagined Gemma lying in her own bed, looking at the ceiling. "Yes, exactly. You're sulking. You don't want to face him at the breakfast table. You're dreaming of the boy you have a crush on."

That was more difficult to approximate. I never had crushes in high school. I thought the whole point of dating was to get the other person to care more than you cared, so I always picked someone I knew I'd never actually like.

"Come on, think about a boy you like. Tell me about him."

I tried to imagine a theoretical boy I might have a crush on, but could only see the faces of actors in various movie roles.

"Ryan," I said finally. "He's got blond hair. And, um . . ."

"Do you want to kiss him?"

I nodded slowly.

"It doesn't look like you want to kiss him. I don't see anything in your face at all. *Feeling*. Remember? Real feeling. Just act how you would act when you were at home, fantasizing about someone."

Gemma. I stretched out luxuriously across the bed, pointing the toe of one foot, an arm reaching above me while the other slid down the length of my body.

"Yes! That's it!"

I felt a pulse of desire between my legs. I was picturing myself through the camera's lens, imagining that Benoit's cock was stiffening beneath his sweatpants while he looked at me.

"There we go," said Benoit. "I want you to touch yourself, there, yes."

I stroked the smooth silk of my panties and imagined I was watching myself from across the room, and was moved with such exquisite egotism—*She is so sexy! She is so perfect!*—that I noticed, with some apprehension, I was genuinely becoming aroused.

"Exactly! Yes!" Benoit had moved closer to the bed, and I imagined myself in his place, walking toward this girl, who was no longer me, exactly, but someone else. I saw the girl on Gemma's bed fondle herself and I imagined climbing on top of her and splitting her open.

"There we go. Now under the panties, yes, come on. No, *under* the panties, yes, there."

I hesitated at the waistband, then slid my hand under. My fingers were like ice, and the flesh beneath them felt foreign and vaguely sinister, like a dead jellyfish. I shivered.

Benoit climbed on top of the bed and stood on it in his shoes, looming over me.

"Don't look at me!" he hissed. "Keep going. Yes."

I tried to get back into it. I closed my eyes and tried to bring up an image of myself from very far away.

"Come on," said Benoit. "Give me something."

I bit my lip, trying to be seductive, letting my eyes roll back slightly. I wanted to go back to being a sex object. To a time when nothing else inside me was relevant.

"Stop it," snapped Benoit. "You're performing."

"I'm sorry—"

"Don't! Don't apologize. Just act natural. Do it like how you'd do it if I weren't here."

Usually, I watched porn when I masturbated, but guys didn't like to imagine that. They liked to think girls just closed their eyes and came, swept away on some romantic fantasy, not that we watched the same kind of twisted BDSM shit as they did.

"Well?"

I removed my hand from underneath my panties and turned on my side, pressing my wrist hard into my crotch and squeezing my thighs together so it hurt.

"Okay," said Benoit. He crouched on the bed and took a few photos of me from behind like that. Then he walked out in front of me and took a few more pictures, though it was obvious he was less excited about it. Deflated, I closed my eyes. Gently, Benoit pushed my shoulder so I was lying on my back. I opened my eyes. "Keep them closed," he said. "You're asleep. You're dreaming sweetly."

He tore the covers completely off the bed. He picked up one of my ankles and moved it so that my legs were spread and one ankle hung off the bed. He pulled my tank top down, so that one nipple was exposed. Then he stepped back and I watched the flash spasm from behind my eyes, as it created sharp red shapes against my closed lids. I pretended I was dead.

Eventually, they had me change into a second outfit: little silk shorts and a matching camisole in shell pink (both Araks). I looked at myself in the mirror as Andy put them on my body, and since nobody was looking at my face, I cycled through expressions, trying to mimic the things I'd seen Gemma do with hers, the far-off stare she would sometimes give, the impish smile. *Not bad,* I thought, and that little bell rang inside me again, and I felt happy and lucky, and a little more sure of myself.

For the next several hours, and in various states of undress, I played the part of the captive teen. I rolled around in bed. I plucked the petals off the dead flowers in the mason jar. I looked at myself in the mirror and pretended to apply lip gloss I wasn't actually wearing. Benoit called me Gemma once, while I was lying on the floor reading *Hot Water Music*, and I thought it was a little weird but then I also thought that it was just because he'd shot her so much, and hadn't I accidentally called Julia Mom that one time, after I'd been home for a week? Besides, it was normal for an editorial to directly riff on the model of the moment, because the model of the moment embodies the look of the moment, and yes, this one was taking it a little literally, and it was possibly a little derivative, but then wasn't everything derivative nowadays?

For the last shot, Benoit had me get back on the bed and jump up and down. I was wearing a thin cotton tank dress with scalloping and a little bow along the top (Calvin Klein), and patterned cotton underwear (Baserange).

"You're doing this to bother your stepdad," he said. "To get back at him. You don't want him to come up, but you actually kind of do."

I tried to imagine what it would be like to be an innocent sixteen-year-old about to be raped by her stepdad.

"Beautiful, beautiful. Give me joy. You're a kid, remember, you have access to joy."

I heard a laugh bounce out of my mouth.

Benoit climbed onto the bed, and crouched near my feet. He shot me like that, from below, with me looking down on him. I felt powerful, like he was someone I could destroy if I wanted to. I thought about kicking the camera into his face and bringing my foot down hard upon him.

"Yes, that's it, wow," he said.

I smiled. I was picturing his face after I'd done it, blood pouring from his nose. It wasn't his pain that would please me but his shock, his disbelief. *Imagine if he knew what I was thinking about right now,* I thought, and laughed a little. That made me feel doubly powerful, to know I had an interiority no one could guess at. I often had violent ideations like this, I didn't know why, though my therapist now says that it probably helped me feel a kind of control in situations where I had none. I'm not so sure. I think I just found them entertaining.

Benoit lay back on the bed, and had me stand over him with my feet on either side of his head. He took upskirt photos, like the kind pervs post on Reddit. He told me to hop a little and I did, my feet landing close to his head. Then he reached around with his free hand and cupped my calf and held it there so I was still. His hand was warm, and it made my calf seem small, like a child's, which I liked. I looked down at him, at his mouth, which was parted slightly in concentration. I imagined him kissing Gemma. I knew they had met at the cheese shop and that he'd made her take out all the cheese in the whole store just so that he could keep talking to her. Later, he'd invited her to a party at his house, only when she arrived, no one was there; it was just him with all the cheese laid out and two bottles of good wine on the table. I thought that was romantic, pretending there was a party so that she would come over when really all he ever wanted was her. Thinking about that, I felt a lurch of jealousy in my stomach, though I couldn't quite work out who I was jealous of. Benoit's fingers slid beneath my cotton panties, and he squeezed my ass gently, his thumb pressing against my cunt. It was oddly unsexual, though I felt something like titillation, an impersonal curiosity to see how it might play out, like when you watch a line of ants struggle and drown against a sweep of hose water. I smiled at him through the camera, part of me wishing he would press harder into me, remove my panties altogether, just to get it over with. The other half still wanted to kick him. I was constantly oscillating between desperately wanting his admiration and hating him for making me want it. His thumb slid underneath the cotton, and I felt the edge of his nail glide roughly against my skin. He thumbed the folds of my vagina gently. Then, as if it were the most natural thing in the world, he stuck a finger inside me. I might have been a little more shocked if it weren't for the expression on his face, which was entirely blasé. The shutter didn't stop. He kept saying *yes, perfect, that's it, yes, like that, feel that,* and my body moved unthinkingly in tandem with his directives. Sometimes it seemed to move even before he'd said anything. I stepped back and straddled him. He wanted me to pretend to be giving him a blow job, and I did, thinking about how strangely familiar it all felt and how performative sex always is, like I'm just following some choreographed skit. It was weird because the whole thing felt incredibly fake and stupid, but then I could feel him getting hard beneath the thin cotton of his sweatpants. I felt embarrassed and flustered—not because I was grossed out or anything, only because I wasn't sure what he wanted me to do. Normally, I'd take the thing out—get the deed over with. But I wasn't sure if he'd think that was unprofessional. He reached down and readjusted his erection so that it was less obtrusive. Then he lowered the band on his sweatpants further—it occurs to me now that's why he wore them. He put a hand on the back of my head and pushed my face down so that my lips were pressed into his skin just above the waistband, and I went to that empty-inside place, like I do in castings, and only my body and nothing else remained. He flipped my hair so that it hid the lower half of my face, so it would look like I was sucking his dick from the camera's obscured angle. I had given plenty of head I didn't want to give in my day, plenty of head I didn't enjoy and only performed out of a sense of duty and obligation, so I didn't really think anything of it. I was nineteen years old, after all. A real adult. I would have gone down on everyone on set if it meant I was one step closer to being famous, loved, revered. It never occurred to me that within those breezy transactions, which I'd been trained to think of as nothing, an act no more consequential than slapping someone across the face, I might also be giving away a tiny, intangible part of my soul.

"Pretend you're choking on it," he whispered, moving the camera so that it hovered above the back of my head. He hadn't actually removed his dick, but I could feel it, hot beneath his sweatpants, somewhere against my neck. He stuck his hand into my hair and pressed my head into his groin, my lips bristling against his pubes, which he had obviously shaved not too long ago. I made a gagging sound and wasn't sure if it was involuntary. When he eventually took his hand from my head, he yanked out a tangle of hair which had gotten stuck in his watch and tears sprung to my eyes, even though I wasn't really upset, and he just kept shooting. Then, after some indeterminate amount of time, he stopped and playfully patted me on the butt, motioning for me to get up.

"Fantastic, Mickey," he gushed. "Absolutely fantastic." He sat up, and his face was flushed and his eyes shining. "I cannot tell you how fucking awesome that was," he said. "I think we made something really beautiful here. Really real and authentic."

All of the discomfort and tension that had been building inside of me immediately dissolved into a bubble of elation. I giggled. "Hey, that's all you," I said. "I just stand there and look good."

"Oh, come now, you do much more than that."

"If you say so."

"You've got something. Different than what I thought."

I didn't know what that meant but I thought it sounded good. I opened my mouth to say something glib, but thought better of it and simply said thank you.

Benoit got off the bed and stretched his arms overhead, revealing a soft, white belly stitched with black hair.

"Come here," he said, bringing his arms together in a circle. "I always close with a hug."

I hopped off the bed and we hugged. His body was warm, and he smelled like sweat.

"You did well today, kid," he said in a faux American accent.

"Well, thank you, kind sir," I said, trying my best Lauren Bacall. We both laughed. I wondered if he might tell Gemma about it later. I imagined her looking through the photos, impressed. The idea lit a warm glow within me.

"Balthazar's downstairs," said Benoit, beginning to pack his flashes into cushioned black bags. When I looked at him blankly, he said, "Dinner. It's a bit of a tradition."

Afterward, we ate dinner like a family. Jack read our horoscopes on his iPhone. Sylvie showed us pictures of her daughter: an elfin child with Sylvie's smooth black hair and big brown eyes. Kiki told us about the guy she'd met at Muay Thai. Andy had gone, and I soon learned that he was not one of Benoit's usual collaborators, that he'd been sent by some other controlling force that nobody mentioned. Benoit sat at the head of the table, resplendent and fatherly. He insisted on creating for each of us what he called a "perfectly calibrated" bite of pâté: he layered it on top of a cracker specially ordered from a gourmet shop—not from the restaurant—and topped it with dried cranberries. I let it melt in my mouth, feeling anointed.

Benoit had ordered us all the same thing for dinner: salmon with green beans and mashed potatoes, cooked without onion or garlic. I inhaled mine—even began, at her suggestion, helping myself to some of Sylvie's. A bottle of white wine was passed around the table. Then another. I drank a lot. My seat faced a mirror and every time I caught my reflection, I startled a little, as if I didn't know myself. I was still wearing all the hair and makeup from the shoot. I laughed and talked without knowing what I was saying.

I didn't *feel* drunk. The sophisticated setting had lulled me into a false sense of sobriety. It was the nicest apartment I'd been to in a long time. Massive, with sleek polished-cement floors that were patchworked with Persian rugs. The palette was beige, white, black, and soft gray, accented by the colorful rugs and large abstract artworks on the walls. The couch looked like something out of Studio 54: low-slung and U-shaped. I pressed my index finger into its ridged fabric en route to the bathroom. It was cut from white corduroy. The lighting was so elegantly orchestrated, I had trouble discerning where it was coming from. It seemed to just exist as an ambient glow, a warmly lit bubble of luxury. Dinner had been served on a large rectangular table at the center of the room. The table was metal, painted matte black, and centered over a large ponyskin rug. Though it was takeout, Benoit had had it plated, so that when we came down to his apartment it was already waiting for us on large slate serving platters. It's difficult to feel out of control when you are surrounded by so much good taste. It's like you're on an island somewhere, insulated from consequences, from the careening madness of the city. I kept downing glasses of wine and thinking to myself wonderingly, *I don't feel drunk at all! Not one bit! How funny!*

The rest of the night passed the way things do in a speeding car; everything comes rushing at you in an indistinct blur and then, through some happenstance of the angle of your gaze, one building will appear in crystal clear definition. Though I had not fallen asleep, I had the sensation of waking up, several hours later, on Benoit's U-shaped couch. Benoit was speaking, and I realized with a jolt that he and I were having a conversation. I looked around the room. It was empty, the food cleared away, glasses half-emptied and abandoned on nearly every surface. Someone had opened a window and the room smelled like tobacco. I blinked and the underneath of my eyelids was purple and velvet.

"Oh dear, did I just lose you?"

"Sorry, no, I'm listening," I said, jamming my eyes open.

"So then Sartre, he gets really clever, and he says—okay, we know the waiter is following the script, but it isn't just the waiter."

I got up and helped myself to more wine. I drank it without sitting back down.

"It's all of us," he went on, waving his arm expansively. "We say 'I am that,' or 'I am this,' and then we act accordingly. But it's all bad faith, you see? So, to answer your question, *that's* why I became a photographer."

He looked so small, and almost pathetic, that I was momentarily dumbstruck by the thought: *Gemma is in love with this person.*

I said: "What about Gemma?" And to cover the digression, I added, "I mean, what does Gemma think about it?"

Benoit looked at me seriously. "You're really obsessed with her, aren't you?"

It occurred to me that I might have asked a lot of questions about her already, and my face grew hot. "I'm not. I'm just making conversation. She's your girlfriend, isn't she?"

"*Girl*-friend." Benoit snorted. "I have never understood the American love of that term. It is a woman we're talking about, isn't it? In Bulgaria we say *priyatelka*. Pleasant friend."

"But she is, right?"

Benoit finished the rest of his drink in one gulp.

"You want to see the pictures?" he asked.

"From today?"

He nodded.

We went out into the hallway, and up the dirty rubber stairs to his studio. Outside the well-ordered walls of his quietly luxurious apartment, I felt a lot more drunk. Benoit led me back down the narrow, blank hallway and into the room that served as his office. He didn't bother turning on the lights. He sat at the desk and jabbed at the keyboard of his Apple desktop until it lit up. There was no other chair, so I stood behind him.

He began near the end. A shot, from below, of my parted legs, the mounds of my breasts visible above. The curve of my chin was the only thing recognizable about my face, which was framed by a halo of blond curls. A complicated mix of emotions swirled inside of me. If you looked at the photo quickly, it could be Gemma. But if you looked only a second longer, it was clearly someone else, just a little off, like a dissonant chord. Still, it was a beautiful photo, suffused with warmth and intimacy. It was shot by *the* Benoit and it was of *me*. There was plenty for me to be happy about. Benoit pressed down on the right-arrow key, and the picture shifted and changed shape as butterflies swarmed inside my stomach. Benoit stopped on a close-up of my face.

"See what I mean?" said Benoit. "Different."

I was horrified. I thought I looked like a psychopath. My smile was far too wide, and there was an evil glint in my eyes. I had too many teeth in my mouth. I ran my tongue over them, feeling ashamed. I looked nothing like Gemma here.

"I think I know what it is," he went on. "Something in the eyes."

Benoit jabbed at the keyboard and zoomed in on one of the photos. He traced the edge of my iris with his pinky.

"You know what I see when I look into them?" he asked. "Nothing. Absolutely nothing. Pure nihilism. Isn't it beautiful?"

I looked at the screen. All I saw were pixels.

Benoit prompted me. "You like it?"

I nodded yes.

Satisfied, Benoit pressed down on the right-arrow key, and the photos slid by until we were back at the beginning, with me lying on the bed. I liked myself better here, farther away so I was less recognizable. More like her. Benoit jabbed at the right-arrow button over and over again, and I watched in mounting apprehension as Gemma, pure and beautiful, opened her eyes and glinted at the camera, grew tainted and lascivious and empty-eyed, morphed into me.

"Gemma—" I started to say.

Benoit scoffed loudly and deliberately.

"What?" I asked.

"That name again."

"Am I not allowed to mention your *pleasant friend*?" I answered archly, trying to regain my composure.

"One's pleasant friend doesn't exactly go about letting one make the sort of art that you and I made today." He looked almost forlornly back at the computer. "That kind of girl would never let me shoot her like this."

"Why not?"

"Oh come now, a fine, respectable lady like her?" he said in an ironic, highfalutin voice. "She'd never sully herself with such smut."

I laughed, though I didn't think it was funny. A series of images flitted through my mind: Gemma and Benoit together, Gemma and Benoit saying how trashy I looked, Gemma and Benoit laughing at me. Even though I thought Gemma was better than me, it enraged me to think that everyone else thought so, too. Was she really so fucking perfect? So fucking untouchable?

Benoit turned to look at me. "That's why I love working with girls like you. Hungry, unformed." He smiled and his teeth glowed a sickly blue in the artificial computer light. "*Shameless*."

I wanted to hit him. I thought about how easy it would be to jab my thumbs into his eyes, and press into them until they bled. I imagined cradling his head in a tender embrace while I did it, his hands pinned under my knees.

Instead I just giggled and said something like, "Guess so."

"I mean that as a compliment."

"Thank you," I said.

"Truly."

I didn't know what he wanted from me, but I knew what I was going to do. Really, there was only ever one thing I could do, one way for me to quench my rage, to avenge myself. I arranged my face to look vulnerable and pensive, so that he would ask what I was thinking about. And when he did, I told him that I was thinking about what he'd said about Sartre. That I'd read him in college (not true) but that no one had ever explained it as beautifully as he had. Carefully, like I was testing the weight of a branch to see how far I could go, I met his eyes as I lied to him.

He leaned back in his chair, and the chair accommodated his weight. His knees were pointed outward. I knew if I crawled into his lap now, he would not refuse me. But it is important, in these situations, to make the man feel it is his idea.

"I think it's really brave, what you do," I said. "Your art."

He scoffed, as if he didn't believe me. But I knew it was a bluff. He believed me.

"A lot of people would probably disagree with you," he said.

"A lot of people are stupid." This, too, I knew he believed.

We held each other's gaze for three seconds longer than normal, which was as good as an admission. My heart thudded in my chest, like I was a hunter closing in on its prey. *One small movement,* I thought, *and I have him—or I lose him.* Almost imperceptibly, I let my body sway in his direction. He grabbed my hand and pulled me onto him, his mouth folding disgustingly under mine, like it was caving in, too soft, like a marshmallow.

We fucked right there on his office chair. I took off my jeans and my panties and sat on him, his dick jamming inside me, scratching at me because I wasn't wet. I made a lot of moaning noises, hoping he wouldn't notice. He didn't. As I thrashed against him, I felt a portal open up, a pathway to Gemma, and the deeper he reached inside me, the closer I got to her. When he came, biting my ear and whimpering like a small child, I finally grasped her fingers and pulled her toward me, and she appeared before me, ghostly pale and artificial, and I just threw my head back and laughed directly in her face.

I woke up gasping, as if coming up for air after a long submersion, swimming through black waters. I could not remember what I had been dreaming of, but I woke with fear and I knew I'd been holding my breath. It was a habit I'd had since I was a child, when, without realizing it, I'd keep all the air inside until my lips turned blue and I almost fainted.

It was still dark out. I checked my phone: 4:30 a.m. I had fallen asleep accidentally. Benoit was in bed beside me. I looked at the hump of his back with such violent distaste that I shuddered. I found a pen and paper in the bedside table and scribbled down a note. *Didn't want to wake you, thank you for everything,* etc., etc. When I was putting the pen back in the bedside table, I noticed a Polaroid. In the dark, I could hardly see the image, but written in big block letters on the white space beneath it, I could make out *My Muse. My Everything.* I knew it must be of Gemma.

I crumpled the note I had written and stuffed it into my purse.

I left his apartment before I even called an Uber, so that I had to stand on the street shivering, even though it wasn't that cold, waiting eight minutes for Yevgen to arrive in his shitty red Hyundai.

My apartment was dark when I got home, and smelled vaguely of rotten food. I glanced at the fruit I'd optimistically placed in a bowl at the end of my island, as if, after being shot by Benoit, I'd be the kind of person that had a bowl full of fruit at her apartment. The banana had already turned black, and I thought I could see fruit flies. I picked up the bowl and tossed everything in it into the garbage.

Then I climbed into bed in all my clothes and fell asleep.

In Montauk, Gemma steps out onto the private deck of her Deluxe Superior King Room. There is a full moon tonight, but it isn't visible. The sky is covered in clouds. The clouds are lilac, lit from behind by the moon you cannot see. Gemma leans against the wooden railing. Beyond it, floodlights illuminate the hotel's winding gravel path and boardwalk in evenly spaced pools, only to be subsumed by the beach's preternatural darkness. You can't see the ocean either, but you can hear it: a soft, cascading hushing sound that belies its hidden power. Gemma could drown out there. If she wanted to, she could walk down the steps, now, and out into its dark waters. She could disappear and drown and nobody would even know.

Gemma tightens the robe around her. She feels the ocean air against her face, a salty moistness that is almost carnal in the heat. She closes her eyes and inhales it. The ocean continues to churn.

She was not even supposed to have a deck. She had booked a Queen with a garden view. When she checked in, the receptionist informed her they'd upgraded her. A manager came out and shook her hand and showed her personally to the room, pointing out every amenity. A bottle of champagne waited on ice, framed by the ocean view. There was a small bowl of raspberries. The manager winked at her. "See?" he said. "We pay attention. We really think it's the small things that make our guests feel at home." Raspberries are her favorite fruit. Everybody knows that.

After he leaves, Gemma stares at the bowl. Beside it is a card printed with the hotel's Instagram account. Gemma picks up one of the berries and holds it between her thumb and index finger. Then she pops it into her mouth and slowly crushes it against her tongue. No one could know that

that is how she eats it, but that is how she eats it. The thought gives her a fleeting sense of freedom and possibility. She pops another one into her mouth. She looks at the California king bed, gleaming in freshly pressed white like a photogenic bride. Gemma stretches herself across it, pushing into its softness, her hands sliding easily against the high thread count. She laughs, feeling self-conscious. Because despite the empty room, Gemma is not alone. The raspberries were not a gift, but a bribe. In exchange, Gemma will parcel out the moments of her life to her hundreds of thousands of Followers, to whoever is watching. She will give everything, until she is unsure what is content and what is her life. She is never alone anymore. Not even tonight, on the deck, is she really alone. She knows that through the clouds the moon is watching.

Everyone is watching.

The next morning, she wakes easily with the sun. The sky is a spotless blue. It is already very hot. She takes a screenshot of the weather app on her phone. It is ninety-eight degrees.

Gemma goes for a walk along the beach. She is wearing a nude one-piece that she received in the mail last week. She had not ordered it. A brand had sent it to her, after she had posted a still of Bo Derek in the movie 10. *She has not seen* 10, *but it is on her list of things to watch, when she has time.* For your own *10* moment, *the designer, or more likely the PR manager, had written on the card that came with it. It was then that she'd realized it had been some time since she'd had a beach vacation. She knew she needed to relax. Get out. Just for a little. She booked the trip that afternoon. Gemma is on vacation, in part, because of a free swimsuit, and a savvy PR strategist. Not that anyone would know that.*

Gemma lies on the sand, and the swimsuit blends into the sand and her skin, making her appear otherworldly, a mermaid washed up on the beach, naked as the day she was born. She splashes into the sea, exhilarated by how the water's cold knifes into her. She dries off with a yellow-and-white striped towel and curls up on a cushioned chaise longue. She spends the afternoon like this. Drinking ice water with sliced cucumber and lemon. Rubbing Supergoop sunscreen oil up and down her long limbs until they shine. Turning onto her front. Turning onto her back. She stares out at where the ocean meets the sky in a solid, unbroken line. The sun's glare is hard and sharp along the waves' edges. She is awed by how flat everything looks. It reminds her of a computer screen. It makes her feel peaceful.

Then the sun is setting. Gemma wraps a towel around herself and walks along the shore. Everything looks dipped in gold. In the fading light, Gemma holds sand in her fist and lets it slowly slip through her fingers until there is nothing left.

Tomorrow, she will return to the city.

I don't know when exactly the idea took hold of me.

It was almost a week after the shoot with Benoit. My mother had called, sounding disturbed, and by the time I was finished speaking with her, I was standing outside of Gemma's apartment.

It was a nice building. Red brick with a green awning, and vines that grew up its sides. I knew Gemma was there. She'd gotten home a few days before from her relaxing beach vacation, a *much-needed breather.* And then, *of course,* she'd said, as if her body had been waiting for a momentary slowdown in order to fully break down, she'd gotten sick with the flu. The poor dear had been holed up inside since. But today, she'd posted a Story of herself sipping tea and promising that she would venture out, if only for a little, this afternoon.

Since the shoot with Benoit, I'd been out of sorts, too. A feeling had taken root inside of me, a dark roiling that I tried to ignore. The person I'd been during those hours spent in the myopia of Benoit's camera slipped away, as if she never existed. I considered the shoot a failure. I told no one about it, and no one remembered to ask me, even though it'd been all I'd talked about in the days beforehand. I bought a jar of Jolen bleach and painted my eyebrows till they stung, then paid a hairdressing student eighty dollars for a perm—I couldn't keep painstakingly curling my hair every day like Jack had done at the shoot. It wasn't a great perm, but it was serviceable, and it was better, certainly, than how I looked before. Still, the feeling of dread persisted. I told myself it was the heat. It got all the way to 104 in the city that week. Otherwise, everything was the same. I went out every night—always the same people, the same places and conversations and questions. *Are you a model? From LA? Where in the city do you live? Want a vodka soda?* I started giving all the wrong answers, openly false and absurd, and watching their faces as their brains short-circuited. It didn't matter. No one was looking for a sensible or thoughtful response, only an answer to recognize you by, the same way birds call out to each other, mechanically singing the same songs in order to identify their species.

During the day, I stayed inside with the lights off, drinking white wine diluted with soda water, pretending I wasn't really there, or imagining myself on the beach next to Gemma. I watched a lot of *Law & Order: SVU*, with my laptop growing hot on my stomach so that I had to put a pillow between its scalding surface and my skin. On my phone, I scrolled through endless online shopping sites, flicking my finger so that grids of empty garments, or grids of empty-eyed models wearing those garments, slid by. I would add everything I liked to my virtual shopping cart, and then, while Stabler and Benson chased down pedophiles, I'd painstakingly edit the cart, deleting items I deemed frivolous, re-adding them later, swapping out colors and sizes until I was dizzy. I couldn't afford anything, and knew I would never buy any of it, but it was comforting to know the clothes were there, and that if I wanted to, I could purchase them simply by moving my finger. I found that in this way, it was like I already owned them. Besides, organizing my virtual wardrobe had the aura of productivity. *It's a kind of self-improvement,* I thought. *I'm making myself better through buying things.* It was while I was debating the relative merits of a black cowl-neck camisole and a

Lurex tank top very much like one I already owned that my mother had called.

I had forgotten about our weekly date.

This was what the call was about.

"I guess I've been a bad mom," she said. "I guess that's why."

"You haven't been a bad mom," I said, trying to be calm, though she was already hysterical.

"But I have! I guess I should just commit suicide!"

For some reason, I got out of bed and put my shoes on. "Mom, I just forgot, that's all. I've been busy with work."

"It's just so *hurtful*. Raise a child just to have them abandon you. Sometimes I wonder what it was all for."

"I haven't abandoned you."

"Your father says he hasn't talked to you in a month."

"It's not my fault I miss his calls!" I grabbed my keys and threw them into my purse.

"I guess we really screwed up as parents."

"I'm trying to spend less time on my phone, okay? For mental health."

"Your father is in *jail*."

"I know!"

I was outside now, walking fast, my heart hammering in my chest like I was fleeing the scene of a crime. I cringed against the sharp sunlight. My armpits were already slick.

"And what am I supposed to do? Just be alone all the time? Just disappear?"

"Mom, really, I'm sorry."

"It isn't easy, you know. I've got things to do. Who do you think is handling your dad's court case? Who do you think is doing everything? Do you think I like getting in my car every Sunday and driving two hours to visit my husband in jail alone? You think that's easy for me?"

I sighed. "How about I go with you next time?" I said, knowing that was what she had been after all along. It felt like the tide was taking me out, like I was standing on the wet sand and everything under my feet was being pulled away.

"Next week?" she asked, as if it were a challenge.

"Sure."

My mother went all quiet, like she did every time I capitulated to her, as if she were somehow disappointed. "That'd be nice," she said finally, smoothing her voice out like she would a white linen tablecloth. "Thank you."

We went over some logistical details, and eventually said goodbye. I felt a gust of cold air as someone opened the door to Gemma's apartment building, and relief washed over me. I was back on solid ground. I knew there was a doorman (she sometimes 'Grammed one of them, Joseph, helping her with her boxes, the free swag brands sent her regularly) but he must have been sitting inside—I could just make out the beginning of a small lobby through the glass double doors. I knew about the coffee shop across the street, too. La Coqueta. Gemma went there every morning for her oat milk latte. It had a slim natural-wood bar along the window that faced the street.

I took up position on one of the café's rickety, artfully distressed stools. My oat milk latte arrived in a rough-hewn pewter mug without a handle. I took six photos of it bathed in the natural light from outside, but I couldn't really focus, I was so jittery, and the pictures all came out lame and not worthy of the Grid, though I uploaded one to Stories. It was too hot to hold even after I sat down (those handleless mugs are really quite stupid), so I had to lean over it and take little hiccupy sips, and still it scalded my tongue.

I focused my eyes on her front door and began my vigil, glancing down at the infinite scroll under my fingertips for only a few seconds at a time.

Thirty minutes later, my phone died. I cursed myself for having been too drunk to plug it in the night before. I asked the guy behind the counter to charge it for me, in a super sweet voice, like it was a big favor he was doing me, and he acted all noble about it, like, *I thiiiiink I can make that work, sure,* when all he had to do was unplug his phone and plug mine in. He was at 85 percent. I saw. Some people are just selfish.

I sat back down. I would wait for her, however long it took. Hours, days, I had the time. But just ten seconds later, my eyes began darting around, looking for a screen, something to grasp on to, like flies that have been trapped inside and keep hitting the wall over and over again, even though the window is open and *it's right there, you fucking idiots.* Intellectually, I knew my phone was plugged in—but still I reached in my bag for it when I wanted to know the time. I bit my lip, took a deep breath, and tried to fix my eyes on the green awning again. I remembered that there were free samples of a brownie up by the register. Keeping my eyes fixed outside the window, I walked up to the counter. I took a sample and then asked the selfish barista for a glass of tap water, and when he turned around I grabbed two more. He handed me the glass and I sat back down. With my back turned to him, I put one of the squished brownie bits to my mouth and nibbled at it, trying to take as long as possible to eat it. When the samples were all gone, I drank the glass of tap water. Then I got back up and went over to the bar, careful that no crumbs remained on my mouth.

"You mind checking on my phone?" I asked the guy.

"It's been, like, five minutes," he said irritably. I thought it'd been at least twenty. He flipped it over anyway, and showed me the blank screen with just the picture of the empty battery.

"Oh, okay, sorry, thanks." *Dick,* I added in my head, and sat back down.

When I was little, I could sit alone for hours, just amusing myself with what was in my head. I was alone a lot. Or I was with my parents, which amounted to the same thing. I liked to make up stories about the various objects in the room. Sometimes I became so attached to, say, a lone and withering helium balloon left over from one of my parents' parties that I'd beg them to let me keep it, and then I'd spend the next few weeks caring for it like it was an ailing pet. I could make up entire plays in my head, complicated operettas with subplots and surprise twists. I used to believe that the world was speaking to me through objects, signs, and noises—at long dinners, I liked to crawl under the table and interpret its hidden language, like, *If my dad coughs in the next thirty seconds, it means that he loves me.* My dad had a bad smoker's cough in those days and was always coughing.

I tried to do that now, to entertain myself. I tried to think of my mind as an empty space, and reminded myself that I could make it as big as I wanted to and fill it with whatever I fancied. Inside, I was free. But all I kept seeing was Benson and Stabler, and I was thinking of the last pedo they caught and how he had a thing for tiaras, and I was just realizing that the whole episode was actually a reference to the JonBenét Ramsey murder, and did her brother really do it? Yes, probably, I thought, he did, even though I knew nothing about the case and had only followed it on the covers of tabloids. I tried to hold on to this thread of thought, this prechewed TV plotline, but even it splintered and got lost in the ether. How many of the stories in my brain were there because some marketing exec thought it'd play well with the 18–25 female demo? Then my heart leapt because the door to the apartment building opened and out walked a tall, blond woman. *Gemma!* I hurried outside, without even bothering to go back and grab my phone. I speed-walked across the street, trying to look casual, but when I got closer I realized it wasn't her at all; instead, it was some other blond girl who looked a lot like her and was wearing a blouse identical to one that Gemma owned, a white blouson-sleeve shirt with ruffles up and down the front from this indie brand that was started by three sisters in California. Everyone had that shirt that summer. I'd bought a knockoff of it at Zara just the other day.

I went back into La Coqueta, dejected. I asked the dick barista to refill my water glass. In fifteen minutes, I told myself, I could take my phone back. *Surely*, I thought, *I can entertain myself for fifteen minutes,* and then I felt a mounting sense of panic as it started to become clear I couldn't. I left the coffee shop and bought a small bottle of vodka at the liquor store on the corner, then filled the paper cup from La Coqueta nearly to the brim and shoved the bottle into my purse. I resumed my watch at the window seat in the coffee shop. The liquor had taken some of the edge off, but it wasn't until I got my phone back and held its cool, rectangular body—*o beloved icon!*—in my palm that I began to feel calmed. I ran my fingers over it and before I could even sit back down, I had opened up Instagram. There was nothing new on Gemma's page, but still I studied it, continuously sipping the vodka so that my upper lip started to tingle from the astringent. Already, I was beginning to feel a dullness at the center of my forehead. The harder I tried to find meaning in her profile, the more it slipped from my fingers. Earlier that morning, the porthole in the top left corner of her page had been ringed in pink ombré; now it was gray, signifying that I had already watched her Stories. The last photo on her Grid was unsatisfying: a bowl of raspberries balanced on the ledge of a balcony overlooking the ocean. *Love a hotel that pays attention and knows it's the small things that make guests feel at home. Thank you @ShorehouseMontauk.* Beside her name remained the indelible white check mark, the symbol of everything I desired. It only reaffirmed what I was doing here. My thumb hovered over the rectangular button inscribed, suggestively, with *Message.* I brought it down lightly and Gemma's profile slid away, revealing the transcript of our last communication, which I had already memorized. Beneath the pale-gray bubble of my last message, in smaller letters, was the word *Seen.* I usually consider that a rebuke, since it only appears when a person has read your message and not responded to it, but for some reason that day I found it soothing, as it gave Gemma's presence a tangible quality. I felt my body flush with warmth, though perhaps that was mostly owing to the vodka. Gemma had looked at the very same page I was looking at, and she was out there somewhere now, probably with her phone in her right hand, just as mine was. I thought for a moment. The girl I had seen coming out of Gemma's apartment was not Gemma, but it had looked a lot like her and theoretically it *could* have been her. I could have seen her from behind or from farther away and if I hadn't run up to her in time, I would have *still* thought it was her—in effect, it was the same as seeing her, like the time I'd seen her at La Boîte. A wild idea occurred to me. I started typing: *Your mirage gets around! Pretty sure I just saw you on W. 12th—La Coqueta is my favorite coffee shop on the planet, best oat milk in the city I swear. Any recos where I should go next?* Before I could think better of it, I hit Send.

Then the most extraordinary thing happened: the body of my text shifted upward and the word *Seen* appeared. Gemma, right this minute, was reading my message, she was touching the screen upon which my words had appeared, and the awareness of her corporeal reality was so overwhelming I had to dig my nails into my forearm to keep from losing all sense of myself. Then I could see that Gemma was responding. The platform let me know she was *typing* . . . right this very minute, furthering the impression of intimacy and immediacy, her fingers pressing against her screen as if she were touching me. I almost felt exposed, as if she were watching me. I glanced around the room and, even though no one was looking, I affected a carefree, cool demeanor, pretending to be dreamily staring out the window. When I looked back at my screen, she had written: *Ha! That was actually me this time, not a mirage—me & Pancakes just popped over to Generation Records. It's worth a gander.*

She signed off with a series of emojis in the shape of shooting stars.

Immediately, I googled the record shop; it was on Thompson, a seven-minute walk away. I clambered to my feet, chugged what was left in the cup, and was out the door within the minute. I wanted to run but I was a little unsteady on my feet, which were suddenly leaden, and anyway, I was worried she might catch me doing it if she was already on her way back. As I walked, constantly scanning the street for signs of her, my skin prickled with the awareness of her presence. I could feel she was close, and when I pushed through the stickered door at Generation Records, it was with a hard bubble of excitement rising in my chest.

But, of course, she was not there. I looked carefully among the stacks, walking up and down the aisles, my head swiveling left and right, but she must have already left. Oddly, though, the exhilaration I'd felt on my way over remained. At the time, I attributed it to adrenaline. Now, I wonder if it wasn't due to some presentiment of what was to come, or rather, what was already underway in that other reality, the one that existed up in the cloud or in my phone, and ran parallel to my flesh-and-blood existence. I should have felt irritated and disappointed then, but instead I stepped out onto the street feeling hopeful—maybe it was the booze, maybe it was a sense of destiny. Or maybe it was the back of a familiar-looking blond head I'd seen go by across the street. I couldn't be sure it was her—I'd only caught a glimpse, a hazy impression of blond shoulder-length curls and a certain gauntness as she'd rounded the corner—but I followed in that direction, hoping, praying, for the best.

The sun is beginning to sink, painting the sky a burning orange and gilding the gentle tips of the waves that lap against the pier. Gemma leans farther out over the railing and watches as the waves disappear beneath her. Black pillars, the husks of old wooden piers, stick out of the water, casting shadows. She should be getting ready right now. It is Thursday, the night of The Rising's weekly Social for Social party, and she is supposed to attend it, because she has always attended it and will always attend it so long as it is relevant. Benoit arranged for that. He will be expecting her there tonight. Waiting for her. But Gemma is exhausted. She does not want to go to that dark, cloistered place, no phones allowed. She doesn't feel like she exists when she's there.

Instead, she moves closer to the sun. The pier is crowded and strangers eye her up and down. She has the impression that everyone is watching her, remarking, if only to themselves, on her hair, and gait, and skin, what she is wearing, and if she smiles. She straightens her shoulders and looks straight ahead, not wanting to make eye contact with anyone, not wanting to give in. Somehow, the possibility of their eyes on her has turned the short walk to the end of the pier into a performance, and she becomes confused and forgets if this is how she usually walks, how she usually holds her head, or if it is the invisible audience that is dictating her movements.

Someone is following her—that much she is sure of as she reaches the end of the pier, where the sun burns before her. She keeps her shoulders squared, refusing to turn around, refusing to give in. The sky is beginning to turn red, as if it were really on fire. Everything is suffused with hot light, the kind of light so thick it appears to have weight and substance, a gauzy film you could hold in your hand.

I watch her in silence—muzzled, invisible, and at the same time omnipresent, a looming force that surrounds her unseen—as I have done countless times when I have held her image in the palm of my hand. There but not there. I watch as she takes out her phone and turns the camera on herself. I watch as she leans against the railing, and then her back arches slightly and her head tilts upward, her body moving unbidden to catch the light, find her angle.

I swear all I do is watch.

PART TWO

It wasn't until later that night, when I finally got home, still drunk and far wearier, and recharged my phone, that I learned what had happened. Numbers in red—numbers the likes of which I'd never seen—blared at me from the bottom of my Instagram app: 147 new Followers, 325 new Likes. I stood there swaying, dumbstruck, my throat gone dry. I was already so exhausted, and the revelation of this new reality was so abrupt, that I could not believe what I was seeing. I tapped on the empty heart; it filled with black and then showed me a list of names I didn't recognize, anonymous faces smiling out of their perfect circles. I slid down the list, found the cause of it all, and in that moment everything changed, although of course in reality the moment had come much earlier, when Benoit had tagged me in a photo.

Hands shaking, I tapped on the miniature image of myself, watched as it flickered, disappeared, and then consumed my screen. I was splayed out on the bed, legs spread open, fingers pressed into my groin. It was softly lit and yet stark, my body and the rumpled duvet outlined in late afternoon sun. Critics often talk about the "naked" quality of Benoit's work. There is a realness to it that feels stripped down, and a little gritty, and all the more poignant for it. You could not really see the face of the girl in the photo. I could have been anyone. I could have been Gemma. But Benoit had tagged *me*. I pressed my thumb against the image and my name appeared, suddenly seeming as anonymous and unknown as all the other strangers online with the identically formatted profiles.

On the one hand, I was a little appalled. I looked like a slut, the way I was arching my back, my eyes half-lidded and lascivious. On the other hand, it didn't matter, because people were Liking it. The image already had 4,614 Likes, 18 Comments, a trail of hieroglyphs from faceless ciphers: Flames. Pink flowers. An eggplant. Another eggplant. Three water droplets.

HAWT

Gross I'd hit it

Porn. Report

Does she have no shame?

Omg, I wish I looked like her.

Uh, I can see her vagina.

I spread my fingers against the screen, zooming in on my crotch. You could see the fingers beneath the silk panties, and to one side a distinct labial fold. That was sort of bad, I thought. I hadn't realized that I'd been showing, and I felt slightly betrayed that Benoit had chosen to post this one, of the thousand photos he had taken.

Maniacally, I began refreshing my screen over and over again, my heart clanging like a bell as the symbols on my screen lit up and disappeared, then lit up again, and the day's frustrations vanished.

One comment read, in all-cap letters: *I WANT TO BE HER.*

I screenshotted it immediately, my brain humming with pleasure. I thought: *Me too. I want to be her, too.*

That the photo would go viral was not something I ever expected. The irony is, if it hadn't been deleted, it might have faded into obscurity. You see, it was the photo's censure that launched it to the Popular page.

Shortly after Benoit put up the image, I reposted it to my Instagram feed. The caption was pretty innocuous and plain—I think I said something like *new work with the talented @ HansBenoit.* But it performed well. By the time I went to bed that night, it had 1,029 Likes, making it my most Liked post to date. I fell asleep feeling a kind of peace I hadn't felt in months. Then the next morning, even before both eyes were fully open, I checked Instagram, nervous, hungover, and excited to see how many more people might have Liked it. But the image was gone. I refreshed my feed. All trace of it had vanished—the Likes, the Comments—as if it had never happened, and I might have thought I'd actually hallucinated it, except for the message I received from Instagram telling me it had been removed for violating "community guidelines." Worse, I saw that Benoit's post had also been deleted. Yesterday, my photo had been next to one of Gemma, our faces staring out side by side from his Grid, but now there was only *her*, people that visited his page today would only see *her*, they wouldn't even know I'd been there at all.

Then I called up Jason, utterly devastated, and while we were on the phone together, I saw that Benoit had reposted the image. Jason read the new caption out loud in a breathless, astonished voice:

"'Female pleasure = Female power,'" he began. "Oh, that is good!" He cleared his throat and kept reading. "'Instagram removed this post, even though there is no nudity, and what is shown is not only natural but beautiful. Instagram is okay with the female body as long as it is displayed for the enjoyment of others—but a woman enjoying HERSELF, her very own body, is deemed inappropriate.'"

I watched the Likes and Comments roll in.

Amen.

Female sexuality has been demonized too long!

Fuck Instagram.

"You need to repost," said Jason. "*Now.*"

After we got off the phone, I spent some time looking around for caption ideas.

I posted a series of three shots, each one progressively zooming in closer on my crotch area so that the final image was of only my hand beneath the panties. The caption read *Give the patriarchy the finger!* I'd seen that somewhere under a picture of two teen girls holding protest signs.

I had a hope that the image would get at least as many Likes as the first. It was more or less a repost, so it was possible that some of my Followers would blow by it without Liking, thinking they'd seen it before. Or maybe some of them would even be annoyed that I was clogging up their feed, even though most of the stuff we see on Instagram is just copies of something else anyway. But then I saw that Benoit's repost now had 20 percent more Likes than his original, so I figured it would balance out, and I wasn't worried anyone would report it again, not now that it was about feminism. I put my phone down and resisted checking it again for as long as I could. I lasted about ten minutes at a time. Within an hour and a half, the post had cracked 1K, and I started to feel a tickle of excitement. Already, engagement was way up. Most of my posts get around twenty-five Comments, which is pretty good given my Follower count, but this one already had fifty. My mother had commented, of course, Jason too (*proud of you!*), but there were dozens of others.

Thank you, one girl, who didn't look older than fifteen, had written.

YASSSSS, another wrote.

This. Is. So. Brave.

Patriarchy, be warned: We're coming for you.

People were tagging their friends, and it was spreading. The post approached 2K Likes and then soared past it. Julia sent a screenshot to our group chat: *DUDE,* she wrote. *You're blowing up!*

It was a pure high, the kind I used to get when I first started doing coke, before the foreknowledge of a comedown was permanently knit into the experience: a feeling of expansion, of rightness within the world, like in those dreams where I suddenly discover a door in my cramped apartment and it leads to an entirely new wing. So much space. Then, almost immediately, there is the urgent desire for more, to inhale it all. Unfortunately, that's also the first sign the high is already slipping through your fingers. (It's a cruel irony that the first high is always the best, the first comedown always the easiest, and, hooked on that one-time illusory experience, you'll spend years chasing that intensity, only to find that it's receding at an ever-faster clip.) The post hit 5K. It hit 10K. I walked around the edge of the bed until it met the wall, then turned and retraced my steps. I did this over and over again, biting my nails, until the ground beneath me blurred and I was dizzy. I noticed my T-shirt was wet. I'd sweated through it. I tore it off. I slid out of my boxers and stepped into the shower, blasting my body with cold water. When I closed my eyes, I saw red bubbles, an imprint of circles and numbers behind my eyelids. I got out of the shower and barely bothered drying off before picking up my phone.

I can't believe this is happening, I wrote to Julia and Blake. Two hours after being posted, the image now had 30K Likes. I got into bed, still dripping wet, and put the covers over my body. My battery was getting low, and I plugged in my phone. I had moved past the exhilaration phase, to that numbed-out feeling of invincibility that comes after the fourth or fifth line. My thumb had ceased being a thumb; it was simply a lever that generated names, numbers, colorful symbols, data for my eyes to process.

Sometimes there was a three- or five-second lag, so that for one instant—sharp inhale—there appeared to be nothing new, and I stared at the screen, holding my breath, heart sinking, until, with one desperate swipe of my thumb, my screen would explode again in an orgy of red bubbles. The release I experienced then was doubly intense, heightened by the delay. *Marry me,* people wrote. *You deserve the nobel peace prize or some shiz,* another wrote. Encouraged by my exhibitionism, perhaps, or simply fueled by a narcissistic impulse, people shared deeply personal stories of sexual abuse and sexual shame and anything else they wanted to read into it. *I'm also a survivor of sexual trauma, and I can't tell you how much it means to me to see another rape survivor sharing this kind of thing,* one person wrote, quite inexplicably.

When the vitriol started rolling in, I really got excited. Everyone knows you're not anyone on the Internet until someone has threatened to rape or kill you, and I drummed my fingers along my lips, feasting on the ugly things people wrote: they called me a whore, a cunt, said that I should kill myself, threatened to rape me *except ur such a slut ud probably let me,* and I laughed because the guy who'd written that looked like he was fifteen; his face was covered in acne and he was on his school's softball team. The Comments that actually creeped me out were from the men proclaiming to be "feminist allies" and then begging me to go out with them. *If I were your boyfriend, I wouldn't let you out of the house,* one guy wrote, apparently thinking that was a compliment.

Jason called.

"Have you seen the *New York* mag thing yet?" he asked.

"No," I said. I'd been too invested in watching my feed skyrocket to even think of looking at anything else.

"Google yourself."

I did, and dozens of headlines appeared:

Model Activist Calls Out Instagram for Censoring Female Pleasure

Why Is Female Masturbation Still Taboo? Model Mickey Jones Wants to Know

Model Flips Off Patriarchy in VERY NSFW Way

Instagram Slammed for Removing Feminist Model's Post on Female Masturbation

I'm Sorry, But This Is Porn: Why Instagram Should Remove Fashion Model's Post

"So does tomorrow work then, three p.m.?" Jason asked, though I was too busy feverishly scanning the headlines to follow anything he was saying.

"Uh-huh," I said, "sure."

"The interview should last just twenty minutes. She'll call you."

I wanted to ask who the interview was for, but I was having trouble stringing together words. We hung up, leaving me once again to the masturbatory pleasure of reading about myself online. Everyone wanted to talk about what it meant that everyone was talking about it, and some people argued that it was a boon to feminism that we were all talking about it, and some people said it was the worst possible thing for feminism, and no one wanted to admit that at least part of the reason why everyone was talking about it was for the immemorial reason that it was a hot girl lying on a bed, almost showing her vagina. My Follower count doubled, then tripled. At a certain point, I looked up and saw that it was dark out. I was still naked, sitting up cross-legged in bed. It occurred to me I hadn't eaten or drunk anything all day, and I forced myself to the kitchen, my head swaying like a helium balloon. I chugged several glasses of water, hoping that might give my body a sense of weight, substance, make me feel less like something that could float away. When it didn't, I dug out a deformed box of freezer-burned Eggo waffles from a block of blue-white ice and popped them in the toaster. Julia called, but I ignored it.

U coming out tn? she texted.

My Eggo waffles dinged, and I ate them leaning over the counter, mentally composing a text to Julia. I could not explain why, but I did not want to see her or Blake or anyone else I knew. I kept thinking about what my Followers might imagine me doing that night, what I could post, but I couldn't think of anything specific.

Gonna lay low I think, kinda exhausted, I texted Julia back, employing the wishy-washy language I used to decline plans. *I think,* as if I didn't already know, as if thinking you were declining plans was somehow different than actually declining them.

Aw c'MON we need to celebrate u becoming famous.

HA HA, I wrote back, though of course I was enormously pleased with myself. *So not famous.*

Ur like the Malala of female masturbation.

That time I actually did laugh out loud.

Lol, I wrote. *You're funny, but still no.*

C'mon, it's La Boite. EVERYONE's gonna be there.

I froze. The last time I had gone to La Boîte, I'd seen Gemma. It was just the beginning; I was nothing to her then. Had that happened now, now that I was anointed, nearly on her level, I was sure that interaction would have played out differently. We would have become friends. It seemed absurd the way I had chased her only a day ago; I remembered—though it was through a thick fog of alcohol—the way I'd trolled around the record store, shifty-eyed, and later sought her out on the street, wandering the winding West Village streets to the pier, where I had passed out for . . . I didn't know how long. I couldn't fully remember what had happened. The rest of that excursion remained a blur, overshadowed by the evening's excitement; indeed, my days before going viral were already growing less distinct in my mind. Idly, I opened up Instagram and gazed at my post again. It occurred to me that Gemma would have seen it, as a close Follower of Benoit's she couldn't have failed to see it—in fact, it was possible she had seen the first post well before me. The thought both thrilled and terrified me, and it was with shaking hands that I searched for her name among the Likers and Commenters.

But it was nowhere to be found. Thinking my eyes must be playing tricks on me, I filled myself a glass of vodka and drank it down. I searched again. Nothing. I visited her profile in a panic; had she seen it then, and found it ugly, juvenile, in poor taste? She was embarrassed by me, and furious at Benoit. She disavowed us, refusing to Like or Follow. I felt sick. But as her page refreshed, I realized she had not posted, not even a Story, since the last selfie she took on the pier that day, her face painted orange by the sun: *Pre-partying for @TheRising tn, and by pre-party I mean gazing forlornly at the sun completely alone.* Relief washed over me. Maybe she had not seen the post after all. She normally posted to her Grid every day and broadcast several Stories, but occasionally a few days would go by without a peep from her and then she'd post something explaining her absence, that she was traveling, or sick, or doing a "digital detox" or taking a "quick mental health break." Probably that was what was going on. I wasn't really worried; in Montauk, she had talked about needing a break, and then she'd gotten sick. So it made sense that she was taking a little time off. It never occurred to me that anything might have happened to her. I didn't think about that possibility until much later. At that moment, all I could do was imagine her reaction when she logged back on and saw what happened. I replayed the scene in my mind over and over again, watched as her eyebrows drew together in consternation and then slid up her forehead in surprise. She would tug on the locket that hung around her neck, as she often did when she was deep in thought. In some versions, Gemma was happy for me; in others, she was jealous. I didn't know which would be sweeter. But every version ended the same way, with Gemma DMing me and asking to get a "coffee or bite or drink."

I poured myself another glass of vodka, and told Julia that I would not be going out that night. *I'm gonna be a grandma tonight and stay in,* though in reality I was in such ecstasy that I could have run a marathon. I wanted to stay in to prolong that happiness and guard it selfishly, as if to expose it to real life might taint it. I got back into bed with my drink and opened up Instagram again, and responded to certain Comments and deleted and blocked certain other ones. I changed my bio to read *Color me a revolutionary.* For the first time in a long time, I didn't want to think about Gemma. Instead, I stayed up late staring at smaller, distorted images of my own face.

It was remarkably easy to slip into her place. At the time it felt like destiny, although now I know it was just the algorithm doing what it was supposed to do, which was to figure out what we wanted to see before we even knew about it, using a set of intractable and unknowable equations that evolved over time based on engagement. The idea was that the algorithm was only showing you what you would have liked anyway—it wasn't corrupting your taste or free will in any way; it was just facilitating greater options. Only sometimes it was difficult to tell if you'd really had any choice in the matter, like in junior high when you thought you liked punk music because the boy you were dating was into punk music but then when he dumped you, you realized you hated it. The machine knew that if you Liked Gemma, there was a good chance you would Like me, too, and since its promise is to serve us more of what we like, forever, always, it promoted me to the Popular pages of Gemma's Followers, and when they Followed me, as the machine knew they would, that was integrated into the equation, too, so I was then promoted to users who were similar to those other users, and so on and so on, echoing out endlessly.

Within the week of that repost, my Follower count was up 170 percent, to almost 70K. I was determined to surpass 100K within the month. I kept obsessive track of how each post performed: Images that showed my face and body received roughly 50 percent more Likes than those that did not. Images that showed my face and body and included a message of empowerment performed best; they received roughly the same amount of Likes, but engagement was far better.

I started reading *The Second Sex*, for something to post about, but it was difficult to get through. I made a list of all the quotes that might make good captions, and brainstormed ideas for their visual counterparts. Books made good content. Yoga, meditating, brunch, smoothies, colorful cocktails, walks in the park: these were all good content, and good content was all I thought about those days. It was my god.

I was so preoccupied that the dread and disappointment I felt every time I checked Gemma's profile and found that she hadn't posted anything in *days* was slightly neutered. I knew she was just taking a break; it wasn't that strange, *really it wasn't,* I kept insisting to myself. She'd be back. Still, sometimes I would visit her profile and a panic would seize me as I gazed upon her familiar Grid, so stagnant and immovable I felt as though she were buried under concrete, suffocating to death, and all I wanted to do was chip away at the barrier between us. *Something must have happened to her, something awful.* What if she was hurt, what if she was in pain, what if she needed me? There could be no other explanation for her silence but catastrophe. *Unless*—my mind turned on itself once again—she was deliberately shutting me out. Or *someone* out, more likely, I told myself, thinking of Benoit. I knew there was no possible way she could have known we'd slept together, but still, it was possible she'd figured out, once and for all, what kind of a person he was. But none of my rationalizing or wild conjectures helped when I went to search for her name among my new Followers, as I did every day, multiple times a day, my heart plummeting when, every time, she was still absent. Thankfully, though, the magnetic appeal of those other Followers, the numbers always going up, up, up, was strong enough to eventually buoy me back to the surface.

Mostly, I was just busy, busy, busy, making posts, doing interviews. At first, I was nervous doing the interviews, but it wound up being easy. All you had to do was say what the interviewer wanted you to say in the same way that everyone else being interviewed said it.

"It just came about really organically," I heard myself say over the phone to a journalist from *Teen Vogue*.

"I love that," she said. "I feel like when things happen organically, it's always better."

"Absolutely—it just feels more real and natural."

The girl's name was Molly, and I googled her while we talked. She was twenty-five, with short black hair cut into weird baby bangs that she probably thought made her look like Amélie. Her face was pretty, but I found a few full bodies of her and she was short and chubby, which was fine if you knew how to pull it off, but she clearly didn't.

"Totally," I said, in response to something she said.

"It's like, we should be out there in the open with it, you know? Girls need to see this so that they know they are allowed to feel pleasure, that their bodies exist for them to have pleasure, too. Don't you agree?"

I said *totally* again, and later, when the interview is written up, her words will be attributed to me. The interview will contain a link to my Instagram, and I will almost immediately get four thousand new Followers.

Molly asked me what I thought my Instagram Following liked best about me, and I told her "Confidence," while I took pictures of my face with my phone.

"I just don't really care what people think, and I think people sense that, and they think it's refreshing and maybe even inspiring," I said, holding down the Capture button indiscriminately and watching a miniature version of my face flicker in the bottom left-hand corner of the screen. "I think a lot of times, girls feel like they can't just be themselves, and I just want to be one of the people that stands up, in my small way, and shows them: you can be yourself, you can be however you want to be, you don't need to apologize."

Molly agreed, as I knew she would. The interview was shared around, people loved it and acted like I was saying something new and profound instead of the same meaningless garbage everyone else was saying. That was what content was; it encapsulated any form of expression, all art, journalism, social media, and it didn't matter what it was saying, or if there was any message; the message was the content; the content was the content. As if all of it were just the contents of something, the guts of some juggernauting beast.

Earlier that month, Gemma had posted a photo of herself perched gracefully on the edge of the fountain in Washington Square Park, one leg extended, the other bent at an obtuse angle, her body turned three-quarters of the way toward the camera, one arm bent, with the elbow gently resting on her thigh. Her hand tilted a vanilla-chocolate swirl soft-serve ice cream near her face, perfectly telegraphing summer nonchalance while maximizing the length of her legs.

It was eighty degrees out, and I bought the vanilla-chocolate swirl at an ice-cream truck parked, seemingly permanently, on Bleecker Street. I waited patiently for a woman to remove two screaming brats from the vicinity, then sat almost exactly where Gemma had sat—with the arch just to my right in the background. My phone was already clamped in the selfie stick. I felt a cold mist against my back and against the spaghetti straps on my Rouje Daria Dress in Night Blue Flowers, and thought about how Gemma's skin had probably been wet by the time she'd finished taking the photos. Expertly, I guided the phone to the correct spot, angled so that you could not see the hand that held it aloft. I bent one knee and extended the other leg straight in front of me. I gently rested my elbow on my thigh, tilted the ice cream toward my face, and smiled.

While I was uploading the picture in a pocket of leafy shade—the ice cream was melting away on the top of an overstuffed trash can— Jason, who had grown, conveniently, into my biggest supporter and number one fan, called to tell me that *JOY* wanted me for a shoot.

JOY, I probably don't need to remind you, was at that time the pinnacle of chic (this was a year before one of its early investors got caught shilling kiddie porn). Founded by the legendary Cate Ancien in the '90s, *JOY* had more recently succumbed to capitalist pressure and sold to Condé Nast, where it had greatly enriched its coffers without losing its street cred.

"Benoit's shooting—he asked for you specifically," Jason said. Then he went all quiet and said in an excited, hushed voice: "And guess who's styling it? Cate."

"Holy fuck." I jumped up and began pacing around the park, zigging and zagging between people.

"We've got a pretty good shot at a cover."

"Holy fuck," I said again—a little too loudly. A trio of NYU students sitting cross-legged in the grass jerked their heads to look at me. I laughed, gave them the finger, then walked quickly out of the park and up Fifth Avenue.

"What about the CK campaign?" I asked. Cate and Benoit did the Calvin Klein ads each season, and it was well known they tried out girls at *JOY* before bringing them on as faces of the brand. I knew the *JOY* shoot would pay nothing—but if I got the cover, I'd be officially sanctioned as the new face of fashion. Ergo, I'd be a shoo-in for the face of Calvin; ergo, I'd soon start raking in hundreds of thousands, then millions . . .

I could feel Jason smiling through the phone. "We've got a good shot at that, too."

I noticed this *we* Jason was all of a sudden bandying about, but I was too excited to correct him on it. "They haven't cast it yet," I said flatly.

"Nope. And it's about that time, too."

Gemma's first cover of *JOY* was almost exactly two years ago, and right afterward she was named the face of CK. So I was right on schedule. Yes. Things were going exactly as they should.

"You just do everything in your power to make them love you, okay?" He wasn't using the *we* this time. "Anything they want."

"Of course."

"Charm their fucking pants off."

"I will." I caught my reflection in a store window and smiled widely.

"This is big for us," Jason went on. "So I just want you to be on your A game. I want you to be absolutely perfect." No carbs, no sugar, no dairy. Actually, try not to eat at all if you can. Water, though. Drink lots of water—except for on the day of the fitting. Twenty-four hours before the fitting and of course the shoot: no water, because even innocent old water can bloat you. For the past several seasons, CK had been pursuing an explicitly sexual image. The glossies called it "porno-chic."

One ad showed a woman on all fours, wearing a horse saddle and stilettos long and slender like needles. That was a lipstick ad. Gemma's was relatively tame. She's wearing a black mesh skintight dress through which you can see a lacy bra, and reclining on a ripped-up couch that seems to have been abandoned outdoors somewhere.

"Think sex," Jason said. "I want you to fucking ooze it, sugarplum."

We hung up. I walked home in a bit of a daze. For some reason I started thinking of my dad—something I'd been trying to avoid since I'd canceled my visit with him. I still felt a little badly about that— mostly because my mother was upset—but not too badly, and anyway work was my priority right now, and my dad had stopped trying to call me altogether, so he couldn't have really cared that much. As soon as the big money started rolling in, though, I promised myself, I'd go see him; I'd finally be able to look him in the eyes and tell him I needed nothing from him, that my mother needed nothing from him either. As I neared my front door, I fantasized about buying my mom a house, or at least renting her a nice apartment somewhere, maybe even in the city, on the Upper West Side. Once I held the purse strings, it would be me she'd have to listen to, not my father. The appeals would stop. Case closed. My dad could rot in jail for the rest of his life, and I'd actually be happy to visit him, my work schedule permitting.

I picked up the boxes and packages stacked outside my mailbox and carried them up to my apartment. Brands kept sending me free stuff, and though most of it was junk, things I would never wear or use, it still gave me a narcissistic thrill to know that I was important enough to warrant unsolicited gifts. I dropped the packages on my floor and arranged them as artfully as I could, then uploaded a picture to my Stories. *Today's goodies*. Getting free stuff was a status symbol that proved my place among the real influencers, and the more I documented it, the more I'd receive—a positive feedback loop, a hall of mirrors.

I took a Xanax and found a sharp knife in the kitchen, then got on my knees and started cutting open and gutting the boxes. Inside the first was another box, and inside that one was a set of cotton pastel underwear with frilled edges and the names of feminist icons embroidered in big, loopy, color-contrasting stitching on the front. I put them back in the box and filmed myself unpacking them. Baby blue was Gloria Steinem. Pink was Ruth Bader Ginsburg.

Another box contained still another box, filled with cardboard chips, which I had to dig through to extract a bottle of nail polish, the color of which was described as Avocado Toast. Apparently, this company had just launched a series of polishes "inspired by your favorite brunch items!" It looked like bile, and I decided to give it to my mother just for the chance to tell her that a brand had sent it to me for free. I knew that would delight her. Next, I filmed myself unboxing a neon-pink spandex swimsuit, necklaces that looked like henna tattoos, beach towels with a hyper-saturated picture of a sunset on them, and plastic pool slides from a company that gives kayaking lessons to kids somewhere with every purchase, or something, I don't know.

Each time I added to my Stories, I got sucked into a vortex inside my phone. *Taylor Swift Weighs In on Sexism, Systemic Racism.* The Brazilian flu had spread northward to Mexico City, which was now contemplating a lockdown after three teenagers with the illness had wandered onto a highway during the disease's dissociative phase and were nearly killed. *Emily Ratajkowski Has a Surprising Trick to Achieve the Perfect Summer Glow.* The "trick" was that she put on bronzer *plus* blush. *Ideas that come to you now, dear Aquarius, particularly about areas related to learning, mental interests, communication, neighbors, connections, and siblings, can be especially important. They may very well kickstart a long-term pursuit.* One of my cousins, Auntie Joey's daughter, had gotten a puppy and named him Chocolate. A gunman had opened fire at a garlic festival in California, killing three, including two children, and wounding seventeen, after spewing neo-Nazi, white supremacist ideas online. An NYPD judge had said the cop charged with choking Eric Garner should be fired, despite the court's ruling. Kendall Jenner wished Bella Hadid a happy birthday. Chocolate played with a butterfly on a patch of grass somewhere.

By the time I was done, there was a mountain of cardboard and packing peanuts and plastic, and I had mixed feelings about the fact that sea turtles were likely to be genocided so that companies like these could send me all this junk I didn't want. I did, however, put aside the underwear that said *Joan Didion* on them, and looked up quotes from *Slouching Towards Bethlehem*. Actually, it would be cute if I was reading the book while wearing the underwear, I thought, getting excited. And I could write something like *Whoa, meta.* That'd be funny.

By then, I had already internalized the algorithm, and I intuitively understood its rhythms and quirks. I had begun to think of all human experience in terms of content, distilling everything I encountered—a beautiful sunset, a funny sign, whatever I ate for breakfast that morning—into neat squares and dispatching it to the void, where it would be gobbled up by Followers while they rode the subway or used what little free time they had on their lunch break to zone out in front of their phones.

Though she hadn't posted in weeks, not since that fateful day by the pier, I continued to pore over Gemma's Instagram, looking for clues to brand-building, content strategy, and post ideas. I slid my thumb up the screen and watched miniature versions of her disappear at the top and new ones appear at the bottom. I went all the way back to the beginning, the first few photos she had posted: a shitty, heavily filtered photo of a sunset; Gemma and a girl I didn't recognize grinning up at the camera without a shred of guile; a picture of a bee, slightly out of focus, crawling on the leaves of a sunflower. These missives embarrassed me, then gave me strength. Clearly, she had posted them before she'd found her brand. I suppose she'd just kept them up for posterity. I was glad, though, that I didn't have anything half so embarrassing in my feed. It made me feel as though I had a leg up on her. In my mind, we were still in competition. I imagined her eyes on me all the time, sometimes enviously, other times derisively. Every once in a while, I'd think of her and feel a pang of longing as clear and sharp as if I'd been stabbed. I missed her. I wondered where she was, what she was doing. But all too soon that ache would turn to anger, and I'd be pissed at her for her silence. I knew her so intimately—could picture her as she slept, as she bit into her favorite slice of pizza from Artichoke, could detail every freckle and mole on her face—that it felt completely unfair for her to just shut me out like that. Especially at such a pivotal moment for me. Though of course it was possible she'd have no way of knowing it *was* a pivotal moment for me. What if she'd missed my viral ascent entirely, what if she didn't even know I was going to be as famous as her? The thought made me shudder.

The only time I felt close to her was when I was creating content. I found myself following in her footsteps and assuming her poses more and more: at Jack's Wife Freda, I ordered what she always ordered; at the Met, I stood in front of her favorite painting (a Matisse); and at Central Park, I bought a hot dog like she always did and ate it on a park bench, half-laughing, as she once had, because ketchup was threatening to drip through my fingers. It wasn't a conscious decision to copy her at first. Her posts had penetrated my brain so deeply, it was not always readily apparent where they ended and my own creativity began. All I knew was that whenever I did it, I was suffused with a familiar warmth. It felt like flowing into a mold, slowly rising until the outlines were filled and I felt something chime within me. Much of the time, I brought Julia and Blake along, and we'd shoot at the Met or in Central Park. Neither of them mentioned the changes I'd made to my appearance. Actually, we all just acted as if I'd always looked like this and acted like this. And if they noticed I'd started to blatantly copy Gemma's posts, they didn't mention it.

Everything was falling into place. Yes, these were halcyon days, with only a few hiccups. There was a mass shooting in upstate New York, and a march was organized around Lincoln Square. I woke up early to make a sign, spending hours drawing and painting a uterus, which I sprinkled with pink glitter. *More regulated than,* I wrote in big block letters, and then painstakingly copied a drawing of an assault rifle I had found on the Internet. It was the perfect sign to bring, and I was itching with excitement to post a picture of it, but I wanted to wait until we'd gotten to the march. Julia and Blake and I made plans to get there at ten a.m., just as things were beginning to heat up, but in my excitement, I left the damn thing on the subway, and then had to put up an Instagram holding Blake's sign, which was subpar at best.

Julia and Blake were both pretty good at taking pictures, though Julia occasionally made snide comments about how she wasn't a *fucking paparazzo,* but I knew they'd both keep doing it as long as I kept tagging them. I was generous like that; happy to spread the wealth. I bought a used copy of Bukowski and had Blake take a picture of me reading it on a checkered picnic blanket I'd bought expressly for the purpose. We trekked out to the beach and drank rosé from mason jars with pink-and-white paper straws. At Coney Island, the content was ironic, a double feint so that we could seem above all the lame, narcissistic shit we were doing, while continuing to do it unapologetically. In the evenings, I opened and cataloged the packages that kept coming to my house, and set aside time to respond to all my fans, writing little messages or at least Liking the Comments they left on my posts. Julia and Blake gave me shit for not going out, but I suddenly had no patience for dinners out with the faceless men, no taste for the rich food, and in the morning I didn't like to be hungover because then I looked all puffy in my pictures.

I'd more or less stopped eating.

Soon, I was walking through the revolving door at the Condé Nast headquarters for the fitting. I remember laughing, thinking about all the castings I'd gone to in the past, realizing only then how pointless they had all been.

The offices reminded me of the airport, which suited my mood fine. Though I hadn't traveled anywhere in a long time, airports remained, in my mind, potent whirlpools of fear and excitement, my father ranting the whole ride there that we'd miss our flight, making us sprint through security, only shutting up when he got to the bar, with thirty minutes to spare before boarding. My mother would say nothing; she'd simply roll her eyes behind his back, and then we'd go buy magazines, gorge on the fantasies they sold us, make shopping lists, and tell each other what we planned to wear on vacation.

The lobby was large, gray, and impersonal, with ceilings as tall as three stories; sunlight poured in through the windowed front, but somehow it still managed to feel cold. The man behind the front desk asked for my ID, made a call to the *JOY* offices, then ran my bag through the scanner. He printed out a sticker with my name and a blurry black-and-white photo I hadn't noticed him taking. I made a mental note to Instagram it later with a cryptic humblebrag. I was wearing COS Limited-Edition Wide Leg Linen Pants in Black, an Equipment Poplin Short Sleeve Blouse with Tortoise Shell Buttons in Black, and the same Totême Flip-Flop Heels in Black that Gemma had worn to The Rising, all of which I had bought for the occasion.

In the elevator, I took a few deep breaths. The point of this, I reminded myself, was not to familiarize myself with the shoot's wardrobe. The point was to charm their pants off. The point was the cover. The point was the campaign. The point was millions of dollars and being able to tell my father to fuck right off. I straightened my shoulders. The metal doors of the elevator showed my reflection, distorted in the imperfect, striated surface. My head was a blur of pink and yellow. My perm had mellowed, but my eyebrows were still pale. It occurred to me that at one point, much earlier, Gemma might have stood in this very spot, she might have stood exactly as I was now standing, a thumb tucked under the strap of her shoulder bag, looking at her reflection and perhaps even thinking similar thoughts about the imperfect, striated surface and the way she styled her hair. I was struck with an eerie sensation, as if I were in two places at once—or rather, that I *could* have been in either of those places, at either of those times. Had a sequence of random events occurred otherwise, I would have been in Gemma's place and she would have been in mine. "I" could have been anyone, had events gone slightly differently. Even Gemma, I thought, as the doors slid open.

There was a girl waiting for me when I got out. She stuck her hand out and introduced herself, then led me through the double glass doors, on which the word *JOY* was spelled out in big plastic letters.

"How's your day going?" she asked brightly, rounding another corner at a fast clip. Besides their labyrinthine layout, the offices of *JOY* were surprisingly banal: fluorescent lighting, gray carpet, hunched figures backlit by the buzzing blue glow of computer screens. The only thing that distinguished *JOY*'s offices from, say, those of a toothpaste brand were the racks of clothing that lined the narrow pathways, and the well-dressed and suspiciously gaunt figures that flitted between them.

"Pretty good, thanks."

"Things are pretty hectic, huh?" Her tone was familiar, knowing; she'd obviously watched my Stories that morning, a series of shots of myself doing yoga and "meditating," waxing poetic about the need for self-care in our hyper-stressed world.

"Exactly," I said. "I mean, that's why this morning was so important."

She jerked her head back a little bit and said something indefinite like "Yeah . . . I'm sure," and I supposed I'd embarrassed her about having watched me that morning. People are weird like that.

"Don't worry," I said, trying to make her feel better. "I mean, that's why we all do it, right?"

She didn't seem to get my meaning, or maybe she was too embarrassed still to acknowledge it. Anyway, we'd come to a halt outside a glass-walled conference room, and I could already see Benoit and Cate.

"Mickey, dear." Benoit had already gotten up and was walking toward me. He kissed me once on each cheek. I turned to say goodbye to the girl but she had already gone. Benoit took me by the elbow and ushered me into the room.

I didn't even have to introduce myself. Cate clapped her hands when I walked in, and smiled at me brilliantly. "There she is," she said, coming up to me and squeezing my forearm. "Lovely to meet you." She spoke with a British accent and was striking in the way that fashion people often are, which is to say that she wasn't attractive in the conventional sense, but nonetheless, you couldn't seem to look away. Close to six feet, pale, with a pixie cut so blond it was white, and a horsey smile. She was wearing a thin plaid shirt, not flannel but something more gauzy, and leather pants—part of her signature punk aesthetic.

A woman made up very much in Cate's image but of Asian descent introduced herself as Kim. She had a pixie cut nearly identical to Cate's, only hers was dyed a pale pink, and I wondered if she had had the cut before she was hired, if a similar aesthetic to Cate's had been a prerequisite for the job, or if she had adopted it once under Cate's wing.

We all sat at the conference table, and I leaned back and felt a rush of adrenaline seeing the way they looked at me. It was the way men looked at me right before I went to bed with them.

Kim cleared her throat, glanced briefly at Cate as if for permission, and then began: "So we're super excited about this shoot. We think it's going to—"

"It's going to push buttons," Benoit cut in, and laughed.

"It'll be a conversation starter for sure," Kim continued.

"A statement," Cate corrected her. "It'll make a statement."

I was listening alertly, scanning for microexpressions, tonal shifts in their voices . . . I sensed it was time for me to say something. "Statements are good," I said, offsetting the banality of the comment with an ironic expression, a little half nod of the head. Repeating what someone said was good. That was charming. Everyone knew that was charming.

"Well, exactly. That's why—when we were looking for a girl, it was like—" Cate snapped her fingers. "We've got her." She pointed at me, then closed her fist as if she'd caught something in her hand.

"You know I found this one in a bookstore?" Benoit said to the others. "I was looking for Rilke, you know, I lost my copy, and this little lady crashes right into me in the aisle."

I laughed. "Right, and Gemma was all like, um, hi," I said. Something passed over Benoit's face, but it was too brief for me to analyze. His mouth opened. I heard the beginning of a word—quizzical, a question—I thought it was the beginning of her name. But then Kim broke in, gushing.

"Oh my *god*," she said. "That's *so* you." She meant me. "Discovered while reading Rilke in the bookstore!" I was impressed at how quickly Kim had transmuted the anecdote, how *I* had become the one reading Rilke, not Benoit, and saw instantly that this was the story that would get passed around as part of my creation myth. It only took me a half second to respond.

"It was *Letters to a Young Poet*, one of my favorites," I said smoothly.

Cate shook her head in appreciation. "Clever girl. That's why you're perfect for this."

Benoit nodded in agreement. "We're just so sick of *models*, you know?"

"Oh god, models bore me to death these days!"

"Exactly. We want *real* girls, you know?"

"Anyone can stand in front of a camera and smile. But, you know, nowadays it's more than that. It's about personality. *Authenticity.*"

Personality was a cozy way of saying *personal brand.* Whereas actual personalities tend to be fickle and elusory, personal brands can be depended upon and easily understood. Personal brands are

SEO-friendly and searchable. Personal brands can be keyworded. Of course, the process by which a personality is transformed into a personal brand is a flattening one—but I like to look at it as a distillation, rather than an attenuation. Make no mistake, though, both personal brands and personalities are performative. What I said: "Oh, I totally agree."

"That's what got me so excited about you, you know, you really *stand* for something. So, okay—" Cate clapped her hands together and stood up abruptly. "The shoot."

She walked over to a rack of clothing, and it was understood that we should all follow. "So we really want this to be about owning your sexuality, owning your body—" Cate extracted a red vinyl contraption of indecipherable utility. "It's 2019, you know? Women want more than just eye candy. They want fashion that *says something*, that means something."

"You know that opening scene in *Belle de Jour*, when she's being whipped?" Benoit asked.

"We thought it was really brave, what you did," Kim put in.

The thing on the hanger revealed itself to be a kind of bra, the sort of thing you usually see in a sex shop: an outline in vinyl. The only thing covering the nipples were two hands holding the middle finger up. The fingernails were painted pink.

"It's really about girl power," Cate went on, and then corrected herself, with a wry smile, over her shoulder. "*Woman* power." Cate turned and held the bra up to my collarbone, and looked at it against my skin. Woman power, but we—the models—were always called girls. That's what they were really after: womanhood slipped over girls' bodies.

"That'll be *rad*," Kim said. Cate did not respond. She was pinching her bottom lip between her thumb and forefinger, a habit I would come to recognize in her whenever she was considering something.

"I'm not sure it'll work with the breasts," she said, returning it to the rack and extracting a pair of high-waisted leather underwear with the words *Fuck the Patriarchy* graffitied on it.

"Chic, yes?" she asked the room. "We had them custom made." She winked at me and then lifted a white men's shirt from the rack. "We tuck a little, leave the rest open, very Helmut."

Kim nodded. "Who makes it, though?"

Cate glanced briefly at the label on the shirt. "J.Crew."

Kim made a note. "Good, they won't care about the stains."

"It won't be a lot of blood."

"And advertising will be happy."

Benoit explained to me, "We're going to do something really exciting—"

"Really raw," added Cate. "Unlike anything we've done before."

Unlike anything we've done before. I was giddy. That sounded like a cover. That sounded like fucking money. I knew better than to ask any further questions. I just nodded coolly. Blood? Who cared about blood? I was going to be rich. Cate handed me the dress shirt and motioned for me to change behind a little curtain in the corner of the room. I had trouble getting the underwear on, leather underwear being just about the most ridiculous invention you could dream up. But once I had the entire look on, I had to admit Cate's genius. It *worked.* I looked like pure sex. It had CK written all over it. I walked outside the little curtained corner and felt their eyes on me. Benoit flipped his aviators on top of his head and peered at me.

"I just realized I'm wearing my sunglasses inside," he said.

"Hans, you always do," Cate said absently.

"I probably look like an asshole," he said, and then he flipped them back over his eyes. "But they're prescription."

"What do you think?" Cate asked, a knuckle rubbing back and forth on her bottom lip.

"I think I look like pure sex," I said, and they both startled, as if a piece of furniture had spoken. Clearly the question was not for me.

"It's not really about sex," Cate said testily.

"Not at *all* about sex," Benoit said.

Fuck, I thought. I laughed nervously and tried to course correct. "Oh no, of course, I meant like, the patriarchal idea of sex, but like, the female empowerment version of it. That's the whole irony, isn't it?"

Cate smiled, and relief washed over me. She wagged a finger at me. "Clever girl."

They took my picture, and they pinned the Polaroid up on a felt wall. Then Cate handed me what looked and felt like a burlap sack, and I went back to the curtained corner. Sweating, I removed the shirt and underwear from my body and slid the sack over my head and found that truly, it was indistinguishable from a burlap sack. In fact, I later learned it was a $3,000 Dolce & Gabbana dress made from burlap to look like a burlap sack. I walked out. Cate stepped back and eyed me up and down.

Kim sucked in her breath quickly. "They'll murder us if we stain this one," she said.

Cate was pinching her bottom lip again.

"Who cares," said Benoit.

"We'll be careful," Cate said.

Kim made a note. I wanted to say something to further redeem myself for my idiotic comment about "pure sex," but I couldn't think of anything. Then Cate was hugging me around the waist. She smelled like tobacco—not cigarette smoke, but the kind of stylized scent common among fragrances that make a big deal about being "unisex." I had an impulse to kiss her on the mouth. She stepped away, and I saw that she had fastened a thick leather belt around my waist. It looked like something a horse might wear. Gemma's cover flashed in my mind: she's wearing a white cotton dress, essentially a nightie, cradling a baby lamb, bits of hay stuck in her hair, her cheeks rosy . . . In the inside spread, she's covered in mud. I mean, completely bathing in it in that white dress, smiling up at the camera.

"I remember Gemma telling me about the mud on *her* cover shoot," I said, laughing nervously. "I'm sure that dry-cleaning bill was no fun either."

Of course, it was bait: I wanted to see how they'd react to the words *cover shoot*. I wanted them to know I knew Gemma, that I was on her level. I wanted them to think I'd done my homework. Cate, who was crouched at my waist, looked up at me quizzically.

"Who?" she asked, having apparently not heard me.

"Gemma."

"Mud?" said Kim. "That's obviously quite different."

Cate shook her head, confused. "You know, I have to admit, the covers sometimes blend together."

"It was her first. Right before she did CK with you guys."

"I mean, mud obviously doesn't stain in the same way," Kim went on inanely. I looked over at Benoit, who was studying me curiously, amusedly, I thought. Cate stood and stepped back to look at me. She bit her lip, seemed to be thinking.

"Was that the one with the lamb?" she asked.

"Yes, exactly."

"Right, right," she said. "We used Naomi for that, though."

I looked at Benoit for him to correct her, but he merely stood there smiling. I let it go.

"Sorry to geek out on you guys," I went on, lowering my eyes as if bashful. "I just think your work together—I mean, those CK campaigns are *iconic*."

Cate smiled. "Thank you."

"Gemma's *was* one of my favorites—" I stopped when I noticed their faces. They looked embarrassed. Maybe there was a backstory to that ad, maybe they weren't proud of the work. Maybe I was right and Gemma and Benoit *had* broken up, and they were deliberately avoiding her name for his benefit. "I mean," I added quickly, blushing, "they're all amazing, though, obviously."

"Oh, thank you," said Cate. "You know, sometimes I swear my memory is going—"

"Maybe you have the Brazilian flu," joked Benoit.

Kim laughed nervously. Cate rolled her eyes.

"Why do we put up with him, I wonder sometimes?" Cate asked, tilting her head in my direction to include me in the "we." That made me feel emboldened, in spite of my obvious gaffe. They had me try on half a dozen more looks and I was careful to scan their faces, though I found no evidence of anything useful. They looked pleased. Benoit would flip his sunglasses on top of his head every time I came out and take a few steps closer so he could "really see me." His fingers often brushed the backs of my arms, the small of my back. I was a little startled at how obvious he was being about it—at one point he actually briefly cupped my ass, while examining the hem on my skirt—but then I started playing into his attentions, smiling coyly at him. Whatever was going on between him and Gemma—perhaps her Instagram break also included a break with him—clearly he did not feel the need to hide his affection for me. While this exhilarated me on the one hand, I found, looking at him under the institutional lighting with his stupid sunglasses, I was more physically repulsed by him than ever.

Eventually they selected six ensembles, which they pinned up on the felt board. Kim took notes. We said our goodbyes: a kiss on both cheeks from each of them. When I came to Benoit, I moved my face a fraction of an inch so that we would kiss halfway on the mouth, and clung to his biceps a little longer than was warranted.

"Can you show me out, Hans?" His first name sounded funny in my mouth. "It's a maze out there."

He shifted uncomfortably on his feet, glanced at Cate, who was busying herself with some papers spread out on the table, and followed me out. His hand was on the small of my back.

"I'm really excited for this shoot," I said.

"It will be grand."

"It makes me excited for the possibility of working with you further," I said, reaching back and covering his hand with my own, pressing it firmly into the small of my back, sliding it ever so slightly down . . .

"I've missed you," I whispered.

We waited for the elevator. He said very little. I understood. It wasn't the place. Once we stepped into the elevator and the doors closed behind us, he turned to me and jammed his tongue down my throat. Then he pushed me away. He sniffed loudly at my armpits, then pulled back and made a face.

"It is repulsive," he said. He was smiling, but it was a disappointed smile. "There is chemicals."

"It's organic."

"You're not to wear it again. You're not to wear any of that again. None of that toxic garbage, you understand? How am I to know if you're clean if you mask yourself with all this chemical stuff?"

I had to keep my face very still so that I wouldn't scream or laugh in his face. I remembered Jason's words. *Anything they want.* It was clear Benoit was testing me. "Of course," I said sweetly. "That's easy. Consider it done."

But this did not seem to appease him. He stared at our blurred reflections in the closed elevator doors, his face stony. His fists were balled at his sides.

"The other thing," he said, "is you must learn discretion."

"Of course," I said, clenching my jaw. *Anything they want. Anything. Anything.* When he didn't respond, I said, my voice as even as I could make it, "I thought I was being discreet."

"No," he said, "you were obvious."

The doors slid open and we walked out together. I had to slow my pace so that I was still beside him. He was walking very slowly, a strained look on his face.

"Are you going to walk out with me?" I asked, hesitating before the revolving door. He followed me out.

"I'm sorry," I said. I wanted to take his hand but I was afraid to touch him. I made my voice flirtatious: "I suppose I lose a little control, being around you."

Benoit stopped walking and turned to glare at me. Then he erupted in laughter. He laughed and laughed and laughed, and just to humor him I started to laugh, too. It was all an act with him. He wanted to control me, and knowing that gave me a perverse sense of power; I would allow him to think he was in control, all the while working to get what I wanted. Thus, I would be the one actually in control, since I would be the only one aware of the true nature of the transaction. I did not, however, account for the pernicious ways in which a person's influence can embed itself within you, changing you from the inside out. I had imagined that my actions, so easily faked, would not impact who I was; yet added together, it turned out those actions amounted to my life.

Benoit caught his breath, then pulled me to him again and bit me lightly on the neck.

"Oh, you are a peach, aren't you?" he said. "I bet you taste just like a peach."

"Thank you," I muttered.

"You'll be at Bianca tonight?" he asked. "Your kind goes to that, no?"

I smiled. That night, there was a party to celebrate the reopening of the Bianca Inn, a fabled club that had been shut down a few years before due to noise complaints. Everyone talked about it like it was the Garden of Eden, an oasis of possibility and debauchery the likes of which simply didn't exist anymore, even though from what I could see from the photos, it was really just a shitty split-level basement bar in an old West Village building. People actually wore shirts that said *Free Bianca*, as if the nightclub's struggle were akin to that of someone wrongfully convicted.

"Of course," I said, though I'd had no intention of going until that moment.

"I will see you there," he said. "You can make it up to me then."

He kissed me again on both cheeks and then roughly squeezed my crotch.

"What about the CK campaign?" I blurted out. "Do you—well, do you have a girl for that yet?"

"Not yet," he said.

"Not yet," I repeated, with a suggestive lilt.

"Maybe soon," he said, and winked. "We'll see how it goes tonight."

Julia and Blake were thrilled. I'd told them I was feeling antsy, that I could use a night out with the girls, and asked if I could come with them to the Bianca after all—this, after I'd turned down the invite twice already.

Benoit asked me to go with him, but I'd rather go with you guys, lol, I wrote.

COME!

Yay!

After a few minutes I wrote: *Benoit's kind of sad I'm not going WITH him, but I think that's crazy right? Like, stop being so needy ma dude.*

Totally.

Like, whatever, I'll just see him there.

I received a thumbs-up emoji, and the details of the night. They would be dining with Joe and the faceless men beforehand at Pastis, the reopened Keith McNally joint in the Meatpacking District.

Living like it's five years ago, wrote Julia. *Act accordingly.*

I wore vintage Levi's 501s, the RE/DONE Classic Tee in Vintage White, Mansur Gavriel Monogrammed Dream Ballerina Flat in Red, and a Clare V. Black Nubuck Wallet Clutch. *Dressed like a 16 yr old boy for the reopening of Bianca, oops,* read the caption on the Instagram I'd put up, though of course no one would mistake me for one: in the photo, my nipples are erect (I pinched them just before, thanks, Julio), and my jeans are so tight I had to lie on my back and suck in to put them on. Still, I knew the deceptively simple outfit would create the right effect, a kind of humblebrag—*Look how good I look and I didn't even have to try*—and when men and women complimented me on how "refreshing" it was to see a woman like me "so natural" and commended me for "not caring so much what I looked like," I would smile at them bashfully and secretly revel in smugness, as if my supposed "naturalness" owed any credit to my character, rather than to the completely arbitrary biological process which had shaped my physical form. Never mind that I paid $425 for the jeans. The photo already had 4,013 Likes, which gratified the effort it had taken to explain to the middle-aged passersby that I didn't want to be looking at the camera; apparently they didn't have the word *candid* in Kansas or wherever the fuck they were from. After some strenuously worded instructions, through which I bit back my rage, they finally got it right and then scurried away as if I were crazy.

I was planning to arrive late, and told Julia and Blake to save me a seat next to one of them. Sometimes Joe liked to split the girls up, to make sure everyone's ego was equally massaged. When I got there, Pastis was busy, low-lit, and successfully passing off its generic, no-nonsense decor—rickety wooden tables, mismatched chairs, juice glasses in place of stemmed wineglasses—as rustic charm. Twelve of them—mostly men, and a handful of girls—were crammed into four pushed-together tables in the alcove behind the bar, coveted and sought after for its relative privacy.

"You look *amazing*," Blake said, her voice aghast as if I'd betrayed her. I knew what she meant was that I looked particularly emaciated.

"Yeah, right," I said. "I'm like a *boy*." An allusion to my Instagram caption.

I kissed Blake on the cheek and then fingered her faux-silk blouse. "And what's this?" I asked, even though I knew it was from Mango. "I love it!"

"Ugh, really?"

I slid into a seat between her and a man with disturbingly pink skin. "Yeah, it's super cute."

"It's just from Mango," she said dismissively, giving the appropriate girl response. This was the language afforded to us women, speaking in brand names and *I love it* and *Where'd you get this?* All of it a white noise disguising the emptiness and rage that yawned just beneath the surface.

"She's *ba-a-a-a-ck!*" Julia sang, rushing from her seat across the table to kiss me. She was wearing a nearly see-through diaphanous dress, through which you could see her nipples and her black thong. I had Blake and Julia wrap their arms around me and took several photos of the three of us, smiling like we're on ecstasy. It took a few tries because the lighting wasn't great, and Blake said her nose looked big in all of them, which really wasn't the camera's fault. Eventually we got it, though. *Living like it's five years ago,* I wrote, tagging Pastis and Bianca, and uploading the picture to my Stories.

By the time we sat back down, the starters were on the table, and I forked a bunch of greens onto my plate indiscriminately. The photo already had 432 Likes, averaging roughly 73 Likes per minute. Beyoncé "throwing shade" at some random woman at a basketball game was going viral. What happened was: This woman leaned over Beyoncé a little bit to say something to Jay-Z, and Beyoncé's face, as captured on film, was unimpressed. Now that woman was receiving death threats. Carli, a blogger I Followed, had a pimple. Chiara Ferragni ate spaghetti. Galveston cops had apologized for leading a handcuffed black man down the street with a rope while mounted on horses, but really they were just apologizing for the photo of it that had already circulated online. Trump had tweeted, *Mental illness and hatred pull the trigger, not the gun,* following another shooting by a white supremacist, in El Paso. Kylie Jackson was *not* dating a basketball player I'd never heard of. A judge had said that Epstein's trial on federal sex-crimes charges could take place in mid-2020. My cousin had had a late-term miscarriage.

At some point, I looked toward the end of the table and noticed that one of the faceless men at the dinner was in fact Andrew. I waved, and he smiled at me awkwardly. It occurred to me then that he did not remember me, and that made me laugh, and then it made me seethe. I turned away from him abruptly and nodded to the man beside me, whose skin had somehow grown even pinker over the course of the dinner, taking on the hue and texture of a pig's skin, and he obediently picked up the wine on the table and refilled my glass. He mistook the gesture as some sort of overture, leaning in to ask me some nonsense or other, and I had to turn from him pointedly, too, leaning over Blake's plate to insert myself in her conversation.

". . . we're in an inflection point, I can feel it," Blake was saying, and I knew she was talking about Blakies, a line of hair accessories she was developing. "After our last pivot," away from hair ties and toward scrunchies, "I knew we were on to something because I just got so many messages from people, and compliments, and people were really feeling them, plus, like I told you, Magda"—that was her psychic—"told me it wouldn't manifest until this year, but it just feels so good, to be putting my money where my mouth is, you know, walking my walk, and—"

I nodded along, not really listening. In my head, I went over my plan. The plan was: find Benoit, impress him, make him want me, get him to a place where he promises me the cover. I had a fantasy that he would see me, preferably surrounded by one or two attentive men, and say something like *Don't you look peachy*, and take out the Nikon he often kept in his chest pocket and snap a photo of me and post it online later. Maybe we could do a whole series of "candid" images of me. I imagined the two of us sitting side by side in a little booth. Eventually, I'd bring up Gemma, very casually. I wouldn't ask him if she was okay, I'd just let him talk. *I wouldn't normally tell someone this,* he would say, his lips just inches from my own, *but you're different . . .* I was jolted out of my reverie as Blake's hand flew in front of me, making contact with my wineglass, which I quickly caught before it toppled. Blake hadn't even noticed. She was gesticulating wildly, her voice gaining velocity like a wheel going faster and faster until it becomes an indistinct blur. I nudged her with my elbow.

"Bathroom?" I asked.

She nodded and followed me in the direction of the bathroom, all without stopping her monologue. The bathroom was even dimmer than the restaurant, almost laughably so. I made Blake chug two glasses of water, after which her steady patter continued, while I cut a line for myself on the back of her gold compact.

"That Andrew guy is here," she said, eyeing my handiwork.

"Yeah, I saw that. Whatever though, he's a douche."

The emotional exchange concluded, I tipped forward and hoovered up the beautiful white stuff. Purity spiked through my brain. I handed her the compact and let her dip her fingers in the remnants and rub it on her gums.

"We need to make sure Joe orders the donuts," I said.

"Ew, why?"

"The 'gram," I said in an ironic, jokey voice.

"Oh yeah, *the 'gram*." Blake's was even more dripping in irony.

We both rolled our eyes and laughed. Then, back at the table, we told Joe to order the donuts. They came, as we knew they would because we had seen them repeated in slightly different variations and angles on our Grids, piled high in a perfectly constructed pyramid of alternating colors. I took twenty-three pictures of them and, feeling almost as though I'd already consumed them, ate nothing. Someone tapped me on the shoulder, and I wheeled around.

"Hey." It was Andrew. Probably come to introduce himself to the "new girl," a new conquest. I wouldn't give him the satisfaction.

"I'm Mickey," I said, sticking my hand out abruptly. "I don't think we've met before, have we?"

Andrew laughed, looking flustered. "Haven't we? I think . . ." He trailed off, clearly not able to place me. The fucking bastard.

"Are you going to shake?" I prompted.

He took my hand, and I tightened it around his, then let it drop. He was staring at me; perhaps only now some sort of recognition was dawning on him. I wasn't about to make anything easier on him.

"And what's your name?" I prompted.

"Andrew."

"Huh. I had a dog named Andrew once."

He laughed, and ran a hand along the top of his receding hairline. Involuntarily and instantaneously I remembered what it felt like to kiss him, his stubble along my cheek, the stale taste he had. Andrew seemed at a loss for words. I looked toward Julia and Blake, who were bent over a cell phone, their hands overlapping around it, almost as if clasped in prayer.

"Is the Uber here?" I called to them. "Benoit's already texting me like, *where are you,* he's so needy! But, like, I feel like we should go soon." I turned to Andrew and said, "So nice to meet you, *Aaron.*" Then I walked away.

By the time we got to Bianca, I was pretty obliterated—we'd done more coke, and I was fucked up enough to think that the weird tincture Julia offered to dose my drink with was a good idea. "It's mellow," Julia had told me. "A good body high." It was mostly psilocybin, something she had cooked up at home with the apparatus she'd bought last year when she thought she was going to get into the essential oils business. Almost everyone I knew was, or had been, the founder of some dubious enterprise; it made doing nothing sound a lot better.

One thousand twenty-nine people had viewed my most recent Story, the one with the tower of donuts. Dozens of people had sent me donut emojis, pictographic echoes.

"Is Benoit here?" Jules asked.

"Not yet. He got held up." I refilled my drink, my body humming with anxiety. Impatiently, I searched the crowd, looking for the glint of his aviators. I held my phone in my hand, flipping it over every fifteen seconds, using the button on the right to make the screen blink suddenly bright, showing me the time, showing me nothing. *If he isn't here in thirty minutes,* I told myself, *I'm going to text him.* In the meantime, Julia and I sat in the booth—which wasn't really a booth but an alcove set with upholstered benches and low tables—sandwiched between the pink man from dinner and a skinny Frenchman who was still dressing like The Strokes and maybe going a little bit bald. They kept talking about how it wasn't the same as the *old Bianca,* which, they wanted everyone to know, they'd *practically lived at.*

"The magic's gone," the Frenchman said, as if this were truly a tragedy.

"Everyone's on their phones," the pink man continued, his face looking more and more like raw meat. "People are posing with the American flag." This tattered remnant of the *old Bianca* had been framed and hung on the wall near the bar. I had taken a picture of it on the way in.

"Millennials, man," Frenchie said.

"Fucking millennials!"

Julia and I exchanged a *gimme-a-break* look that not even these two obtuse fools could happen to miss.

"I mean, no offense," the pink man said.

Julia let out a bark of laughter. "We're not even millennials, you old farts," she said. "We're the generation after that."

"*Fuck.*"

"What do they even call you?"

"No one knows yet," I said, standing suddenly. I stuck out my hand, and Julia took it. "Let's dance."

We topped off our glasses with vodka and headed into the crowd. My eyes strained against the anonymous, useless bodies gyrating in the dark. Julia followed my gaze.

"You see Benoit?" she asked. "Is he here?"

"I don't know, my phone lost reception," I lied.

We started dancing, but it was difficult to concentrate; I kept turning my head this way and that, trying to spot Benoit without looking like I was trying. Every once in a while, I'd contort my body and close my eyes in a way that made it look like I was really getting into it, but as soon as my little performance was finished, I'd snap my eyes open and anxiously scan the crowd, each time expecting to find Benoit watching me, and each time disappointed that he was not.

"Maybe we should look for him at the bar?" Julia said, even though I really hadn't been obvious about my impatience. I figured she had her own reasons for wanting to meet Benoit, beyond the fact that I'd halfway led her to believe he was my boyfriend. She probably wanted him to take her picture.

I got us two waters at the bar. We noticed that a lot of people were wearing these T-shirts featuring a big wave on them, and Julia said that it was Julio Ronaldo's design, to support the humanitarian efforts in the Philippines following the recent typhoon.

"He sent them out to a bunch of people. You know, to raise awareness."

We both laughed as we watched two girls grinding on the dance floor, raising awareness in a West Village bar that charged twenty dollars for a glass of wine.

"Fuck," I said.

Julia finished her water and wiped a hand over her lips. "At least the design's cool."

"Yeah, if you're into performative wokedom." This was something I'd seen someone else say on Instagram. Of course, I was really just pissed I hadn't been sent one.

"Wait," said Julia, pinching my forearm. "Isn't that Benoit?"

He'd walked in with a group of people I didn't recognize. He was wearing aviators, a loose black utility shirt, and a leather cord tied at his neck, and was flanked by a guy in a fedora and a woman with a shaved head.

Like Me

"Who's he with?" Julia asked.

"Oh, just some *friends* of his," I said vaguely. "He told me he was coming with them, but I'm just so shit at remembering names."

"That girl's buzz is fucking rad."

"Yeah, whatever," I said, hardly looking at the girl, my eyes fixed on Benoit's aviators, willing him to look in my direction.

"Oh wait, shit, that's Karma Black," Julia continued. "She's been, like, all over my feed recently. You know she shaved her dreads off in protest of the abortion ban? Or maybe it was because of climate change. Whatever, it looks fucking sick."

I remained silent.

"Aren't you going to go say hi?"

"I will," I said, but I didn't make a move. We watched as one of the door guys clapped Benoit on the shoulder; they embraced and soon were walking toward the back, where the enclave of booths provided a shred of privacy and space for those who had forked over thousands for the privilege.

"You know, I think you'd look pretty fucking sick with a buzz," said Julia, running her hands roughly through my hair.

"Ew, yeah right. I'd never."

Blake strode up, and put her arms around us. She was clearly annoyed that we'd left her but trying to mask it. "What're you hoes talking about?" she asked with juvenile bravado.

"How Gemma should get a buzz."

"Oh my god, that'd be *maje*," Blake said, turning to look at me appreciatively.

The world tilted slightly. There was a strange clamoring in my head. "Wait, what'd you just say?"

"That you should get a buzz cut."

I shook my head, and the noise disappeared.

"What?" Julia asked.

I laughed at my own foolishness. "Nothing, sorry. I thought you said Gemma for some reason."

"Gemma?"

"Who's Gemma?" asked Blake.

"Nothing," I said, getting annoyed. "I just thought you said Gemma should buzz her hair. I *misheard* you."

"Yeah, but who the fuck's Gemma?" said Julia, and Blake laughed.

"Ha ha, you guys."

"Honestly," said Julia, grinning. "I've no idea who you're talking about."

"Okay, good one."

Julia put her hand on my shoulder. "My darling Mick, I think you've had too much of the tincture." She patted me on the head, and I wanted to slap her. It was true, perhaps, that I'd overdone it a little with the tincture, but then why was she deliberately trying to fuck with my head?

"Oh, P.S.!" Blake exclaimed, uncomfortable at the obvious tension between us. "Joe said we can charge shots to the bar."

Julia's face lit up comically. She rubbed her hands together like an evil villain. "Three shots of tequila?"

"I thought I was already too fucked?" I asked, my voice edgy.

"A nice shot of tequila will sober you right up," she said, and like magic she turned around, immediately summoned the bartender, and ordered three shots of tequila. I decided not to be annoyed anymore, it wasn't worth it when Jules was in a mood where the only thing that mattered was partying.

"Fuck it," I said, and when she doled out the shots, we threw them back in unison.

Afterward, we went to find Benoit. He was in deep conversation with two old guys: not middle-aged like Benoit, but really old, fifty or sixty. One of the dudes had a cotton-white beard and wore a cowboy hat. The other was completely bald, with fashionable clear-rimmed glasses. They wore thoughtful, bemused expressions and sat with chins on hands, bent over and sprawled out, discussing something with the leisure of three powerful men, as if they were seated not in the city's hottest new bar but in a quiet little sidewalk café and the world carrying on around them was just background for their discussion.

"Hi!" I had to say it really loudly to get their attention. Benoit looked up without even taking his chin off his hand. When he saw me, he leaned back and spread his arms along the back of the booth, a wide grin on his face.

"Ah," he said, gesturing toward me for the other men at the table, "this is my new peach." He winked. The men nodded.

"These are my friends," I said, introducing Julia and Blake, then squeezing into the small remaining space at the end of the banquette. Benoit put his arm around my shoulder but did not move to accommodate me, so that half my butt cheek was hanging off the edge and I had to flex my abs and squat a little to keep myself in place. Benoit looked from me to the man with the cowboy hat.

"Perhaps you two know each other?"

"I don't think so," I said.

"No," the man said.

"Ah, well, you should." Benoit put a hand on Cowboy Hat's shoulder. "He's the man you gotta blow to get a job in this business."

Everyone laughed.

Blake and Julia stood there awkwardly, smiling, shifting on their feet—there was nowhere for them to sit. Eventually, I gave them a dismissive nod and they wandered away, Julia with an irritated look on her face. Whatever. I turned my attention toward the men. Benoit poured me a glass of vodka, and I drank it down quickly. They went on talking as if I weren't there.

"Genius," one of them said.

"So fresh."

"It all happened so organically," Cowboy Hat said.

"She was into it?"

"She was game."

I nodded along, smiling.

"Good girl."

"*Smart* girl."

"I was inspired by Grace Jones."

"Genius."

What were they talking about? I didn't know. Not then. I was having trouble following words. Things were looking slippery. I'd drunk two more glasses of vodka, forgetting, in my nervousness, about the not-insubstantial amount of drugs I was on. I was so stupid I thought I was still in control, even though the next thing I remember clearly was being helped off the ground.

"You all right there, little lady?" Cowboy Hat asked me. I think it was the first thing he'd said to me the whole night.

"Just dandy," I said, sliding back in next to Benoit. Their eyes lingered on me only a fraction of a second before they resumed their discussion. I had no idea how much time had passed, but all of a sudden I understood they'd been talking about the CK campaign. I took a swig of my drink, but it was empty and the ice cubes knocked against my teeth and left a slippery, cold feeling on my lips. I smiled, showing my teeth.

"The CK campaign," I said. "That is *so* exciting."

"Is it, my peach?" Benoit put his arm around my shoulders.

"Are you guys all working on it?"

The men exchanged a look, the meaning of which was so obvious to me I didn't need to press them further.

"Of course," I said, smiling slyly. "Never mind. I'm sure I'll know soon."

They laughed, looking a little embarrassed at their transparency. I excused myself for the bathroom. When I came out—nostrils stinging, heart singing, and only a little bit unsteady on my feet—Benoit was waiting for me, alone, standing at the table where he and the others had been sitting. He was bent over his phone, his face shining corpse-blue in its glow. He was still wearing those fucking aviators.

"Hey," I said, but he didn't hear me. I covered his phone with the palm of my hand. "Hey," I said again. He looked up, but two smaller versions of myself flew up in front of his eyes, reflections in his aviators, and the music was loud and it was suddenly very late. The ground slanted, and I sort of tipped over . . .

Benoit kissed me hard on the mouth, holding me upright with one arm underneath my armpit, his teeth gnashing against mine.

"Peach," he said.

I was still leaning into him, finding it difficult to stand on my own, but I knew exactly what I was doing.

"Take me home and fuck me," I said.

He called an Uber. Or someone called an Uber. I don't really remember. Benoit and I clambered into the back seat. I was unsteady, and kept pinching the inside of my arms, trying to sober up.

"Shhh," Benoit said, though I didn't think I'd been saying anything. "Just lie down here." He patted his lap, and I lay down.

The next time I opened my eyes, it was with the understanding that we were moving at great speed, probably on a highway, and that Benoit's hand was beneath my underwear. Gold filtered through the windows. It had rained. I thought the rain looked like stars. Gold water droplets on a shimmering sky, shivering, the city behind them like a blur. Benoit turned my head and pressed my face into his crotch, his zipper biting into my lip. I moaned and tried to push myself up. When he resisted that, I rolled away from him, hitting the back of the driver's seat and banging my head on the side of the door.

The driver yelled something.

"Don't let her be sick in my car," he said, after calming down.

"She's fine."

I giggled—or tried to giggle. It gave way to an unpleasant gurgle.

"I'm going to pull over."

"Don't pull over," said another voice. I bolted upright and peered toward the front of the car. The man with the cowboy hat and white beard was riding shotgun. I figured we were giving him a ride home. I didn't say anything. I thought they'd probably told me something and I'd forgotten.

Benoit helped me back into his lap. He stroked my hair, my cheek.

"Relax, baby, we're almost home," he whispered. I shivered.

"Unroll the window," I said, comforted to hear my voice loud and clear.

The cold false sky disappeared down a shaft, and the stars, too. The outside air, which was warmer than the air inside the car, washed over me. I closed my eyes. Gemma was here, she was right there in the front seat. *Gemma, don't worry,* I thought, *you're fine, Gemma. It's okay, Gemma, I'm here, Gemma.*

"She's fine," I heard Benoit say again.

"She's fine," Cowboy Hat echoed from the front seat.

They had a difficult time getting me out of the car and up the stairs. I kept falling over, and they kept giggling, making jokes about it as if it were surprising.

The men stretched me out on the sumptuous corduroy couch.

"We'll take pictures some other time," I mumbled to Benoit.

"Yes, my peach."

"We'll do a shoot like last time."

"Of course."

"Exactly like last time. But for CK."

"Yes, peach."

"I'm a CK girl, don't you think?"

Benoit giggled.

"I can't do pictures right now, though. I'm pooped. Just utterly pooped."

The men laughed. Benoit went into the kitchen to fix more drinks. The couch was soft as a cloud. I felt its pleasant, velvety ridges all along my back and arms, cradling me. I started calculating how much something like this might have cost. I remembered a time when it never would have occurred to me to wonder such a thing. We used to have things like this. My mother made sure of it, decorating our house the way she cared for her hair: every few months she made a little tweak, though the discussion and worrying were constant. I had been on intimate terms with Egyptian cotton sheets, custom-made Italian sofas, and antique rugs, but I never had any idea of their cost. The price of things only becomes striking when you can no longer afford them. Like I said, ignorance is the most pernicious kind of entitlement. I must have drifted off to such ruminations because the next thing I remember, I was lying on the bed naked, and Cowboy Hat, now hatless, was kneeling on top of me, trying to get his pitiable stiff to work. There is nothing more womanish or pathetic on a man than a soft penis. It evokes both revulsion and a kind of tender pity in me, like when you're looking at a slimy, squirming, pink-skinned litter of puppies. The man began choking me, I suppose because I'd uttered something of my thoughts to him. I might have called his prick "little lady." I may have pointed out its resemblance to a mole rat. The man could not take a joke, apparently. I squirmed beneath him, his hands tightening around my windpipe. I slapped him across the face, and then I heard Benoit shouting, and the man was pulled off me. Benoit held the man's shoulders; they were both panting. I started laughing. Not a little titter either, but wild peals of laughter. The man grew redder in the face.

"You're fucking crazy!" he screamed, then stalked off.

Benoit nodded appreciatively. He climbed on top of the bed. "Oh, peach," he said, lovingly stroking my hair. "I think you're quite deranged." He slapped me lightly across the face, more playful than anything, but for some reason I couldn't stop laughing. Then, probably in an effort to get me to calm down, he covered my mouth with his. But I just laughed harder, my teeth knocking against his, or maybe I was screaming by then, it was difficult to tell the difference, though at that point I would've sworn I wasn't afraid at all. Quickly, deftly, and not without a little gentleness, Benoit flipped me over so that I was lying on my stomach, my laugh stifled in the pillows. He stroked my hair while my head sank deeper into the pillows. I heard the metallic bark of his zipper as he undid his pants. A wave of revulsion ran through me. On one level, I knew I didn't want this to happen, even that I was afraid and repulsed. But on another level, I was telling myself that it was okay, it was worth it, no big deal, a few hours of my life, *whatever*. And it wasn't *even* a few hours of my life, it was a few hours of my *body's* life, which was separate from me. I'd been training for this, after all; every girl has. Why else do they teach us to hate our bodies, to treat them as expensive machines? Then it's easy to do whatever you have to do, since you're not really involved; everything's happening on the outside, but inside you're completely untouched.

On the outside, I could feel Benoit's cock pressing up against my ass. Soon after, pain tore through me and I heard a muffled scream escape my mouth, but it didn't feel like it was happening to *me*, but rather to some actress on a TV program. It was all scripted. I knew the lines and, inexorably, found myself playing the role. I heard myself whimper, then moan, and when Benoit told me to turn over, I did, still whimpering, my hands clutched into fists, though now I was only pretending to resist. Pretending, or believing I was pretending, gave me a false sense of security and control and so I leaned into it, and when hatless Cowboy Hat came back in, his pneumatic system fully functioning now, I didn't even flinch. I watched it all on a tiny TV screen at the end of a hallway, and the hallway kept stretching on and on forever until the scene was the size of a postage stamp.

I suppose it was rape. That's what we argued at the trial, that I was raped—because a woman's sexual past still explains everything, is both cause and effect of everything in her life. She is necessarily good and sweet until a man corrupts her, and then you can't blame her—it's not her fault, it's the man's fault. I've heard people say that rape is worse than murder, which is to say that a woman's sexual purity or dignity is more important than her life. Needless to say, I don't buy that. Under threat of violence or death, my dignity means nothing and my sexual purity even less. Besides, I didn't process it as a rape at the time. I know it sounds crazy, but right to the end, I nursed the delusion that I was somehow in control of it all.

After they had finished, the man put his cowboy hat on and left. Benoit stayed, stroking my hair and calling me "peach." It was light outside, the sky a luminous white. I took a shower. You're probably wondering why I did that, why I stayed. There's no deep psychological reason. I just felt like a fucking shower. I turned it as hot as it would go, and then I sprayed diarrhea all over his toilet bowl. After I'd flushed, and used toilet paper to wipe away my mess—hilarious, but I was humiliated at the thought that he might discover my waste—I stepped into the shower and stood there until the water started going cold. When I got out, Benoit was fast asleep. I stood there watching him, my chest going up and down, though I had the strange sense I wasn't really breathing. Water dripped from my hair down my back, making me shiver.

I had a sudden compulsion, as clear and reflexive as a knee jerk when the doctor brings his tiny hammer down, to rifle through Benoit's things. The idea made my heart pound in the most sickeningly delicious way. I told myself it was not a good idea, and I shouldn't do it, even as I quietly and carefully opened a drawer in his dresser. *Don't do it,* I kept thinking, *don't do it,* as I cataloged the items. In the next drawer, I found his diary. I turned to look at Benoit to make sure he was still sleeping. He was. I opened it up to the middle, and saw the words *fuck* and *millionaire*. The rest was in Bulgarian. I flipped further ahead, and looked at sketches he had made of a naked woman sleeping. Though the face was not filled in, and bore only hints of features—a Cupid's bow for lips, simple curved lines for eyes—I thought I recognized Gemma in it. I had broken into a cold sweat all over my body. There was a strange ticklish feeling in the pit of my stomach. I wanted to wake Benoit and throttle him. I wanted to rip him limb from limb. Instead, I forced myself to close the book quietly and slid it back among his things, telling myself I could come back for it later, that I could take it home with me—he wouldn't notice—even as another voice inside of me implored me to stop, to not go forward, to leave. I knelt at the bedside table and very carefully opened the drawer, glancing every three seconds at Benoit's immobile form, my entire body humming with the fear that he might wake and see what I was doing. I was looking for the Polaroid of Gemma. *My muse.* I wanted to look at it again, to get that sick twist of pleasure that comes when you've picked a scab and the blood starts dribbling. There were dozens more Polaroids in the drawer, all of them of women in various stages of undress. I flipped through them impatiently. None were of her. Almost all were young, thin, beautiful. But not *her*. One was even of me, though I had no recollection of it being taken. Benoit snorted in his sleep, and I hurriedly put the pile of photos back into the drawer. He rolled onto his stomach and began to snore. I sat back on my heels, trying to slow my breath. A feeling of disappointment and dissatisfaction settled in my stomach—but what was I disappointed about? That I hadn't found anything more incriminating? That I hadn't found a better tool to self-flagellate with?

I watched my hand open the drawer back up and, as if I were sleepwalking, as if it had nothing to do with me, I searched the rest of its contents. That was when I found the locket. It was inside a little zippered jewelry case, wrapped in a soft velvety fabric, at the back of the drawer. I recognized it instantly: the heavy gold chain, and the fine engraving, which spelled the word *paix*, with the little ruby set on one side of it. There was never any doubt that it was hers. I had always known it was expensive, but the weight of it clarified that assessment. It was not just expensive, it was priceless. Hands trembling, I opened it up. There was nothing there, though that did not stop a thousand images from dancing through my mind. Benoit had given her this precious thing, he'd wanted it to rest against her chest, hitting the bones of her clavicle every time he fucked her. And even now, he held on to the thing: a symbol of their love, both precious and weighty, something I could never understand. He kept it swaddled in velvet, it was so important to him; he slept beside it every fucking night. How foolish I'd been to believe he might one day grow to find me interesting. Oh, I'd never fallen for any of his cheesy *peach* business, I never imagined he *liked* me, but I thought he might come to value me in a certain way. I thought *I* could be his muse. Now I saw how pointless that had been. Even though Gemma's Follower count had plateaued, and even though the industry had clearly begun to tire of her, he still loved her. He would never see me the way he saw her. I told myself it was irrational to fault him over that; he was allowed to feel how he felt. He couldn't help it if things were still unresolved with her. But rage bubbled up inside me all the same, and I wanted to do violence to him, not just physically but emotionally. I wanted to hurt him—bad—and part of what made the desire so intense was the knowledge that I never could.

I probably knew I would take the locket as soon as I found it. All the same, I pretended to hesitate before stuffing it in my purse.

I found the rest of my things in the living room and dressed quickly. I left without saying goodbye, but not before I had found Benoit's aviators and snapped them in half.

On the car ride home, I comforted myself by watching last night's Stories. I looked beautiful and happy in those images, and that instantly calmed me. Things could not be so bad if you looked like that. I watched the bones move beneath the skin on my chest as I raised a glass of champagne; absentmindedly I touched the same bones today, trying to reconcile the image with the reality. Julia posted a photo of the three of us hugging sloppily near the bar. I didn't remember her taking the picture. *In the huddle. Hut! Hut!* read the caption. I hit Like. Chocolate, my cousin's dog, was learning how to sit. The episodes of amnesia and dissociation were found to be recurring, potentially permanent, in a small percentage of Brazilian flu patients, though the vast majority go on to recover from the disease without any lasting side effects. It was still unknown whether the antibodies could be properly detected, and how long they would last. Joe Biden's son Hunter was being accused of buying off public officials or some sort of other shadiness, which I was having trouble following. Kylie Jackson's pole-dancing video was banned by some universities and other institutions in the U.K. Julia sent a video to our DM thread with Blake. *How fucking rad?*

The video was a close-up of Karma Black's face, framed by navel-length dreads. In it, she has full lips, a strong nose, sparkling black eyes, and light-brown skin, with a heavy dusting of freckles across her nose and cheeks. She cocks her head to one side to accommodate a pair of clippers that has appeared in the upper right-hand corner. Her tongue flicks out and presses against her upper lip as she drags the clippers back from her temple, along her scalp, and her dreads fall away.

There were 8K Likes. I studied her name, @KarmaIsaBitch, wishing briefly that I'd been given a cool name like Karma, to facilitate a clever Instagram handle. I tapped my thumb against the blue Follow button; *Follow* shivered and disappeared and was replaced by *Following*. I pressed her name and my screen opened up into a vista of small squares of Karma Black's face.

Karma Black is dancing in the center of her living room, or a living room; there's a bulbous vintage leather sofa to her right, the kind that looks like a beat-up baseball glove, and a midcentury coffee table laden with books and empty wineglasses. The carpet is a Moroccan thing, the kind West Elm started copying, though Karma Black's is obviously vintage, the real deal. Karma is wearing overalls and nothing else but a choker around her neck. Her tattoos, all black ink drawings: a butterfly just below her collarbone, a snake coiled around her wrist, indecipherable cursive along her shoulder, an arrow up one inner forearm, and a feather on the other. One hand in the air, the other out in front of her, she rides an imaginary horse. I tapped Unmute, and Lil Nas X's "Old Town Road" blared in the back seat of the Uber. I scrolled down.

Karma Black is wearing a Hawaiian shirt and hugging a skinny white girl with a bowl cut, both of them falling over as if from the force of the embrace. *Happy dyke day,* the caption reads. The photo is geotagged *The Rising.*

Karma Black is marching in the street, a fist raised in the air; she's wearing Vans, a wifebeater, shredded army pants. I don't bother reading the caption to find out what she's protesting.

Karma Black is—

A red bubble exploded on the upper right-hand corner of my screen. My mother, who was probably just waking up, had commented on my Stories from the night before with dozens of heart-eyed emojis.

So beautiful! she wrote. *Have fun!*

I called her, thinking she might be able to console me, even though I would never have admitted at the time that I needed consoling. But all she wanted to talk about was the appeal hearing.

"Saul's got a really good feeling about this one."

"Doesn't he always, though?" I snapped.

She didn't seem to catch the irony in my voice, and answered earnestly. "It's true. What a godsend."

From the beginning, Saul had wanted me to be highly visible at my dad's trial. He said it'd look good to the jury that he had such a beautiful, sweet-faced blond daughter. "Even if you don't say much," he'd said, "even if you don't say anything at all, it'll count for something to see you, this beautiful young woman, well bred, articulate, and kind." I asked him how they'd know I was kind. "People aren't that deep. They mostly look at what's on the surface. And they'll think, *Well, how could he be that bad if this is his daughter?*" He actually patted me on the head when he said that, then sent me off to be interviewed by one of his associates, who coached me on being a character witness. Of course, I couldn't remember anything about my father that might qualify as character-building. Even my best memories of my father usually involved him performing some irreverent act, or saying something outrageous. Eventually, though, we landed on something that could work, and on the stand, I'd told a story about how my father had taught me to ride a bike. It was something I'd seen in an AT&T commercial once. Everyone ate it up. My dad's eyes even started watering. He actually believed it, that's how deluded he was. I still don't know how to ride a bike.

"Anyway," my mother went on, "we're still on for Thursday, right? Don't forget."

"I won't."

"Well, last time—"

"I know, Mom. I'm sorry. I'll be there."

"Let's go somewhere fun," she said in an excited, girlish voice. "Maybe we'll have something to celebrate!"

"Sure."

"Oh, but you know what, I'm supposed to be eating keto." She paused, I think waiting for me to tell her that she didn't need to diet. "That's when you eat only high-fat and protein so you train your body to—"

"I know what keto is, Mom."

"Well, I'm just trying to get in good shape for when your father comes home."

I sighed loudly.

"If I can lose five pounds, just *five pounds*, I'll be happy."

My mom always said that if she could lose *just five pounds*, she'd be happy, and she always said it exactly like that, with the *just* and everything, as if she were haggling over the price of happiness with some unseen overlord. But no matter how thin she got, she never shed those five pounds that were keeping her from happiness. I wanted to tell her to give it up, finally. To forget the fantasy of my father's return and stop dieting; to for once in her life figure out what *she* wanted to do, take pottery classes or learn to speak another language, do *something*. But I knew from experience there was no point. She wouldn't even understand the concept. It's not really her fault, since she grew up in a generation of women that did everything to please their husbands, because that was their best shot at any kind of financial security. Women in my generation have other options, and know that the best way to build their wealth is to build their own personal brands, not their husbands'. Building your personal brand means getting people to want or admire you so they'll give you things, whether that means impressing someone at a job interview or making good grades to get a scholarship or fucking a photographer and a dude in a cowboy hat because it gives you a better shot at booking a lucrative campaign. It's all the same, it's just about knowing what to capitalize on.

Instead of saying all that, though, I told her I'd look up some keto-friendly places in the city.

"Thanks, darling," she said. "And give your father a call, if you can. Wish him good luck."

"Sure," I lied.

"He misses you."

"Uh-huh. Mom, I'm just going through a tunnel."

"Okay, well, if you do reach him, just—"

I hung up before she could finish. I took the locket out of my bag and felt its weight in my palm. I secured it around my neck, just to see how it felt, what it was like. Every time the car drove over a bump, it bounced against my chest, hitting bone. I thought about how it would have hit Gemma like that, thwapped like a heartbeat against her rib cage. I remembered how once, in a video, she had popped the thing in her mouth absentmindedly while she flipped through magazines.

In fact, she was often touching it. How many times had I watched her play with its chain or—in a habitual, instinctual way—readjust it so that its clasp hung at the nape of her neck? Every time the clasp would sneak down toward the locket, she would pinch it between her thumb and forefinger and slide it upward and back, while she gently held the locket in place with her other hand. Come to think of it, I had never seen Gemma without it, except for when she did a fashion show or was photographed for an editorial. I felt a growing sense of unease.

I texted Julia and Blake: *You guys were just fucking with me last night right?*

Of course they had been. I wasn't really worried. But I recognized that last night had had a deleterious effect on my anxiety levels, and I didn't think there'd be any harm in having them actually say it. The sky was still white; it was overcast. I unrolled my window to see if the rain had diminished the heat. It had, only slightly. But there was little reprieve, since the humidity was far thicker than days previous. I knew it would rain again, and soon, possibly this afternoon. I looked at the people walking on the street and thought everyone looked a little gray, and depressed.

Blake responded: *Lol.*

We pulled up to my apartment and I got out, still wearing the locket. My legs were stiff. I felt bruises developing along my knees. The homeless man was still sleeping beside my door in an upright position, his face like a waterlogged gourd. I was waiting for Julia to say something, to make fun of me for being so gullible. As soon as I got into my apartment, I stripped naked and drank a tall glass of water, cold, from the tap. I placed a fan on the bedside table and lay down on top of the covers. I closed my eyes and let the fan dry the sweat from my body. When I checked my phone again, Julia still hadn't written.

I wrote: *I'm serious guys.*

Julia responded right away. *Lol.*

So you ARE just fucking with me.

Lol, from Blake.

So they were trying to make me feel bad about ditching them last night. Fine. Ordinarily, I'm down for such jokes. Really, I like a good ribbing, I can take it. But, as spent as I was, I was not in the mood.

C'mon, I wrote, not wanting to seem dramatic. *I feel like I'm being gaslit.*

Lol.

Lol.

Okay, seriously, I don't think this is funny. I was growing irate. Maybe it wasn't cool of me to leave them last night, maybe it was even a little bit rude. But it wasn't as if either of them hadn't ditched me before. When Julia started fucking this bartender and thought she'd fallen madly in love with him it was like we didn't even exist for a while.

I wrote again: *I'm sorry about last night, but like, you guys have done the exact same thing before. Remember Admiral?* That was actually the bartender's name. Julia had made him show her his driver's license.

Wtf does that have to do with this?

You disappeared for a month, I wrote.

Wtf, I'm lost.

Me too.

So am I!!! I wrote.

I just thought it was funny to write lol, I had no idea what it was even about.

I started to type *about Gemma,* but stopped myself. It suddenly seemed juvenile to drive the point home. Clearly, they had been upset about last night and had wanted to let me know, in their passive-aggressive way. Now that I had apologized, they were dropping it. I couldn't be too annoyed about it. After all, I'd thrown a fit before when Julia went MIA at a party or two, sneaking away to be with Admiral while I was forced to . . . entertain the male guests that she herself had insisted on tailing.

Forget it, I wrote. *Sorry. I had a rough night, not in the best mood.*

It's cool, wrote Julia.

What happened? asked Blake.

Yeah, tell us about it! We want to hear all the deets!

Ugh nothing, I went home with Benoit.

How was it.

I started typing. Then deleted what I wrote. *Meh,* I sent.

Then I wrote, *He's kind of obsessed with me it's a little awk.*

These would be used against me, of course, later on. The prosecution would have a field day with them.

Also, I continued, *the guy with the cowboy hat was like hitting on me the whole time, right in front of him.*

Oh God.

Creeeeeep.

I think they're working on Calvin together. He's big-time, apparently.

Omg, you're totally going to get it.

They more or less told me I had it.

Gaaaah that is so exciting!!!!!!

I don't want to jinx it. But Benoit said it was 95% going to happen.

Typing it out had the effect of convincing me it was true. Though my memory from the night was blurry, I was sure that a transaction of some sort had transpired and that, ultimately, it would benefit me. The more unsavory elements were already beginning to loosen in my mind, much like when I cashed a check from a catalog shoot and instantly started forgetting the hours of excruciating boredom I had spent earning it. I saw myself on a billboard looming over Houston Street, large and untouchable, and the vision temporarily blotted out what was left of last night's pain and embarrassment. If I told no one about it then, when it did completely drop from my mind, it would be like it never happened, and I'd be restored to myself. Like if I put up a post, but no one Liked it or even saw it, then it basically never existed. The funny thing was that if that happened—if no one Liked one of my posts—I'd probably end up deleting it, bringing its effacement to fruition.

Btw that dude Andrew came up to me and asked about you, Julia wrote. *Wanted your number. Said there'd been some kind of miscommunication. He's a dick.*

He said you ignored him or something?

Um, he didn't even recognize me.

He said YOU pretended like you didn't even know him.

That gave me pause. Was it possible I'd misread him?

He liiiiiikes you, she wrote. *He told me.*

Ugh, I wrote. *He just wants to get back into my pants.*

I dunno, he said he had real feelings for you—that he thought "there was something real there."

At first, I was a little flattered. It was nice that Andrew thought he liked me. But the more I thought about it, the more it enraged me. Andrew didn't even know me!

Men, I wrote. *Fuck them all.*

Literally or figuratively?

Lol, I wrote. *Both.*

Suddenly, I felt the weight of my exhaustion settle over me. I had not slept last night at all. Still naked, I got up and looked at myself in the mirror. The locket beat against my chest, like another heart. I swayed my body and it caught the light, piercing a hole in my naked reflection. I climbed into bed and fell into a fevered sleep.

I woke, several hours later, in a panic. I'd been dreaming of Gemma—she had been speaking to me but I couldn't understand anything she was saying. I tried to get her to explain it, it was clear that she was in distress, that something was wrong, but when I opened my mouth I found I could not speak. It was my screams that woke me up. I was saying, *Where are you?*

Instinctually, my hand reached for my phone, which was plugged in at my bedside table, and sightlessly navigated to Instagram. I began typing her name in the search bar. I was not seeking any news or updates—I was used to the static quality of her page by then, had stopped hoping for anything else. I wanted only to look at her face, slide my thumb over the glassy surface of her life. It's true, her name usually populated at the top with the first quick tap of the *G*—another way the algorithm served you, nudging you in the direction of what it knew you wanted—but I didn't think anything of having to type out the rest of her name, it flowed so fast from my fingertips, *e . . . m . . . m . . . a.* A list of @Gemmas appeared at the top of my screen, and I almost tapped on the first one before a flicker of discordance ran through me and I realized it wasn't her. I scrolled through the stream of Gemmas peeking out from perfect circles. None of them was her.

There was a sickening twist in my gut. I typed out her username, just her full name—classy, simple—@GemmaAnton. Gray forms took shape on my screen, then disappeared.

No results found.

I tapped on the words again and again as if they might yield something, some new information, as my heart raced. The screen didn't so much as blink—it just stared at me, relentlessly blank and unchanged. My stomach gurgled and I had to run to the toilet to throw up, seized with a horrible sensation. An image appeared in my mind as clear liquid streamed from my mouth: Gemma, standing at the edge of a pier off the West Side Highway, the setting sun blazing in front of her. I call out to her and she turns to look at me with her mouth open in surprise . . . I pressed the butt of my hands against my head, dispelling the strange daydream, then wiped my mouth and flushed. Still, I could not shake the heavy dread that gripped me, and I began to think, and then to really *know*, that something truly terrible had happened to her. On *Law & Order* it is always the husband, the boyfriend, the closest man who is responsible, and I began to think of Benoit, and what I knew of him, and feel increasingly panicked.

I forced myself to drink some water, trying to calm down. It was then I noticed a distinct atmospheric shift in the room. I looked outside and saw an iridescent sheet of pouring rain between my window and the brick building, like a curtain of glass beads blowing in the breeze. I took a deep breath. I walked to the window and stuck my hand in the water. A plan had already taken form in my head, though I didn't want to admit it to myself. I spread my fingers out wide and turned my hand over in the rain, letting the water splash both sides, and at the same time I turned the idea over. I sighed resignedly, as if it weren't my idea at all but an order from a micromanaging boss.

Finally I said, "Well, that's all there is to do." The rain responded with a hiss.

As soon as I said it out loud, all hesitation evaporated. It was the right thing to do. It was the only thing to do. I dressed quickly. Bruises were darkening along my neck, thighs, arms, and knees, and I chose a white sail of a dress that went to my ankles and billowed at the chest and sleeves. Even though I was in a rush, I reflexively took a few photos of myself in the mirror.

It took me fifteen minutes to get to her apartment. The doorman was standing under the green awning, his hands in his pockets, looking at the rain. He was portly and balding, with light-brown skin and a trim black goatee. And he was whistling.

"Hi!" I said.

He stopped whistling and looked at me, his mouth falling open in surprise.

"Oh wow," he said, "you needa umbrella?"

I looked down at my dress, which was drenched and revealed the pink of my skin where it clung to me in uneven patches. The bottom of it was gray and speckled with flecks of black. My nipples protruded like pencil nubs as my chest heaved. I laughed. I had filmed myself on the way over. I had thought it'd read as carefree and romantic.

"Oh, thank you," I said. "I don't mind the rain. I'm here to see Gemma."

"She's a tenant in the building?"

"Oh yes, she's my cousin."

Had I been a man, had I not been white, had I been anything but a dumb blond in a soaking, see-through dress, he might not have let me through. But because I was so obviously not a threat—just a little sweet trifle, a kitten, nothing to worry about—he opened the door with a nod and waved me in. It is not a very nice feeling to be the beneficiary of a racist and unjust system, but back then I was not about to deny myself the benefits. I walked purposefully through the lobby, as if I'd been there a dozen times. I froze in front of the elevators. I walked back out.

"You know," I said to the doorman, "I always forget her apartment number."

He looked at me blankly. I think he was just really enjoying the rain.

"I texted her," I said, flashing him my phone's screen, "but you know her . . . total space cadet."

He sighed, looked one last time at the rain coming down, and went inside. I followed him. "What was the name again?" he asked, making his way behind a tall, semicircular counter.

"Gemma," I said. "Gemma Anton."

"Let me just look her up real quick. I'm new so I'm still getting to know everyone's names." He stood in front of the swivel office chair but did not sit in it. Instead he hunched over the ancient-looking desktop computer, his tongue pressing against his upper lip so that I could see its purple, veined underbelly, and typed with his pointer fingers.

"Gemma . . ." he said, drawing out the name as he painstakingly click-clacked on the keyboard. "Is that with a J?"

"No, a G."

He hammered on the backspace key.

"It's G-e-m-m-a," I said helpfully. "A-n-t-o-n."

The tongue came out again. Click-clack-click-clack.

He shook his head. "I don't see her."

I sighed, trying to hide my irritation. In a louder voice I said again, making sure to carefully enunciate, "It's G-e-m-m-a. A-n-t-o-n."

"Yes, I understand, but she's not in here."

"G—as in George. E—as in elephant. M—as in—"

He laughed, also trying to hide his irritation. "Yes, I hear you, but she's not here."

"Just try Gemma, without the last name, maybe there's a typo."

Reluctantly, he hit the backspace key, then clicked enter. I leaned over the top of the counter to watch him.

"No, I'm sorry, she's not in here. The system can be like that sometimes. Maybe try calling her again?"

I sighed as if this were an inconvenience of unconscionable and unimaginable proportions, and took out my phone. I pretended to hit a few buttons, then pressed the phone to my ear. I wandered away so that he would not hear there was nothing on the other line. After a few moments, I "hung up" and put the phone back in my purse.

"See?" I said aggressively. "She's not picking up."

He shrugged apologetically. "I'm sorry."

"Try Anton, then, the last name."

The man's patience was clearly wearing thin, but he acquiesced, this time taking a heavy seat in front of the computer. I followed his fingers on the keyboard carefully, making sure he typed correctly. I knew it was insulting, my leaning over like that, as if he couldn't be trusted to type a person's name correctly—but then people's incompetency never fails to amaze me. Even with my oversight, however, his persistent click-clacking yielded nothing. Or so he said. I was starting to worry that he had become suspicious of me. His eyes had taken on a shifty quality. Instead of looking at me straight on as he had done before, he now snuck glances sideways, his eyes darting away before I could ever meet them. Maybe he was only bluffing, trying to get me to leave.

"Look, I'm her cousin, I swear," I said. "I mean, seriously, look at me. I'm obviously related."

He laughed uncomfortably. "I believe you. But I have no way of knowing her apartment number."

The man was lying. He was fucking lying to me! I pulled out my phone again and hesitated briefly, remembering that her account had been deleted. Then I scrolled through my camera roll, millions of little squares, mostly showing some miniature version of myself, until I found the pictures of the two of us together at the Strand.

"See?" I said, showing him the screen. "Cousins."

He looked at it wonderingly, then shook his head.

"I don't recognize her, you, whoever," he said slowly and carefully. What an actor! Looking at his face, anyone would have thought he'd never seen Gemma before in his life.

"Yes, I know you don't know me. But she lives here."

"If she does, she must be new." He added, in an upbeat, helpful tone—the sly devil, the fucking theatrical genius—"Maybe that's why she's not in the system."

"She's lived here *for years*!" I was getting really exasperated now. It was one thing if he wasn't going to let me in. But to carry on this charade was absurd. Who did he think he was?

"Ma'am," he said, which everyone knows is code for *bitch*, "I'm sorry I really can't help you." His tone was icy, and his eyes, which he was no longer afraid of pointing directly at me, were flat and calm, as if he'd brought a metal grate down over them.

"Oh, come *on*."

"Maybe you should come back another time."

"This is getting ridiculous."

"I'm sorry."

The elevator doors opened, and a middle-aged man holding the hand of a small girl came out. I lunged toward them with my phone, and the man's eyebrows rose in surprise. The doorman stood up behind me, and quickly followed—no doubt eager to keep his unprofessional behavior from the eyes of tenants.

I put on my sweetest voice. "Excuse me," I said, "I don't mean to bother you. But I'm having a little trouble reaching my cousin. Gemma. Gemma Anton. You know her?"

The man shook his head. His daughter took a step closer to him. I smiled down at her. She was not particularly beautiful, but she had good bone structure, and long, thin limbs, and I saw instantly that she'd one day make a good model. Not a great one, but a good one. I looked back at her dad.

"She's the blond model who lives here, tall, beautiful," I said, taking out my phone and showing him the picture. "That's her. It's us. She's on the right, there."

The man frowned at the photo and shook his head. "I'm not sure . . ."

"I've asked her to leave," the doorman said to the man. "I told her she should go."

I rolled my eyes theatrically, letting the man know that I thought the doorman was being ridiculous. "I'm just trying to find my cousin!" I shouted. "She lives here!"

At that moment, an older woman with frizzy yellow hair walked in from outside with a little black dog on a leash. She smiled at the four of us standing there, and her smile seemed to ask a question. I took a deep breath, and smoothed out my voice until it was calm and syrupy.

"Maybe you can help," I said, smiling my best smile. "My cousin lives here, Gemma, the model, do you know her? You see, I've forgotten her apartment number, and she's not picking up. I'm worried about her and—"

The woman looked at me as if dumbfounded. "I'm sorry—what—"

Before she could finish her question, I flashed her the photo on my phone. "See—it's us. Well, do you know her? Maybe you could help me knock on her door? Her name's Gemma."

"Gemma . . . ?" the woman repeated, a confused, stricken look on her face.

"Well, do you?" I shook the phone in my hand, and the woman picked up her little dog and tucked him into the crook of her arm, then stepped forward to get a better look. The man and his daughter stood nearby, as if waiting to be dismissed.

"What's going on?" the woman asked, looking at me. She'd barely even glanced at the phone screen. It was then that I noticed she was holding Pancakes! She was holding Gemma's dog right there in her arms, and pretending to not know Gemma! She saw me staring, open-mouthed, my entire body rigid in astonishment. Gently she touched my forearm.

"Are you okay?" she asked, in a low whisper.

"That's Pancakes!" I shouted, my hands clawing the air in front of me. "That's her dog!"

The woman stepped back, clearly startled and afraid. She hadn't counted on me recognizing the dog.

"Of *course* I recognize Pancakes!" I said. "I'm not fucking dumb!"

The doorman put his hand around my elbow. The man and his daughter moved quickly away. I ignored all of them and continued to yell at the woman, who was clutching Pancakes to her body.

"You think I'm not going to notice you kidnapping Gemma's dog or something? You think I'm that fucking stupid?"

The woman bore an expression of frank shock and fear. I don't know who she was scared of—possibly the lobby was being surveilled, and whoever wanted Gemma to remain MIA was watching to make sure everyone kept their mouths shut. My head swiveled around, looking for cameras. The doorman tightened his grip around my arm. I looked back at the woman, and the more I looked at her, the more obvious it became that she was wearing a wig, and a horrible-quality one at that, with bad, streaky highlights. If you looked at the frayed ends, it was clear they were synthetic.

"Well?" I said harshly.

She said in a trembling voice: "I don't think you're stupid." Ha! So she wasn't denying it! She went on, "Let's just all calm down a little bit."

I relaxed for a brief second, and the doorman took advantage and began moving me toward the door. When I struggled against him, he took hold of my other arm and said, in a chiding, parental tone, "I'm sorry, ma'am, but I need you to leave now, or else I'm going to call the police."

"Call the police?" I screamed. "I'd love you to call the police! Then maybe this woman can tell me why she's got Gemma's dog and is lying about it! Bet the police would get a fucking kick out of her disguise, too!" I turned my head to look back at her—but she had fled to the elevator and the doors were sliding shut in front of her.

"Coward!" I screamed. "Fraud!"

The doorman held my wrists with one hand and propped open the door with the other. He pulled me through it, and I could feel his disgusting sweat leaking from his palms, contaminating my skin. Outside, the downpour had turned into a light drizzle. The father was standing under the awning with a protective hand on his daughter's chest (Or was it even really his daughter? The two looked nothing alike—they were probably just actors), and when he saw us come out he moved backward, so that rain was splashing against the back of his neck and shoulders.

"All right already, I'll leave, you got your way!" I shouted, trying to wrench my wrists from the doorman's clutches. After a brief hesitation—a searching look toward the father and child—the doorman eased up his grip and finally let go. I rubbed my wrists dramatically, breathing hard like an animal. I'd no intention of leaving. I wanted to get to the bottom of this. I rounded on the doorman, just as the man with the child spoke up:

"I called the police." His voice was almost apologetic. He was clearly embarrassed to be party to the whole business. So he was a liar and a blackguard like the rest of them, but at least there was some part of him with a conscience. I knew because when I looked him in the eyes, his gaze was one of compassion and concern (with only a tinge of fear). He said, his voice incredibly soft and gentle but at the same time firm—a real father! The father I never had! The father I always wanted!—"I hope you get some help."

I nodded. Looked at the two of them, his large hand pressed against her scrawny little chest as if protecting her heart, as she backed herself into him so that her body was practically wedged between his legs, knowing herself to be totally protected and safe, trusting that everything would be fine, because Daddy was here.

"Your daughter's lucky," I said. "I hope she grows up ugly. But if she doesn't, she could be a model one day. She could be just like me!"

I took off at a run. I was not afraid of the police. The police would sort it out, they would see my side of it. But that would take time, and I did not want to invest any more of it in this farce. No, it wasn't the police, but the prospect of paperwork and labyrinthine bureaucracy that sent shivers down my spine. The father's words had given me courage. *Get help.* Yes. Without delay. I must get help. Gemma was missing. There was something seriously wrong with this picture. Gemma was gone. The image returned to me out of nothing: Gemma, standing on the pier, a red sky behind her, an uncertain expression on her face that gives way to terror. I thought I heard her scream. I began to run faster. The strap on my sandal broke. I tore off the whole contraption and flung it into a garbage can. It was starting to get dark. Gemma was drowning in black waters, the waves of which reflected the red sky at their apex before turning black again. I kept running, one bare foot slapping against the pavement. Gemma was surrounded by red streaks in the water, her mouth was open and calling out—she was calling out to me as she drowned. What had I done? Why hadn't I helped? Where were Benson and Stabler?

I was having a million thoughts, one after the other, clear bolts of lucid comprehension, divine inspiration, where everything seemed perfectly straightforward, but they were coming in quick flashes, and somehow they were not connecting in my head. It was as if fireworks were spreading across the night sky, but just as I was beginning to make out their shape they disappeared, swallowed up seamlessly by the dark. The night before I'd gone viral, I'd followed Gemma to the record store. I had wandered in the streets, followed her all the way to the pier, on which I'd watched . . . I'd watched . . . I'd only watched. A rushing sound swept across the street and the rain intensified. I felt a shudder of guilt. Big wet drops splashed along my collarbone and down my back. It was then that I felt the weight of the locket against my chest. *Her* locket was against my chest. This fact stunned me. Why was her locket against my chest? Who took it from her? Its discovery in Benoit's bedside table now seemed distinctly ominous. I saw Benoit snatch it from her neck. I saw the thin line of blood it left on the tender skin of her nape just before he strangled her and threw her into the river, just like on that episode of *SVU* where Olivia only put it together because she identified the bloated corpse's ankle tattoo . . . No, it didn't make sense. None of it made sense. Gemma was okay. She *had* to be okay. It could not be otherwise. All I needed to do was find her.

I passed under a scaffolding. There was another person there, swaddled in layers, a hood up over their head, and they were leaning against one of the metal supports and moaning softly. It was now dark. I waited on the other side of the scaffolding, and the person's moans were drowned out by the sound of the rain. Cars made noises like waves as they drove through the water on the street, disturbing puddles and creating lurid streaks of red and yellow along the wet pavement. There was a ticking inside of me, growing louder and louder until I thought I would burst. My hands trembled, and I realized they were clenched around my phone. I ran my fingers over its smooth surface as if it were a talisman. Where else did I have to turn, I ask? Where else was I to go? I opened up Instagram. Of course that was what I was going to do. It was all I knew how to do. A circle appeared at the bottom of my screen, and I pressed my thumb to it. I began filming.

"Hey guys," I began. A car passed, briefly illuminating my face, and I was momentarily dazed by the magnetism of my own reflection. Even though I felt like shit, I couldn't help noticing I looked good: my skin was wet with rainwater, making it shine in the light. My eyes were large and penetrating, like those of a film star about to get murdered. I already felt calmer, looking at myself in the glassy mirror. Then the stranger, still slumped against the metal support, made a small, animal noise behind me, and I cleared my throat and went on: "So I know this is a little weird, but honestly, I'm not sure what else to do." I took a deep breath, heart hammering in my chest. "I've started to become very worried about someone. Someone who has wound up being very important to me. I won't say her name, because—well, for a lot of reasons. Her privacy, for one. And also because I'm not sure it would be safe just now . . ." I glanced at the person slumped at the scaffolding but couldn't make out their face, if they were watching me. "Anyway," I continued, turning back to the camera distractedly, forcing a smile. "You guys are smart, so I'm sure you know who I'm talking about." I gave the camera a knowing look. "She looks a lot like me. She's a model. Dated a certain photographer about town . . ." I could feel the faceless person staring at me, the heat of their attention. I turned to glare at them—but they turned their head away too quickly, and somehow managed to get into exactly the same position they were in before. This frightened me because it suggested a kind of skill I hadn't suspected. I hurried away, and the circle completed itself and appeared anew on my screen. I kept filming. I was walking fast, my face glowing orange when I passed under streetlights. Rain fell lightly on my head. Rain fell onto my eyelashes and filled my eyes with water until I blinked. I didn't even realize I was crying until I heard myself speak. "What I want to know," I said, my voice cracking, "is why everyone is lying. Why is everyone lying? What is everyone trying to hide? I don't understand. Can someone tell me? You know who you are. What are you trying to hide? What is it!" I was screaming at the end there, and it felt good; I felt a release. A new video began. I was walking. I was walking in the rain, hair matted to my head. I was walking in the rain, walking fast, and I was dripping wet, and I should have been freezing, but I wasn't. I was starting to feel calm, and that's when the anger began to set in. Oh yes, I'd show them. I'd get right to the bottom of this. I was unstoppable. I continued, in a lower pitch: "Something very disturbing happened to me just now, which is that twice today I was in a position where a *guy*, who was sort of in a position of power, was trying to tell me that I was wrong. He didn't believe me. I knew what I was saying was true and right but he didn't believe. He denied it. He denied my reality, and, to be honest, it just really fucked with my head. But you know what I realize now?" I began screaming again. I wanted him to hear it all the way back in his house of lies. "Fuck him," I shouted. "*Fuck him!*"

A message popped up on my phone alerting me to a perilously low battery.

"I'm going to die soon," I said, picking up my pace to a run. "But it doesn't really matter. What matters is—well, what does matter?" I'd pretended not to notice that I'd lost my train of thought. The rain was covering my face, it was getting in my mouth. I suddenly wanted to laugh out loud. "Yes, exactly, that's the thing, isn't it? What matters is the truth, and I want to know it, is what I'm saying. That's what matters." I was starting to lose steam. I was panting. The circle completed itself, and I lifted my thumb off it. The video was uploaded. Message sent. I looked at my feet. My bare foot shimmered in the light. It looked like a fish. It looked exactly like a fish, with silvery scales that shimmered in the light. For the first time, I felt the cold against my skin. I didn't remember why I had been running, and when I looked at my phone I saw that it was dead. Without my phone, there was no time. Where time should have been, there was just an empty container. And within that void, I began to feel a tickle of freedom. I began to feel giddy, even. Yes, giddy. It was a glorious night, and I knew exactly what

I was doing. I kept walking for I don't know how long, but eventually I did get home.

The next morning, before I even woke, dread was upon me. Between dreams, I'd remembered parts of what I'd done. How I had acted. Details, memories returned to me, surfacing like sharks in the water, black, amorphous shapes that grew larger and then emerged only when it was too late. I tried to block them out. I turned on my side, but like a relentless alarm clock, my anxiety kept pinging me with new details. Ping! My eyes, clearly unfocused. Ping! Had I cried? I had cried. I had cried in front of my entire Follower list. Ping! I'd lost my fucking sandal! I'd run through the streets half-barefoot like a maniac. I could recall my thinking at the time, but could not connect it to any sort of reality I had experienced. When I remembered that I had begun to suspect something violent or criminal about Gemma's "disappearance," it was like peeking into the mind of another person whom I didn't know or understand at all. I couldn't believe how melodramatic I'd gotten! It was all the hours I'd spent watching *SVU*, surely. I'd let the show seep into my subconscious. I was sure the image that had plagued me—the one of Gemma out on the pier, Gemma drowning in the waters—was in fact the climactic scene from one of the most recent episodes I'd watched. A thought—one I couldn't even bring myself to articulate at the time—kept occurring to me, no matter how many times I tried to ignore it: Benoit might have seen the videos. I wasn't sure if he even watched my Stories, but if he did, he would see them, and that made me want to die. Eventually, I couldn't take it anymore, and I picked up my phone. It was six a.m., I was covered in sweat, my heart was racing, and my skin was still flecked with mud—I was filthy. I steeled myself and then opened up Instagram.

It turned out I needn't have worried at all.

Everybody had loved it. They thought it was brilliant. Someone actually wrote that: *This is brilliant!* Relief flooded over me so powerfully, I was dazed. Everyone thought I was saying something profound, though some people thought I was calling out rapists and victim-blamers, and other people thought I was making a statement about the facades we all put up, the roles we play, especially on social media.

So brave. You tell that fucker! #believewomen, someone wrote.

This happened to me once in college, and I can't tell you how much it means to me to see it on someone else's feed. Makes me feel less alone. Thank you, wrote another.

People had DMed with personal confessions, the things they'd been hiding. Most of it was mundane shit, like they were embarrassed about their thighs, or they told a lie once, or kissed their best friend's crush, or they were broke and hid it from their friends—though one girl confessed she'd had sex one night with her first cousin and was in love with him.

I'd gotten so many responses and messages, it took me a moment before I noticed *his* name among all the strangers. Benoit.

Tee hee, he wrote. *You're WILD ;)*

I recoiled, briefly, at the use of *tee hee* from a middle-aged man, but I was too delighted to care. In fact, I was so delighted that soon my relief matured into complacency, then bloomed into full-blown self-assurance and cockiness. I began to feel that it had all unfolded as I had planned; that I'd intended exactly what everyone thought I'd intended. Of course, I'd had to subvert that intention subconsciously, in order to pull it off in the moment. Truly, the foresight of my genius astonished me.

As for Gemma, I decided it would be better if I didn't think of her any longer. For whatever reason, she seemed to provoke in me a juvenile thirst for melodrama. I had imagined all sorts of impossible, insane things, when in fact there could be nothing more mundane than a girl deleting her Instagram account and going on vacation. That is what I told myself at the time. That is what I tried to believe.

In my camera roll, I found the photos that Benoit had AirDropped to me of the two of us standing next to each other at the Strand bookstore. They were the only reminders I still had of her. Taking a deep breath, I deleted them all.

The next morning, I walked outside, and watched myself walk outside in a two-by-six-inch liquid crystal display. I walked outside and I smiled and breathed in the world as if I were happy, and it began to feel, as the sun fell across my tilted face and reflected in the mirrored lenses of my sunglasses, that truly, I was happy. My thumb lifted from the screen, and immediately my posture transformed itself from convex to concave. I stooped forward, bending my neck almost perpendicular to my body. I flicked my sunglasses to the top of my head and clutched my phone with both hands and squinted at the screen, but all I saw was a malformed reflection of some black, bulbous face, backlit by the sun. I found a sliver of shade in the shadow of a building and watched myself perform my life of fifteen seconds ago. I watched as I walked out of the building, smiling, as the sun fell across my tilted face and reflected in the mirrored lenses of my sunglasses. I watched as I smiled and breathed in and looked happy and was happy. I watched myself. *Feeling strong and healthy and lucky,* I wrote. Then I hit the delicate white arrow at the bottom corner of the screen, and the me of seventeen seconds ago was dispatched to the ether. I resumed my walk. I was going to meet my mother. Like a good daughter. Like a perfectly normal human.

You'll be experiencing stronger motivation to pursue your goals, dear Aquarius, but you might also need to let go or back off a little today. It was seventy-nine degrees. Chance of rain: 0 percent. Humidity: 15 percent. Air quality: moderate. Julia was having a bath, pink bubbles foaming up to the neck. More victims had come forward to accuse Jeffrey Epstein of rape. "He was a sociopath," one said. He had a familiar look to him, in his zipped Harvard hoodie, like Andrew or Joe but older. Prince Andrew and Bill Clinton were also possibly implicated in the case. Two women stood in a field holding hands, wearing blazers and long dresses and imploring me to check out Zara's summer sale. Flat Leather Bow Sandals, $35.99. Tuxedo Trousers with Side Taping, $39.99. Tuxedo-Collar Blazer, $49.99. Embroidered Voluminous Top, $19.99. Global climate temperatures were set to rise two degrees by 2050. Blake "ate" a donut with blue frosting. A hurricane was en route to New Orleans. *Kylie Jackson's "Revenge Body": How the Star Toned Up After Breakup to Wow in Pole-Dancing Video.* No one talked about the Eric Garner case anymore. I wore All Access Rush Stretch Biker Shorts in Black, Jacquemus La Chemise Bahia Shirt in White, By Far Sage Croc Mini Bag, and Balenciaga Mirrored Rimless Sunglasses.

My mother was waiting for me outside the restaurant. I saw her from a distance, her head bent over her phone. She was wearing skinny jeans and old Tod's loafers with an oversize blazer I recognized from J.Crew, which made me want to cringe, that my mother shopped at J.Crew now. From far away she looked so small and insignificant, I felt a pang of protectiveness.

"Hey," I called out. My mother's head shot up. She broke into a wide smile and, seemingly unable to wait the ten seconds until I got to her, half-jogged over to me with arms outstretched. We hugged.

"My Mick," she said, and kept her arm over my shoulder even as we walked into the restaurant, a place called Wishbone that specialized in bone broth.

"Oh, it's counter serve," my mother said, taking in the restaurant's low-key setup with obvious disappointment.

"It's supposedly got the best bone broth," I said defensively. I'd spent a not-insignificant amount of time looking up Yelp reviews.

"Oh no, this is fine, really! It's cute. We don't need anything fancy, do we? Any old place will do."

"Well, you said you wanted something keto, and so I looked it up, and this was ranked number one."

"I'm sure it was," she said. "It's very cute in here. Different."

I should have known this was not her idea of a restaurant. It was bright and deliberately unfussy, with a counter cut from untreated plywood, white tiled floors, and small round tables and stools scattered throughout. It was 10:30 a.m.—there was plenty of time before the lunch rush—and there were only a few people seated at the tables, all of them hermetically sealed in the attention orbit of their phones.

"Well, let's look at a menu. We can go somewhere else if you want," I said, shrugging her arm from my shoulder and picking up a menu from the counter. I could feel my mother's eyes on my back, raking over my body.

"Have you lost weight?"

I scoffed, shaking my head, though I had in fact winnowed myself down to the smallest I'd ever been.

"You look like you've lost weight."

"Supposedly the Original Badass Bone Broth with Chicken is the thing to get," I said, ignoring her and studying the menu.

"Don't lose any more weight, okay?"

I rolled my eyes. "Fine, Mom."

"I get it—because you're young, you want to look good, everyone else around you is so skinny, it's easy to start comparing, but you just have to do what's best for your body."

"Uh-huh. So what do you want?" I asked, pushing the menu at her.

"Oh, I'll just have whatever you're having. Did you have breakfast today?"

I nodded.

"What'd you have?"

"Eggs."

Whenever I lost weight my mom kept meticulous track of everything I ate and tried her best to copy it.

"What kind of eggs?"

"I don't know, scrambled? Why don't you save our seats there," I said, pointing to a table next to the window. "I'll order."

My mom passed me her credit card. At the counter, I took a deep breath, trying to soothe my irritation. Almost immediately, I felt a surge of guilt—my mother meant well, I didn't get to see her all that often, I should learn to appreciate my time with her. But my self-recrimination over my irritation with her only increased the irritation I felt toward her.

The woman behind the counter was white, had a nose ring, and wore a shirt that said *End Racism* on it. "Did you want a boost for your soups?" she asked me.

"What was that?"

"A boost. You can have a love boost, a passion boost . . . brain boost, empathy boost . . ." She articulated each boost with a dip of her head.

"Uh-huh, what's in them?"

"It's a proprietary blend of ingredients."

When I didn't answer but just stood there in consternation, she went on, "Personally, the love boost's my favorite."

"How much is it to add?"

"Six dollars."

I laughed. Six dollars for a splash of salt, probably. "We're fine, thanks."

"Are you sure?"

"Oh yeah, we've all the love we need."

She handed me a number and I sat back down with my mother, who had her reading glasses on and was painstakingly typing something on her phone with her index finger.

"Sorry, one sec," she said.

"It's fine."

Apparently finished, she flipped her phone so it was facedown and then threw her reading glasses back in her purse, a large black hobo bag I hadn't seen before.

"That new?" I asked.

She picked up the bag, a sheepish smile on her face, and put it on her lap, stroking it gently as one would a cat. "A celebratory purchase."

It was then I noticed the gold lettering on the front. Celine. And from the looks of it, real, too. *Celebratory?* I thought. *For what?* And then I realized that she must have been thinking of the *JOY* shoot and my obviously imminent rise to fame. It was just like my mother to get ahead of herself like that. She was like a child in that way, I thought, though not unkindly. I laughed.

"Mom, you should've waited."

She pursed her lips together and raised her eyebrows excitedly. "There's no need to wait," she said, barely containing herself. "It's already official, honey! We won! He's out! It's all over!"

I stared at her, mouth agape, as I tried to process what she was saying.

"I know, I know, it happened yesterday, and I was going to call you, but then I thought, I'll tell her in person." She was beaming at me; her whole face was a bubble of joy. I felt the sand give way beneath me, the tide taking me out, icy waters rising to my throat.

"I don't understand," I said, my voice catching on an awkward laugh. "What're you talking about?"

"Well, his appeal started yesterday, *as you know*," she began, though I had of course forgotten all about it, or perhaps blocked it from my mind. "And we were expecting it to take a few weeks, but the judge overturned it on the spot! We couldn't believe it, we were so happy." She shook her head wonderingly, still stroking the leather on her handbag.

"What do you mean, he just overturned it?"

"Something about jury misconduct," my mother said, narrowing her eyes in concentration. "I think, anyway? I don't know how Saul pulled it off."

"Just overturned it in one day?" I asked again, my body cold and my heart beating fast from treading water in the icy depths, trying to keep my head from going under. "I mean, doesn't that seem kind of . . . weird?" I had wanted to say *shady*. I had wanted to say *corrupt*.

My mother shrugged, a delighted look on her face. "Who knows? The point is he's out. He's home."

"*Home?*" I swallowed. We had sold our home to pay for the trial.

"Well, the Four Seasons for now."

I glared at her, unable to speak.

"I know it's expensive, but give the guy a break, he's been in jail for two years, and anyway it's just for a few days, while we celebrate. Then it's back to Joey's. Of course, that'll only be temporary, too. He's already gotten back in touch with some of his old partners, and now with all this behind him, we can go back to normal, and I know we can get back to what we were. It'll take time, but then your father is persistent, isn't he? I told him he should think about taking some time off—Saul said best to keep a low profile. The prosecutors are already working on a new filing; there'll likely be a retrial, though I can't imagine they'll reconvict, I mean"—she laughed a little—"you'd think they'd have learned their lesson by now, right? The whole thing just seems so silly to me. So . . . unsportsmanlike, don't you think? If you lose, you lose, that should be it."

I neglected to point out that my father had lost his first trial and that hadn't stopped him from appealing. I was too preoccupied with a question that had just occurred to me, completely urgent in nature. "So, wait . . . he's in the city?" I blurted out.

"Yeah, at the Four Seasons," she said, making it clear that this should have been obvious. "He almost came down for this, just to give you a real surprise, but then, you know how he is." She rolled her eyes. "Taxis make him nauseous, he can't walk, the traffic, the crowds . . ." She laughed. "Anyway, we thought it would be more special to do it tonight, something fancy, you know. We thought—"

My phone vibrated with a new text message, and I practically fell over myself retrieving it from my purse, which was slung over the back of my chair. My mother continued to prattle on about the night, while with shaky hands I caressed the cold metal surface of my phone, which I held hidden beneath the table in my lap. Julia wanted to know if she should get bangs. She sent three selfies with hair positioned over her forehead.

Do it, Blake responded. *Also, srsly, I'm now considering a buzz cut am I crazy?*

She sent a screenshot from Karma Black's Instagram; in it, she stared out vacantly in front of a dilapidated wall with large strips of paint torn from it. She was undeniably beautiful and she had a raw, unvarnished quality, as if she really didn't care what she looked like. In other words: nothing like Blake.

Lol, I think that only works on Karma because she's like a badass, biracial renegade, no offense, wrote Julia.

I'm just so bored with my LEWK, I wanna dooooo something, y'know?

I hear you so hard girl.

I sought further distraction on Instagram, droning out my mother's excited speech with Likes, and Views, colorful squares of other people's lives, wishing more than ever that I could see Gemma. Even though I had promised myself I wouldn't think of her, wouldn't even care if she did come back online, I still sought her face—that familiar visage that instantly calmed me—in my feed, like an amputee continues to feel that phantom limb. But it was just the usual bullshit. My old best friend from high school had gotten engaged, and the ring was ginormous and very ugly. A man was holding up a cardboard sign as if in protest, only it read *Why does it feel like Mercury is always in retrograde?* Corey Wang, an A-tier blogger, had gotten a new puppy. A sponsored post for a leopard bra asked if I was feeling down. *We'll support you, always, no matter what the mood. We got your back, girl. And you got THIS. (Whether this is just getting groceries or going on a date, and general #adulting.)* A baby was caught saying good night to its cat on the nanny cam.

"Two Original Badass Bone Broths," the waitress said, and I tore my eyes away from my phone to see two steaming bone broths set down in front of us.

"Oh wow, these look lovely," my mother said, evidently unaware that for the past several minutes I hadn't been listening to her. I felt a twinge of pain in my jaw and realized I'd been grinding my teeth.

"Are you two mother-daughter?" the waitress asked cheerfully.

"Oh, you could tell?" my mother asked, beaming. "What a compliment!"

I managed a thanks, still gripping my phone, itching to vanish back within its comforting dimensions, of which I alone was in control.

"We're very close," my mother went on, nodding in my direction to signal my cue.

"She's basically my best friend," I muttered.

"Well, aren't you two sweet." The waitress shook her head wistfully and returned to the counter. Immediately, I depressed the button on the side of my phone, lighting up the screen. Four new red bubbles blazed on at the bottom of my message app, but before I could open them up, my mother placed her palm against my cheek, forcing my eyes up.

"You really are just so beautiful," she said. "Your father will be so happy to see you."

I shifted in my seat, feeling the magnetic pull of those red bubbles. I knew they were probably just Julia and Blake, but what if they weren't? What if it was Benoit, or even—my brain flailed wildly—Gemma, somehow? What if there was something that would change everything, render it all okay? That was always the hope that glimmered, however briefly, every time I refreshed my screen; it was like pulling the lever on a slot machine.

My mother stroked my cheek again. "So what do you think you're going to wear tonight?"

"Uh, I dunno."

She squeezed my shoulder. "Well, whatever it is, I'm sure you'll look great." She leaned back on her stool and regarded her soup dubiously, letting her spoon hover just above the rim of the bowl. Hurriedly, I checked my phone. There were five more new messages.

Speaking of changing one's lewk, did you guys watch the new Botched last night?

Omg those boobs!!!

I was dying!

I scanned the rest of the inane exchange. Yet though there was a sense of completion afterward, there was no contentment; the anxiety I had felt anticipating its contents did not dissipate. If anything, I felt even more frustrated.

"Honey, aren't you going to eat your soup?"

Regretfully, I put my phone down on the table, then carefully dipped my spoon into the bowl, swirling the unappetizing contents.

"I'm going to wear this black lace blouse that's new. And guess where I got it from?"

"Where?"

"J.Crew! Same as this blazer. Can you believe it? They actually have really cute stuff right now. Have you been?"

I shook my head and stared at the amber-colored liquid in my spoon. A wisp of steam rose off it.

"You should go," my mom went on. "They have a lot of stuff I think you'd really like."

I nodded solemnly and then swallowed the entire spoonful, which burned the back of my throat and tasted, to me, like blood. The photo I put up later, of the half-finished soups artfully arranged on the table, my mother's Celine purse posed just beside them, had the following caption: *Bone broth with Mom > chicken soup for the soul.* It got 3,356 Likes. A good mother-daughter relationship was part of my brand.

I arrived at the Four Seasons at seven p.m., the appointed hour. We were to have a drink in my father's suite, then head down for dinner shortly after. At the front desk, I gave a false name, which my mother had told me in advance. Apparently, they were afraid of press, even though this wasn't Illinois and no one in New York City knew or cared about my father; in the pantheon of the city's con men, he was small fry.

It had taken me hours to get ready. I'd found my brain strangely muddled when I got home. I tried on dozens of outfits, but everything felt wrong, juvenile and unimpressive. In the end, I went to Zara and bought a black suit: Tuxedo Trousers with Side Taping for $39.99 and the Tuxedo Collar Blazer, $49.99. I thought my dad would think I looked "sharp" in it. My perm had frizzified a bit in the rain that night, but I got it under control with some mousse and pulled it back into a low bun and put on Glossier Generation G Sheer Matte Lipstick in Zip. At least an hour before I had to leave, I put up a photo of myself in the ensemble with the caption *boss bitch vibes* and a briefcase emoji. Immediately, my feed was flooded with Likes and Comments. Each one fortified my sense of self-worth.

In the elevator up to my father's room, I surveyed my look again. I smoothed back my hair and reapplied lipstick, feeling a certain satisfaction that dulled my nerves slightly. In orchestrating the right outfit, I had believed I was exercising a small amount of control over the evening. But when the doors slid open on the fourteenth floor, I felt myself tense up. My father was on this floor. This was already the closest I'd been to him in almost a year. Heart pounding, I tried to make sense of the gold plaque that directed guests to the appropriate rooms, only it appeared to me as a jumble of numbers and arrows. I set off in one direction, then another, before I realized that I'd gone the right way the first time and had to double back.

My mother opened the door, a little breathless. She was wearing a lot of makeup, but it looked good; she might have had it done professionally, perhaps at Bloomingdale's nearby. Certainly, she'd gone for a blowout. Her hair was parted on the side and fell in waves across her face. She was wearing a black lace blouse and a black pencil skirt with the Manolo Blahnik heels she'd had for years. We hugged for the third time that day, and she stepped aside to reveal my father, nestled into one of the armchairs with a foot on the coffee table and his cane supported at an angle by the nearby sofa.

His face lit up when he saw me. I noticed there was a bottle of champagne, half-drunk, in a silver ice bucket on a console. The weather channel was playing, muted, on the TV behind him.

"Mickey!" he called out. He did not get up, and I did not approach him.

"Hi, Dad," I responded, and was surprised by the sweetness of my voice, how it seemed to hold a note of optimism. I resisted moving toward him. My mother gave me a gentle push on the back.

"Come here, girl," my father called in a gruff voice. "Give me a hug."

Reluctantly, I went over to him and leaned down to embrace him briefly around the shoulders. He patted my back. My cheek brushed his neck on the way up and it felt clammy, like the skin of some dead sea mammal. His face was slick with a fine sheen of sweat, and he looked unhealthy. He had always been a large, broad man, but jail had turned him fat; he sat as if balancing a ball on his stomach, a large round drum of fat, which stretched his shirt tight. Otherwise, he was the same: wild, unruly eyebrows, neatly combed salt-and-pepper hair, twinkling dark-blue eyes, which he wiped quickly with the back of his hand as I straightened up. I realized he was crying.

"It's your perfume," he said, smiling sheepishly, not even bothering to disguise the lie. "It makes my eyes water."

I laughed involuntarily. It was the same excuse he'd given at his own mother's funeral, only then it was the flowers that irritated his eyes and made them water. I was eight then, and took it for fact, not able to catch the nuance in his voice. For the next few years, any time there were flowers nearby I'd ask my dad if his eyes were okay, until one day he explained to me it had to be a very particular kind of flower, only found at mothers' funerals.

"It's the kind of sensitivity one can develop when divorced from the general population," he went on, a humorous lilt in his voice. "One may find the smell of one's daughter oddly stirring, particularly to the tear glands."

"Sure, Dad," I said, embarrassed. "Whatever."

He cocked his head to one side, staring at me with a vaguely perplexed look, his eyes still misty, and I worried for a moment he was going to say something else oddly sweet, until he asked: "So what the hell happened to your eyebrows?"

I blushed.

"I told you, she dyed them," my mother said, gently defensive on my behalf, or maybe it was only on my face's behalf.

My father looked aghast.

"It's the look nowadays," my mother continued. "It's high fashion."

"And I'm frightened to see you so thin," my father said, moving on from my brows to my body.

Another memory surfaced: It was my twelfth birthday and my mother gave me two bikinis. I had always been a skinny child—something my parents had led me to understand was a virtue—but I was going through a chubby phase at the time. I remember my father pinching the flesh at my hips and exclaiming gleefully: *Soon you'll be getting tits, too.* My mother had slapped him irritably on the shoulder, but he'd just laughed harder. *What?* he'd said. *Should I have called them breasts? Is that it?*

"You're skeletal!" my dad exclaimed now. "You're like Annie when I first met her and her idea of cooking dinner was to boil water. I'm telling you, your mother couldn't have eaten more than a cracker a day."

My mother didn't contest it, but quietly poured me a glass of champagne.

"I've just been busy," I said irritably and, shooting a derisive look at his belly, added, "Anyway, I wouldn't talk."

He laughed and patted his belly contentedly. "I imagine some prisoners in Club Fed eat better than the average American. Steak and potatoes almost every day, followed by a glass of ice cream. And it's all free! Now tell me, where can you get three squares a day, a solid bed, a roof over your head, and not pay a penny! No, jail's not too bad. I wouldn't mind staying in jail. I fell in love with jail! Wonderful group of men there, and it's nice, too, being around only men. We became brothers, those men and I. It's a heck of a whole lot less stressful than bloody running my own business and taking care of my family. The problem is: I'm innocent. So it's simply not proper for me to be there. I wouldn't have minded, had I done it, but the fact of the matter is I'm innocent, and I can't stand for that kind of miscarriage of justice."

In the course of my father's ramble, his eyebrows had danced up and down on his forehead, his cheeks growing pink, while he kept a delighted smile from broadening into a maddening grin and I accepted another glass of champagne from my mother. His eyes were really sparkling now; truly, that's what they do, they sparkle. It's not a figure of speech with him. That sparkle is what allowed him to get away with what he did. I have his eyes, but not the sparkle. Still, everyone tells me they're my best feature.

"Well, maybe you'll get a chance to go back one day," I said, draining the rest of my champagne.

"No!" shouted my mom in a childish, high-pitched voice. We ignored her, as we often did when the three of us were together.

"Well, the sad truth is the DA's got a grudge against me. I don't know why. It could be that his wife has taken a liking to me, I don't know. Did you see her in court? Oh, she's got legs! Oh, she does! And I've got experience to know when a woman is ogling you, and let me tell you, she was ogling me right there in court—"

"Honey, why don't you sit down?" my mother asked me in a lowered voice so as not to disturb my father's soliloquy, patting the couch next to her. Instead, turning my back to her, I lifted the champagne bottle by its neck, refilled my glass, and walked a few paces away, where I leaned against the wall, regarding my father.

"So, you know, he's got a bee in his bonnet, and you know what they say: bees make you crazy. The man is like a mutt with a bone, and don't get on me for being racist; I know he's half something, but that isn't what I mean, I mean mutt in the sense of a determined beast. I've got nothing but respect for him. Mutts are scrappy, aren't they? No, I like a good mutt, I do. But this mutt's just on the wrong track, that's all I'm saying."

"So are they refiling charges?" I asked.

My father shrugged dramatically, then motioned for me to refill his champagne glass. I did. After taking a large gulp, he went on, "They tell me they're refiling, I don't know. But what I do know is: I'm never going back to jail. You can mark my words."

"That may not be up to you."

He downed the rest of his champagne, and let out a monstrous burp. "There are ways," he said, "of making sure. Every man has at least one option."

I didn't press him on it, and neither did my mother. It was difficult to think in his presence. I felt like a pile of leaves that had been blown by a sudden gust of wind and formed into a small eddy, with scraps of garbage getting mixed in. At the same time, I felt heavy, as the weight of the past bore down on me. I had stopped thinking of myself as his daughter, but now, faced with him, there was no avoiding it; I felt myself inexorably drawn in, confined to the role I had always played: dutiful listener, sometime accomplice, a pretty doll to be put on display at parties. I managed snide remarks here and there, but I'd never stood up to my father. On some level, I had hoped that this time it would be different, but that hope was quickly draining away.

When the champagne was gone, we headed downstairs. The restaurant was cavernous, bathed in beige and dominated by a massive art deco chandelier that gave off a golden light. Its carpet was so thick, I felt myself sink half an inch with every step and had to fight the impression I would soon be swallowed up and disappear beneath its plush pile. We were seated at a square four-top table, replete with a crisp white tablecloth and three place settings. My father promptly ordered a bottle of white wine, and when the waitress poured him a taste, he made an impatient gesture with his hand for her to continue.

"I trust you, my girl. No time for that. Fill it to the top."

The waitress, blushing slightly, did as he asked. My mother unfurled her napkin and placed it delicately on her lap. I used the opportunity to check my phone. The photo I'd put up had 4,170 new Likes. I scrolled through the hearts and Comments. *Damn girl, get that money,* someone had written. *If you were my boss, I'd work for free*—from an unknown male. And, from an earnest-looking young woman, *So inspirational! I love it.* Some woman had had *DRAKE* tattooed on her forehead, in homage to the rapper. Gwyneth Paltrow had gotten married. Karma Black was standing on a street corner somewhere, holding a cardboard sign that read *Protect Our Future.*

"Mickey!" my father exclaimed, aghast. "Now, don't tell me you're one of the zombies that terrorize my dreams."

His grubby fingers plucked the phone from my hand but, being clumsy and ill-coordinated, he dropped it and it tumbled to the carpeted floor. I snatched it up.

"No idiot boxes at the table," he said.

"Dad, it's work."

"Yeah, okay," he scoffed. "It is."

"Michaela's a really big influencer now, Pete, she's doing really well. She's got—I mean, hundreds of thousands of Followers or something like that."

"One hundred and twenty-six thousand," I said proudly.

"You know, your mother explained this to me, but I still don't understand it." My father cut me off before I could answer. "I know, I know, an *influencer*. But an influencer of what?"

"That's just what it's called. Influencer."

"I know, but of what, Mick? That's what I don't understand. What exactly are you influencing?"

"Don't be obtuse, Dad." He was probably the only person I knew with whom I could use that word, and I did so with relish, feeling deliciously smart.

Meanwhile, he had begun absentmindedly cleaning his fingernails with a fork. "I mean it," he said, studying his work as he talked. "Who're you influencing? Other zombies glued to their idiot boxes?" He smiled ruefully. "Isn't that a little bit like saying you're Leader of the Lemmings?"

"It's a billion-dollar business—"

"Garbage removal is a billion-dollar business."

"Yeah, but this is a platform that people, whoever, can build their careers on. It's a tool—"

"It's a figment, Michaela," he said, putting the fork down. "It's just another gymnasium for the masses to exercise in, so they don't become disgruntled and rebel against their overlords. It gives the appearance of power, but don't be fooled, daughter of mine, there is no power there."

"Kim Kardashian has 151 million Followers on Instagram. How is that not power?"

"I don't know who this person is, but I'm guessing she makes her living, at least in part, from having all these Followers, right?"

"Exactly. She's a millionaire now. You can get rich—"

"So," he began, looking down at the silverware and straightening it so it lay perfectly parallel to the table's edge. "In a sense, this woman is being paid by her Followers."

"Sure."

"So her Followers pay her money, and she—Kim, you said it was?—works to please her Followers so they will continue to give her their attention and their money."

"I guess so," I said uncertainly, sensing despite his even tone that he was cornering me.

"And who generally pays whom? The boss or the employee?"

I sighed irritably and looked at my mother, who quickly avoided my gaze. Whenever my father and I tussled like this, she remained utterly silent, a tight smile on her face. I took a large sip of wine and held it in my mouth in an effort to cool down.

"Kim *whoever* has no more power than a bottle of Coca-Cola sitting on the shelf. She is a slave to her Followers, as the factory worker is a slave to his boss. She is *dependent* on them."

A waiter placed a bread basket at the center of the table, and my father, hardly waiting for the man's hand to withdraw, flicked away the white napkin covering it and extracted a roll.

"Real power comes from breaking the mold," he went on, slathering his roll with butter. "Although of course, the establishment will use any chance it can get to silence such innovations—just look at what happened to me."

"That's not why—"

"It's a conspiracy against free thinking," he went on, not looking at either of us, his concentration bound up in carefully coating his roll in butter.

"No, Dad," I said quietly. He bit into his roll. Grease shone along his lips and on his chin as he chewed, the roll still in one hand, readied for the next bite, and the knife still poised in the other. He saw me glaring at him and opened his mouth into a wide grin to show the macerated bread. Then he swallowed with dramatic effort.

"What was that?" he asked. Up until now, his tone had been almost exaggeratedly pedantic; annoying, to be sure, but not dangerous. Now, as he straightened up and stared at me, I could see the familiar flatness in his eyes that always presaged an outburst. I knew it was unwise to go on, but the words fell out of my mouth anyway, like hot bile. He wasn't just attacking me, he was also attacking Gemma.

"You didn't go to jail for 'free thinking,'" I said.

"Oh no?" Though he was not looking at me, I could feel his building anger in the intensity with which he was now slathering butter on the innards of his bread roll, the white stuff he'd revealed after he bit into it.

"No," I said flatly, knowing all too well what was to come and yet unable to stop myself. "It was theft. You stole. You committed a crime."

My father shoved the remainder of the roll into his mouth with such violence, I flinched. He stared at me, and this time I could see the fire burning in his nostrils. I remembered the first and only time he had hurt me physically—after coming home drunk one night, he'd slammed me against a cupboard, making lewd jokes. *You like this?* he'd said, and then, to my horror, he'd ground his pelvis against mine—only for an instant, though, and then he'd burst out laughing.

I suddenly wished I could take back what I had just said. Desperately, I tried to think of how I might walk back the statement as I watched my father force the lump of bread down his throat. He put his knife down carefully at his side.

"You know what," he said, his voice almost playful as he flicked the napkin on the bread basket aside and picked up another roll. "Why don't you fucking eat something." He slammed the roll down on my plate, making the silverware clink. Immediately, and without thinking, I brushed it away with the back of my hand. It bounced onto his thigh, then fell to the floor, where it rolled along the thick carpet.

"No," I said.

He was already bending over to pick up the roll. He plopped it back down on my plate and then, with surprising agility, grabbed my wrist as I went to flick it away again, and brought it to rest on the tabletop.

"You *will* fucking eat this," he said through clenched teeth, his face close to mine. I could smell his familiar smell of soured wine, and saw the spittle that had accumulated in the corners of his mouth.

"I won't."

He tightened his grip around my wrist.

"Michaela," he said, slowly and seriously. From an outside perspective, it might have looked as though we were only holding hands. I looked down at the roll, on which I could see small threads of carpet fiber, black. My mother whimpered beside me.

It was for her sake, and for the sake of avoiding the stares of other diners, that I begrudgingly muttered, "Fine." My father let go of my wrist and, through increasingly blurred vision, a hot fear burning in my chest, I picked up the roll and ferociously shoved the entire thing into my mouth, eyes bulging.

"Oh, honey!" my mother said, fingers rising to touch her mouth in surprise. She reached for me, and I swatted her away roughly, fleeing for the bathroom. The carpet was so cushy, there was no noise as my chair fell away behind me.

I heard my father say, in mock innocent surprise, "Yeesh, what's the big deal?"

In the bathroom, I hung over the toilet and spit out what was still in my mouth, retching painfully. After, I did what I often did when I was feeling out of control. I stared at my reflection for a long time. But this time, it brought me little comfort. All I saw were my father's eyes staring back at me. I put on another coat of Glossier Generation G Sheer Matte Lipstick in Zip. The counter, the floor, the walls, were all marble. It was so quiet, and the marble so cold, I felt like I was in a mausoleum. I opened up Instagram, and my fingers blindly typed out a name, *her* name, as if feeling a face in the dark. I knew it was stupid, that it would yield nothing. If anything, it would only open back up the door to a room I'd decided would be best shut off. Still, I felt the heaviness of my disappointment when those paltry gray words appeared on my screen again. *No user found.* I was frustrated. I wanted to see her, as if seeing her might reveal something to me—might help me know her and therefore become a little more like her, which was to say, a little less like my father. I scrolled through my camera roll, searching for the photos of us at the Strand bookstore—until I remembered bitterly that I had deleted them. I flew through more of my camera roll, looking for a distraction. Eventually, I landed on a photo Julia had taken earlier that month of me suntanning in the park, a book—Bukowski's *Hot Water Music*—half-shadowing my face. At the time, I had decided not to post it, since it was too literal a copy of a photo Gemma had posted a month before. Now, it occurred to me that if Gemma's Instagram account actually had been deleted, if she was not returning, I could post the image and no one would know that I'd copied her. I thought for a moment, then uploaded the photo to Instagram with the caption Gemma had used, to the best of my memory: *Can you miss something before it's even gone? Already mourning the end of summer. #tbt #takemeback.*

I knew the image would perform well, and I was not disappointed. The second I refreshed my screen, the heart that my hopes were forever pinned to pulsated and bore the numbers of Likes and Comments my post had already elicited. I breathed a sigh of relief. I felt I'd been restored to myself.

When I returned to the table, my mother had moved her chair closer to my father's, and was giggling like a teenager in love. He was stroking her hand, speaking in low tones. I wanted to wrench my mother away from him. How could she accept him, how could she—after everything he'd done to her, done to me—still allow him to touch her? The one piece of comfort was that I was not confined to the same duty.

I sat back down stiffly.

"Are you feeling better, sweetheart?" my mother asked me, as if I were a child that had just had a temper tantrum. Without waiting for my response, or perhaps with the knowledge that I wouldn't respond, she went on. "We ordered you the salmon. Is that okay? You were gone for a while."

"It's fine."

"Well, you certainly are emotional, my girl," my dad said, pinching me lightly on the shoulder and laughing. Seeing me recoil, he went on, "I mean that as a compliment! A woman with emotions. I approve."

When I continued to stare at him, stone-faced, he added, in a tone that was either pleading or mocking a plea, "Oh, come on, please? Humor your dear old dad. Forgive me."

I glanced at my mother, who was watching me anxiously, her hand clutching my father's forearm.

"Fine," I said, through gritted teeth.

"Oh good," my mother said, her body immediately relaxing. "That makes me happy."

My father raised his glass in a grandiose gesture. "We have a lot to celebrate."

My mother quickly followed suit. "We certainly do." Reluctantly, I raised my glass to meet theirs. I was thinking of the *JOY* shoot next week, how excited I'd been about it only just that morning, and how small it now seemed next to the grief which my parents always drew from me. I knew they were not thinking of my own imminent success and I didn't want to remind them of it, since I suddenly felt that anything they knew about my life would be irretrievably tainted.

"To freedom," my father said, and we all touched our glasses together. He drained his glass, then signaled with a twirl of his hand for our waiter to bring another bottle.

"I do hope we can go on being friends, Michaela," my father said tenderly. His eyes were watering again. "Because, well, I'm your father. And it's only natural."

I smiled and squeezed his hand. "Of course, Dad." Hiding my true feelings was innate, it came naturally to me, especially with him. Being false, letting someone think one thing while privately you schemed another: I'd learned it at his knee. Everything was a calculated performance.

The new bottle of wine arrived, along with our dishes.

"Oh, yum," my mother said. She'd also ordered the salmon. It was a golden-skinned fillet swimming in a pale-yellow sauce and topped with three slender asparagus spears. I sliced into its pink flesh with a knife. It came away easily and my stomach turned over. The meat, which was slick and dotted with white slime, trembled at the end of my fork as I slid it into my mouth, and I swallowed almost without chewing. I didn't want to taste the food, I only wanted it as an excuse not to speak. Though I had calmed down somewhat since our altercation, I could still feel a chaotic mix of emotions churning just below the surface. My phone was resting in the palm of my hand on my lap, and surreptitiously, while my father was absorbed in draining my mother's glass of wine, I checked it: 421 new Likes. I resumed eating, nodding along to my parents' chatter and saying a word or two where appropriate. My knife scraped against the plate, making me shiver, and goose bumps sprouted along my arm, but I remained silent. I checked my phone again: 120 new Likes.

Soon we were finished, and a waiter was clearing our plates. My mother excused herself for the bathroom, my stomach lurched, and I was left alone with my father. I felt nervous, as if we were strangers and the person who had introduced us had just left. My father, perhaps sensing this, cleared his throat and attempted to smile. He leaned back in his chair and, lowering just his bottom lip in a familiar, efficient gesture, let a burp escape his mouth. I scowled at him.

"Oh, don't look at me like that!" he said, laughing, but without my mother's comforting presence, I could not bring myself to respond. His laughter subsided. He began toying with a corner of the napkin he'd carelessly discarded in front of him.

"You know," he said, pinching the napkin and, with a flourish of his wrist, letting it flutter briefly in the air so that it settled flat on the table, "you and I are more alike than you think."

I snorted. He began carefully folding the napkin crosswise. "It's true," he said, his eyes not meeting mine. "I see you. I know what you're capable of."

"I've no idea what you're talking about," I said, a little too urgently. I wanted, desperately, for him to stop talking.

"Yes you do," he said, raising his eyes to meet mine, as the napkin became smaller and smaller. "You're more intelligent and cunning than I think you even realize. Oh, yes, I know what you're capable of—because I'm capable of the same."

"I highly doubt that."

He patted the small triangle of a napkin briefly with his fingers. "I'm not trying to insult you, Michaela. I'm trying to tell you something. You'd do well to listen. You should be proud you are the way you are. You and me are survivors. It's in the blood. There's no escaping."

When I was sixteen, my father gave me a black BMW as a present. By then, I already had a taste for drunkenness, the luxuriousness of a dulled consciousness, and though I promised to take good care of the car, I was not about to temper my habit. So I drove drunk a lot. One night, coming home from a party, I was more intoxicated than usual—I'd chugged half a bottle of vodka on a dare, just to show those idiots I could. I remember very little about what happened, except the sick *thwap* of something going under the tires. I had sped up, trying to put distance between me and whatever had just happened—and the next thing I knew, someone was shouting at me, and I felt strong arms under my armpits. Miraculously, I was unhurt. But the car was totaled. I'd driven it into the trees on a winding road a few blocks from our house. When the cops drove me home that night, they'd already called my parents to tell them I'd be charged with drunk driving and I'd heard my mother, hysterical, all the way from the back of the cruiser and felt sick with guilt. But when we got to my house, it was my father who answered the door. He made me go into the kitchen and told me to pour myself a cup of coffee, then he took the cops outside. I drank my coffee slowly. Through the thick fog of alcohol, a beast of remorse and terror was beginning to rear its head. I felt badly for what I'd done, but worse that I had gotten caught. It had been stupid, I should have been more careful. Tears fell from my eyes as I mourned my life, which I was sure was already over. After what felt like a long time, my father came back into the kitchen and poured himself a cup of coffee. He sat down next to me at the table.

"Well, they've agreed to drop the charges."

"How?" I asked, flabbergasted.

He sighed, leaned back in his chair, and looked at me frankly, turning something over in his mind. "If you're old enough to get in trouble like that, you're old enough to know: I paid them off." After I didn't say anything for some time, he went on, "Don't look so shocked, Michaela. I did what I had to do. Any father would."

This was a few months before he was charged. I knew nothing of his exploits, but, though he had read shock in my face, I wasn't actually surprised. On some level, I always knew my father was capable of that kind of thing. And though I'd later come to despise him for it, that night my whole body was suffused with gratitude for him. I got up from my seat and hugged him tightly. "Thanks, Dad."

"You're lucky to be alive," he said, and his eyes were wet. "Don't ever do anything so stupid again."

"I won't," I promised. "I won't."

We never spoke of the incident again, not even when my father gave me a new BMW. Not even when we saw the Robinson kids with tearstained faces, and learned that some maniac had drifted into their yard and run over their dog in the dead of night. Not even when he got arrested and everything he'd ever done was put under a microscope.

Now, I stared at my father and felt the weight of that transgression like the weight of a heavy promise: destiny, dread. He held my gaze, as if he knew what I was thinking. To my embarrassment, my eyes had welled with tears; first one crossed the threshold, tickling my cheek like a fly to be swatted, and then that pregnant, inevitable second one, too: I felt them catch on my jaw, hover tremulously, then fall.

"Oh, come now, there's no reason to cry," he said, unfurling the napkin and dropping it in my lap. "Wipe those away before your mother comes back."

On the subway ride home from the Four Seasons that night, I missed my stop. I didn't get off at the next one either. Instead, I transferred trains and, all while pretending I wasn't doing what I was doing, rode to West Fourth and then walked to Gemma's apartment. It was dark out, and I made sure to stay in the shadows. The entrance was silent, unforgiving. No one came or went. I wished I knew which window had been hers, was still hers for all I knew, and I studied each one, praying for some sort of sign, an identifying mark. But they were all the same, indistinguishable squares of glass; anything, anyone, could have been behind them. I began meandering along the streets, feeling comforted by the fact that Gemma had once walked them, too. It occurred to me that I'd been foolish to only look for her at her apartment building. After all, in New York, one's apartment is hardly the most likely place to be. I went into the dive bar she always used to go to and ordered a gin gimlet, which was her favorite drink. Time passed, in the uncertain way of growing drunkenness. I had another gimlet. When that was drained, the bartender, a nice-looking kid with a scruffy beard, asked if I'd like another. Startled from whatever reverie I was swimming in, I blurted out Gemma's name instead.

"What was that?" he asked.

I straightened my shoulders, trying to sober up. "Do you know Gemma Anton?"

He shook his head. "I don't think so?"

"She comes in here a lot," I said and then, to my embarrassment, hiccupped. I added quickly, to erase the hiccup, "She's a regular."

"Lots of people are regulars in here."

"She's tall, blond. A model"—*hiccup*—"kind of hard to miss."

He looked at me strangely.

"She wears a locket like this," I said, sliding it off my neck and showing it to him. I closed the back of my throat, trying to prevent any more hiccups.

He gave the locket a cursory glance, then laughed. "So, like you, you mean?"

Hiccup. Fuck. "Yes, we look alike."

"I mean, there's a blond girl who used to come in all the time with that photographer guy."

My heart leapt. "Hans Benoit?"

"She does look a lot like you," he said.

"Was it Benoit?"

"Yeah—that's right, that's his name. I like his shit, actually."

"Do you—I mean, have you seen her recently? Do you know where she is?"

His face darkened. "Why do you ask?"

"Oh, no reason, it's just"—*hiccup*—"never mind—"

"Is something going on?"

"No!" I said, though I'd accidentally raised my voice. "Everything is *fine*. Just give me another gimlet."

He looked on the point of refusing when I rudely jammed a crumpled twenty-dollar bill on the table, and he reluctantly turned to mix me one. So she had been here with Benoit. Often. The old illusions boiled up in my head: Benoit had strangled her and tossed her in the river. Benoit had banished her from the industry. Benoit had done something awful to her, he had broken up with her, insulted her, and she was so heartbroken she went to extremes, did the unthinkable, deleted her Instagram.

More time passed at the bar. My brain was awhirl with images, which shape-shifted as soon as I tried to pin them down—they became violent, less real. I asked the man next to me if he knew Gemma, only he didn't seem to understand me. I stumbled from my stool, and it fell over behind me. A girl helped me pick it up.

"D'you know Gemma?" I croaked.

She shook her head and hurried away. I worked my way through the rest of the bar, asking everyone if they knew her, trying to show them pictures, then stumbling over my words, getting confused over what I was saying, forgetting where I was. People started whispering. I could feel them staring at me, growing alarmed, or maybe they were only disgusted. But I couldn't stop. Eventually I was reduced to murmuring her name repeatedly, my body jerking with hiccups as I paced back and forth, phone in hand, until they threw me out.

I stumbled away from the place, found a darkened doorway to lean against and get my bearings. I closed my eyes and pressed my fingers into them, trying to keep the rising nausea at bay, and the Grid appeared in red behind my eyelids. Gemma's last Instagram reared up, her face growing pink from the fading sun—*or is it from something else? Something just out of the frame? No—no—no—Gemma,* I repeated to myself again, strenuously, *her face growing pink from the fading sun, standing out on that pier.* Her caption had read *Pre-partying for @ TheRising tn, and by pre-party I mean gazing forlornly at the sun completely alone.* Was it strange that I could recall, down to the punctuation, all the captions she had ever posted, almost as if they had come from somewhere deep inside myself? I didn't think so at the time. Instead I had a flash of inspiration. The hiccups subsided almost instantly. I knew what I should do.

I hurried back out onto the street.

"Is it Thursday?" I screamed at the closest passerby, a white guy with long, scraggly hair, who looked up at me with alarm, then confusion. "Today is Thursday, right?" I asked impatiently.

"Uh, yeah," he said, and then before he could ask me if I wanted a drink or needed help or some other bullshit, I turned on my heel and jogged toward Seventh Avenue. It appeared in my mind like a beacon, calling me toward it: The Rising.

Gemma had religiously attended the Social for Social Thursday parties, and though it was true I hadn't seen mention of them anywhere else on my feed, I was sure they were still going on. The Rising had probably only become more exclusive and under the radar—from the get-go, they had never allowed photos inside—and I was sure that if Gemma was anywhere on a Thursday, it would be there. I cursed myself for not going there sooner. My lack of interest in any sort of nightlife had, for the most part, benefited me, allowing me to concentrate on what mattered—content, content, content—but it was stupid that I hadn't thought about how it might be costing me a Gemma encounter. More determined than ever, I shot up Seventh Avenue and veered toward the Meatpacking District. I knew the club was located somewhere on Bethune Street, which only had three blocks to it. I made it to the street in five minutes, paused to catch my breath, and recognized it instantly: the weary-looking awning and the innocuous sign, *Bethune Street Body Work*, and the neon signs in the window alongside the chart of the human body sliced in half with all its organs showing, poor thing. I took out my phone and reapplied Glossier Generation G Sheer Matte Lipstick in Zip to the shadowy, slightly cross-eyed woman in the screen. I walked purposefully toward the door, perfectly calm.

Of course, there was a sign in the window saying it was closed, but this did not deter me at all. I would have figured as much. I waited patiently at the door for the bouncer, whoever he was, to see me and let me in, usher me into my rightful place among the anointed, where, if I was unable to find Gemma, I was sure to meet someone who knew her, who possibly had been with her that very night she'd last posted. But when nothing happened, I grew impatient and tugged on the handle. The door rattled but did not budge.

"It's Mickey Jones," I said, barely suppressing a smile as I imagined how embarrassed, how apologetic, they'd be when they realized it was *me* at the door, *me* they kept waiting. Proof that my father was wrong, proof of my power.

After a minute of silence, my smile faded. I moved closer to the glass and looked past my blurry reflection into the room. I had to laugh—it was a perfect imitation of a massage parlor, complete with a money tree behind the cramped reception desk (the handmade sign Scotch-taped to a jar, marked *Tips*, was a particularly brilliant touch) and an aquarium in the corner, which was giving off an unnatural blue light. Obviously the bouncer, or the host, was ushering whoever had just arrived inside—the club must be hidden somewhere, perhaps at the end of the long, dark hallway just to the left of the reception desk. Sure enough, a figure emerged in the hallway, moving toward the door. I knocked loudly and stepped back, relieved, trying to calibrate my smile so that it conveyed both my annoyance and my gracious forgiveness.

When nothing happened, I began to grow angry. Could they really not recognize me through the glass? Couldn't they tell I was somebody?

"Um, hello?" I called through the door, this time not bothering to hide my irritation. I yanked at the door again. "It's Mickey Jones," I yelled, and this time I tried to push through the door, though it wouldn't budge. "Hello!" I pounded at the door with my fist.

Finally, the door opened halfway, and a middle-aged Asian woman wearing a pink sweatshirt, white slacks, and rubber sandals stood in the slim gap in the door.

"Can I help you?" she asked in a thick accent, which was obviously fake. They had really gone the extra mile.

"The Rising," I said breathlessly. "I should be on that list."

"What?" She drew her eyebrows together and tilted her head to one side, as if trying to hear me better.

"Yeah, yeah, yeah," I said impatiently. "I know it's supposed to be *secret*." I made bunny fingers around the word. "But I'm okay, I come all the time."

"I'm sorry," she said, smiling and shaking her head, already beginning to close the door. "Wrong place."

I heaved a dramatic sigh. "Please," I said. "Don't give me that. I *know* this is The Rising. I've been here, like, fifteen times."

"I'm sorry, no, no, no," she said, shaking her head and smiling and stepping away from the door like I was going to rob her, like I was going to bash her head in and step over her dead body.

"Stop the act," I said in my gentlest, most coaxing voice. "It's *fine*." I made a calming motion with my hands, smoothing everything down, smiling wide. The woman's face relaxed slightly, her grip on the door slackening just enough—I lunged forward and pushed through the door. The woman yelped and ran behind the tiny reception desk in the corner. I blew past her, past the fish tank, down the darkened hallway, down, down, down, searching for the elevator.

I heard the woman speaking loudly in Mandarin behind me. I'd reached the end. The elevator was ingeniously concealed behind plain drywall. I slid my palm against its smooth surface, searching for the button, for whatever trick would make it open up and ferry me above.

"Let me in!" I screamed, slapping my fist against it. I knew it was here, it had to be. What devilish lengths they would go to, whoever they were! I breathed in eucalyptus, and it burned my nostrils. It didn't make sense. None of it made sense! I pressed my entire body against the hard surface, shivering all of a sudden. A strange strangled sound erupted from my throat. I was sobbing.

"What're you doing?"

I whipped around to see a twentysomething guy, probably this woman's son, wearing Air Jordans and clutching an iPhone in one hand.

"Where is she?" I asked.

"You have to leave," the man said patiently. "Or we'll have to call the cops."

I saw that his phone was pointed at me, his face illuminated by the screen, and my stomach dropped, the ground giving way beneath me fast as the power dynamics swung like a seesaw. I felt suddenly afraid, indignant, trapped.

"Don't film me!" I screamed, taking a step toward him.

The man remained impassive, his phone pointed at me like a gun.

"I demand that you stop filming me!" I screeched.

"You are trespassing on our property. I will continue to film you until you leave."

His voice was calm, as if he knew he held all the power, and that was what really irritated me, that was what really drove me nuts. I was breathing fast and hard like an animal, trapped in the corner. He took a few steps forward and said something in Mandarin over his shoulder. A spark flew in my chest—I knew I had to escape, I couldn't allow him any closer. With superhuman agility, I barreled toward him, my body cutting the air like a knife, the wind rushing in my ears—the man was so surprised, he didn't have time to react as I wrenched the phone from his hands and flew, soaring, soaring, soaring past him, the room blurring behind me, until I was outside gulping at the air, and I was still running until I reached the river just a few blocks away, just barely missing a car whizzing by on the West Side Highway, and tossed the device, that wretched all-seeing eye, into the Hudson River.

In a trance, I walked back over to Gemma's apartment. The doorman, a different one from the last time I'd been there, nodded at me familiarly. "Welcome back," he said. "Good night."

I took the stairs, all the way to the top floor, where there was unlikely to be anyone passing through. Then I curled up on the landing, and slept.

A week later, the day of the shoot arrived, blown in on the most perfect summer's day. Since the dinner with my father, I'd hardly eaten or slept. But the funny thing was: I felt fucking great. Best I'd felt in years. I'd discovered new depths to lightness. The hunger had calcified and hollowed out. It felt like a glass ball I carried around with me, balanced in the palm of my hand: hard, but light, so light! Sometimes I felt like my toes would lift off the ground, like I would rise and effervesce and disappear into nothingness.

Trust your intuition, dear Aquarius, and nurture faith and positive thinking. If you find that obstacles to the realization of goals always seem to pop up, then it's important for you to take an honest inner inventory of what you really believe you deserve. New York City had confirmed its first Brazilian flu case. Sixty-three Likes. A mall had been shot up in Pennsylvania, the second mass shooting in twenty-four hours. Forty-two Likes. Jeffrey Epstein was found dead in his cell, an apparent suicide, the fucking coward. Two new Follows. Comment: *Hi! I'm a big fan of your page! It's my birthday coming up. I suffer from lupus and it would mean a lot to me if you Followed me on my birthday. Thank you!* It was going to be seventy-five degrees and sunny, with a cool breeze at night. I had 132K Followers.

The night before, I'd submitted a request to be verified on Instagram, utterly confident that I would qualify. Every time I blinked I could see it; the white check mark danced in my mind as I readied myself for the day to come. The car came for me at five a.m., a big, shiny black Lexus, and because it was still dark out, and because I hadn't slept in days, and because I usually only ever rode in cars like this with Joe the promoter and the faceless men on their way to some club, I had a moment of confusion, thinking, disoriented, I was returning from somewhere rather than leaving. I would have wondered briefly if I'd been dreaming, except I didn't dream anymore, because I didn't sleep. I was wearing Le Specs The Flash Sunglasses, a black-and-pink Balenciaga hoodie, Adidas Alphaskin Sport Shorts, Adidas Classic Stripe Socks, Nike Air Force 1 Sneakers, and an Off-White Basic Nylon Fanny Pack.

I greeted the driver warmly, wrapping my arms around him in a professional, formal hug, then considered, rather smugly, how much sleep he had probably gotten last night—what? At least five hours?—and marveled yet again at the amount of time humans were willing to waste every day. He laughed nervously, probably flattered and impressed with the level of personal attention I was giving him, and I slid smoothly into the back seat. Now that I wasn't sleeping, I'd become super productive. Everything in my life was optimized. Instead of wasting calories on imperfect food that left gaps in my daily nutrition and often made me feel bloaty, I kept myself alive by consuming vitamins and PowerBars at thoughtfully scheduled breaks during the day. At night, I exercised: yoga, Pilates, videos I found on the Internet that seemed to mostly involve jumping around . . . I'd streamlined elsewhere, too: instead of thinking up new things to say to Followers or friends, I just copied and pasted from a memo I had in my Notes app.

Lol okay.

Lol, thanks.

Um, no, lol.

Lol, thanks mamma.

Lol! I miss you!

In the back of the car, I took a selfie, pretending to drink from a coffee cup I'd already drained before leaving the house. I remembered something Gemma had written on Instagram, en route to one of her shoots: *When your call time is 5 a.m., and you have to pick up your coffee the night BEFORE.* When we crossed the Brooklyn Bridge, I filmed myself, the lights of the city streaming behind me: "And why, you might ask, am I up so early? Something I'm really excited about and really want to tell," I said in a breathless, excited voice. "Buuuut I can't, because lawyers. Stay tuned, though."

Someone from *JOY* had sent over an NDA and some other paperwork, which I'd hastily signed without reading. *You're welcome to take behind-the-scenes pictures, but everything specific to the shoot—your makeup, the team, set, etc.—is under strict embargo until further notice.* I knew the deal. I'd seen it hundreds of times on the Instagrams of other models and influencers, even, I suspected, when there was no actual embargo—they just wanted to feel important, and also they'd seen other, more famous people do it, and they thought if they parroted those famous people, they might become more famous, too. *Under embargo.* What a scintillating phrase! I knew Gemma had probably used it at some point. I had a distant recollection of that. I tried to remember her posts from her first shoot with *JOY*, but strangely the images blurred in my mind. I thought there was a farm animal involved, but I couldn't remember if it was a pig or a goat or a lamb. I felt a pressure build between my eyes, a headache coming on, and pressed my fingers against my forehead. I was hot to the touch.

The car turned onto a nondescript residential street in Park Slope, then pulled over. It was still dark out, eerily quiet, and I made a joke to myself, trying to ignore the headache: *What if he kills me! What if this is all a ruse, and I'll be dead soon, ha ha ha ha!* But no: the driver opened the door and let me out, smiling distantly, and I noticed two trailers, humming with air conditioning, parked outside a weary-looking brownstone. Figures milled around a white-tented craft table. As I got closer, I noticed Benoit, Styrofoam cup in hand, head bent in thoughtful consideration, nodding occasionally while Kiki spoke to him. As far as I could tell, he was wearing the exact same outfit he'd had on at our last shoot: navy sweatshirt, cuffed navy sweatpants, and Gucci loafers. He was wearing aviators, too, and it was only then that I remembered I'd snapped them, and again I felt the satisfying crack between my fists. The impression startled me, emerging from a mass of blackness that I'd buried the night under. I felt vaguely ashamed. I tried not to think about it. Instead, I stared at his aviators, trying to ascertain whether they were a completely new pair or if he'd managed to get the old ones repaired. It didn't matter either way. He was wearing them. Of course he was.

I called out to him, forcing my voice a few octaves higher than normal to convey cheerfulness.

Benoit, who was swinging one of his legs back and forth so that the sole of his shoe made a pleasant scratching noise on the pavement, did not look up, apparently lost in thought. Only Kiki acknowledged me.

"Hey, Mickey, welcome," she said, coming over and almost touching me, her arm jerking forward and then falling back. Even still, this was a remarkably warmer welcome than I'd received before. To Benoit she said, in a slightly lower voice: "Talent's here." Benoit instantly came to life, spinning on his heel to face me and opening his arms.

"Ah, my peach!" he said. He kissed me on both cheeks and sniffed my neck, and I stared at the smaller versions of myself reflected in his glasses.

"Those new?" I found myself asking him, or thought I did anyway—it was getting more and more difficult to decipher the line between what was happening in my head and what wasn't.

Benoit readjusted the frames on his nose. "Hm?" he asked. "Did you say something?"

I shook my head no. And then, maybe because I *had* asked the question or maybe because I was staring at them, he tapped the lenses. "You know, my peach, the longest monogamous relationship I've had is with these glasses. I've been wearing them since I was twenty-six. Isn't that beautiful? Some objects are worthy of love, no?" He lowered the glasses and winked at me. I smiled. Benoit nodded. "So," he said, looking at me sideways. "How are we feeling today? Are we ready?"

"Absolutely."

"Marvelous," he said, with his signature out-of-time bravado, and I had to keep myself from rolling my eyes.

"Do you want coffee?" he asked me, walking toward the craft table, then carrying on without a reply: "Cate and I have been thinking a lot about the run of show today, how best to get what we want, because of course, it might get messy. It will be taxing. I told you the working title, yes? 'Human Being.' Isn't that beautiful? When I saw the shows, and everything looked so slick—*yech*—you know? Aren't we tired of everything looking the same?" Black coffee streamed into his Styrofoam cup in a swirl of steam. I clutched my hand harder around my phone. "This is a rebellion." He turned to face me, leaning against the craft table. "It's a fucking revolt, that's what today is, that's what it's all about.

A fucking revolt. Against the fakeness and the slickness and the LED lighting. The average American adult consumes eleven hours of media *a day*. Isn't that absurd? Or maybe it was twelve hours a day? Wait . . . now I can't remember, it's something like six months in a year—"

I nodded and knit my eyebrows together, like I was blown away by what he was saying and really concerned, though all I was really thinking was that this was a fashion shoot for a large media conglomerate, and that Benoit was probably getting paid six figures to do it.

"Kiki," he called, and I turned to see her ferrety face pop up from behind her clipboard. "What was that stat—Americans spend how many hours—"

"Eleven," she said.

"Right, I knew it." He nodded to himself. Then he leaned backward, his ass inching ever closer to the perfectly chopped kiwi artfully arranged on a plastic plate. "Eleven hours!" he screamed. "What about people? No, it's an epidemic. Bringing people back to people: that is what this is about today. Not media. Not fashion—I don't even want you to think about fashion today, okay? This is about humanity. Humanity with a fucking capital *H*. By the way," he said, suddenly calm, readjusting his stance at the table so he was facing me at a three-quarter angle, "you're not on your period, by any chance? We could possibly use that. But if you're not, then that's okay, too."

I shook my head, taken aback by the question.

"Ah, that's too bad. I had this vision—you see what I mean, we want this to be human in every way. In all the grotesque glory that is humanity. But," he added, cocking his head to peer at me, "you're not on it." As if he thought I could bring it on by will or something, as if his power over me extended all the way to menstruation.

"No."

He sniffed sharply, and I could see the mask of affability falter ever so slightly, only for a split second, but enough that my reflexes kicked in, and I found myself, to my horror, mumbling an apology to him.

He assured me it was fine, and I was left with the shame of having apologized to a man, *this* man, for not arbitrarily having my period at that moment.

"Not to worry, at all," he said. "It's all cool, cool, cool." He nodded several times, as if to emphasize that he was entirely laid back about this issue.

I said nothing. The sky was turning a pale gray, the color of something empty.

Benoit righted himself and reached his arms in the air, groaning quietly. He clasped his right hand in his left and stretched sideways, revealing his soft belly. I turned away and filled a Styrofoam cup with coffee. Four thousand Views. Sixteen new Followers. Comments:

omg she's totally shooting Vogue
fucckkk why can't I look like her
best of luck babes
dyinnnnggg to know
i'm single & lonely & u look like a nice girl. can u follow me?

I pressed my thumb against the miniature version of my face ringed in rainbow, and watched the video on silent. I watched as my mouth formed words like invisible bubbles. I couldn't now remember what I had said, but it didn't matter. My skin looked impeccable, I'd caught the morning light perfectly. My perm, which had finally recovered since that night in the rain, had dried nicely—it helped that it didn't suffer hours smushed against my pillow at night anymore—and the curls pooled attractively around the collar of my hoodie.

Benoit suddenly called out for Cate, and I startled, my heart hammering unnecessarily. Maybe it was the coffee, which I'd drunk so quickly. I turned and saw Cate emerge from the semidetached brownstone we were parked in front of. For the first time, I got a really good look at it: the paint trim was peeling, the yard overgrown, and one of the front windows had been smashed and then boarded over. It looked condemned. Benoit strode purposefully toward her, and I heard him say, "Cate, she doesn't have it."

Cate spurted Purell on her hands and worked them over carefully. She was wearing a mechanic's suit cut entirely from paper-thin suede, which was halfway unbuttoned to reveal a plain wifebeater and lots of gold jewelry. Ignoring Benoit, she walked straight toward the craft table and filled a cup with hot water, then plunked in a lemon slice, while he trailed behind her. She took a sip of hot lemon water and turned to me.

"Has he explained to you about the hair?" she asked, eyebrows raised.

Benoit, obviously irritated, snapped, "She'll be fine with it."

Ignoring him still, she continued to look at me.

"Because it's a big change," she said, gently like I was a little kid, her voice as smooth as calamine lotion.

"Why wouldn't she be fine with it?" Benoit asked loudly behind her.

"Yeah, I'm fine with it," I said easily.

Cate put her cup down and then, without warning, stuck her fingers into my hair and pulled it back into a tight ponytail at the top of my head, intensifying the dull ache at the center of my forehead. She transferred the ponytail to one fist, then twisted it over and over again so that my hair was pulled as tight as possible against my scalp and I had to screw up my face to keep from crying out. All the while Cate just looked at me curiously.

She sighed. My scalp screamed and tears sprang to my eyes. "Well, we have to do it regardless," she said, but it wasn't to me, it was to Benoit.

"Of course. It's essential," he answered.

She let go of my hair. I worked to catch my breath.

"You're going to look like a real badass," she said to me.

"Good." I tried to smile. My head was pounding. The headache had morphed into a full-blown migraine. I turned to refill my coffee cup and wiped the back of my hand quickly across my eyes, to steal the wetness there.

"You okay?" Cate asked, as I took my first sip.

I nodded, forcing the hot liquid down my throat. "Oh yeah," I said, smiling. I felt Benoit's eyes pressing against me. "I'm great. I'm just *peachy*."

Benoit smiled appreciatively, then motioned for me to follow him to the hair and makeup trailer.

"You know Bill, right?" he asked over his shoulder.

I frowned. "I don't think so."

He whistled. "Oh, wow," he said. "You're in for a real treat. Imagine Picasso, but with a pair of scissors and a blow-dryer. A real artist."

He opened the door of the trailer and called inside: "Maestro, I have your first victim—well, your only one, today." A gust of air conditioning made the hair on my arms stand up. I walked up the small steps and looked into the narrow space, then stopped short, inhaling quickly and nearly tripping over the threshold.

"Whoopsies," Benoit said. "You okay?"

The man, the man who could only be Bill, was already getting up from his seat. I noticed his cowboy hat first, the same pale-gray felted job he had worn that night, the night that . . . I pushed the memory from my mind. He put his hand on my forearm to steady me.

"You okay there, love?" he asked.

I looked into his eyes, which were the color of antifreeze fluid, and gave him the most evil smile I could muster. "Oh yes," I said. "I'm absolutely perfect."

He laughed lightly, then removed his hand from my forearm and tucked it almost shyly behind his head, just beneath his hat. "Oh, good," he said. I heard Benoit screaming something to Cate outside. Our eyes met, then Bill stuck his hand out for a handshake. "I'm Bill. I'll be doing your chop today—don't worry, we're going to make it as painless as possible."

I laughed. "When have I ever been scared of pain anyhow?"

He looked at me curiously, then ushered me toward the leather chair in front of the mirror. I realized he had no idea who I was.

Bill got right to business, gently probing my skull, lifting strands here and there and rubbing them between his thumb and forefinger.

"Are these your natural curls?"

"Uh-huh."

"Lucky girl."

He let my hair fall around my shoulders, then slid a hand underneath it and lifted it like a curtain. His hand was warm and moist against the nape of my neck. Could he really not remember? I bored into his reflection in the mirror, and he shot me a polite smile. He really didn't remember!

He started by using a spritzer to dampen my hair, then he combed it through, and even though he was gentle, unimpeachably gentle, my head throbbed with pain. I had let myself be defiled by a fucking hairdresser. Vacantly, I watched him pick up a pair of long scissors. They flashed silver in the mirror as he cut, five inches in two swift chops, sending a sheaf of golden hair to my feet. My stomach lurched forward. I smiled as if I had expected this. I thought about how small and harmless his dick had been. He tried to make chitchat but I was having trouble following it, distracted by the sudden weightlessness of my head, the way my hair now stuck out around my chin.

"Uh-huh," I said to something Bill had asked, as I watched him unfurl a gadget from the coil of its black cord, his cowboy hat bent in concentration.

"That's great," he said soothingly. "Happy to hear that." The gadget free, he paused, smiling kindly at the two of us in reflection. A hairdresser! A fucking hairdresser! "So, are you ready, lass? There's no rush."

It was then that I noticed he was holding clippers.

"Oh," I said. "Are we, um—how much are we doing again?"

He cocked his head curiously. "We'll probably buzz you on a three—is that what you mean?"

"Oh, yeah, um"—my eyes darted around the room—"is there a bathroom in here?"

"It's okay to be nervous," he said, winking at me. "I know women and their hair. But you're in good hands, promise. Buzz cuts are really having a moment now, I mean since Karma—"

"You know, it's just that I have a headache, actually."

"Oh, I can give you something—"

"And I need to pee," I said, standing up so quickly that I knocked his hands, which had been hovering around my head.

"Sure," he said, totally unbothered. "It's over there, at the back."

I shut the door behind me, and pressed my hands against the cold metal sink, fear-choked and gasping, my eyes darting back and forth in the mirror, studying the contours of my hair. I thought about how painstakingly I'd cultivated the curls, how long I'd studied those images of Gemma. Okay, so it wasn't perfect, it could certainly use some styling—still, it was *mine*. More than that, it was *hers*. I could not believe they wanted to strip me of it, they had to be mistaken. Didn't they understand, didn't they know, wasn't it obvious that without it I'd be—I didn't know what I'd be, actually, but I knew I'd no longer see Gemma when I looked in the mirror. Pain strobed across my forehead, forcing my eyes shut. I pressed my fingers against my temples. Outside the bathroom door, Bill cleared his throat. I opened my eyes, flushed the toilet, and ran the tap water for a second, never taking my gaze from the reflection in the mirror. I took a deep breath.

"So," I said lightly when I got out, trying to sound calm, reasonable, careless as I made my way back to the chair. "I'm totally game—really, I'd be thrilled—I'm just wondering if we really think a full buzz cut is the way to go, I'm just not sure . . ." I faltered when I saw Bill's face, stony and red, the same frightful mask he wore that night that I couldn't let myself think of. "It's just my face . . ." I trailed off, lost.

"We really don't have time to reconceptualize the entire shoot," he said with obvious impatience.

"Or if we just pulled my hair back really tight and—"

Bill snorted in laughter, banishing the mask, though not entirely. I could still see it just below the surface. "Look," he said, putting a hand on my shoulder, and helping me into the seat. "I would be open to it. But, unfortunately, my dear lass, I get paid to take orders." He leaned over so I could feel the heat of him right along my cheek, and spoke into my ear, his antifreeze eyes locking on mine in the mirror. "And last time I checked, you do too."

I laughed nervously, his breath on my neck, the casual, even kind, derision in his voice spurring on a deep shame inside me. I was instantly embarrassed by how juvenile I must have sounded. I was lucky to be here at all. I would, of course, do whatever they wanted, anything, anything, anything, anything at all.

He straightened up, satisfied in having elicited the appropriate change in my attitude, and smiled widely and warmly into the mirror. "Welcome to the big leagues, dearie." He picked up the clippers, then nodded to two small round pills laid out on a towel on the vanity ledge in front of me. "Those'll help with the nerves. And the pain."

Anything, anything, anything. Hands trembling, fully chastised, I scooped up the pills without even asking what they were—but the fear still churned in my stomach and frantically I reached for my phone, searching out its comforting solidity and clasping it to my chest, where my heart beat against it.

"You want to film it?" Bill asked brightly, softening, almost solicitous now that I was fully in his control. "Karma's did really well. Even got some news coverage."

I nodded, recalling the video of Karma, head tilted, tongue pressed against her upper lip, her nose ring glinting, as her dreads were sheared away.

"Here." Bill handed me the clippers, and held out his palm for my phone. "It's better if you do it yourself, and I'll film. Authentic, you know? That's how we did it with her."

I took a deep breath and delicately placed my phone into his palm.

The girl smiles. Soft blond curls frame her face, ending in a jaunty choppiness at her chin. There is a buzzing in the background, an incessant insect. The girl cocks her head sideways, her smile faltering only slightly as her tongue flicks out across her lip. The smile returns; the girl's smile is industrial strength. Her face is made of plaster. The clippers travel back again, cutting away a new strip of hair. Golden filaments, parts of her body no more, fall to the floor. A few are stuck to her neck.

The girl, newly shorn, smiles maniacally at the camera. Without her signature blond curls, she is somehow more striking and also less distinct: her features, always malleable, are almost unrecognizable. Her eyes shine black in the overhead lighting.

The girl presses her cheek into the shock-white beard of an older man with a ruddy complexion and kind eyes. He is wearing a cowboy hat. She is smiling the same industrial-strength smile. She pulls her head away and jerks a thumb at the man.

"This is the man who deserves all the credit," she says. "He's the dude."

The man lowers his eyes briefly, then beams at the camera, clearly pleased with himself.

I don't know when the drugs took effect, or what they were, but sometime during my shearing I began to feel as though my body was slipping away from me, a strange dislocation of self that was freeing and exhilarating and disorienting and terrifying. My head was weightless, practically floating. The hair on the floor was no longer mine, was alien to me. Bill swept it up and shoveled it into the garbage.

Six thousand Views. Hundreds of Comments. *So brave!, omg! Wish I was this brave!, badass, killer, fuckin hot*, etc., etc. Who were all these people, and who were they talking about? I didn't know.

@BlakeyBlake: *You DIDN'T! I'm DYING. Love it so much!*

Jules texted me: *Um, not cool to buzz your hair when Blake said she wanted to and you were so not into it.*

It's for work, I wrote, the New Me, the Buzzcut Me, adding, *It wasn't my choice and it's not my problem. Also: She can get a life.*

Seven hundred new Views. Eleven new Followers. Twelve Comments.

I went to the bathroom and cut two fat lines of coke on the sink, inhaling them sharply, one after the other. They interrupted, briefly, that sense of intangibility, of not being there, just long enough for me to catch my reflection and feel the slap of betrayal. I tried to picture Gemma's face, but found that every time I thought I'd gotten hold of it, it slipped away. I would get glimpses—the curve of an earlobe, the way her nose upturned slightly—but they wouldn't coalesce into a cohesive image, like trying to grab smoke in your hand, or maybe like trying to take a picture of the moon, only it just shows up blurry and super small and doesn't even look like a moon at all, but more like a smudge in the sky, the most frustrating thing ever.

When I came out of the bathroom, Leone—the absurdly attractive makeup artist who had taken Bill's place—was waiting for me, and the fog swept over me again, and this time I was relieved, even pleased. Leone swiveled my chair so that I faced away from the mirror, her knees on either side of my knees as she leaned in close and attended to my face, rubbing all sorts of things onto my skin, even my scalp. My body pulsed and those white fireflies danced before my eyes as she mixed various skin tones of tan and light brown on the back of her hand. Was I seeing things? Surely I had to be seeing things.

"Won't that be too dark?" I asked, as she dipped a brush into the mixture.

She shrugged. "That's how they want it."

All of a sudden I was standing in a different trailer, shivering because of the artificial cold, or maybe it was the coke, or maybe it was this feeling of existential emptiness that was slowly choking the life out of me, but whatever it was, it was making my nipples stand up attractively, and it was with this observation that I fully recognized that my body (not me) was naked but for a pair of leather underwear that said *Fuck the Patriarchy* on the ass, only it wasn't my body anymore, it was somebody else's, somebody I recognized but could not place.

"You're so brave," cooed Kim, who was unclipping something from a clothes hanger.

"Oh, totally," said a small man crouched at my feet, lacing up my boots, which were black leather and came up to my knee with a six-inch stiletto heel. "That's some serious balls."

The man's name was Andy, and he looked a lot like the Andy who had worked with me at my last shoot for Benoit, but I wasn't sure. I was having trouble recognizing things unless they appeared on that beautiful crystal LCD screen, the portal to another world that was currently tucked away in my robe hung up on the other side of the trailer.

"I mean, I would have cried, honestly, I know that's pathetic but it's true," Kim went on.

"You just look so . . . like, dangerous or something."

"Renegade."

They had painted my skin brown and dusted my hair with black powder. My eyebrows had been filled in with pencil. Freckles dotted my nose. A terror rose within me, and reflexively I reached for the locket, hitting bone instead, because of course they had removed it, of course, of course, they had banished anything left of her, removed all traces, replaced it with—what? Who? A profound loneliness tore through me, making me dizzy; I swayed forward and braced myself against the mirror.

"Whoa," Andy said, his hands still on my boots. "Sorry about that."

"It's okay," I muttered, peering at my reflection inches away, as an eerie sense of incongruity crept over me. "I just got light-headed."

Kim helped me straighten up.

"Do you think my skin is . . . ?" Kim gave me a curious look, cocking her head to one side as I struggled to find the right word. "Too, um, brown?"

"I think it looks perfect," she said as she turned and went to retrieve something from one of the jewelry boxes laid out on the vanity shelf.

"But—"

"Cate and Benoit are *geniuses*," chimed in Andy. "You gotta trust their vision."

"You just look really *tanned*," Kim said, briefly cupping her hands around my nose as she inserted a thin gold ring into one of my nostrils. "There," she said. "Complete."

I heard something wail in the distance.

"What's that?" I asked.

Andy looked up at me from his crouch. "Hm?"

"I thought I heard a baby crying."

"Oh . . ." Andy glanced around vaguely before returning his attention to the laces. "Yeah, it's for one of the shots. Benoit wants to use it as a . . . prop."

"Is it real? I mean, is it actually a baby or is it—" I shuddered involuntarily.

He sat back on his haunches and knit his brows together. "I think it's real," he said, clearly considering the question for the first time. "I mean, I saw it earlier, and it looked pretty real to me."

Kiki came in at that moment, holding a clipboard and looking vaguely harried. "Ready?" she asked.

"She's good," said Andy, standing up and dusting off his knees.

Outside, I saw the baby, strapped into a soft pink Fisher-Price sleeper beside the fruit plate on the craft table. It was wearing a cream-colored hat, beneath which I could see little wisps of black hair, and was wrapped in a chunky blanket that looked hand-knit. It had light-brown skin and a small little plum for a mouth, and its eyelids, closed in peaceful slumber, were shiny like flower petals. Its singularity, how alone it was, positioned there on the table as if it were just another object, startled me.

"Is its mother—"

"Come on," snapped Kiki. "Everyone's waiting for you."

I walked slowly up the path to the house, trembling because of the shoes, which were incredibly difficult to walk in. Inside, the building was falling apart. Huge swaths of the drywall, painted a pale green, had been ripped away in white tears, revealing bare wood beneath it. Parts of the ceiling were hanging down, and the floor was covered in desiccated leaves and a thick layer of dust. The hall opened up into a big, open room, the former living room of the house, surely, with a once stately fireplace and large-paned glass windows. The ground here was particularly filthy and mottled, and I wondered if they'd trucked in extra dirt for effect. Studio lights loomed like giant insects around a torn camelback sofa, their black spindly legs set at just the right distance, their massive umbrella heads angled down, ready to devour me. Cate and Benoit stood with their backs to me, studying a bank of monitors set just behind the lights. The screens showed an image of what was in front of them almost exactly— the shredded sofa with the musty fireplace in the background—so that it appeared as though we were looking through separate tunnels, and the screens were simply the rectangular mouths of those tunnels. Only on the screen the set looked haunting and romantic, instead of merely depressing. I was willing to be devoured then, if it meant stepping into that same light. Benoit murmured something to Cate and she walked over to the sofa, smoothed out its cushion, and flicked away an invisible piece of dust. Then she tended to me, while Benoit began pacing back and forth, muttering something to himself, seemingly oblivious to my presence. Cate touched me all over, fingering the buttons on my shirt, adjusting the rolled-up cuff on one of the sleeves. Circling me, she bent low and peered at my ass, gently shifting the leather underwear around my right butt cheek. The outfit that humanity, *capital H*, wears.

Benoit ceased his pacing, finally, turned and saw me.

"Goll-lee!" he exclaimed. He came over and kissed me on both cheeks, ran a palm over my scalp, and I felt my stomach drop and then rush forward like a roller coaster. I was just so excited to have his adoration again. "Wow," he said, grinning. "Astonishing, really, almost uncanny, how close it is. Cate, I told you, did I not?"

Cate nodded.

"Cate, come feel her head, it is like velvet." His palm was warm and heavy against my naked scalp, and I felt a crick in my neck as I tried to hold my head as straight as possible.

"I've felt a shaved head before, Hans," Cate deadpanned.

"Divine." He slid his hand down the back of my neck, all the way to my ass.

"You like, my peach?"

"I love it," I said, trying to convince myself I did, that it was all okay. Cate and Benoit were *geniuses*, after all. What did I know? But something in my tone apparently did not satisfy Benoit.

"Be honest, peach," he pressed.

"Well the makeup—I was a little worried—"

"Nonsense, nonsense." He cut me off. "You look marvelous. Just right. Cate was a little skeptical at first. We were *so, so* close to booking—" He hesitated sourly over the words, "*someone else*, but you have proved my point beautifully." He cocked his head, as if I'd asked a question, and added, "That I can create anything, any*one* I want." But I was hardly listening, the words *someone else* having upended the floor beneath me, making me suddenly afraid. The casting that seemed so long ago, the one with Julio Ronaldo, swam into my head, and I thought about all those girls staring vacantly in that hallway, their images repeating ad infinitum on either side of them. I felt something sharpen inside of me, that instinct for survival. I could not go back to that place. I could not fuck this up.

"Totally," I said, trying to recover, forcing my smile as wide as it could go, and stumbling all over myself, telling him what a visionary he was, how grateful I was to be working with him. As if to emphasize the point, I brandished my phone. "Should we take a selfie?" I asked, still grinning.

"*Bien sûr.*"

He reached around my waist, and pulled me close. I held the phone away from us, tilting it slightly down, my best angle, and held down the Capture button so it would take a burst of images while I moved my head from side to side, smiling, pouting, looking at Benoit.

"We should get started," Kiki said from somewhere behind us, and Benoit broke away and patted me on the butt one last time.

"I am curious about the reaction," he said, nodding at my phone screen, and smiling mischievously. "No doubt there will be some shock, but shock is what we love, right?" Without waiting for a reply he continued, more gravely, "But, now dear, be clever about hiding my face."

He strode away and immediately the grin vanished from my face, and I bent over my phone and rushed to upload one of the images into Instagram.

"Mickey?" Kiki asked, clearly not pleased.

"Just one sec." My heart raced as I frantically cycled through filters, trying not to notice what was so glaringly obvious in the photo, telling myself it would look different under the professional lights.

"We really need to get going."

I opened up my keyboard and selected one of the classic happy-faced emojis. Then I spread my fingers wide, enlarging it to cover Benoit's head. *Guess who's shooting me today?* I added a winky face.

Kiki cleared her throat dramatically.

"Coming, coming," I said, trying not to feel too irritated as I dispatched the image to my Stories, even though I wasn't sure the filter was exactly right.

I slid the phone into my robe pocket, and Kiki took the robe off my shoulders with cold hands and hung it up on a rack in the hall. Then she led me over to the sofa, as if no one expected me to find it myself. Benoit dragged a stool over and sat, one leg tucked up on a rung, his face half-covered by the camera.

"What is humanity?" Benoit began, his tone suggesting that he'd prepared this little speech. "What does it mean to be human? Sit back now, lie, with your arm up like that, yes. Why do we venerate only the noble emotions? Are we our most human when we're at our best, or when we're at our worst?" Kiki stuck a light reader next to my face. The room exploded in flashes. "What about ugliness, death, decay, piss, and shit— those are the cornerstones of the human existence, or if not cornerstones, then integral . . . how do you call it . . . essential parts . . ." Benoit was distracted by something on his LCD touch screen. "Kiki, can you turn the light down—I want her to look really dark, tormented . . . impoverished."

Kiki made a few adjustments, held the light reader to my face again, more flashes. "Birth, death, love, suffering, sex, loss: the entire human experience, that's what we're after today. Nothing sanitized. Nothing left out. Everything: even the gross and the grotesque and the gritty." He started taking pictures. "Can you look a little more . . . bleak? Trauma, I want trauma, I want you to go there in your mind. Think of a time when you were powerless, abused, in pain . . ."

I must have partially blacked out, because when I opened my eyes, after what seemed like a blink, Benoit was gone and the flashes had stopped. I was lying on the floor, breasts exposed, and my face was wet with tears. Gingerly, I raised myself on bent elbows and saw Benoit and Cate studying the computer monitors. Cate said something I didn't quite catch and they both laughed.

"Mickey?" Kiki loomed over me, appearing from I don't know where. My headache had returned and I winced as she handed me a Styrofoam cup of water. "You did great," she said gently, a chastened look on her face. "Benoit's really happy."

"Thanks," I said, then drained the cup and gave it back to her.

She put a hand underneath my elbow and helped me stand. "Let's go for look two."

I tried to shake her off because I was sick of the infantilizing way she was suddenly talking to me, but I was wobbly on my feet and actually did need her to lean on. She helped me into the robe. I felt the familiar weight of my phone knock against my thigh and was instantly calmed and more myself. I opened up Instagram as she led me toward the wardrobe trailer.

Forty-two thousand new Views on the image I'd posted of Benoit and me. Dozens of Comments.

U look fucking sickkkk

So rad

Holy shit woulda never recognized you

Ummm guessing that's Benoit cuz I know his tats and also you guys are the perfect couple.

Couple goals.

Love goals.

Relief washed over me, swiftly turning into gratification. Any worry I'd had evaporated. I was loved. I was anointed. I imagined that the "someone else," whoever she was, seeing the photo, was seething with jealousy. Though my white check was still pending, I was more certain than ever that after this shoot—especially after this shoot, *especially* if it went viral like the last one—I'd be verified.

You didn't actually shave your head right? A text from my mother.

No, I wrote back. *It's not real. Don't worry.*

Below my mother's name in my Messages app a blue dot lay like a bomb beside Julia's name. I had ignored it earlier, but now, with new validation, I allowed it to detonate.

Get a life? That's funny coming from you considering you basically stole someone else's. You're such a fake it's crazy.

Andy helped me into a seat and began unlacing my boots. Immediately, I felt everything loosen, followed by a stinging pain as the blood flowed back into my calves, which looked as though they'd been crisscrossed in red marker.

"Oh god," Kiki said. "We can't shoot those for a while."

Are you seriously not going to respond? Julia had written again, almost an hour ago.

I know you're busy or whatever—

A notification slid down from the top of my screen, a text from my mother: *Phew! That would have been bad. Have fun! Love you, xo Mommy*

—getting famous, but it's just sad to me because if you stopped pretending for like, one second, you'd actually be a lot cooler. But you're so afraid of letting go of that control, you won't ever—

"Stand up for me, sweetie," Andy said, helping me to my feet and stripping the leather underwear from me in one fluid motion. I looked down at my bald vagina. "Can you jog up and down a bit?" Andy asked. "It'll help put the blood back into your legs."

So I jogged in place half-naked while he removed my robe and top, and then I jogged fully naked, my vagina lips flapping to my disgust, until he slid a shredded silk chiffon sheath over my head, and still I kept jogging, trying to fight the growing unease that had returned swiftly now that I had read Julia's message, now that I had tucked my phone away back in my robe pocket. I kept jogging all the way to set, up the creaking death trap of a staircase to one of the bedrooms on the second floor, where the overgrown black insects with their umbrella heads circled a bare mattress on the ground. The walls here had once been papered in a chintzy floral pattern that, as in the rest of the house, had been torn away to reveal planks of wood and plaster. It was even filthier than downstairs, and I coughed, inhaling a cloud of dust.

Kiki directed me to sit on the mattress so my back was against the wall. I flicked away a spider with the back of my hand. Benoit entered wordlessly, carrying a stool, and began setting up his shot. After the lighting had been sufficiently calibrated, Benoit settled in: he ran a tongue over his lips, cleared his throat, and began another diatribe while he started shooting, something about the cruelty of human nature and about how that's where the beauty really lies, in that capacity for cruelty, and I started to think about Gemma, and what had happened to her. Was she okay? She was probably okay. But if she wasn't . . . What duty did I have? What if her family was looking for her, worried sick, what if her brother—or wait, was it her sister? Didn't she have a twin? With a shudder of fear I realized I couldn't remember—couldn't picture their faces, didn't even know where they lived or where she had grown up. A cold sweat broke out along my neck. I could feel my body vibrating. It didn't make sense. How could I have forgotten? I became aware that Benoit had stopped taking photos.

"Okay," he said, standing up. "I think we're ready." I wasn't sure who he was talking to until I saw Kiki scurry out of the room. Benoit paced around the small space, drinking coffee. Kiki returned, carrying the Fisher-Price carrier like a purse in the crook of her arm. She set it down in one corner, well out of the shot, and began unbuckling the baby, who was looking around with wide, curious eyes. Cate appeared in the doorway with a filthy-looking canvas rag in her hands. Kiki pulled the baby's cap off, revealing a head of tight black curls, then unfastened its onesie and slipped off its socks. The baby fussed, whimpering gently.

"Shhh . . ." Kiki murmured.

She removed the baby's diaper and, in one quick motion, as if she wanted to handle the baby as little as possible, she lifted it naked from the carrier and passed it to Cate. The baby let out a plaintive wail as Cate wrapped it in the rag and advanced toward me. I cowered, pushing myself flatter against the wall behind me. I had never held a baby before.

Cate squatted near the bed and transferred the sniffling bundle to my arms. The baby quieted down in my arms and stared up at me with beseeching eyes, but as soon as it saw that I was not its mother, its face crumpled. It opened its mouth and began to cry even louder than before.

"What should I do?" I asked, almost screamed, looking up in obvious panic. I wondered where its parents were. I hadn't seen anyone who looked like they could be related. But maybe it was adopted; maybe it was Cate's, for all I knew. Or—I thought with a shudder—maybe you could rent out baby models, just like you could rent out girls like me.

Benoit shrugged comedically. "Don't look at me!"

Cate rolled her eyes. "It'll calm down, don't worry."

But it didn't look as though it would calm down. It was heavier and warmer than I expected, and its cry was surprisingly powerful.

"What's its name?" I stammered. "Maybe that'll help, if I call its name."

Cate laughed. "It's not a dog."

"I know," I muttered, shamefaced, as if my inability to comfort this poor child laid bare my myriad inadequacies as a model, as a woman, as a person.

"Go on, rock it," Cate said.

"Okay," Benoit said, clapping his hands together. "We can get started already? Yes?"

Cate and Kiki left the room, taking the carrier with them; I had already been told the rest of the day was to be a mostly closed set. "Benoit wants it to be really intimate," Kiki had said. I had no problem with closed sets, I might have actually preferred them, but the thought of being in a room alone with Benoit and the baby made me uneasy. I shook it gently in my arms, whispering for it to shush. The baby quieted slightly and I felt a rush of warm gratification.

"Look up here, please."

I stared up at the camera, cradling the baby closer to my chest. The flashes flickered rhythmically throughout the room. The baby whimpered. I wondered if the flashes were hurting its eyes—I glanced down at it—

"Up here!" Benoit shouted through gritted teeth.

"The flashes—are they okay—"

"No talking!"

I swallowed hard, trying to choke back my painful discomfort, as the baby stirred in my arms. The flashes continued.

"Can you be a bit looser with it?" Benoit asked, after some time. "See if you can get one of its arms out."

I reached into the bundle and found one chubby arm. Its sure, strong fingers clasped my thumb and held fast there, and something inside me tightened and seized. I tried to bring the hand out of the blanket but as soon as I pulled it, the baby started crying again.

"I don't think it wants to do that."

"It's a fucking baby," Benoit snapped. "It doesn't know what it wants."

"But—"

"Just do it."

I used my other hand to loosen the blanket, and gently moved the baby's arm. I could see its small chest—so smooth and soft—going up and down as it heaved sob after sob, and I couldn't believe that such a small vessel could contain all the vital organs, would grow into a man or a woman—I never did learn what its gender was—just like everyone else. Like me or Benoit, even. The thought pained me.

"Can you let go of its hand? Your arm's blocking the face."

I tugged my thumb out of its grip, and the baby—whose face showed the betrayal immediately, contorting as if cracked open—emitted a bloodcurdling scream. It was so small, so helpless, growing hotter in my arms—I was wrenched with a profound and sickening wave of guilt.

"Up here," Benoit snapped, and I dragged my eyes up toward the camera in time for another flash to wrack the room.

Gently, I tried to comfort the baby, rocking it from side to side and whispering for it to shush like I'd seen mothers do in TV shows, *shh, shh, it's okay.*

The baby kicked its feet and arched its back, pushing its head into my thigh as it let out another bloodcurdling scream.

"Please," I whimpered, but Benoit could not hear me over the metallic shudder of the flash, or maybe he just ignored me. "Please," I said again, and this time I was sure he was ignoring me.

"Jesus Christ, just put it down if you can't manage it."

"Put it down?"

"Yes, yes," Benoit snapped.

Reluctantly I leaned over and placed the baby on the bed. I was startled at how red its face had grown, blaring against the white of the mattress.

"Are you retarded?" Benoit screamed. "Not in the shot!"

I snatched the baby up quickly, instinctually.

"No—put it down!"

"Where?" I had to shout because of the baby's crying.

"Wherever!" He gestured impatiently at the floor, a few feet from the bed. "There!"

I stared at the spot, which was as filthy as the rest of the house. Tiny pieces that looked like wood chips were scattered about it. I cradled the baby closer to my chest. Its face was soft and wet. I could feel the hard-soft of its gums as it thrashed openmouthed against my skin. I wanted to run, to take the baby far away from here and never come back, but I knew I wouldn't do that. I couldn't fuck this up. The white check danced in my mind, even as terror rose inside me. Part of it was a visceral, bone-deep aversion, a feeling of *wrongness*, about placing the baby down on that floor, and the other part was the foreknowledge that I would do it anyway, I would do whatever Benoit asked.

Benoit sighed dramatically. "Please stop wasting my time."

I stood up slowly and carefully, a feeling of dread roiling my stomach, making me queasy. I squatted over the spot Benoit had gestured to; I could feel his eyes boring into my back, while the baby went on crying. As gently as I could I placed the baby on the ground. I tried to wrap the blanket around its small body, but it kept flinging it away and waving its little fists in the air as it wailed.

"Get back on your mark," Benoit said. "We've already lost too much light."

I got back onto the mattress, my body shaking, hot and cold at the same time. Where was the baby's mother? Why did they keep it so unsafe? Benoit was giving me directives but I couldn't concentrate; all my thoughts were drowned out by the plaintive insistence of the baby's wails. I pressed myself as hard as I could into the wall, as if I could disappear through it. The baby's sobs sounded almost violent now, as if it were being strangled, and I kept looking over to make sure it was okay, that it was still in the same spot—

"Kiki!"

Benoit had shouted it down the staircase. He was close to the door. I hadn't seen him get up.

"Kiki!" he screamed again.

Without the camera pinning me in place, I sprung up and scooped the baby into my arms and rocked it, did my TV-mom *shh shh* thing, only this time it didn't feel scripted, it felt real in a way I hadn't experienced in a long time. The baby started quieting down, and I wondered what it was thinking. I thought about how I could have been anyone to this baby—it didn't matter, I was a pair of arms that was comforting it, and that was enough. That was all there was. I thought about how this baby looked like a lot of other babies, but that there was something about it, even at such a young age, something ineffable that made it only itself.

Kiki appeared breathless in the doorway a moment later. Benoit nodded at me, and she pursed her lips in displeasure. Without a word, she strode over to me and slid her hand between my arm and the baby's back and lifted it out of my arms, and a devastating wrench twisted my insides as the baby's scream pierced the room.

"Get it out of here," said Benoit, pressing a hand to his ear, and I watched Kiki walk briskly out of the room and saw her shiny, black-haired head descend the staircase. The baby never stopped crying; its cries only grew fainter and more faraway. A lump rose in my throat. I felt Benoit turn to me, glaring, but I could not bring myself to meet his eyes. I kept looking at the empty stairway.

"Look at me," Benoit finally said.

I turned. His face was burning with such disgust, I shuddered.

"What the fuck was that about?"

My entire body went numb. I opened my mouth to speak but no words came out.

Benoit laughed unpleasantly, hands on his hips, shaking his head as if he couldn't *believe* what was happening, what *I* was putting him through. "You know, you girls are all the same," he began, fixing me with hard eyes. "I give you opportunity and you respond with shenanigans. The games. You have no idea how many girls, almost exactly like you, I've seen before. And you wanna know where they are?"

I swallowed. A face, *her* face, swam before me—the overlarge eyes, the soft blond curls, everything so familiar to me and yet somehow elusive. As quickly as it had appeared, it was gone, and all that was left was my body vibrating with longing. *Yes!* I wanted to know. Where was she? *Tell me!* I shouted, only it was just inside my head. On the outside, my head jerked back and forth in a nod.

"Nowhere!" Benoit took a moment to relish the word. Then he jabbed a finger at me. "They are nowhere because they try to pull something like this on me." It was almost an admission. He was talking about *her*, I knew it. I imagined her in my place, and my stomach flipped. Of course he had done it—whatever *it* was.

"Is that what—" I started to say and then froze. My mouth went dry, bile climbing up the back of my throat. I could not remember her name.

"What *what*?"

"Your ex—" I said in a rush, unable to recall the Bulgarian term either. "Nice friend? Lady friend? You know what I mean."

He gave me a strange look, and I searched my mind desperately, but it was as if a white screen had descended, an oppressive blankness

I could neither see through nor grasp, everything just sliding, down, down, down when I hit against it.

"What is her name?" I almost shouted it.

He flung my hands away—the hands I had raised without realizing, the hands that trembled in anticipation, as if I could pull the answer from him—and growled in disgust.

"Jesus, have you gone mad?" he shouted, but I was too busy blindly probing that white screen, hitting upon its emptiness again and again and again, to respond.

"Okay, this is too much," he said, the corners of his mouth twitching in anger, his hands flying up. I thought he was going to hit me. Instead, he pinched the bridge of his nose and closed his eyes, took one deep breath, slipped his aviators from his jacket pocket, and put them on. It felt like that was his true self: nothing but cold mirrors for eyes. "I am going to go downstairs for a coffee," he said, enacting a stern dad voice. "And when I come back, you better have gotten your shit together."

I nodded.

He stared at me, or I thought he was staring at me, since all I could see was the reflection of the room in his glasses, one long streak of light. "You know, without me you'd be nobody," he said finally. "I want you to think on that. *Nobody*."

The word reverberated through my body as he left the room, and I listened to the staircase scream with each step of his descent. *Nobody*.

Blindly, instinctually, my hands sought out my phone in the pocket of my robe, which was hung over a chair in the corner. I clicked on Instagram, in search of soothing metrics, red bubbles, numbers that kept going up, the indisputable reassurance that I was who I thought I was. Or, if not that exactly, that I was at least *someone*. Someone who was Liked. The screen opened up into a colorful vista, someone's sunset or colonoscopy, I didn't know—I only saw the numbers at the bottom of the screen as my thumb alighted on that black heart, making it shudder and reveal its contents: 70K new Views, 175 new Followers, 1,225 Comments.

I slid my thumb over the screen, watching the names fly up and disappear and new ones appear. It was more than I had imagined, more than I had dreamed of. A thrill ran through me, pure excitement. I could feel myself grinning as I began to read the Comments that had flooded in. At first, I didn't notice what the Comments were saying; I was only scanning and registering them as they slid up my screen. But then the familiar shape and size of a certain word began to appear with such frequency that eventually its meaning connected itself to the form.

CANCEL
Cancel this B
Um, ok. CANCELED
CANCEL
CANCEL
CANCEL

My stomach lurched.

No, no, no, I thought frantically. There had to be some mistake, a misunderstanding. Cate and Benoit were *geniuses*, this was fucking *JOY Magazine*, what was wrong with everybody, why were they being like this—

Blackface in 2019 r u fucking serious?

How could they say that? I was just *really, really tanned*. Wasn't I? Wasn't that what Kim had said? I could make them understand, I could make them see—

She is literally ripping Karma Black wow

My hands trembled with rage. It wasn't my fault! I was just doing what I was told, I was just doing what the market wanted! How could they be so stupid, overly sensitive, naive—

So sick of fashion brands co-opting black culture to sell expensive shit.
Disgusting example of a long history of appropriation
@KarmaIsaBitch: Um, wtf is this.

She had also reposted the image of me to her own Stories with a long caption. I felt the ground give way, the tide rushing in.

This is so deeply disturbing to me, Karma's caption began. *This photographer @HansBenoit asked to shoot me. I said sure, and asked how much he'd pay me. He said it would be FOR FREE. Well, I was not about to get down with that slave fuckery. So I said no. Next thing, he's hired a WHITE MODEL and made her look like me??*

I was still constructing counterarguments in my head, pleading for leniency with some unseen God. The problem was that even back then, lost as I was in the morass of narcissism and self-delusion, I knew deep down they were right, though it would still be some time before I fully understood. Even though it hadn't been my decision, even though I was just doing what I was told, I can see now how self-serving my willful ignorance had been, my lack of thoughtfulness. It was the same complicit ignorance that had allowed my mother and me to luxuriate in the proceeds of my father's shady doings, the same deadly carelessness with which I had gotten into that car blackout and killed my neighbor's dog all those years ago. I wish I could say that I would have realized this on my own, even if what happened hadn't happened. I've tried to make peace with this personal failing. My therapist says that while, on the one hand, it's true I chose to be ignorant, it's also true I was raised to it. Men like my father and Benoit—men I thought I needed to survive—encouraged it, fostered it, wouldn't tolerate anything else. In the moment, though, all I could feel was desolation—that I'd been caught, that I'd *let* myself be caught.

My phone screen lit up in my hand with another notification, another blistering comment pleading for cancellation, for the termination of my existence. I had always done what my Followers wanted and now would not be different. Hands shaking, I went to my Instagram profile settings, searching for an exit, a gun, a way to disappear. My frantic eyes could not navigate it—or maybe the app had made it deliberately difficult to delete the account. I opened up my web browser and, heart racing, googled *delete Instagram account*, typing so fast it was as if my fingers were moving independently from my brain. I found the right link, I logged in. *Are you sure you want to permanently delete your account?* A brief, shuddering moment, and then I clicked Yes, my stomach free-falling into emptiness.

She had also deleted her account. *She* had also disappeared.

I pressed my fingers against my skull, hitting it over and over, as if I could knock it into some clarity. I knew now that she had been discarded, forgotten as if she had never existed at all, and then replaced. And I—I had helped it along, destroying her even as I poured myself into her mold, believing it would bring me power, never realizing that the mold was itself inconstant. I would never find solid form if I always sought relevancy; that wasn't what Benoit and his ilk wanted, they wanted me to remain malleable, pliable, a *nobody*, so they could shape me into whatever role suited them. I had betrayed her for nothing, and now I was being betrayed in turn. *Her, her, her.* I still couldn't remember her name, *why couldn't I remember her name?* I beat my palms against my forehead. I didn't remember her name, but she haunted me. I didn't remember her name but I saw her—I saw her clearly, and suddenly she was standing under a red sky at the pier with Benoit beside her, and of course, it was Benoit. Benoit was responsible. He must have done something. Benoit pushed her—or no, *I* had pushed her, or—

I remembered what Benoit had said about the shoot. How he had laughed about "outrage." How he had said he wanted to shock people. Anger seethed inside of me. I felt suddenly cold and sober. I wandered over to where Benoit had left one of his cameras on the stool. I picked it up. It was surprisingly heavy, and I hefted it in my hand. I tilted it up and looked into its insect eye, peered at a tiny version of myself that stared back out of a long tunnel. I ran my thumb over the hard metal rim of the lens.

"What're you doing?"

I turned to see Benoit standing in the doorway. His face was unreadable behind his aviators, but his voice was irritated. I froze.

"Put that down!" he snapped.

I swallowed and took three steps back, sidestepping the mattress on the floor.

"You knew," I said, surprised by the solidity of my voice. "You knew what would happen."

Confusion, then rage, rippled over Benoit's face. "What the fuck!" he screamed.

"Is that what you did to her too? Did you drive her to—"

"Who?"

"Her!" I spluttered. "The girl . . . the one who . . . *her*!"

Benoit took a few steps forward, and I retreated in tandem until my back was against the wall.

"Give that to me *now*," he said, holding his hand out for the camera.

"I just want to know her name!" I was sobbing now. "Just tell me her name!"

Benoit lunged for the camera and I moved it behind my back, holding it tightly in my right hand. His face contorted into rage, as familiar to me as my father's, as he tried to wrench me from the wall, only to push me back into it—hard.

I could feel his hot breath on my neck now, see his gray spittle, something beginning to tick inside me as he used his forearm to press me against the wall. He was so enraged he'd forgotten all about the camera, and I let it hang by my side, pressing it into my thigh.

"You disgust me," he said. He moved his forearm so that it was against my neck, and continued to press, choking me.

"Tell me," I said again, my face wet. "Please." The *please* came out a whisper. The ticking was so loud now it drowned everything out. Pain shot through my ears. Everything was too loud, too close.

Benoit laughed. "What're you going to do, huh?" *Tick, tick.* "You think you can do *anything*? You are nothing, you understand?" *Tick, tick.* "And you'll be nothing—" My head hurt with all the ticking, I felt sick, I wanted to make it stop, needed to make it stop—

I didn't even realize I had swung the camera around until I felt it connect—hard—with the back of Benoit's head, sending a ripple up my arm. He fell forward and I pushed him away. He staggered back, tripped over the side of the mattress, spun around, then crumpled to the floor, landing with a thud. I only hesitated a moment. Then, positioning myself over his body, I brought the camera down again, and again, and again.

The rest is a blur.

I remember walking quickly and quietly down the rickety stairs, wild-eyed and covered in blood. No one seemed to notice anything was amiss. Leone, who was on her phone in the hallway, glanced up at me and nodded. I looked around for the baby, who I had been sure was close, had to be in the house, but he or she was nowhere to be found. I forced myself to walk down the brownstone stairs calmly, taking measured steps, past craft services, past the trailers, but there was nothing to worry about. Everyone on the crew was bored, waiting, either hiding out in a trailer or stooped over their phones.

I'm not sure how long I wandered around after that. I was barefoot, covered in silt and bits of Benoit's blood. No one on the street seemed to notice either. A man told me to smile. Another called me G.I. Jane. I hummed myself something that I didn't even recognize. Up ahead, I saw a green oasis and walked mindlessly toward it. Benoit would not be found for another hour.

The girl runs a hand over her buzz cut, a sly smile on her face. There is an artful smudge of dirt across her cheek. She is looking directly at the camera, and in her pupils the white space around the phone is reflected. She touches the dirt on her cheek and winks. "Oh, the glamour of fashion," she says. Behind her, trees blow in the wind.

The girl sits on the edge of a fountain, Bailey Fountain, according to her caption. A thick white spray of water shoots out behind her and lightly caresses the bronze bodies of Wisdom and Felicity. Mist falls on the girl's face, and she half closes her eyes and tilts her head back, as if in ecstasy. Then, with some difficulty because it is difficult to balance with her hand still holding the phone, she bends forward and splashes water all over her face.

"I'm really obsessed with being clean," she says. "If I have stuff on my skin for too long it drives me nuts. Obviously, in my line of work it happens, so I always keep a pack of these in my purse to use on the go."

With that, she uses the sleeve of her bathrobe to scrub at her skin. When she looks back up at the camera, her lashes still wet, she is mottled: her face is pale and white, while her neck and temples remain dark. She is smiling wide. Then, apparently having just noticed the nose ring still in her nostril, she extracts it with a thumb and forefinger and flicks it easily away.

Now she is dancing in the fountain, tilting her head back as the streams of water cross behind her, just barely misting her still-wet face and body. Her feet, bare and pale, hop and splash in the shallow water. She is singing something, but it is difficult to pick out what it is.

The girl lies sprawled out on the grass, basking in the sun, one hand tented over her eyes, one of which is squinting.

"I think true beauty is about being real," she says. "Authenticity. That's the most beautiful thing in the world to me."

A no-nonsense marquee advertising pancakes, eggs, and free refills beckons from a diner across the street, tucked between a hardware store and a dry cleaner's. The camera flips: the girl is walking, a little out of breath, in the direction of the diner. She makes a show of looking at her wrist, which is naked.

"It's never too late for breakfast," she says.
She pushes through the glass door of the diner.

In front of me was more food than I'd eaten in months. I'd ordered the Lumberjack Special: two pancakes, a pair of sunny-side up eggs (yellow eyes staring up at me), home fries, sausage, and a vomit of beans. I ate the pancakes first, not even bothering to cut them up into small pieces like I normally would, but just shoveling them in almost whole with my fork, until I tired of my fork and began using my hands. By the time I got to the sausage, my hands were coated in grease and there were pieces of egg stuck to my chin. Sweat beaded my brow. I was becoming short of breath. I drank a tall glass of water and ordered more pancakes. The waitress—stern, Eastern European expression, matter-of-fact, braid down her back—was too busy or dulled by the city's absurdness to notice anything amiss.

I liked the diner. It was cozy. The dingy windows gave everything an indistinct gossamer glow, and it smelled like the inside of our childhood Suburban after a long drive to our cottage: a smell of stagnation, restlessness, inevitability. I used to think about how we were transporting air on those trips, trapping it and then releasing it only hours later, when the trip was over, we all got out, and something else in my life had ended. I never slept on those trips even though my mother said that when I was a baby, the only way she could get me to quiet down was to strap me into a car seat and drive around. But that was before, when it was enough to know I was in motion, and I didn't have to think about where I was going.

Round two of the pancakes arrived and I poured more syrup than was warranted onto them. Once I'd finished, I dipped my fingers in the syrup and licked it off. I ran my tongue along the circumference of the plate.

Now it was growing dark out. I waved over the waitress and, feeling entirely sick with myself, ordered another stack of pancakes and a large jug of water. This time, she did eye me, slightly unpleasantly. I realized I was beginning to smell. She disappeared into the kitchen, and I looked forlornly out the window. It was then that I saw her, walking purpose-fully down the street in yoga pants and a tank top, a Whole Foods bag swinging at her hip, and at the sight of her dear face, a spark flew inside my chest, and I remembered her name. *Gemma.* Gemma! How could I have forgotten? My face was streaming with tears of joy as I ran out into the street in just enough time to see her round the corner up ahead and disappear out of sight. I took off at a run. But when I turned the corner, she was not there.

"Gemma?" I called out. "Gemma, is that you?"

A hand landed on my shoulder, and suddenly I was back in the diner. It was well into the night, and an average-looking man was stooped over my table, peering into my face.

I frowned, waiting for him to say something moronic, to tell me to smile, but he only asked me what my name was. I was in such a state of confusion that I couldn't think what to say. I looked at my hands, which were trembling and covered in syrup, filth, blood. It was very quiet. The waitress, *my* waitress, stood a ways off, an anxious look on her face.

"Are you Michaela Jones?" he asked gently. "Michaela Jones, née Heffernan?"

I did not want to answer the man—in fact, I had no intention of saying anything—but the sound of my name provoked a strange reaction (I thought I heard something breaking) and I started to sob. The man nodded slowly and sadly as if he understood all, and for one delirious moment I thought I'd finally found a trusted confidant, that he'd take me with him to his two-story home on Staten Island to live a normal, mundane life and all would really be well—and then I saw the two offi-cers, summoned by some invisible signal of his, enter through the diner's swinging front door, dressed smartly in their matching navy and match-ing badges and matching stern, implacable expressions, and soon I was being lifted; professional, tender hands caressed the recesses of my being and then I was guided, flanked by two pairs of strong arms, out the door.

EPILOGUE

They had me plead temporary insanity. I kept telling them I wasn't insane, that I'd meant to do it. I was *glad* I did it and would have done it again if I could. But nobody listened. They just patted me on the head, told me I was a *good girl* and didn't mean what I was saying.

"You're lucky he didn't die," Saul said. "Now shush."

He had stepped in as my lawyer almost immediately after I got arrested—we Heffernans are a real family business for him. I remember seeing his shiny bald head as he waited for me in the visitor's room at the Brooklyn city jail ahead of my arraignment. He had a thick moustache and black eyebrows, and the top of his head looked exactly like an egg in an eggcup, ringed as it was with that coarse salt-and-pepper hair of his. I tried to fire him. But he just laughed, said, "I don't work for you, I work for your father—you'll have to talk to him, he's the one paying my bills." Then his face went all soft and he inched his hand closer to mine, though not touching me since that's verboten in the visitor's room, and he shook his head sadly. "You poor girl."

I was too exhausted to fight it. They'd kept me up all night in an interrogation room, asking me why I'd done it: *What did he do to you? He obviously did something to you. If you'd like us to call in a female officer . . . If there was assault, we'd have to administer a rape test . . .* All I wanted to do was drink the ice-cold Cokes they kept bringing in at my request, and relish the feeling of sugar coating my teeth, the taste of needless calories. I had the strange thought that maybe it had all been worth it just so I could get to drink a fucking Coke again in peace. In prison, where I assumed I'd be living for the indefinite future, nobody'd care if I got fat.

They brought up that rape thing again and I looked at them for a long time, then opened my mouth and let a burp roil through me and blare in their concerned faces.

"I need another Coke," I said, after we'd all recovered—them from disgust, me from laughter.

"That's the sixth one you've had already." This from the patient cop, the one I'd thought might take me to Staten Island one day.

"I can't think without a Coke." I enunciated every word slowly and exactly.

"You're going to have to tell us something if you want another Coke," the other cop said.

"What led up to the attack?" the nice cop asked gently. "Did he do something to you? You can tell us."

"It wasn't what he did to me," I said finally. "It was to someone else."

"Who?"

I put the empty Coke can to my lips and tipped my head all the way back. The ceiling was made of those god-awful papery tiles. I almost felt bad for the detectives that they had to sit under it all day. A drop of cold sweetness hit my tongue, but only a drop. I sat back upright and put the Coke can on the table, resigned.

"Gemma," I said. "Gemma Anton."

After I got my next Coke, I told them everything—well, most of it. About Gemma and Benoit and how Gemma had gone missing suddenly, and I was pretty sure Benoit had something to do with it and—*no, I only met Gemma once.* And—*no, I don't know any of her friends or family* or *have any "evidence," but I did know her, I knew her better than anyone, perhaps. I'd been following her for years.* The officers nodded vigorously and made quick jabs with their pens on their notepads—only toward the end I started noticing they weren't taking nearly as many notes, and their nods had taken on an apprehensive quality and they kept sneaking little looks at each other like, *Are you getting this?*

"How'd you come up with that bit about the other girl—the doppelgänger?" Saul asked me before the arraignment. "Absolutely brilliant."

The judge released me on my own recognizance, pending trial, with the condition that I undergo psychiatric evaluation and treatment at a mental health facility. They sent me to a place up in Westchester, where they pumped me full of lithium and confined me to my room for most of each day. I tried to explain to them about Gemma, but all the nurses would do was smile real nice and say they understood and *don't worry, it'll get easier.* Only one of the other patients ever believed me, an elderly lady who'd been there I don't know how long and who everyone called Minnie, even though she introduced herself to me as Dolores. I tried to get Minnie to search for Gemma during Internet Free Time, since I wasn't yet allowed to use any devices, but she couldn't get past the Safari welcome page. She'd just keep clicking on the Yahoo! logo ("Sounds fun!") and open up a million new windows, trying to get back to the welcome page.

My mother came to visit me on the weekends. Dad said he couldn't stomach being back in a state facility, and really, I didn't blame him. I knew at least part of the reason he wouldn't come to visit was that I hadn't visited him in jail, and I understood that, too, petty as it was. Yes, we were alike; there was no denying it any longer.

"Sometimes I just wonder why this is happening to me," my mother lamented one Sunday. "I mean, obviously it has to be somewhat my fault. No, no"—she waved away my protest—"I have to take responsibility for my role here."

"You didn't do anything," I said. "It has nothing to do with you."

Her head bobbled back and forth on her neck. "Everyone knows that a child is just a reflection of the mother. It always goes back to the mother. That's what everyone says."

It just about killed my mother—not so much my arrest, although she was obviously upset about that, too, but the publicity that surrounded it.

"I'll just never understand it," she had said. "I mean, I'd get it a little bit more if it were, I don't know, one of those creeps who sleeps in alleys—"

"A homeless person, you mean?"

"Sure—or whatever. But *this* guy? I mean, you know, when I was a beauty queen, some of the judges—they took certain liberties. You didn't *like* it, but you didn't *bash their head in* about it."

"You're right," I'd said. "You'll never understand."

But I did have some sympathy for her. She'd been fielding calls from reporters almost since the day it happened. I was now the "Fashion Killer," and my father the "Crooked Daddy Warbucks." At least I knew she was secretly pleased when the press dug up a photo from her pageant days and dubbed her the "Tragic Beauty Queen Mom." Still, she could forget about ever going back to Neiman's again.

"And after your father, I thought we were finally—" That Sunday she dissolved into tears before she could finish the sentence, taking a shredded Kleenex from the jacket of her tweed blazer (Sandro, but an obvious nod to Chanel, just purchased) and pressing it to her eyes. It came away spotted with black. I'd meant to reach out to her, put a hand on her shoulder, but the lithium made me slow—they always gave me higher doses on visiting day—and by the time I realized I hadn't done or said anything, she was already getting up to go and it was too late.

After about a month in there, I decided I'd had enough. Even though the court-appointed psychologist said I was making fantastic progress and we were finally getting to the bottom of some of the trauma I experienced as a child, I couldn't stand the food, and I hated the pale-blue smocks they made us wear over our own clothes, and I had none of my good underwear there, just a bunch of cotton briefs my mom had bought at the Gap for me.

"What do I have to do?" I asked Saul during our twice-weekly tactical phone call.

"They're not going to release you until they think you're mentally fit to care for yourself and stand trial."

I looked out through the shatterproof glass and made eye contact with the nurse, who was sitting behind a desk, monitoring me. Regular personal calls were made from the pay phone in the hall, but calls with lawyers took place in this small, soundproof room, more of a closet, with an entirely glass wall. I felt like I was in an aquarium. Actually, it reminded me of the room I'd had my fitting in for that doomed *JOY* shoot. Behind the nurse there was a large photo of the Grand Canyon. It was part of a theme—scattered throughout the facility were framed photos of the natural wonders of the world. I wondered if they'd hired an art consultant to come up with that, or if Staples just had a sale one day on nature landscape photos.

"How do I convince them I'm mentally fit?" I asked, though I was pretty sure I already knew the answer.

"Quit it with the Jenna stuff." It was golden hour in the photo of the Grand Canyon, the best light, turning the river at the bottom into a silvery snake and the tips of the uppermost rocks amber. This was not the first time Saul had instructed me to stop talking about Gemma. "After some time, tell them you're beginning to think she was a delusion."

A few weeks later, at my exit interview, the psychiatrist asked if I was still concerned for Gemma's safety.

"No," I said, repeating what I had already told the nurses and the psychologist. "Because I no longer believe she was a real person."

The psychiatrist nodded and made a mark on her notepad.

"So you have no intention of trying to look for her?"

I shook my head. "No. She doesn't exist. She was probably a composite of a handful of young women I was fixated on."

Another nod, another approving mark on the notepad.

I was released the next day.

I spent the next few months preparing for trial, living with my mother under house arrest at Auntie Joey's apartment. My father was in Chicago, crashing in an empty house his developer buddy was trying to sell and reconnecting with his old associates. Some of them still wanted nothing to do with him, but others were apparently convinced enough by his verdict of "innocence," or were able to look past it all for the promise of a quick buck. Maybe some of them felt bad for him, what with his own ordeal having been followed so closely by his daughter's shameful fall from grace. I didn't really know. My mother didn't ask any questions when it came to his business, preferring not to know for legal reasons, but also because I don't think she really cared, so long as money was coming in. Though neither of them would admit it, I think they'd both realized during my father's incarceration that they got along a lot better the less time they actually spent together. Saul visited at least once a week, and often stayed for dinner. Other than that, and the occasional brief phone call from my dad, I spoke to and saw no one. It wasn't intentional at first. I just didn't remember anyone's number without my phone. And without my phone—or Instagram—they had no way of contacting me either. Julia, Blake, Joe . . . I realized I knew very little about them beyond what they liked to drink and the brands they wore. I imagined they were still going out every night, to the same places with the same people. It all felt very far away.

Looking back, these were probably some of the most peaceful and stable weeks of my life. My mother and I fell into a rhythm. We did Pilates together in the morning and played cards and watched *Jeopardy* at night. During the day, my mom would go out to run errands or to "do emails" at a Starbucks, since, for whatever reason, she took very seriously the psychologist's recommendation that I not have access to the Internet or social media right away. I guess she was concerned about how I'd react to everything they were saying about me, since it was all so disturbing for her. She always made a big show about locking her laptop away in the closet whenever she came home. But it was an unnecessary precaution. A strange thing happened during those weeks: I hardly thought about the Internet, or cared if people were thinking of me. It might have been the antidepressants they'd put me on. Or it could have been that I was reading again (I'd started *Anna Karenina* and couldn't put it down). Then again, I suspect it was largely because I'd given up. Even if I somehow managed to escape jail time—which looked doubtful—my future was over. I would probably wind up working the cash register somewhere shitty that didn't mind hiring felons for the tax breaks. I'd get fat and probably wouldn't even bother with what I wore or how I looked. Who cared about going online if you didn't even have a presence? If no one even Liked anything you did?

You'd think this realization would have depressed me, but strangely it had a freeing effect. I went on long, solitary walks, circling the five-block radius that did not violate my release order. For the first time since I was very little, I appreciated the fall foliage. When I finished *Anna Karenina*, I started on *War and Peace*, working my way through all of Tolstoy. I slept better than ever. One morning in late December, I woke while it was still dark out and padded to the kitchen to make a pot of coffee while my mother continued to sleep. The kitchen opened out into the living room, which had a small balcony off it. Pigeons often congregated on the railing, but that morning, I clocked a much larger bird through my morning blear. It was white and stocky, with black stippling along its feathers. My heart started beating fast. I walked slowly and cautiously into the living room to get a better look. I became aware that two large yellow eyes were looking at me, so suddenly that it was as if the bird had grown them in the back of its head. It was an owl and it was beautiful. We looked at each other for what felt like a long time. Then, without a hint of forethought, it spread its impressive wings and took off. I felt as though I'd just been given a key to the universe. I went back to the kitchen and finished making coffee, feeling a profound sense of well-being.

A month before the trial began, the fan mail started arriving. Someone had figured out my address and posted it on Reddit. There were homemade signs and postcards, sympathy cards, and long letters. Apparently, I'd become a cause célèbre, half counterculture hero, half circus-freak oddity. I realized the extent to which the case had been covered in the press. Suddenly, it made a lot more sense why Saul had appeared to be going the extra mile on my case.

Give the patriarchy the finger! the cards read.

Mickey, we're with you!

Don't lose hope!

We stan you forever!

We believe Mickey

Believe Mickey

Often my fans included the hashtag #FreeMickey, as if they'd forgotten you couldn't click on the page and be redirected to an entire thread. No one talked about me being canceled. I don't know if it was because they didn't care, or because they didn't remember. Karma had deleted her account—she'd gone on to become a painter, quite a talented one, and was notoriously reclusive and press-shy—so it's possible there was no record of it. But more likely there was a screenshot of it, or many screenshots, saved somewhere on the Internet—but, though the Internet is endless, our memory and attention spans are embarrassingly finite.

My mother and Saul were thrilled. Apparently the tabloids had been putting me through the wringer, and since neither of them really understood social media, they'd missed the strange birth of a small but ardent fan base. My mother liked to go through the mail with me and set aside her favorite cards. I was far more dispassionate. It all felt so impersonal, even though it was about me. That's how fame works—it's like love without the personal connection. Since fame means having a bunch of people love you without ever knowing you, being known is therefore antithetical to it. You are only adored where you are absent, in a permanent form of dissociation, like what I used to do at casting calls—becoming a body only, becoming a shell. And yet, even still, I didn't want the cards to stop.

Often, the cards included a photo, usually from the first shoot I'd done with Benoit: in it, my eyebrows have been bleached and my hair curled, only it's in black and white and looks like a mug shot from an old-timey newspaper. Meanwhile, in real life, my hair had grown into an awkward bowl cut the color of dishwater. My eyebrows, which I'd neglected to pluck since my arrest, were dark and bushy. I looked nothing like the woman in the pictures.

"We're going to have to do something about that," Saul said one day a few weeks before trial, as he sat at the small dining table in the living room, drinking tea.

"What do you mean?" I was lying on the couch, pulling one side of my sweatpants drawstring and then the other, creating a kind of pleasant rhythm.

"We want you to appear consistent, stable," he said. "What happened that day in question was an aberration, an unfortunate consequence of tremendous mental stress, which led to temporary insanity—"

"Yes, yes, I know, I went nuts," I said, rolling my eyes.

"In the public's mind, this is what you look like," he continued, ignoring me and holding up a recent card, another close-up from the first Benoit shoot, in which I'm staring wide-eyed at the camera, mouth slightly parted, like a deer in headlights. "We want to stay closely associated with this image. Otherwise you look inconsistent, and that makes you seem erratic and untrustworthy."

Saul knew his stuff. He'd met with an image consultant earlier that week to discuss my presentation during trial. He reached into a paper bag I hadn't noticed him bring in and extracted a Styrofoam head wearing a blond wig, and set it on the table in front of him. I shuddered.

"Lori"—that was the image consultant—"told me this is top quality, from a wig supplier she's worked with in the past and had great experiences with. Made from real human hair."

My mother walked in carrying a load of laundry at that moment and saw the head, with its soft shoulder-length blond curls, sitting on the table. She nodded—clearly Saul had already discussed this with her—and put the laundry basket down in the hall.

"Should we try it on, sweetheart?"

Mom used bobby pins to pin my hair out of my face and then fitted the mesh cap that came with the wig over it. She tented her fingers inside the wig—where my skull would go—so it would keep its shape as she carried it over to me. But she couldn't get it to sit right on my head.

I sighed. "Let me try."

I went to the bathroom mirror and pulled the wig down, a little bit to the right, and tucked in some stray hairs.

"There," I said. I looked good, better than I'd looked in months. I felt something squirm inside, like a worm coming to life again, something repulsive but oddly compelling.

Saul brought over the card with my face on it, the old face, and put it next to mine in the mirror.

"Perfect," he said.

"Perfect," my mother echoed.

That night we plucked and bleached my eyebrows.

Trial began in mid-February. On the first day, I wore a navy cashmere turtleneck and cream wool trousers with brown faux-croc boots. I walked in holding the hands of both my mother and father, who flanked me on each side, another suggestion by Lori. "We want her to look supported," she'd said. Also, the presence of my mother and father highlighted my youth. I had only just turned twenty. Outside the courtroom were a dozen or so protestors holding signs, many of which said *Free Mickey* on pink bristol board. My favorite read *Guilty of Fucking the Patriarchy, Innocent of Everything Else.* A few people came dressed as me, in curly blond wigs and long white dresses like the one I'd worn when I showed up at Gemma's apartment that night in the rain. A thrill went through me, and the worm burrowed deeper inside, so that I couldn't help but smile a little even though the fact that I was happier than I'd been since this whole thing started terrified me.

In their opening statements, the prosecution argued that though I was narcissistic and disturbed, I was hardly insane—not by a long shot. In fact, throughout my relationship with Benoit, I'd exhibited a level of cunning and manipulation that revealed a well-ordered, if mal-intended, mind. The insanity plea was further evidence of my shrewdness; after I'd been arrested, I'd cobbled together a story about a woman who didn't exist. It wasn't until the fifth hour of my interrogation that I had even mentioned this so-called Gemma. The prosecution conceded that Benoit and I had had a sexual relationship, but they asserted it had been brief, consensual, and conducted outside of working hours. Benoit was an eccentric, true, but of the sensitive-artist ilk. If he had trouble negotiating workplace boundaries, it was only because he felt things so deeply, was too easily swayed by emotion and what other people wanted from him. He had always been a big supporter of women's rights—he'd even once shot the portraits for a domestic abuse PSA! For free! Even if what happened between Benoit and me constituted workplace harassment, it certainly did not give me license to viciously maim him, leaving him blind in one eye and unable to walk without a limp for the rest of his life—and that was only because he'd gotten lucky. He could have died. According to the prosecution, I'd tried to kill him that day not because of some imaginary woman but because he wasn't giving me enough attention. And I was pissed about my haircut.

Their argument might have gone over better had Benoit not been such a shitty witness. Twice on the stand he seemed to have forgotten my name. He insisted on wearing his damn aviators, claiming that because of his injuries, his eyes were extra sensitive to light. Though you could just make out a thin scar that ran down one side of his face, and though I could sense a certain frailness to his bearing, he looked perfectly normal otherwise. He'd started off hoarsely, seeming almost embarrassed, but when he'd been talking for long enough, his old bravado and cockiness snuck back in. I'd had moments, before the trial, when I'd felt bad for him. I'd imagined him taking the stand with a cane and a bandaged eye. But nothing had changed for him; actually, he was setting up for a solo gallery show in Berlin in a matter of weeks. His eyes still gave nothing, but were only shiny, implacable mirrors. Any pity I'd had melted away.

"She begged me," he said, recounting our first sexual encounter. "She said she loved me as an artist. I was naive. I believed it."

"And now?" the prosecutor asked.

"Now I understand that she was just using me to get ahead in her career."

I knocked Saul's thigh under the defense table when Benoit said that. Saul leaned his head close, keeping his eyes on the stand, so I could whisper in his ear: "That's complete bullshit! He was the one with all the power! At the very most, we were both using each other!"

Saul nodded and moved his head away from me. I had wanted him to nail Benoit for that comment during cross-examination, but he mostly tried to avoid the topic. "Since we can't one hundred percent prove it was rape, it's best we don't bring it up," he'd explained.

"It *was* consensual the one time, but the other—I mean, I had bruises."

"That's too confusing for the jury to understand. Juries' minds are binary—either you consented to sex or you didn't, it can't be both at different times."

Instead, Saul focused on my fractured mental state. He argued that despite my obvious psychological distress, Benoit ignored the signs and took advantage of my vulnerability to get me to agree to a perilous shoot in a dilapidated building that had not been permitted properly.

"Did she ever mention this Gemma to you?"

Benoit shifted uncomfortably in his seat. "She had, yes," he said.

"What did she say about her?"

"I don't remember."

"Did she call her your ex-girlfriend?"

"I believe she did, yes."

"So you do remember." Saul flashed a small, ironic smile at the jury. "And was that true? Did you ever know a Gemma?"

He sighed. "I mean, I meet a lot of people."

"But did you ever date a model named Gemma?"

I saw Benoit hesitate a moment. His body jerked awkwardly to the left. You could see a flicker of a smile as he bit back a response like, *I date a lot of models, too.*

"I don't think so," he said finally. "No."

I wanted Saul to press him on that. Why wasn't he sure? But Saul wouldn't have wanted to go there. Our whole case rested on the premise that Gemma was not real.

"Is it true that you texted one of your colleagues saying that you believed, quote, 'Mickey is crazy'?"

"I was trying to be humorous."

"The text continues: 'She'll do whatever we want. She's that insane.'"

I hadn't known about that. It stung.

I was to take the stand on the last day. We had rehearsed extensively over the weeks before the trial, crafting a narrative as pitiable and believable as it was divorced from reality. I had been a girl unusually attached to her father. Traumatized by his wrongful conviction, devoutly loyal to him, I had taken it upon myself to earn what I could in order to support my family. An instant modeling success, I immediately began booking high-level jobs, despite my relative inexperience. Working almost non-stop, grossly underweight, my mental state frayed due to exhaustion, I was so emotionally and mentally depleted that I was unable to fend off what we called Benoit's "attention"—a harmless, nonsexual word—and I, an innocent, helpless, hapless female (the most desirable kind of female), soon found myself "in way over my head." My brain, in an effort to cope with the exhaustion, trauma, and immense pressure to succeed, latched on to the delusion that there was another young woman, very much like me, who was in trouble. My mental state grew so weakened that I began to believe that this woman, who I called Gemma, had been murdered, and I even occasionally nursed a harrowing guilt that I'd done it. When Benoit badgered me that day, after several weeks of hardly eating or sleeping, something inside me snapped and I began to believe that *he* had been the one to kill her. I had acted then, in my confused state, out of the desire to *protect* rather than to *harm*.

"But there was never any person named Gemma, was there?" Saul would ask.

At this point, I'd be crying gently. "No," I'd say. "No, there wasn't." I would go on: "I cannot tell you how much I regret that I let my mental state deteriorate to the point where a human being was hurt. Though my memory of the day is very blurry"—consistent with PTSD—"I know that I never would have acted that way had I not, in my own deranged way, been afraid for my life and the life of someone I thought I loved."

Saul coached me on diction, inflection, tone; the point was to appear remorseful but not too remorseful (which would indicate guilt), mentally fragile but not actually insane, to be pitiable, girlish, and above all, likeable. I was surprised how naturally it came to me, like sinking into a favorite chair already imprinted with the shape of my body: *pretending*. I'd forgotten how good it felt, being someone else.

Right before court began that day, I went to the bathroom, even though I didn't have to pee. I was wearing a camel crewneck sweater, navy slacks, and a small Cartier watch borrowed from my mother. The wig was itchy. I was nervous at the thought of having all those eyes on me. I didn't really care what happened to me, but I didn't want to disappoint the people who were clutching cardboard signs outside the courtroom. The thought of even one of them giving up on me felt like a jab in the gut, and I knew I had to put in a good performance for their sake—they'd be able to forgive a guilty verdict, but never a subpar performance. I stared at myself in the mirror, feeling the thud of my heart in my chest. I adjusted my wig, trying to scratch without scratching, and peered at the unfamiliar face in the reflection, barely suppressing a laugh. Pretending I was someone else was what had gotten me into this mess, but it was also what would get me out of it. I realized then that everybody was pretending, all the time, but that for most people, for the people we call "normal," the pretending part eventually falls away and the act simply becomes their life. It's exactly what Anna thought right before she threw herself onto those train tracks. I wasn't about to be so foolish.

I took a deep breath and walked into the courtroom with my shoulders back, head straight, and for the next five hours I didn't just pretend I was some hapless victim driven to madness in the wake of PTSD, I *believed* it. I went through a dark tunnel and didn't come out until I was stepping down from the stand, and Saul put a hand on my shoulder, and I realized my cheeks were wet and I'd been crying and it was all over. My mother and father were standing at their seats behind the defense table, and both of them hugged me over the little fence.

"That's my girl," my dad said, his eyes twinkling. I wondered if he would have been as proud of me had the narrative actually been true. I suspected not. I realized that in the annals of the American court system, our father-daughter relationship, twice documented in our respective trials, would live on as one of the most intimate and cherished. I laughed a little, flushed and slightly embarrassed by the irony of it all, and my father, who seemed to be thinking the same thing, laughed lightly, too.

Five hours later, the jury delivered a verdict of not guilty by reason of temporary insanity.

I was shocked, frankly. Even though I could tell at trial that our side was doing well, I hadn't really believed I'd be let off the hook so completely. My parents were gleeful. My mother wept as she hugged me. Even Saul put an arm around me and squeezed my wrist, a wide smile on his face. It began to sink in. I'd hardly thought about what I was going to do after the trial, not so much out of fear for what the verdict would be, but because the level of uncertainty blanketed everything in a thick layer of fog I couldn't see out of. Now that I'd been proclaimed not guilty, visions of a quiet life flooded into my mind. The arrest and my confinement before the trial had humbled me, and I was almost startled to see how simple my desires had become. I didn't want a lot of things for my future—I mainly hoped to get my GED and find some sort of work, nothing fancy, maybe as a barista or a bookstore clerk, which would leave evenings free to write. I planned to burn the wig.

I had a big smile on my face when I left the courtroom that day— *No interviews, please. Not now. Maybe later.*

I thought I was free. Finally free.

At sentencing, the judge wanted to send me for a forty-five-day mental health evaluation whereby I would be released on my own recognizance, but Saul argued that since I had already been treated at a mental health facility prior to trial, I should not be obligated to undergo another internment. "What's more," he continued, "due to the Brazilian flu epidemic, to place this young woman into the custody of a women's state mental health facility would be to unduly expose her to the risk of contracting the disease. The forty-five-day stay may turn into a death sentence." In the months since my arrest, the Brazilian flu had burst forth from its home country like a thousand flies, and cases were now surging on practically every continent. Beyond its symptoms and the fact that it was highly contagious, little was known about the disease except that women, particularly those under the age of thirty, were disproportionately likely to contract it. The judge reluctantly agreed that the risk was too great, my privilege at work again. Even though I had bashed a man's head in, as a pretty white girl, I was still a thing to be protected. Still, the judge feared a possible relapse, the repercussions of which could be severe, and he did not feel comfortable releasing me into my own care "for my own good."

After some deliberation, a settlement was reached. I was released into the temporary guardianship of my parents under Article 81 of New York State's Mental Hygiene Law, which gave them complete control of my health care, finances, and living arrangements.

It's three years and several hearings later, and that "temporary" conservatorship has continued to drag on. My father and mother believe it's for the best, and apparently the judge agrees: "You seem to be making progress," he says. Owing to my public persona, I am considered particularly vulnerable to grifters and scammers. The arrangement, then, is for my "own protection," I am told.

Saul, one of my few friends these days, says I shouldn't complain. "Your mother has made you into a star," he says. She's certainly tried, though I wouldn't exactly call myself one, per se—I still have no talent, and if you asked anybody on the street, most of them wouldn't recognize me, though my name might ring a bell. Mickey Jones is more of a niche brand, a cult icon. Most importantly, I am now a passive income stream.

At MickeyJones.com, we sell T-shirts, hoodies, key chains, lip balm, posters, USB cords, shot glasses, eye masks, yoga mats, door signs, underwear, mugs, stickers, beaded bracelets, iPhone cases, water bottles, mouse pads, robes, pens, measuring tape, one blond wig, a mirror that comes with an overlay so it looks cracked (my mother's brainchild), and sets of two matching blond dolls called Doppelgängers. My new Instagram, @TheRealMickeyJones, has 578K Followers. My bio reads *Remember me? Yes, THAT Mickey Jones.* Every morning I log on to the Cameo app and record messages for those who want to give their loved ones the kitschy thrill of seeing my face on a small handheld screen for a birthday or special occasion and are willing to pay $150 for the pleasure. Half my appeal lies in what one commenter described as my "randomness. Like, remember her? Lol." The other half owes largely to the fact that I am still, I have to admit, quite beautiful, especially from the neck up, where the fifteen pounds I've put on since trial have softened my features and made me appear more womanly. I trade in nostalgia, impermanence, whimsy, irrelevance. For my clients, I am the human embodiment of how much time has passed since I first entered their orbit of awareness, and how much things have changed. In considering my face, they are invited to fathom my transformation from relevant to irrelevant, and in doing so are reminded that what seems like a big deal in their lives today will likewise seem insignificant in just a few years. Most of all, I represent the Punished Beauty, the Insane Woman Tamed and Chastised, the female Icarus—I flew too close to the sun, and look how I burned! Look how repentant and servile I am now! Twenty-three and trapped at home with her parents, how normal and yet oddly sad! Everyone loves to comment on how "crazy" my eyes look in certain videos, or that the way I talk makes me sound like a hostage. They complain about it, but secretly they love it. Sometimes, I deliberately upload videos that make me seem unbalanced—ones in which I dance a little offbeat, or sing a song I made up. These are always my most popular posts. No one wants to hear me talk about Tolstoy or New Jersey's snowy owl population, or hear about my monk's life: up at dawn, asleep by nine. They want the crazy.

I suppose it's a comfort to my fans, who probably all work normal jobs and have to struggle to pay off debts, and scrimp and save to send their kids to college. I am the gentle assurance that all too often the price of beauty and fame is madness. And yet even still, many of them appear to want a chance at it.

Almost every other day, I get a DM from a girl asking me how I got into modeling. What are my tips? Do I have a diet they could follow? The same girls will post something about me being a "tragic beauty. So so so SAD what happened to her!" They'll send me pics of themselves, sometimes wearing T-shirts with my face on them, other times bikinis, or crop tops, whatever is the trend of the moment. *Do you think I could be a model?* they ask. Or, *Will you follow me?* Or, *I want to be an influencer. Any advice?* They all have the same empty look in their eyes, and the same desperate, self-conscious way of posing. Most of them aren't much older than thirteen.

I'm resigned to it, this life of mine. Sometimes I even think I'm happy. This is what I wanted, after all. Hundreds of thousands of Followers, millions of Likes. My mother says I deserve all the credit for what I have, what *we* have, now. "It's *your* brand, darling," she'll say. "I'm just the manager." As a manager, she is very hands-on, always making sure I respond to the right amount of DMs and Comments—not too many, not too few—constantly monitoring and evaluating my posts and keeping my Cameo page up-to-date. It surprised me, at first, how quickly she took to it, how easily she absorbed the algorithm's mandates, but then, as she always likes to remind me, she did win the Miss New Jersey crown. She understands pageantry, contests, rules. And I figure, after all she's been through, after what I've put her through, it's the least I can do, to go along with it. I always wanted her to have a career, or at least a hobby—and now she does. It's me—or, at least, the brand of me.

My father is supportive but hands-off. He sees how much money we bring in, and since his real estate comeback has yet to fully materialize, he can't really complain. My mother still defers to him everywhere else, but when it comes to MickeyJones.com, she's the one in charge, we all know that. She negotiated this very book deal, sold it as a "frothy, lightly fictionalized memoir with never-before-seen photos." Over several Skype sessions with my editor, my mother and I hammered down a narrative, one that adhered very closely to the one set forth at trial.

They wanted me to use a ghostwriter—it would be easier, better, and one could be got for not much money—but in an act of self-assertion that surprised even me, I insisted that I write it.

"The book is just so we have something to talk about online," my mom reminded me, after I'd spent what she passive-aggressively insinuated was too much time writing. "Just consider it one giant billboard for your digital channels."

I know it sounds risky, being so active online when that was one of my big triggers before. But with therapy and the encouragement of my family, I've been able to manage it okay. Most days, I don't even notice the yawning emptiness that threatens just beneath the metallic shine of my iPhone screen as I respond to Comments and Cameo requests—that is, I didn't, up until six months ago.

One night, I was doing a routine sweep of Comments on my most recent video—I'm twirling around outside on the grass—and noticed a message from a middle-aged woman. *You remind me so much of my daughter,* it read. *She worked briefly as a model, and I remember how tough it was on her too. Sadly, we lost Liz about five years ago. I miss her every day. I wish you two could have met. I wish she could have seen someone like you talking about your mental health struggles so openly and honestly, and known that she wasn't alone. Thank you so much for all that you are doing. God bless.*

The message was not so unusual, but I was immediately struck by the woman's last name: Anton.

Of course, by that point, I knew, or I thought I knew, Gemma had just been a delusion. But even after all those years, hundreds of hours of therapy and as many pills later, there must have been a small part of me that believed in her still. I clicked on the woman's profile. I scrolled down. Almost immediately, I was confronted with a face indelibly familiar to me, even though it was staring out from the head of a small, blond child. *Liz at 8. Will never forget that mischievous gap-toothed smile of hers.* She'd added several heart emojis. A strange fluttering beat against my chest. I scrolled further down. The woman's daughter was named Elizabeth Gemma Preobrazhensky, but it was her. It *had* to be her. I saw the two of them hugging in a more recent photo: in it, Gemma was an adult, her smile wide and dazzling, her eyes squinting unphotogenically—a real smile. She looked different than I remembered, less beautiful, less polished, but it was her. I swear it was her. She had been pulled out of the Hudson River shortly after my arrest. I had the feeling of something giving way, like when I take the stairs too fast in the dark and accidentally miss one. I understood immediately that she had used her mother's maiden name professionally, as I had also done. The realization opened up a vista of discovery for me. I spent the next several hours holed up in my room, well into the night, later than I'd been up in years, scrolling, googling, and piecing together what I could. Her life—her real life—unspooled before me: She had been born in Canada, the daughter of a Jewish Russian refugee and a Quebecois woman. The family had eventually made it to California. Her father was a high school teacher—not a professor—and though her mother liked to garden and make ceramics, her day job was that of an HR rep for a marketing company. She had three brothers, not four; in one picture on her mother's Instagram she is standing next to a young man in a wheelchair who looks vaguely related, but he isn't tagged. I think he might have actually been her cousin. She'd suffered from dyslexia and bulimia for most of her life. She'd struggled as a model, finding success only after years of casting calls—and then, for no clear reason, her career stalled. Her body was found, bruised and waterlogged, floating in the Hudson River. She was twenty-three, and $35,000 in debt. It was ruled a suicide.

I let the information circle me like a drain, until I could take it all in. I knew that if I shared any of this information with my mother or father, Saul, or even my therapist, they'd tell me I was hallucinating again; it wasn't real. If I showed them pictures, they'd just say the resemblance was a passing one; they'd point out that her name was completely different from the one I knew her by. It was a coincidence, her mother's name, there had to be hundreds of Antons out there. Nothing else about her matched up. Part of me sensed the logic in those arguments and was terrified. After what I've been through, I can't help but be suspicious of my own mind. But worse than that was the realization that even if this was the real Gemma, this Liz, she was nothing like the Gemma that had existed in my mind. All the time I'd spent following her, copying her, doing my best to be her pale reflection, it had never occurred to me that she had been doing the same.

I think of those young women who write to me, wearing my face on their chests, who don't know anything about me really, but seem eager to take my place. I think about that vacant look in their eyes and I remember the young woman I used to be. We are all of us trapped inside a hall of mirrors, our shiny, hard exteriors reflecting both to each other and on each other, ad infinitum, forever and ever so we can't escape.

I know that as long as I'm a marketable product, I'll never be let out of that hall of mirrors. So long as there are people willing to shell out $5.99 for a key chain with my name on it, so long as the eyes never look away and there are people to Like me, there is too much money to be made, too much time invested, for me to move about unencumbered by that pressure. Plus, my father would never allow it.

But if I were to become unlikeable, if I were no longer viable as a brand, I might finally allow myself to be a person. This book is my final act of defiance, my last hope, and I've done the one thing that nobody, not my mother and not even me, expected: I've written the truth. Not anything so neat and tidy as what you read in the news, or see on TV. But it is the truth, as I experienced it that summer.

I've no illusions about being liked after this. But at least I'll be understood.

ACKNOWLEDGMENTS

This book began as my very first submission during my very first semester at NYU's Paris MFA workshop. It would probably not have gone much further than that, and certainly it wouldn't be what it is today, if it weren't for the support of the program, the careful early readings by my fantastic peers, and, most importantly, the infinite wisdom of my irreplaceable teachers. Under Helen Schulman's patient tutelage and exacting (yet supportive) advice, I first found Mickey's voice. Nathan Englander taught me the importance of "pressurization." Katie Kitamura, who generously worked with me over not one but two semesters, deserves double the credit: Her enthusiastic support and incredibly insightful edits and feedback proved indispensable. I could not have finished the project without her. My thesis advisor, Matthew Thomas, provided the final push to polish. Throughout the process, classmates supplied much-needed feedback, commiseration, and laughs—there are too many to name here, though I'm thinking in particular of Andrew Porter, Stephen Fishbach, Jenni Zellner, Liz Riggs, An Yu, and Avery Carpenter.

Endless gratitude to my agent, Ellen Levine, whose tireless support of this novel amid a very difficult year was nothing short of superhuman. During the editorial and publishing process, two major life events turned my world upside down: my father passed away and, two weeks later, I gave birth to my first child, a beautiful baby girl. The

Lake Union publishing team, and Jodi Warshaw in particular, were incredibly supportive and patient as I tried (and often failed) to juggle deadlines amid grief and the grueling days of early motherhood. I will always be thankful.

Finally, I have to thank the people who have been with me from day one, before I had any idea about this writing business (or anything else). To my mother and late father: thank you for encouraging me to do something as crazy as pursue a career I actually liked. Paul, Jamie, and Jennen, you three have always made me feel incredibly supported. I'm so glad we were born into the same family. And to friends and early readers, family not by blood, I wouldn't be here (or half as sane) without you: Thank you. You know who you are. Last but most certainly not least: Amit, my first and last reader, most honest critic, biggest supporter and deepest love, thank you for everything. And to Ajooni, for making our little family complete. I am so lucky to be sharing this life with you.

ABOUT THE AUTHOR

Hayley Phelan is a writer and journalist whose work has appeared in *Vanity Fair, ELLE, Vogue,* and the *Wall Street Journal.* Her column in the *New York Times,* Browsing, ran for two years in the Style section, where she continues to contribute. She was born and raised in Toronto and currently resides in Los Angeles. For more information, visit www.hayleyphelan.com.